THE
TORRIL
CITY
MYSTERION

A PINCH OF PERIL

JAMES McLEOD

Published in 2021 by James McLeod & Wondercrab Books.

First Edition.

Publisher and wholesale enquiries: orders@wondercrab.com
For press and other enquiries: press@wondercrab.com

Cover design by James McLeod
Map design by Oleg Dolya and James McLeod
Fonts by Dan Sayers, Andrew Hart & Andrew Paglinawan licenced or used under the Open Font License initiative.

Thank you for supporting this author — way to keep reading alive!

www.torrilcitymysterion.com/code
CODE: TC1-A24U-973

21 22 23 | 10 9 8 7 6 5 4 3 2 1

To Mo, my glowing chair-leg in the dark,
without whom I'd be lost.

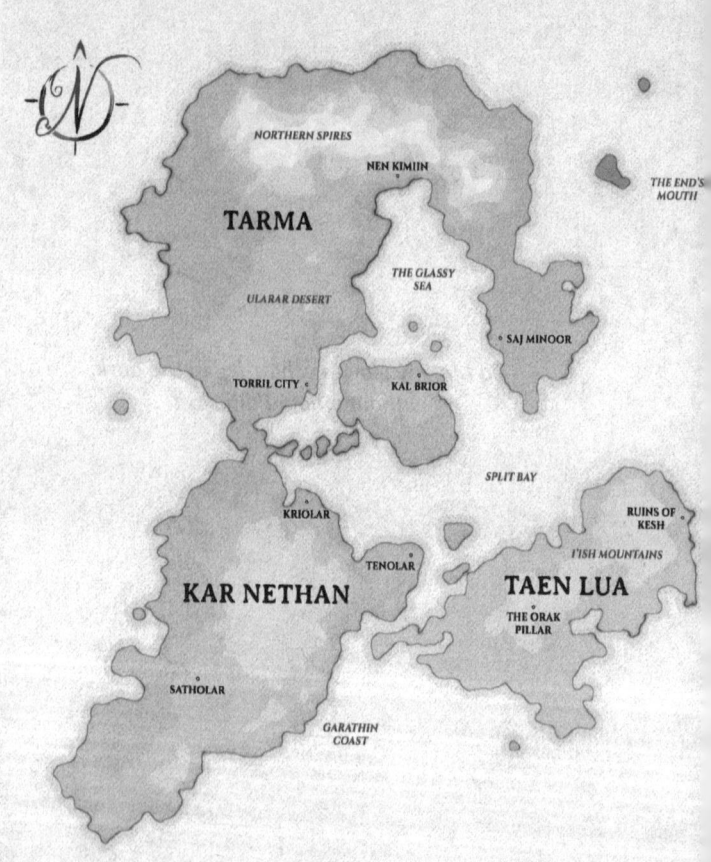

THE FROZEN SEA

SILTARI

THE TWISTING
SEA

TIJAN
ISLAND

DRIFTER'S
STRETCH

NAT'ITH

THE EASTERN
WASTES

TE'ERAM

BA'AL TERAT

KAR TAAM

LOCUN
BAY

BLADE
CANYONS

HUKAN

TILOI

KINTH'ORA

MAKUUA JUNGLE

KUAHUK

SATKU

SARAL

ALIRU
WORLD MAP
TORRILIAN ERA

TABLE OF CONTENTS

PART ONE

CHAPTER ONE
LIGHTS OUT

"Alright, worst fish you ever ate," Akteron whispered, watching Piria lie back in that armchair.

"That's not easy," she replied, "I did eat at Garleon's before the big crackdown."

"You *didn't*..."

"I had to see if the rumours were true." Her shrug was innocent. "You can't tell me you weren't curious, too. When a whole city condemns a place, it's either truly horrible, or so good that the wrong people get jealous."

"...and?"

"Stuck in bed for three whole days."

Akteron gave a quiet chuckle. "I don't trust most of the official departments, but the Bureau of Metropoly don't throw around food poisoning charges on a whim. Glad I listened on that one."

"To be completely honest, Garleon's linnfish seasoning was *preeetty* good. Maybe better than yours."

He loosed a small cushion in her direction.

"Impossible."

Silence then fell, over which a gaudy clock ticked softly in the corner. Its hands reached well into the early hours and faint moonlight spilled through the windows, making the sitting room seem even more enormous than it really was.

A good dozen ticks sounded before Piria sighed.

"Are you sure about tonight?"

"Not at all. But it's either now or tomorrow night. Or the night after tomorrow. Or next span."

"I wouldn't mind coming back here tomorrow night," she said, shifting in her cushy seat.

"You like it? No, it's all too much," Akteron replied. "The self-portraits? The chandelier? That lamp with the silk shade?"

"She's a Seat Official..."

"It's too much. I'm surprised the painting isn't bejewelled."

Piria snorted and glanced at the clock before turning back to her partner. "So, how's about we give this another hour. If nothing has happened by then, we hit the cobbles?"

"We have to stay until we have something. We can't send Official Gaussi to different lodgings every night."

"Like you said, it might not even happen tonight."

"We have to give it a good shot. I need this, Ri." Akteron gestured to his ingot-belt. "I'm almost empty again—"

"Wait. Psshht." Piria motioned him quiet and sat up, head swivelling, Akteron doing the same as a faint, scratching sound caught their ears.

Lips pursed, Piria then nodded to the window behind their chairs, through which Akteron turned to see a silhouette edging past on the building's ledge, outside.

Well, by the Blue Robes. It was him.

Akteron raised a hand, gesturing, *easy now, don't move*, before reaching into his donvul pocket and pulling out a slender, metal gadget. A palm-sized grip with a trigger, terminating in a long, polished barrel. Nothing fancy. He didn't have the charge to buy more than the plain, undecorated option.

Sliding to the edge of his seat, Akteron then observed as the figure outside bent to make a final inspection of the darkened room and, without wasting time, produced what appeared to be a small pair of scissors. These he lifted up towards the window frame and there, in the air, he began cutting.

Akteron nodded, watching pulses of purple light radiating outwards at each motion.

So. That's how he does it...

A moment later and after thoroughly snipping the air, the man seemed to have deemed his efforts sufficient. The scissor-like tool was stuffed back into a pocket and something thin and metallic withdrawn, instead. This, he drove between the two window panes, manoeuvring it until the latch clicked open. All that remained to do was lift the glass pane, then, and within another breath the figure was sidling over the sill and lowering himself into the room.

Akteron had to admit, this was impressive. This burglar wasn't young or particularly fit, by the looks of that silhouette. But he moved with a strange...*elegance.* Professional and absolutely silent, each movement seemingly rehearsed.

No wonder nobody had caught him, yet.

Ah, it was a pity. If this guy's pal hadn't been such a loudmouth, perhaps he'd have gotten away with another heist, tonight.

Oh, well, Akteron thought, allowing the man no more than two steps before pulling the trigger of the metallic gadget.

A soft – *PECK!* – rang out and a second later, the would-be-thief stiffened and tipped like a felled tree, hitting an ornate side table on the way to the marble floor. The very fine crystal vase upon it followed, smashing into a thousand fragments before Piria hit the small switch by the door, at which the room was bathed in light.

"Ouch," she muttered, wincing at the fallen figure, bleeding from his scalp.

"I didn't want him getting *too* far," Akteron said, stepping over to the fallen burglar. "He might have seen us and turned around."

"Not him, the vase," Piria said, eyes on the diamond-like

fragments, "looked Kal Brioran. Would have been expensive..."

Akteron seemed not to be listening.

"Alright, let's see who you are," he said, kneeling beside the figure and pocketing his gadget again, before he reached out to roll the man onto his back–

"Wait!" Piria grabbed his shoulder, "*Thief*, remember? You saw how he handled those wards, outside. He's got experience. He might be protected."

"A fine point...well, what better opportunity would I need to test a certain new, novel powder I've recently come into possession of?" Reaching once again into his donvul pocket, the young man now retrieved a small, glass phial.

"*Akteron...*" Piria said, her tone dripping with disapproval. "That's still experimental. I did not say you could take that."

"I know. I just figured you need more field tests outside the confines of Riallo's agreement." Akteron uncorked the bottle and sprinkled a fine powder onto the unconscious man before Piria could protest further.

Making contact with the limp form, the pair shielded their eyes as the powder reacted immediately, crackling in sparks of orange and pink which lit up the room.

Piria's annoyance seemed to have been shed by the time it died down again. "*Great Wastes*...it works! It actually *works*! Pink...that's a shocking-ward, and orange, too...he's got *two* hexes on him."

"I don't know why you ever doubt yourself. Two hexes, though? A bit much. What's the second?"

She crinkled her nose. "I don't know. Orange...orange. I don't remember ever observing an orange one in my tests."

"Well, it's enough just to know he's protected. Your powder just saved me a possible heart-attack. Raise the price when you decide to sell it."

"I need to know what that orange ward is, though..."

Akteron shrugged, then feeling around a belt at his waist

12

where his fingers brushed over a series of small, metal ingots fastened there. "I have just enough charge to petition its removal. And thank the Blue-Robes we got this guy now. My account at the Dispensary is looking pretty dry..."

"I'm no better off, Ro," Piria replied, "End of the threespan. Everyone's running on empty."

Finally, Akteron's fingers met a pair of ingots near the end of the row still imparting a decent tingle, and he gave a small nod. "Perfect."

Slipping the small metal bars from their little holsters, he held them before himself and closed his eyes.

"Ath viraan, Kandaar...I send my respects and appeal for aid."

There was silence for a moment before he noticed a slight coolness descending around them, the air shifting, and he cocked his head as if listening to something.

"Always so formal..." Piria muttered. "Does he actually like that?"

Akteron raised an eyebrow but held his concentration. A moment later, he felt the answer and nodded. "Wonderful, Kandaar. I'd like you to remove the wards on the man lying before me. I can offer two ingots, in return."

Again, silence. He heard Piria take a deep breath and shift on her feet.

Then, there was a slight pulse in the air. The pressure in the room seemed to shift, as if the space were inside a bubble being poked by some invisible finger.

A soft hissing sound then issued from the body at Akteron's feet and following this, a pink mist began radiating from the man's skin. It drew into the air, spiralling about before vanishing with quiet – *SCHLLOOCK!* –

"Brilliant!" Akteron said with a grin, waiting for an orange mist to emerge as the first had done.

It didn't.

"Erm, no removing the other hex, then?" Akteron prompted,

13

glancing hopefully into the air. He pursed his lips as he experienced a conversation Piria couldn't, imagery flashing through his mind before he gave a light, disbelieving grunt.

"No, no, never mind, then. Viraan chath, Kandaar."

"That's odd. He's usually so reliable," Piria said, and returned her gaze to the unconscious man.

"Nothing to do with reliability, just my charge," Akteron replied. "He wanted another six ingots"

"*Six*? To remove a *hex*? *Great Lights*, that's extortion! Why?"

"It's not his fault. Whatever that hex is, it cost a lot to put there. And that means even more to petition its removal."

Piria glanced to her own ingot-belt and shot him an apologetic look, "I don't have enough, either, Ro."

"It's fine. We'll just have to risk handling him with the hex in place, and make sure we let the Security Bureau's grunts know about it before anyone touches him and explodes...or whatever it might do."

"Actually, I'm just thinking. It might *not* be a protective ward, after all."

Piria had cocked her head and Akteron glanced up. "What do you think it is, then?"

"Well, look at him." Piria gestured to the man's patched clothing. "Does it look like this guy could afford to put a hex like that on himself? Surely he's only on a couple of ingots a span..."

"I suppose that's why he's a thief, Ri. Maybe he did something extreme to get the job done. Or maybe he has another belt, somewhere..."

"Hah!" Piria barked, before her face grew thoughtful. "But really, though...two hexes seems too much. One would have been strong enough for a simple burglary. This is something different."

"Hmm." Akteron cast that curious glance back at her. "You think someone else hexed him?"

As the pair let that settle, that gaudy clock in the corner began to chime two hours to sunrise and the noise seemed enough to rouse the unconscious man. He groaned and began to turn himself over and instinctively, Akteron leapt to pin him by the wrists. Realising his mistake, he sucked a breath through his teeth and gave an expectant wince while a breath or two passed in nervous anticipation...

But nothing happened.

"There," Piria said, "you didn't explode. I suppose it's not a protective hex, after all."

Akteron unclenched his jaw. "Hand me the irons."

From a small satchel hanging over her shoulder, Piria did.

"And just for the record," Akteron added, locking the man's wrists one after the other, "he broke the vase."

———■———

"Dianon Scaa, born under Tesbri," Riallo said, dropping a small pile of papers in front of Akteron and leaning against the wall.

Riallo did that. Leaned on things in his office even though he had a fine, wooden desk. It was that same kind that all office-types had, really, but in all of Akteron's visits, Riallo had never sat at it.

"His Sharak's name is Ganaar. Pretty strong welding and you were right on both counts, he was behind the other break-ins. All five. List of well-to-do officials was found in his donvul pocket," Stuffing both hands into his own pockets, Riallo shook his head. "I can't believe he was actually moving down them alphabetically...but we aren't exactly dealing with masterminds here, are we?" He then gestured to another stack of papers. "My unit found a small fortune in boxed goods at his apartment, including the fabrics he stole from your clothier. Seems he was planning to exchange the textiles at the wharves in a twospan for a shipment of copper and tin ore."

"Hah!" With a clap, Akteron leant back in his seat and crossed one leg. "Your brilliant detective knocks another one down! Oh, and Sendil's going to love me."

Riallo raised an eyebrow. "*Going* to love you? You're already a walking advert, for Sevellan's sake. That shirt. It's one of his, isn't it?"

Akteron smoothed out one sleeve of the vibrant garment. "He makes the best shirts in Torril..."

"Well, now he can keep making them, thanks to you both. The textiles will be returned to him in two days — after Wards And Pests clear them of tampering."

"And did you find out what that tool was?" Piria asked, leaning against the opposite wall. "The one he used to get in through the window?"

"Ah." Raising a finger, Riallo stepped back to the desk and opened a drawer. "That was interesting. I haven't ever seen one of these in the wild, before."

Rifling around, he produced another sheet of paper upon which a delicate, two-handled implement had been sketched. It looked — as Akteron's glimpse in the Official's dark apartment had suggested — like a pair of scissors. Yet this tool had four curved blades instead of two, and each seemed to lock into one another as the device closed. The accompanying text on the paged named it a *Decessor*.

"These are rare. Rare as lizard feathers," Riallo explained. "It's a type of magickal deactivator used to cut weak to moderate ward-lines. No idea where he got it. These things have been banned for over thirty cycles and cost more than I make in two. No chance he just stumbled upon it at some pawn-shop."

"*Interesting*," Akteron muttered. "I assume the Bureau has an inventory of units still out there."

"And a list of every craftsperson capable of making them," Riallo finished for him, "not many are on that list."

"Alright, so let's just take a moment here," Piria said, "and take stock of all this. The guy not only had access to a powerful thaumaturgical relic, but he also has knowledge of where the finest textiles and materials in the city were stockpiled. *Private* stores, mind, including Official Gaussi's stash of rare silks, *and* he had one hell of an expensive hex on him."

"Sounds serious, doesn't it?" Riallo nodded. "But Dianon's snitch of a buddy kindly filled a lot of those blanks for us."

Still at his desk, he reached into a small, ceramic pot and strode to the window. There, he strew a handful of seeds about the sill and a cluster of small birds immediately descended to vacuum up the offering.

"About a cycle ago, a certain reporter for the Daily Warble ran a story on Torril's best marketplaces. She did her research well and when the piece was finished, she threw that research into a paper-bin. Thought nothing of it. Well, who should come along, then, but Dianon Scaa Tesbri, freshly freed from lockup and carrying out city waste-duty? And what should he find but a detailed report listing the city's most expensive imports? The names of big buyers, dates, amounts, even contact information... he had everything he needed."

Akteron gave a thoughtful nod as a larger bird landed and began to peck about with the others.

"Oh!" Piria exclaimed, eyes locked onto its bright plumage. "A tektek!"

"Mm?" Riallo glanced to the sill. "Oh. A brute, you mean. He's here almost every day, that one, and the others barely get a nut once he arrives."

As if in response to that, the tektek waggled its brilliant, emerald wings, shooing the others away and using the ensuing lull to steal one of the larger nuts.

"Aren't you afraid they'll poop everywhere?" Akteron asked.

Riallo gave a chuckle. "It's worth the mess. They bring a bit of life to this place."

"And sound, too, I'll bet," Piria said. Akteron could see her studying the bird's long, sweeping tail. "Tekteks can learn to mimic, you know...you can teach them poetry or even to sing."

"I'll give it a shot sometime..." Riallo told her, clearly trying to pull them back on topic. "The interesting part of all this is really that hex." Turning back to Akteron, he leant against the wall again. "Now, I'm going to guess that the lack of detail in your report was on purpose, because, *'Unknown, possibly benign hex still in place,'* lacks your standard, descriptive flair. But I also need one of you to elaborate, now, because Wards is asking about it and I don't know what to tell them."

A series of squawks filled the room and Akteron pressed his lips together until it had settled.

"As we reported," he said, "Piria found a shocking ward on the guy, along with the second, mystery one. I wasn't trying to be secretive, we just didn't know much about it. We still don't. Only that Kandaar wouldn't touch it for less than six ingots..."

"*Six?*" Riallo's eyes became moon-like. "Beaks in the night, that's steep!"

"I know. That's why we were kind of hoping Wards would tell us what it was."

"I see," Riallo said, recovering from his shock. "Well, nothing yet. They're still unpicking it and the best guess they have is that it's some kind of tracking-hex."

Akteron's brow furrowed further.

"It's common enough," Riallo went on. "Fall in with a bad crew for a while and then try to get out, and they slap you with a tracker to make sure you're not fraternising with the enemy. To keep tabs on you for a while."

"They'd use over *six ingots* to mark this nobody?" Piria asked.

"Not sure," Riallo tilted his head as if weighing that up. "I mean, if they were planning on hitting his stash, later...maybe cleaning out all that loot he'd collected, then it would pay off nicely. But who knows?"

"Alright," Akteron said, "so, if Wards are making progress then why are they asking about it?"

"Because," Riallo made sure to stress the next words, "this hex took a team of four to detect..."

Akteron winced, for the implication was clear enough. If it took four Bureau professionals, then how in *Aliru* had he and Piria found it?

A small silence fell, and under Riallo's stare, it seemed Piria was reluctant to explain. Akteron knew why. She hadn't considered that powder 'ready' — even though his application of it had proved otherwise.

Piria must have realised that secrecy was no longer an option, though, and finally gave a relenting sigh. "It's something I've been working on," she said. "A new powder that reacts to the trace particles and fields magick emits. Think of it as translating an invisible, magickal signature into visible light. It's taken me cycles to get working."

Riallo remained silent.

"I know," Akteron told him, "but she's *my* girlfriend. Hands off."

Piria gave an amused snort. "You wish. But I will allow that because you cook better than half the chefs this side of the Glassy Sea. And because you agreed to make last meal tonight, as an apology for stealing that powder..."

"Oh! I can make that cloud pastry and sautéed mushrooms!" Akteron's face lit up. "You just reminded me, there's a fresh shipment of garinians coming in today from Tenolar! They're really the only ones that taste any good, sautéed."

"Can we focus?" Riallo asked. "Please? So, this powder...what else can you tell me?"

"Not much," Piria went on, "it showed the signature of this hex as bright orange, which I'd never seen in my tests. At first we thought it might be protective, but then Akteron grabbed the guy and nothing happened–"

"*Great Lights*, you two," Riallo shook his head. "What if it *had* been? Some kind of time-based detonation? Or a contagion? It could have been dangerous!"

Akteron glanced to his own hands, turning them over. "*Contagion*? I didn't think of that…"

Piria shook her head and raised a hand to calm them both. "No. Any decent destructive hex would cost more than six ingots"— she then turned to Akteron —"including a contagion. That's complex, even higher-level stuff. Officials might be able to afford it but not this schmuck. Also, I *may* have used the powder on you, Ro, on the way here. Just to check." She shrugged in apology. "You're clear, so at least it's not transmittable."

Akteron allowed his clenched shoulders to relax but Riallo grunted, shaking his head. "Mr. Scaa is in confinement behind our own wards for now, and seeing as the big kids think it's a tracking hex…and the fact that you two are alright after touching him…I'd like to assume it's nothing too dangerous. But you need to be more thorough in reports in the future, secret, experimental powder or not. We need to know if we're bringing something unknown into the Bureau."

Both Piria and Akteron nodded.

Riallo then took a breath. "In any case, I have to congratulate you both. We *have* been trying to nab this guy for over a cycle."

Piria flashed Akteron a knowing smile and he returned it, for those words spoke of a decent reward for this job.

"But before we get to that," Riallo added. "I have something else we need to discuss. Remember that little chat we had over dinner? A chat about you not being able to take on high-profile cases for the Bureau?"

"Oh," Akteron brushed a hand absently through his hair. "You know I was only kidding about that. Really, Riallo. Don't get me wrong, we'd love a big case. But I know where contractors sit in the Bureau's eyes and how they like to handle things."

Riallo merely smirked. "Today, that might change."

Huh. Well, that *was* intriguing. Akteron cocked an eyebrow. "Meaning...?"

Riallo stepped towards the office door. "Well, I could tell you about the people I've had to sweet-talk. The strings I've had to pull. The paperwork I've drowned in...but instead, I'm just going to introduce you both to your next client. Come on. You're going to like this one."

Akteron stood and turned to straighten the cushion on the seat.

"Leave it, neat-freak," Riallo's voice came back from the hall outside.

Akteron shrugged and collected his donvul from the back of the chair. He could hear Piria chuckling as he pulled it over his shoulders and left Riallo's office.

CHAPTER TWO
THE CURATOR

The Bureau of Security's corridors were bustling as Akteron, Piria and Riallo emerged into the main thoroughfare and turned towards the central stair.

Agents, clerks, and officials flowed in two streams up and down the marble edifice, and the trio joined those moving upwards, making for the briefing rooms on the third level.

It always occurred to Akteron when they took the stairs that even though Riallo had been a coordinating officer three cycles already, he hadn't applied for that shiny, triangular badge, yet. The one which would allow him to ride the elevators and dine in the more private, senior-official's hall. But perhaps it was to do with exercise? If he were confined to an office all day, Akteron would relish a few stairs, too.

He dodged a trio of stylish women in clopping shoes who powered by, their painted cheeks and fussy, ornamented hairstyles betraying them as guests rather than part of the Bureau. They did seem to ooze control but they wouldn't fit in, here. Too much style. While the Bureau desired to project both those things, they did so in a different way. Marble floors and brass doorframes were polished with military precision, while ranks of alphabetically-sorted plaques adorned the walls and directed the flow of foot traffic. Everywhere else, banners of proud, Bureau-lilac lined the corridors and presided over staff who whizzed by with folders, scrolls and charts.

It *was* admittedly a nice shade of lilac but in such quantities tended to singe one's retina, Akteron felt–

"Palaman!"

It was mid-way down a hall and amidst a succession of identical doorways when a call broke over the trio's muffled footfalls.

"Kendara, take me. What now?" Riallo groaned, and all three pivoted to see a balding, jowly man stomping the hall towards them, his moustache leading the charge.

"Ah, Nomos! What brings you down to level three on a day like this?" Riallo chirped.

Face sweaty and eyes determined, the man simply bucked his head to peel Riallo off the thoroughfare and the two converged behind one of those banners.

Akteron barely exchanged a glance with Piria before following to hear a low-voiced exchange.

"You know *damned well* what brings me here. Just...*assure* me, right now, that it'll be managed quickly," the jowly man said as he wiped his brow with a tatty, grey handkerchief.

"It will be," Riallo said.

"Good. Great. Because, *Great Sands,* you know what's at stake..."

"I do."

"I mean, this whole mess could throw sparks into an already very stacked tinder-box. The last thing we want right now is-..." At that moment, he leant around Riallo to find Akteron and Piria standing there. "Who in blazes are *you* two?"

"They're with me!" Riallo said, and held up his hands. "Nomos, you remember Akteron Uusei Nisbri, and this is Piria Kii Kasbri. They're–"

"Ohhh no," the man cut him off, eyes scanning the badges on their donvuls. "No, no. Don't tell me you pulled *contractors* on this one? On *this* one!"

"I'm telling you," Riallo said, raising his hands. "I have this. They've both been vetted. Extensively. They're professionals. I trust them."

"Palamann..." Nomos's face reddened further and Akteron could see his jaw tightening.

"Come on, where's that famed bravado?" Riallo said convivially, leaning into the man's gaze. "Where's the guy who told me *'grab every chance by the reigns. Be bold, out there,'* two cycles ago?"

"He didn't mean on a high-profile case and with two unknowns!"

"Oh, they're not *unknown,*" Riallo said, brushing the comment off. "I've worked with Mr. Uusei before many times. There was no other choice, really. And we have a great dynamic."

The older man's expression remained unimpressed as Riallo then bent over and whispered something in his ear. It wasn't a particularly long something, but the effect was swift and seemed to finalise the discussion. Akteron watched as the older officer's jaw relaxed, and he stepped back to eye Akteron and Piria head to toe.

"Fine. Your decision," he grunted. "Not much we can do in that case. But if this all falls apart, you hired them and *I* hired *you.* Understood?"

Riallo nodded, and that moustache spun from the trio. "And for the love of all things green, get it sorted. *Quickly!*"

Nomos ploughed off down the hall again, and a moment passed as Riallo made sure there would be no change of mind. Then, he turned back to his two agents and gave a puff through his lips.

"Nomos Bessoram, Head of the Department of Crime," he said. "He's-....hmm. I was going to say he's not so bad when the fate of two nations isn't on his plate, but actually, he is."

"Fate of what, now?" Akteron asked, eyes widening.

"Yes, we'll get to that. Come on."

Past more lilac banners and dodging more staff the three tromped, Akteron's thoughts barely having time to convene before they drew up to a door, upon which a temporary slip of paper read, "CASE 7266"

Opening it, Riallo ushered them inside. It was a small briefing room, and barely had the three crossed the threshold when a portly, balding man leapt from his seat and bounded across the carpet.

"Ah!" he cried, running a hand along his arm in customary greeting before taking Piria's hands in his own. "Good morning, good morning! *Thrilled* to meet you both!"

The two contractors returned the gesture.

"Akteron, Piria, this is Mr. Kabonn Saal Nisbri, curator of the Torril City Museum of Antiquities," Riallo explained, cocking one eyebrow to check that Akteron looked sufficiently impressed.

Akteron did. *The* Kabonn Saal Nisbri?

For a coordinating officer with only three cycles behind him, hooking a big-client like this for his contracted detectives was definitely nothing to squawk at...

Akteron felt a flush of pride. Sure, Riallo *did* still owe him for that exemplary bottle of Kal Brioran Kassoon...

But this wasn't just a favour. No, Akteron couldn't help feeling this more of a *sign*. A sign that maybe, all his small wins so far were finally starting to be recognised. Riallo wouldn't have picked him out nor whispered praises into the Head of Department's ear if he didn't believe in him, after all.

"Pleased to meet you, too, curator," Akteron said with a light bow. "Can I just say, I thoroughly enjoyed your article in *History Now* about tribal poison rituals. Not to mention your take on the drowned Saj Minooran consorts."

"Oh? Good, good! Glad to hear it. Yes, curious topics, indeed," the curator's answering bow threatened to split his tight trousers.

It was no difficulty to detect that, despite his air of formality and control, Kabonn was holding a current of nervous energy, within. His worried glances and flushed cheeks made it seem he'd been holding his breath before their arrival, damming-up words which would have breached his lips now, if they hadn't been stifled further by a glum looking Security Bureau Official with a plait of grey hair and unusually smooth skin.

"Before any further discussion," this woman said with all the warmth of cement, motioning to the round table before her. "Please sit to allow a review of the proposed contract."

Akteron's face crinkled.

Yep, there it was. The one, real reason the Bureau would never be too stylish. Bureaucracy.

The official didn't smile as the four took their places, and her expression remained flat as the busts of past Officials in the halls outside as she ran through the standard, droning preamble and ticked and signed agreements.

Perhaps she lived in this room, Akteron wondered. Never seeing the sun. That might keep one's skin smooth...

Seated, and evidently only half-listening, the curator shifted constantly, gripping the tabletop impatiently with his thick thumbs as the various details of their contract were stated, and the usual yaying and naying came and went.

But it wasn't over, yet.

A sharp clap from the official and a timid looking young woman entered from the hall, outside.

"Agent Kiralla? If you would..."

This young agent took the newly penned documents that were passed to her, left again, and over a pair of small spectacles, the grey-haired official then proceeded to shuffle a *second* stack of papers, reading them to herself over her thin nose.

Akteron sighed and started a count inside his head.

It was always a mystery to him, why officials didn't read these documents *before* coming to briefings? Last time he'd counted to four hundred and seventy three before this part was over...

Across the table, Kabonn's reaction was far less veiled. The man loosed a flurry of nervous glances upon each of them as each page was scrutinised, taken, and laid upside-down.

Akteron ignored it all, counting instead the ticks from a clock mounted to the wall and scrutinising the fixtures.

As with all the briefing rooms, this one was thoroughly devoid of vitality. The geometrically patterned wallpaper, wood-panels, and angular chairs were restrained and matched the dark carpet and wall-clock. Outside that pool of light in which they sat, it all looked so dull, too. So *retrograde*. Copper, dark-wood and red feathers hadn't been in for twenty cycles or so.

But he supposed it all served its purpose.

Twenty cycles ago, the Security Bureau had celebrated the longest period of peace in Torril City and the surrounding states. It had been a time of great strength for them and Akteron couldn't help but feel they were clinging onto this decor as some kind of subtle reminder of all that. A reminder, as things slipped downwards again...

"Freshleaf?"

Another official had entered and Akteron leant aside as a tray was set on the table, its centrepiece a pot of steaming freshleaf encircled neatly by five porcelain cups, set at equal distances from one another.

Pouring one for himself, then Riallo, Akteron was about to pour one for the curator, too, when Kabonn absently snatched his in such a jittery grip that the cup slipped from its dish.

– *KATASH!* –

It smashed on the edge of the table and everyone started.

"Good gracious! I-...oh-...my apologies," Kabonn blurted, grabbing a serviette and trying to dab up the mess.

When he was done, Akteron eyed the last, empty cup before him, dreaming of the rich, woody flavour and the kick freshleaf would deliver. Then he sighed, pouring it full and sliding it towards Kabonn.

"Oh! Very kind of you, very kind," the man said.

"So." The awkward moment ended as the lady opposite removed her spectacles and laid her hands on the table. "Mr. Saal, your museum has been robbed."

Darnit. Akteron had lost count.

"Yes," the curator replied at once, barely able to contain himself. "Yes. Last night. Three very precious artefacts, missing. A *disaster!*"

"And do you know of anyone who might have been involved?"

"What? Do I know who the thief was? I imagine I wouldn't be here if I did...what kind of question–"

"Madame Official," Riallo prompted quickly, "perhaps we should acquaint Mr. Saal with our detectives and get them up to speed?"

Recieving a ceding gesture, Riallo turned to his client.

"Mr. Saal, this is Akteron Uusei Nisbri, and Piria Kii Kasbri, contractors I've chosen personally for their excellent track record. As I mentioned earlier today when we met, I feel them the perfect duo for this case. In fact, just this morning, they caught a textile thief the Bureau wasn't able to capture in over a cycle."

The official gave an incredulous grunt.

"I mean...I'm sure the Bureau would have, eventually," Riallo stumbled. "What I mean to say is that these two are highly competent, and due to their lack of attachment to the Bureau, are able to work swiftly and outside the complications of bureaucracy. I have every confidence that they will be able to solve your case and return these stolen artefacts in no time."

"Contractors..." The curator glanced to Akteron and flexed his knitted hands around his cup. "Yes...good, that's very good... pressure to do a good job, reputation on the line and all that. You have experience with thieves and robberies, I take it?"

"We do," Akteron said, keen to get things moving. "So, Mr.

Saal, could you perhaps begin by explaining what happened this morning? At what time you discovered this theft had taken place and what your security team has already determined? Perhaps start by telling us how you discovered things were awry."

"Ah, yes, the bones of the matter." The curator now shifted in his chair. "Well, I arrived at the museum just after the dawn bell, as ever. I like getting in early, you see, the place is just so peaceful, it's like another world. And I like to make sure the cleaners did a good job."

"And these cleaners..." Riallo prompted.

"Oh, no, absolutely not. They have worked there for cycles. They all pass a routine security check each and every shift, not to mention I know them all personally. Friends of the family. Lovely people."

"Right." Riallo scribbled notes onto a small pad as he talked. "I had to ask, you understand. Please continue."

"Well, after I arrived," the curator continued, "I checked my desk for mail, turned on the lights." He looked into the table as if picturing his routine. "Then I began to wander the circuit. I check every exhibit, every day — the whole museum — before we open. It truly is the best time to see the artefacts, when the sunlight is peeping in at the right angle..."

"So, there are windows?" Piria asked.

"Have you never been to the museum?" Kabonn looked shocked.

"Many cycles ago, as a girl," Piria replied, "but not again, since."

"Indeed, there are windows. But I think we can rule them out," Kabonn said, "they don't open. Also, they're only about this high." He estimated the size with one hand, then used both hands together. "And this long."

"So, about the size of a brick?" Akteron asked.

"Yes. Three rows of them. None big enough for someone to get through, even if the glass was smashed."

Akteron nodded. "I see."

The curator's eyes glossed over slightly. "Ah, how pristine the first two exhibits looked in the morning light! We have a new display there of some pottery which is really quite exquisite. I highly recommend it! Early pieces, fashioned before the Kal Brioran Descendency, you know, and the descriptions Kardia wrote for the presentation's placards is art, in itself!"

"So, you wandered the museum's exhibits..." Riallo tried to bring the man back on track.

"Yes. I wandered the circuit. And it wasn't until I left the fourth-age relics and passed through the main hall into the *fifth*-age exhibit, that I saw all the glass..."

"Damaged display cases?" Piria guessed.

"Two display cases," Kabonn confirmed, "completely smashed in and visible from the hall, and if that weren't bad enough, a *third*, not much further on. Now, I tell you this, the glass there is the strongest we have, and it's protected by tamper *and* impact wards...all of which proved utterly useless..."

"So, the thief had some kind of special implement with him or her?" Piria asked.

"Him. And what he used, I can't really say. The vision was inexcusably awful!"

"But you have to have seen *something*, surely..."

"As I said, one of my security detail petitioned to determine exactly what happened, but the man's Sharak made such an utter muck of the vision that we barely saw anything. Truly disappointing. Still, that's only one element of the whole. The more worrying question is how this thief was able to enter the museum at all."

"You can't find the entry-point?" Akteron asked.

"Oh, we found it," the curator said. "The problem is, it's a solid wall."

The room fell silent for a moment.

"Wait, so your thief entered the museum through a solid

wall," Akteron confirmed.

"It seems so."

"You mean, brickwork? Concrete?" Piria pressed. "Are there windows at that point? What kind of wall is it?"

"As I said, a solid one. A full two dashes thick. No windows. Just solid granite. That whole wing is made of marble and granite, floor to ceiling. From the days when construction of public buildings was a little more decadent, you see..."

"Marble and granite," Riallo muttered as he continued scribbling on his pad.

"And can you tell us anything else about these smashed cases? What was taken from them, exactly?" Piria then asked.

"Why of course! And this is the most important and tragic part," the curator replied, his thick eyebrows drawing together. "It is truly disastrous timing, and why this case needs such urgent attention! You see, in four days' time the museum is due to hold a most prestigious event...an exhibition, the likes of which Torril has never seen."

Akteron sat up. "You wouldn't be referring to an event placarded around the city, right now?"

Kabonn gave a nod. "We named it, *'The Power of Unity'* and it was supposed to be a show of friendship...of common ground and shared history between Torril and Kriolar, in which treasures from both cities were to be presented, side by side."

"Two nations..." Akteron muttered, Riallo's earlier words suddenly acquiring gravity.

"Indeed. And I dare say, the ramifications of this would be dire, should the relics not be recovered."

"So, what kind of relics were stolen?" asked Piria. "Are they dangerous?"

"Oh, not just dangerous, *treacherous!*"

Akteron raised a brow. "Treacherous? Does that mean weapons? Are we talking swords and daggers?"

"Oh! That you should land on the answer yourself is a very

good sign," the curator said. "But before we get to that item, allow me to acquaint you with the first two pieces..."

Turning to Piria, Akteron suddenly smirked. "First guess! Sword or a dagger. That's a tin of madigan-flower tea, *Piriaaaa*."

Her response was to punch him in the shoulder. "That doesn't count! You don't know which one it is, and you only got one of three, anyway."

Across the table, the curator blinked at them.

"Our apologies, Mr. Saal." Rubbing the spot, Akteron turning back to their client. "The, erm, first two items?"

"Yes...oh, where did I put them?" The curator rifled through his papers for a moment, before the official slid a pair of sketches across the wooden surface. "Thank you. Yes, here they are. Oh, it hurts to see them. They're like my children, these relics..." It seemed Kabonn wasn't simply being dramatic, now, for Akteron noticed tears welling up in his eyes.

"It took almost four cycles to arrange the loan," he explained. "Four cycles of planting seeds, of careful prodding and assurances that it was for a good cause. The Kriolar Museum's curator, not to mention the sea of officials I had to wade through, were so suspicious and hesitant that I had serious doubts my idea would ever flower! Yet, the relics did finally arrive, and I duly arranged for them to take the most prominent position in the museum. I designed a lumstone lantern array specifically to show off their intricacies and had their mounts crafted from sappelwood, themselves worth a small fortune but well worth the effort, for these items are true beauties! And now...*now*...*great sands,* they're gone..."

"A bell?" Piria asked, looking at the first sketch.

Taking a deep breath, the curator calmed himself. "Yes. A treasure which was originally the possession of the empress of what would eventually become Kriolar. In Old-Krio, its name was, *'Hara Genn',* which means, 'Bell of Tongues.' What an absolute tragedy...a tragedy! She was truly unique."

"She?" Akteron asked. "Is it...alive?"

"Alive? It's a bell," Kabonn said, eyeing him strangely. "*Genn* is a feminine noun in Old-Krio..."

"Ah. Well, why is she-...erm, why is it named the Bell of Tongues?"

"Isn't it obvious?" Kabonn answered. "Striking this bell causes all in the vicinity to lose their capacity to communicate."

"Not obvious," Piria said.

Akteron shook his head in agreement.

"Yes, indeed. Its effect can be calamitous! Rebellions, coups, ferocious campaigns were begun, fought and lost under the influence of that object," Kabonn explained. "The Day of Blood-...well, surely you learned about that as youngsters?"

"Of course, but—" Akteron began, wide-eyed. "Four thousand people dead. A massacre! Because of a bell?"

"It is both beautiful, and dangerous," Kabonn replied wistfully.

Piria cleared her throat. "Alright. So we have a powerful and dangerous bell. The second object?"

Akteron scanned the sketch before him. A decorative, circular band with a clasp at the back and what appeared a closed eye etched into the front side.

"We antiquarians refer to this next item as 'Gildran's Collar', named after its discoverer," Kabonn said, "its true name is unknown but is believed to have originated in the ancient kingdom of Kesh, based on this unique, etched pattern. You see, here? The rippling, wavelike details?"

Akteron nodded. "But I thought these two items were supposed to be Krio?"

"Oh, I don't intend to kick up dust on the matter," Kabonn replied. "Kriolar taking possession of the item many centuries ago has become a matter of pride to those who enjoy military conquest. One of Kriolar's last, great victories, you see. And in any case, the collar no longer functions. As far as I and other experts can tell, its key mechanism is damaged and has been for a long time."

Akteron look up from the paper. "What kind of function did it use to perform, when it worked?"

"A most fascinating one!" Kabonn said. "The collar has a twin, you see. A twin which we have never found, though we see it in records from long ago, and utilising both collars, an individual was able to see through the eyes of whoever wore the other."

"*Interesting*," Piria muttered to herself. "From the optic nerve into the thalamus...and the signal has to be diverted through the collar, into the consciousness of the other wearer...but *simultaneously*?"

"What, now?"

"If it's damaged," Riallo cut in, looking up from his pad. "Then the collar isn't really dangerous..."

"Well, that depends on if it can be repaired. Or, indeed, if there is some trick to it we are still unaware of."

"But, supposing it can't be repaired," Akteron now added. "If the twin is lost and if the piece itself is damaged..."

"It does seem unlikely that the collar could be used in its current state, that is true." Kabonn finished the thought.

"So, then. We have a missing bell and missing collar. What's the third piece?"

"Ah." Kabonn's expression grew distant. "Well. Now we come to that, most troubling relic." Standing, he then began to pace, as if the words he needed could only be grasped by doing so. "This last piece has quite a history. Although, as with the collar, it's origins are uncertain..."

"Yet, it's in the fifth-age exhibition?" Piria asked.

"The fifth-age is guesswork, it should be admitted," Kabonn said, "made by scholars who haven't much to go off. Its true chronology is still being debated and in all likelihood, it was fashioned far earlier. The style and materials used are quite indicative of a culture predating the Torrilian, a culture capable of advanced metallurgical and thaumaturgical techniques."

"And, it's a sword?" Akteron asked.

"A knife. Or, more specifically, a dagger," Kabonn explained.

"Sharp?" Riallo asked, and the curator almost laughed.

"*Great Lights*, lad, we never tested it, I assure you that much! Yet, as with all these relics, this knife has most troubling properties, and my fear is that if it *were* used in any capacity, it would have dire consequences." He took a breath and stared through the desk for a moment, as if seeing the relic before him. "It is known as the Umbral Blade and fittingly, what we *do* know of its history is shadow and portent. Its theft is one of the single most distressing developments in my long career."

"Alright. You'll have to elaborate on that," Akteron prompted, sitting up.

Kabonn returned to his seat but didn't sit, placing his hands instead upon its back. "Of course. I will tell you all I know about it," he then said, "but I must warn you, what I will now say about this blade must never become known outside this room. Only a select few have been granted access to the Seat's Deep Archives and have read the records therein. Naturally, I, as curator, have that privilege. But as you are being entrusted to find this object, this information may also be crucial to your success. I therefore trust the Seat will allow me to share it…"

The lady official bristled. "As we agreed at the beginning of this session, you have freedom to speak as you will within this party. The Seat recognises your predicament. All present are bound by contractual secrecy."

Kabonn nodded again and located a pair of large, sealed rolls against the wall. "Lovely. Then I will do my best to fill this room with secrets…"

———————■———————

CHAPTER THREE
THE UMBRAL BLADE

Kabonn Saal Nisbri made some ceremony as he donned a pair of white gloves, one after the other, then withdrew a large, aged piece of parchment from the first roll.

"Would you be so kind Mr. Uusei?" he asked Akteron, who stood and cleared the freshleaf service to make space.

"Thank you."

The curator then spread the parchment out, lay it down, and tacked each corner with a small stone.

Akteron at once realised that it was a map, aged and tattered and with mildew spots pocking its face, but still readable.

"Now," Kabonn said, sweeping his hand over an area of land as Piria and Riallo stood to watch, "this continent is of course familiar to you, our continent, known today as Tarma. And you surely recognise Torril City, here..." His finger was aimed at a small smudge, sitting atop an inlet which swept east and met the familiar seas of the Split Bay. "Most Torrilians are very aware of the history of this region and I assume you are all equally well schooled, so let us leave the obvious parts unsaid. The relevant part for us to know is that in the second-age, there was–"

"Sorry, that was when, exactly?" Piria interrupted.

"Around four thousand cycles ago," Akteron whispered.

"Yes, very good." Kabonn nodded. "That's when the *great* tribe of Tarma, from which all of our ancestors descend, fractured.

Legends and scholars both tell us that this was due to disagreements and difficulties between the people, leadership, and shamans." He now spread his fingers out. "In the end, three tribes formed from one. Two went their separate ways, one north, one south, and as you all know, the last stayed in the central region and founded what would become Torril City."

Perhaps to test if he was still listening, the curator turned to meet Akteron's eyes but he needn't have bothered. Akteron was soaking in every word. Good books on Torrilian history were frustratingly sparse, yet before him now stood a professional historian positively itching to share what he knew. A fine opportunity to save himself some research.

From the second tube, Kabonn now withdrew a slightly transparent document and lay it atop the map, taking some care to align small circles at each corner. Seen against the underlying map, this provided a tangled mass of lines — travelling paths or routes, it seemed — which snaked across the continent. Some terminated in dots, others looped back upon themselves and still others merged with partner lines.

"Now, as the second tribe, the Kasria, moved northwards," the curator said, tracing one of these trails up the parchment, "their internal struggles continued. Their leadership was locked in disagreement, you see. Many still wished to return to Tarma, to fight and take the region for their own, but most were interested only in travelling north, away from here, to start their own civilisation. The tribe fractured once again. A small fracture, yes, but significant."

"Those who continued north," Akteron started, "they founded Nen Kimiin?"

"Correct," the curator answered. "And Tramin, and Kas Koshir. They were very prosperous in the north."

"And the others who split off?" Piria asked.

"Ah. That second, fragmented group settled here," the curator replied, his finger smacking the middle of the continent where one, faint line terminated in a splodge of red, "in the mountains and deserts of Ularar."

It was a huge, lonely expanse from what Akteron could see, spreading from one side of the continent to the other.

"Unfortunately for them, they no longer had the numbers to dare their desired rebellion. So instead, they planted their roots in those inhospitable wastes and it seemed for a time that they had not survived, for they vanish from the record at that point."

"Though...not for good, right?" Akteron asked. "They reappear."

"Indeed," Kabonn confirmed. "I take it you're familiar with the tale?"

Akteron looked to the blank stretch on the map. "My understanding is that the deserts were silent for almost three hundred cycles. Then, some kind of cult appeared. An odd people with odd beliefs, who eventually spread around the whole continent."

Kabonn beamed, nodding. "Go on."

"...they called themselves the 'Kiira-Vesh,' didn't they? I don't remember what that means, but their culture revolved around blood. Their art, their homes, even their bodies were decorated with it. That's about all I know."

"Brilliant. That sets a fine scene." Kabonn took over again. "Yes, the Kiira-Vesh had unusual, dramatic customs, indeed, most of which need not detain us."

"But they survived out there. In the desert?" Piria asked.

"Oh, they thrived!" Kabonn replied. "Developing a unique and complex language, novel social structures, that style of art and architecture...and that brings us to the heart of things!" He gave a small clap, almost seeming to enjoy himself, now.

By contrast, Riallo's eyes had entirely glazed over. He was absently turning a coaster with one finger while staring through the maps. Kabonn didn't notice, drawing out a smaller piece of paper covered in strange glyphs and setting it down.

"Over the last few cycles I've developed something of a hypothesis, despite some rather *spirited* scholarly disagreement." He chuckled as he slid the paper towards Piria and Akteron. "Look, here. This here is a charcoal rubbing from a tablet found in the Ularar mountains, a rare, intact story from the Kiira-Vesh, themselves, and it begins by speaking of a ritual. A very dark, bloody ritual, indeed, in which members of their society were murdered before their sacred leader, their 'outstretched arm of light,' as they called him or her."

"*By Sevellan*...they made ritual sacrifices?" Akteron asked.

"Where do you think they got all the blood?"

Akteron shivered. "That wasn't in the book I read."

"Most probable," Kabonn replied. "The penalty for sharing stories and lore outside the Kiira-Vesh was death, after all. That's part of the reason it's so hard to research them, you see, and why this tablet was such a boon! This particular story is the account of a man chosen to be the victim of just one such gruesome display." He then furrowed his brow. "And admittedly, it would be difficult to write such an account after being murdered, so let us speculate that this tale was written by another. All the same, according to our mysterious author, this so called 'sacred leader''s immortality depended on this brutal bloodletting. Moreover, human sacrifices went to his aid willingly, apparently finding it a great honour to be sliced open..."

Perhaps unsettled by the grisly visuals, Riallo cleared his throat. "Not to be rude, curator, but how does all this relate to finding the stolen artefact?"

"Don't fret, the reason for this dramatic interlude is this passage...*here*." Turning the paper back to himself, Kabonn whipped a magnifying glass from somewhere and, peering through it, translated aloud. "*The sublime master's order was clear. Thus, did I mount the stair. Thus did I go to the figure-blade, the black, vitreous god, through whom Ulgim's power flows, and* *utter the secret words of...*erm, *sparking...*" Kabonn looked up. "*Ulgim* was another name for this leader, I presume..."

"And 'sparking'?" Akteron asked.

"A mistranslation, most probably," Kabonn waved off the disruption and looked down, again. "*My end was swift. The point met my flesh. I was made infinite, my soul gladly given up and now in the starless domain.*" He then prodded the document triumphantly. "There, you see? Sacrifices and religious babble aside, this is undoubtedly a reference to the Umbral Blade!"

Akteron cocked an eyebrow. "What makes you so sure? It all sounds a bit ambiguous to me."

"Oh, not at all! You see, there are two curious features of the Umbral Blade which make it such a beauty to behold! Firstly, it's dark, glass-like structure..."

"Ah. Black and vitreous," Piria said.

Kabonn pointed to her and grinned in satisfaction. "And secondly, the shaft was fashioned into human form." He looked to Akteron expectantly.

"A figure-blade..."

"Indeed. And, what do we have to add to this rather convincing start? Well, as I see it, the pottery and artistic style of the Kiira-Vesh match the style of this human figure perfectly. Yes, yes, I am in no doubt of that. Nor that the blade was fashioned in truly ancient times, for its forging is said to have been done under the converging moons and we can date that precisely with astronomy, you know. Cycle five hundred and forty-two, as it were. *Truly*, the blade is an ancient treasure!"

"So," Riallo sighed, "that was thrilling, but what we've learned is that the blade was made by these people in the desert, that it's not Torrilian, and that now, it's gone missing."

Kabonn looked a little hurt. "And that it's treacherous!"

"I don't see why," Riallo said. "It's just some blade used in old sacrifices, right?"

"*Great Wastes,* no!" Looking flustered, Kabonn glanced down to the paper, again. "Did I forget to mention that whoever wields this blade is considered a bringer of calamity?"

The room was silent for a moment.

"Mmm," Kabonn muttered to himself. "I did forget. It's down here, somewhere..."

It took another few breaths from them all before Akteron finally spoke. "Well, we don't have much reason to believe such a claim, do we? That's just myth and legend, right?"

Kabonn bobbled his head. "Actually, there are numerous sources to corroborate past 'calamities'. The Kiira-Vesh considered their sacred leader unstoppable and this belief led them to conquer much of Tarma. Records from these vanquished peoples all say that the Kiira-Vesh often infiltrated and soured from within, bolstering numbers with a 'convert or die' approach, then attacked when society was weakened and panicked. A terrifying prospect, indeed. And it all centred around their leader and this blade." Kabonn motioned back to the maps. "Now, as far as we know, the blade's last *definitive* use in ritual was around the fifth-age...we have images of its use in Nen Kimiinan reliefs, for example. Then, at some point after that, the Torrilians took the dagger into their possession."

"Ah, it *became* Torrilian. Another prize of conquest," Akteron uttered.

"Alright," Piria piped up, assumedly trying to tie things off. "So–"

"So what happened in the fifth-age?" Akteron cut back in, and she rolled her eyes. "How could these people let such a precious talisman slip out of their hands?"

"Tricky to say, exactly..." Kabonn rested his hands on his prodigious midsection. "The Kiira-Vesh had enjoyed an age of prosperity and unchallenged rule, even establishing their own capital. They held huge sway over the continent for roughly fifteen hundred cycles. But around the middle of the fifth-age, *something* happened, an unknown disruption, opening the way for the Torrilians — who had already deemed them a threat — to launch a decade-long campaign. They were eventually victorious and the Kiira-Vesh destroyed, all their hierarchy and satellite settlements collapsing. The blade was seized at this time, brought here, and has remained in Torril ever since. I bartered for it about eight cycles ago from the private collection of a Seat official who thought it was a cheese-knife."

Akteron raised an eyebrow.

"Oh, I don't think he really used it as such," Kabonn said, "from what I recall of the episode, he mentioned it was too dull even to cut a loaf of Torrilian Rye."

"In any event," Riallo said. "We need to plot the next steps on this very carefully. You mentioned you wanted to prepare a press release, curator?"

Kabonn withdrew a handkerchief and blotted his forehead. "Oh, yes. I wished to be prepared to inform the papers–"

"No! Don't do that," Akteron interjected, giving them all a start. "Apologies, Mr. Saal. But considering what we've just heard, that might not be the wisest decision. These objects are very dangerous, after all, and if the press gets word and starts digging, and rumours of some plot to revive the Kiira-Vesh start circulating..."

"The Kiira-Vesh no longer exist," Piria reminded him. "They've been gone for two thousand cycles."

"I know, but you know the media. They spin everything out of proportion. I can already see the headlines, 'CONSPIRACY! ANCIENT BLOOD CULT RETURNS TO THREATEN TORRIL CITY!'...and that's all before we even get to the other two relics."

Piria seemed to weigh that up before she also turned to the curator. "Another thing to consider is that if word gets out, it may actually make finding the relics impossible. Thieves melt down or jettison risky goods when they know they're being hunted, rather than trying to pawn them off. But we want the thief to try and pawn the items off. It's our best chance to get them back."

Kabonn merely nodded. "Both fine points. However, had you two allowed me to finish my earlier sentiment, I was going to say, *'but I hope I don't have to publish that release'*. I am very aware of the implications this caper might have. *Goodness*, yes. That is precisely why I requested the Bureau assist in this matter as quietly as possible!"

"Ah." Akteron pressed his lips together.

"Honestly, for me the greater concern is the political factor. Imagine if Zikaron somehow got wind..." Riallo then said.

Akteron crinkled his brow. "Zikaron Feriin? The Krio ambassador?"

Kabonn gave a concerned grunt. "Yes, I had entertained the notion. Wildly nationalistic, hot-tempered. Really, about as unpleasant a force as you could hope for and we have come to verbal blows over far less in the past. I hate to imagine what he'd do with the knowledge that two of Kriolar's most precious artefacts have been loosed into the wild...it would spark international furore!"

"The exhibition is due to open in four days..." Piria muttered, almost to herself. "We'd need to find these relics before then."

"Absolutely," Kabonn agreed, giving his forehead another wipe. "As soon as possible, or all of these very unpleasant scenarios may become reality..."

Giving a slow nod, Akteron then tapped the table. "Alright, what now?"

A voice piped up from across the table, drawing all eyes to her. "Now, you all have to sign your names on this paper, waiving the Bureau of all responsibility in case of injury or death."

It seemed everyone had forgotten that official was still sitting there.

"If you two are taking the case, that is," she added.

Akteron glanced at Piria, and the answer came from her lips.

"We're taking it."

———■———

"So," Akteron asked as their small troupe trod the carpeted halls back towards the main hall of the Security Bureau. "When can we visit the museum, Mr. Saal? I'd like to see the scene as soon as possible."

"I can escort you there right now," the curator replied. "Yes, yes, the sooner the better."

"Great. We just need a few moments to collect our effects, then." The four approached the entrance hall staircase and Akteron gave the curator a small bow. "We'll meet you below."

Riallo waited until Mr. Saal bowed back, descended, and was out of earshot before turning to Akteron. "Your *effects*?"

"Actually, I was hoping we could negotiate an allowance for this next job before we leave," Akteron said quietly. "I barely have enough charge to petition a cracker at the moment and could really use a top-up."

"I imagine that might come in handy," Riallo agreed. "And I don't think there'll be much negotiating. The Bureau is keen to have this one solved, they'll part with a small fortune to see it happen. That said, I still have to justify it all to C&T, so make it easy for me and don't blow it all on fancy meals, alright?"

"You really are no fun."

The coordinating officer gave an amused grunt.

A short while later, Akteron and Piria descended into the entrance hall as well, their now-fuller ingot-belts giving off a pleasant buzz. It was common for ingots to radiate a small charge-aura when newly filled and the sensation was comforting, though Akteron knew it would fade in a few hours. That served as a reminder of how fickle ingots were. They couldn't hold charge forever and if not utilised, would slowly deplete over a couple of span until they were nothing more than pretty paperweights.

"Feels good, having a full set," Akteron said, running his finger over the dozen metal tokens as he trod the stairs.

"What exactly did you tell him we needed it for?" Piria asked. "They didn't question me and barely glanced at my request slip. Just charged them up."

"Apparently, that's what high-profile cases are like," Akteron replied with a shrug. "And I'm not about to question it. *Great Wastes,* a few cycles ago, I'd have slapped a knifebeak in the face for the charge at my waist right now..."

Piria smiled at him as they reached the ground floor to find Kabonn waiting by the large, revolving doors, his round cheeks red with nervous excitement as he bounced on the balls of his feet.

"Is Mr. Palaman coming?" he asked, peering over Akteron's shoulder.

"Riallo doesn't usually accompany us on cases," Piria answered, "more of a managerial type."

"Ah. That is a pity. I'd have liked to show him the Kal Brioran collection..." he said, before his expression brightened again. "Well, then, let's away! No time to waste."

The curator stepped through the main revolving door and Piria waved Akteron through before following.

Emerging into fresh air, Akteron found the city alive with chatter, footsteps, and birdsongs. Discs of orange sunlight pierced the endless canopy above and danced on the pavement, while a crispness to the air hinted that the cold season of the second tack was approaching.

Even Torril City was subjected to the occasional cold day, after all.

Spying a coach in the main avenue, Akteron hailed it with a loud whistle and the vehicle veered into the Bureau's U-shaped entrance way to halt before them.

"Where to?" A wiry driver with a large nose asked from his perch, brushing aside a pair of long, hanging vines.

"The Museum of Antiquities," Akteron answered.

"Seventh of a chunk," the driver offered.

"A ninth," Akteron parried.

"Hah! Find another coach, skipper," the driver said, and turned away. Rather than pulling into the street again, though, he seemed to take an awfully long time to adjust his seat and inspect his teeth in his rear-mirror.

"Fine. An eighth," Akteron relented.

The silence lingered a moment longer, before the driver pulled a small lever beside him and the doors of the coach clicked open.

Catching a cocked brow from Piria, Akteron shrugged. "What? It's the principle..." he said, then leant over to whisper, "and no use letting on that we've a threespan's wages at our hips, is there?"

The curator was the first to enter, the coach tilting as he manoeuvred his bulk through the small opening. Akteron followed, allowing Piria to climb in last for she liked sitting near the door, he'd noticed.

Then, with a lurch, they were off.

A number of vines knocked against the carriage's wooden roof as the wheels juttered over the cobbles and the vehicle swept into the main avenue, turning towards the Trade Quarter.

"Remarkable, these new coaches," Kabonn said. "So quiet! When I was a mere exhibit custodian way back when, the coaches were still pulled by animals! And the stink...my word! The city used to have to pay cleaners to tend the streets. During the warm seasons it was almost unbearable..."

Akteron smiled.

He and Piria barely ever took coaches, choosing usually to go by foot as was common in the city. Its lattice of alleys and avenues were easy enough to navigate once one knew the way.

Still, Akteron had to admit it was pleasant being driven and, sitting back, he contented himself to watch the main avenue pull past. It was a grand stretch, paved in white like most of the city was, and sliced through the expanse to Splitsack Market, in the main square. To each side in almost triumphal procession stood a series of stelae, indicating that this was an official road, while at the far end, the Seat's imposing, curved tower loomed, sweeping into the canopy above the sprawling, jungle city.

It was not alone. Closer by, the more modest Bureaus of Atmosphere and Information stood as if in reverence of their grand sibling.

All these official edifices spoke the same architectural language. Rounded, white, and tiered, Akteron had always thought they looked like giant, sliced eggs, leaning against one another at a slight angle. And they were impressive, even four cycles after moving here.

But that was what the Seat wanted with all these buildings, wasn't it? That they paraded grandeur. That they proclaimed themselves not as mere offices, nor meeting places, but as showpieces for the wealth and prestige of Torril...

"I see the next season is arriving early on the streets." The curator chuckled, gazing to the sidewalk where throngs of people wandered. Most were reflecting the brisk temperature with slightly thicker ensembles — scarves and cloaks replacing shawls and skirts — though as ever, a few others chose to remain with their light donvuls.

Those sticklers would inevitably capitulate once the temperature dropped further.

One thing that never changed, however, were the colours. Nearby was a lady swathed in aqua garments, and passing her were a pair of men wrapped in reds, oranges and yellows.

"It's *kaleidoscopic*," he went on. "I've always found the clothing here so vibrant."

Akteron had to agree. "It's like the people are competing with the plant-life. Trying to outdo it," he said, the coach pulling past a billowing asrelia with its orange and pink blooms.

Such decorative plants were common, spilling over the bounds of their planter boxes up and down the streets. But Akteron's comment had been accurate in another sense, too, for humans weren't just competing to be colourful, here. Behind those planter boxes, behind *everything*, stood giants — mighty trunks which punctured the cobbles, blocked alleys and filled courtyards, their branches filling the sky in every direction. It was these quiet colossi which provided the city's green blanket and dropped the flowering vines which swayed in the temperate breeze, brushing over pedestrian, coach and wildlife, alike.

The coach jostled over some rough cobbles and Akteron spied a small team of youths, working away. Clad in brown and green, some plucked weeds while the others trimmed branches. Others still swept the sidewalk and collected refuse, but all bore triangular badges with a tree motif at their centre.

Yes, Torril's inhabitants faced another, endless struggle against the green, and if they failed, the jungle would not hesitate to flood in, engulfing every stone, step and structure. Without constant tending, every crack and crevice here became plugged. Roots drilled through stonework, leaves clogged the drainage systems, and vines webbed up alleys and lanes. It was a tiring, constant challenge for those teams of official green-thumbs.

That was the downside of a city in the jungle, Akteron supposed.

The birds would love us to fail, though, he imagined, watching two giant pteranars stalking amongst the tenders and pecking idly at fallen seedpods.

So majestic, with their fiery plumage and lengthy necks. They effused an elegance and power which definitely justified their selection as the symbol of Torril, and could roam about freely, the Bureau of Nature seeing to their protection. One could find pterenar images on certain ingots and their brilliant, shed feathers everywhere else. And not just theirs. Myriad birds called Torril City home, most with similarly thrilling plumage, and as feathers were such an integral part of fashion here, this was fortunate. It meant a surplus was always lying around, waiting to be collected.

"When did you take your Kav ceremony?" the curator asked, turning to Akteron.

"Huh? Oh, erm-...when I was seventeen," Akteron answered.

The curator nodded. "Forgive me. I noticed your markings earlier but didn't want to presume or put you on the spot. Do you return, often?"

Akteron absently touched the small row of vertical lines above his left eyebrow. "To Kriolar?"

"Mmm. I heard there's been more trouble — waves of it at least, rolling in, these last few span."

"It's-...honestly, I haven't had much news in a while," Akteron replied. "I moved here five cycles ago. I send letters but I don't get many replies. And I don't tend to keep on top of it all as well as I should."

"Ah. You left it behind," the curator said.

Akteron's face reddened slightly as he shifted on his seat.

"It's all right," Kabonn reassured him. "I did, too. My father was Krio, you see. I was born and raised down in Kriolar and that side of the family, they'd been there for generations." He bobbed his head in thought. "But when the uprisings started again, well, I decided enough was enough."

"Understandable," Piria uttered, still gazing out the window. "It's not the kind of place I'd want to live."

Akteron's brow bunched up.

"I mean, it's not the kind of situation I'd want to live in..." she corrected herself, realising how that had sounded.

"Well, I just hope they sort themselves out," Kabonn said. "We don't want a repeat of that mess...the Torrilians won't put up with any whiff of rebellion, now. They'll end it quickly and forcefully. It won't be pretty. And then the Krio will lose even more of their heritage..."

"Do you ever think of moving back there?" Akteron asked.

"Oh, *Great Lights*, no." Kabonn almost laughed, though his face remained serious. "I'm curator of Torril City's most prestigious museum, lad! I've held that post for eleven cycles, now, and it was a dream of mine since I had spots. No. I'm quite happy here. Quite happy." He turned to gaze out his window again.

Akteron did the same.

The drive through the city was otherwise silent.

Akteron opened his window as the coach wove into the market and the delicious aroma of baked, seasoned burrins and simmering kama-butto wafted in, joined by the calls of stall-owners and customers heckling and trading. Akteron could almost pick out each spice on the wind.

Over the market's sea of noise, the midday bell had also begun. One temple's song echoed through the square while others, more distant, were muffled, unable to completely conquer the stretch intact.

"Oi, out the way!" the coachman's voice called to some pedestrian ahead.

To no effect, it seemed. People did not respect the road, here, for it dissolved over the market square into stalls and meandering masses. The coach might as well have been passing through a flock of pteranars. It jerked abruptly, stopping and starting until at last, Kabonn straightened, took a breath and smacked his knee. "Well, this won't do. Whatsay we walk the last twenty paces?"

Akteron and Piria agreed.

Rapping on the roof to alert the coachman, the coach's door swung open with a – CLACK – and they all stepped out, Akteron pausing at the driver's window to conclude their business.

Palming one of his newly charged ingots, he touched it to the driver's, top to tail, and a small tingle passed through his fingers. Two-seconds was enough to cover the fare.

"Thanks, skipper," the driver said with a tip of his cap.

Akteron nodded and slipped the metal back into his belt. Then, he followed the other two as they filtered through the crowd. Kabonn led the way to a building which could only have been the museum, its stone torso stretching towards the canopy with that imposing style classical buildings held. Stepping into its shadow, Akteron immediately noted the barricade of Security Bureau guards, their crisp, cream uniforms and lilac sashes bright against the museum's vine-covered front walls.

"They were quick to arrive. Been here since sunrise," Kabonn muttered as the trio reached a security cordon, where one of the guards straightened.

"Curator. Welcome back," she said, giving a stiff, security-guard nod and lifting the rope for them. She then turned back towards the market and Akteron found himself relaxing. It wasn't because of the security challenge. It was because once beyond the cordon, he was suddenly free of the seething mass, no longer having to dodge limbs and shift people aside.

He followed Kabonn as the three stopped momentarily to gaze at the museum's imposing entrance.

"My second home," Kabonn said with a smile, and began climbing the wide staircase to the front doors.

CHAPTER FOUR
SMASHED CASES

"And here is the wall, whence the vile villain vanished," Kabonn Saal Nisbri said, making a sweeping gesture across the polished floor and into the white stone wall beside him.

Akteron followed the invisible line and his brow bunched up.

It wasn't possible. It simply didn't make sense.

He'd certainly seen some odd things since posting that *DETECTIVE!* advert in the papers, sure. There had been that tree-feller whom everyone had thought vanished, until he was found in the river, pinned under a log and breathing through a reed. *"CASE SOLVED! TREE HAD ITS REVENGE!"* the headline had read. Then, there was that oddly dressed Saj Minooran lady who had sat on fire in order to prove that she was a deity. And when Akteron had tested how long, exactly, she could stay there, they had both found that while her clothes may have been magickally shielded against fire, the concealed metal plate inside them had not. The resulting headline, *"DETECTIVE BURNS TO BOTTOM OF DECEPTION!"* was Akteron's favourite, thus far.

Ah, and then there was his first murder case.

That one hadn't been so odd, really. Merely an unfortunate combination of a heated argument, a rotten balustrade and a poorly-timed shove. Admittedly, less sinister than he'd imagined his first murder case would be. The headlines had refrained from any witty quips, that time.

But walking through stone? That was altogether new territory.

A few paces from Akteron in the middle of the cavernous exhibit hall, Piria stood beneath a hanging banner upon which the words, *'THE POWER OF UNITY'* were rendered in mocking capitals. They weren't the focus of her scrutiny, though. Bent at a clean angle with narrowed eyes, she was studying one of the three smashed cases from which the three relics, Gildran's Collar, the Bell of Tongues, and the Umbral Blade, had been stolen.

Remaining shards of glass stuck up like jagged teeth from their rims and as Akteron watched, Piria scrunched up her nose and began sniffing them.

He cocked an eyebrow and turned back to the curator. "And you're sure he went through *this* wall?"

"One hundred percent," Kabonn replied. "The head of my security team showed me that much, at least — or rather, his Sharak did. Right after grabbing his prizes, the thief swept this way." He gestured again across the floor. "Right through this wall. I wouldn't have believed it, but when you see it...well, it's clear as the dawn bells. He simply passes into the stonework and–" He made a – *VUUSH!* – sound. "Gone."

Akteron cleared his throat, looking at the wall, then the floor, then the cases. "Impossible..."

"Akteron," Piria suddenly said in her 'I've got something' voice.

"Curator, excuse me." Akteron left Kabonn admiring his wall.

"Well?" he asked, drawing up beside her.

"Mmm," she grunted. "Nothing. You?"

"What? I thought you were onto something? Why did you call me over?"

"I just wanted to know if you'd found anything."

"Nothing, yet," Akteron replied, nodding to the case. "So...did it, erm, smell nice?"

"Huh?"

"The glass..."

"Oh. I was checking for traces of alkamium," Piria told him. "It's used in a relatively simple mixture which expands glass on contact. With enough, it *could* theoretically blow out a panel like this."

"And what does it smell like?"

"Hard to describe. Like mud, and carrots, and alcohol...but colder."

Akteron stared at her. "It didn't occur to you that Kabonn already said the thief used some kind of tool?"

"Well, yes. But I thought of another possibility..."

"What, then?"

"That maybe the vision was faked."

"Sharak don't fake things like that," Akteron replied.

"Not intentionally. They can be tricked, though. Remember that case, just after you'd moved in with me? That woman at Millet Docks?"

"That was a unique case, and she was a shaman..." Akteron said, recalling the small, keen-eyed woman in her feathered garments. The wooden necklace with a flat, aqua stone hanging from her wrinkled neck...

"Yes, but she still tricked the Sharak into showing a false memory. People like her still exist."

"She didn't *trick–*" Akteron sighed, watching Piria's eyes narrow and deciding not to enter that debate again. "Never mind. I just doubt that elder mystics are in the habit of robbing museums. And the Bureau has most of them on record, now."

Piria gave an accepting hum.

"I feel the motivation here is pretty obvious, anyway," Akteron went on, turning back to the wall. "I mean, if you go to all the trouble of breaking into a museum like this, it's clear why you'd nab those three objects. Even if it had only been those two,"— he motioned to the farthest pair of cases where the Krio relics, the bell and collar, had been housed —"I would have assumed political motivation. But with the blade also gone, the whole thing smacks of some kind of stunt. Some attempt to stir up trouble."

Piria didn't look convinced. "That's a leap. It's *also* possible our thief isn't that smart. Or bitter. What if this was just a 'smash, grab, go,' deal?"

Akteron pressed his lips together. "Happenstance, you mean? Done on a whim?"

"I don't see why we should rule that out."

"So, you think someone decided to break into the largest museum in the city, days before a high-profile event, and steal three irreplaceable artefacts, two of which were on loan and could spark a national crisis...without thinking it all through?"

She shrugged. "You know I don't like speculating."

Akteron tilted his head in acceptance. "Alright," he said, then closed his eyes. "Alright, well, I *do* like speculating, so let's go with 'on a whim'. Say the thief hears about the event. Maybe he sees the relics on the posters and that whets his appetite. They do look like big-buck items and he knows where they'll be, days before the exhibition. So, he enters the museum...*somehow*. Let's not deal with that, yet. Then, once he's inside, he beelines for the relics, deactivates the wards around the cases and smashes them. Another big *somehow*, there. Oh, he also misses this one, in between." He waved vaguely to an intact case. "And he *also* ignores the rest of the museum. Ignores the valuable, priceless objects on open display which are far easier to snatch." Opening his eyes again, he glanced at Piria. "If it's not to do with international relations, then I can't say I understand the motivation properly..."

Piria studied that lone, intact case, inside of which was a kind of three-headed goblet, each bowl extending from the shaft like roses from a stem. "Why would *you* say he left this?"

"Because it's ugly as a cachak's arse?"

She chuckled. "It's hideous. But really, we shouldn't close off any options. Not until we have something conclusive..."

Akteron didn't respond. He was staring through the case, considering her remark as he began thinking aloud.

"It's true, there's been no shortage of press and posters advertising this exhibition..." he said. "Any thief seeing them would realise these relics are highly valuable. So, perhaps he finds a way in, takes his chance, grabs what he can, then flees again before security gets here. Perhaps he didn't get distracted by the rest of the items because he didn't even see the other displays. It was nighttime, after all. It would have been really dark."

He tried to picture the museum in shadow. No light streaming in from those small, brick-sized windows. No lamps glowing softly above. No case-lighting to show-off the valuables. The whole space would have been like a gloomy, echoing sepulchre.

Piria cleared her throat. "Alright. Enough speculation, for now. Time is a factor, here and I think we need to get a more solid idea of how it played out."

Akteron nodded.

Sliding his fingers across the metal tokens at his belt, he removed a trio of ingots and weighed them in his hands.

Kabonn appeared beside the pair. "Ah, yes, I do wish my security team had waited for your arrival before petitioning their vision," he said. "It would have saved you this effort, and the charge."

Akteron gave him a shrug. "It's no problem, curator. Another round will likely prove beneficial and shed more light on things. Sharak never seem to do the same thing twice, after all."

"To be honest," Kabonn said, standing back from the cases, "even a mudslide would shed more light on things than that last petition did."

Akteron chuckled as Piria stepped back as well, leaving a few paces between them. He then allowed a moment to pull his senses from the echoing exhibition hall, to ignore its stale mustiness and the distant clamour from the market, outside.

Closing his eyes, Akteron imagined the presence circling just outside the sphere of his own consciousness — drifting, watching, listening.

"Ath viraan, Kandaar," he then said. "I send my respects and ask for your aid."

He only had to wait a heartbeat for a response. The air in the exhibit hall seemed to shift as a feeling descended over them all. A coolness. And Akteron's closed eyes searched about before they seemed to find something.

"That's kind of you," he said, choosing his next words carefully. "Kandaar, I ask that you show us the space we currently stand in as the three cases before me were smashed this morning, and the relics housed within were stolen. We would like to see the act of the theft, and how the culprit escaped with the artefacts. For this, I offer you three ingots."

A faint breeze tickled the stillness and Akteron raised his brows in surprise.

"Four...? Well, I do have another, yes." He removed another metal chip from his belt. "So, if you please?"

A tingle met his fingers as the charge was accepted and immediately, that subtle breeze picked up, ruffling Piria's hair.

It began in the lumstone lanterns, hanging above, each glowing core's luminance draining into faint trails that swirled down towards Akteron. These threads re-converged before him, spinning into a single, glowing ball about the size of a fist and shielding his eyes, Akteron stepped back to join Piria and the curator.

He hadn't seen Kabonn's face at the beginning of the communion. He'd missed the man's evident skepticism and perhaps a hint of helplessness, but if Akteron had glanced to his side now, he'd have seen a very different expression.

The orb rose above them and on the museum's stone floor, shadows began to bloom. Swiftly, they formed a blob, a dark mass which extruded upwards, upwards, until it began to take on human shape. Even so, its undersides remained connected to the floor in pillars, as if that glowing orb above were projecting solid shadow downwards — or *pulling* one out of the floor.

The dark figure was in motion before it had finished forming.

Trudging from the first case, which it had apparently just looted, it reached the second, whereupon he — for it could clearly be discerned as a he — lifted what appeared a sizeable work tool and struck the case with a blunt, powerful swing.

"A hammer?" Piria tilted her head in confusion.

Invisible glass shattered, shards of black shadow scattering into the air and evaporating as the man reached into the enclosure to seize the relic within, the metal circlet known as Gildran's Collar.

Then he paused, as if listening to something.

"Ah, yes..." Kabonn said distractedly. "He probably suspected our security team had heard the commotion. Alas, they had picked that moment to patrol the perimeter, outside."

The thief didn't wait to find out. Bounding at last to the third case, that hammer was raised once more and within seconds, the shadow was bolting past Akteron, past Piria and Kabonn directly for the wall, relics in hand.

Just as the curator had described, he didn't hesitate nor slow. His dark form ran directly through the stonework as if mist, and vanished from sight.

Silence lingered in the exhibit hall as that floating orb of light began to descend, again. When it reached Akteron's eye-level, with a quiet – *KSSHHP!* –, it then burst, tiny strings of light streaming back into the hanging, lumstone lanterns, above.

"So," Piria said. "That looks like a smash and grab, after all."

Akteron nodded. "It does."

He then turned to Kabonn. "Did this vision match the one you saw earlier today?"

Kabonn opened his mouth but no words came for a moment.

Then, he turned to Akteron and seemed to register the question. *"Good grief,* no...I mean, yes, in a way..." he broke a wide smile. *"Great Lights,* lad, what a spectacle! My security team's vision amounted to nothing but an incomprehensible eddy of smoke! This...*this* was truly something!"

Akteron mumbled something and glanced to the floor.

"Your welding...strong, I imagine?" The curator eyed the young man intently.

"I figure it's a ninth or tenth-grade," Piria answered for him. "Unusually strong for a nobody. And Kandaar is a bit of a freak, as well." She shrugged to her partner. "Sorry, Akteron. But it's true."

"Indeed, indeed." Kabonn gave a nervous chuckle. "I'm lucky if I can get Kanliira to acknowledge me, let alone grant a petition! Luck of the draw, I suppose."

"Truly unfair," Piria grunted.

"Alright, well, if we're done analysing me and my Sharak," Akteron said, "I'd like to have one last look at the wall outside, before we return to the Bureau and puzzle things out."

"The outside wall! Yes, indeed, of course." Kabonn turned at once to plod back towards the central corridor off which all the exhibits branched. "Though I must say, it *is* just the other side of this same wall, and my team and I did survey it, earlier..."

"You mean you saw the thief emerging from the stone?" Akteron asked.

"Emerging, yes, but also entering. We petitioned to see both moments and didn't glean anything of real value. And it cost a grievous sum! My security team used all they had. I dare say calling for another show — regardless of how fine it might be — won't unveil much more of use."

"Maybe not," Akteron said, "but we still need to examine the spot and gather any information we can."

Kabonn took the stairs down into the main entrance at a slight canter. He reminded Akteron of a festival showman, that round stomach leading the way while his little arms hovered at the sides as if gripping some tiny, invisible reigns.

Presently, the three were in the midday warmth again. Birds chattered in the canopy as they skirted the perimeter to enter the dappled sunlight on the museum's eastern flank and there, the curator finally halted his little trot.

They stood before one of the hulking wall-stones — a monolithic slab in a line of alternating red and white, each wider than Akteron's reach and a full storey tall — which Kabonn smacked with his palm.

"Marvellous construction, is it not?" the curator asked.

"Very impressive," Akteron said, brushing the wall with his fingers. It had been worked to a perfectly even, silken-finish and felt soft to the touch, yet rapping on the slab brought the familiar, cold immovability of stone to his knuckles.

"This is where he came out?" Piria asked, moving from one slab of dark granite to the next, lighter one.

"Indeed." Kabonn made that whooshing sound again as he gestured to indicate the thief's trajectory. "Out of that block like a fleeing cachak, he came. Then, down the steps here, over the street and, it appears, into *that* alley."

Akteron pivoted.

Encircling the museum was a wide, cobbled ring-road, which began and ended at the market square. Closed to carts and wagons, its bulging, rippling cobbles were unnavigable, pierced as they were by the beige gargantuans whose flowering vines festooned the city streets, and whose branches spread out to form Torril's boundless canopy.

Looking at the way each was staggered down the road, one might imagine that these sentinels had been planted. Placed about the city as part of another human scheme to shape nature, perhaps. But Akteron knew that, in fact, the city had grown up around *them*.

"Into one of those alleys," Piria muttered, peering at a dark opening opposite them. It lay about twenty paces away, between a wall of squat houses and shops that lined the ring road. Beyond lay the coiled mass which comprised the eastern edge of the city all the way to the wet quarter.

Kabonn nodded.

"It's the perfect getaway route," Piria went on. "Branching alleys, darkness, plenty of opportunities to hide himself or the items, or to change his clothing. Perhaps he's already found passage on a ship and is half way to Saj Minoor..."

"Let's hope your initial guess was right, then," Akteron replied, "that it was just a smash and grab and the thief wasn't that organised."

"Let's hope," Piria said, stepping forward to run her fingers over the wall, and barely a breath passed before she crinkled her nose. "Huh..."

"What is it?" Akteron asked.

"Not sure," she replied, leaning forward. "It's some kind of-...I can't say, exactly. A residue on the stone."

Whatever it was, Piria traced the perimeter of it with her fingers and reaching into her donvul pocket, then withdrew a handful of items. A metal scraper, a small phial, and a square of paper, the last of which she held out to Akteron.

"Help me out," she told him.

"You just happen to have all that with you?" he asked, taking it and stepping over to inspect the stonework for himself.

It wasn't clear what Piria had felt on that cool surface, but as she proceeded to scrape, Akteron caught a light grey substance which came off in flakes and collected in the paper he held.

"I knew I'd be on a case," she replied with a grin, "and prepared accordingly. Not that you'd know much about that."

Akteron snorted as she took the paper back.

"I also don't know if this will tell us anything, but based on the fact that it's only on our stone, I'd say it's not supposed to be here." Pouring the flakes into the phial, she finally stoppered it and pocketed the effects again.

"Good stuff."

"So?" the curator then asked, turning to Akteron and glancing to the young man's ingot belt. "Whatsay you? Shall we request another vision?"

Akteron could sense eagerness in Kabonn's grin but running his fingers over those tingling chips of metal at his waist, gave a reluctant wince. "Two such petitions in the space of an hour is pushing it," he muttered. "And I'm still not convinced it's necessary."

"I can try this time, if you like," Piria said, dusting her hands off. "Who knows, maybe Lathiik is feeling charitable, today."

"It's fine. If Kandaar is willing, his vision will probably be worth the ingots it'll cost."

She shrugged. "Your choice."

"Or..." Kabonn suddenly spoke with an air of drama. "Perhaps, *now*, after all these cycles, Kanliira will come through for me. Now, when it counts most. Perhaps after witnessing your display, inside, my old friend will find it inside herself, the *courage*, the *resolve*, to help us in this most important time..."

Akteron glanced unsurely to Piria.

"Be our guest," she said, and stepped back. "But it's really no problem for us. We can always return to the Bureau and request a recharge."

Kabonn simply waved them aside and planted himself a pace or so before the wall, face serious and eyes narrowed in concentration as he closed them.

"Kanliira..." he whispered.

A closeness fell around the three as it had in the exhibition hall, the air growing slightly cooler as it had inside, and Akteron watched with interest as the man continued in a low voice.

"Ath viraan," Kabonn said. "I know we haven't had the greatest of relationships. And I know I have neglected you of late, but I beseech you now, from the bottom of my heart...grant me a petition."

A slight breeze kicked up, Akteron not entirely sure if it was from the communion or just normal wind, yet a moment later, the curator's face flashed astonishment.

"She answered..." he said softly, eyes widening. "She *answered*!"

"Uhuh..." Piria gestured him on with her hands.

"Oh, yes. Kanliira, I would like to see what happened, here." Kabonn gazed into the air and swished his hands toward the granite wall beside them.

"Show me, in your way, whence the thief emerged and where my artefacts went, and I shall reward you with a three whole ingots."

The breeze shifted.

"He needs to work on specificity..." Piria uttered quietly. Akteron grunted in agreement.

Apparently dumbstruck that his Sharak was responding at all and clearly out of practise, Kabonn fumbled with his ingot-belt but managed to remove three of the metal nubs. His face was hesitant as he lifted them before himself and he gasped aloud as the tingling of his Sharak accepting the charge met his fingers.

"*Great Lights...*" he uttered. "She's actually going to do it..."

Akteron was equally surprised. After what the curator had said, it seemed this was quite a momentous turn.

Now, as if a prelude to the request, a small patch of ground before the three began to spark. The air popped and fizzed while leaves and small, fallen flower buds began to shift, vibrating, jittering, almost dancing across the stonework. This vegetable detritus then began to disintegrate, grinding itself into a fine, pastel-hued dust.

As it did, Kabonn's eyes became like the full-moons, his mouth ajar in astonishment.

"Beautiful," Piria uttered as the powder streamed into the air and drifted past her face. Upwards, upwards, until quite suddenly, it was out of sight.

For a moment all three remained, staring into the air. Then, they turned to watch the stone wall of the museum for whatever imagery the Sharak decided to occasion.

They waited an anxious breath. Two. Three.

Around the fourth breath and just when Akteron was about to give up on seeing anything, the sheet of dust appeared again, wheeling through the air to collide with the great granite block beside Kabonn.

It smashed against the stone, spreading out to coat the surface and formed an elongated, pink disc.

Then, that powder-disc burst into flame.

Piria raised her hand against the heat and light, and when she lowered it again, there was nothing of the dust left to be seen.

A second later, Piria began batting Akteron's head.

"You're on fire..."

"*Cragspit!*" he hissed, joining in as Kabonn muttered behind them.

"*I see, I see...*"

"I have to admit, I'm more confused than before." Piria turned to him. "What was that? What do you see?"

"That Kanliira is still a tempestuous *lout.* That's what!"

"Well..." Akteron was feeling gingerly through his plume of dark dreadlocks for damage. "We shouldn't judge her *too* quickly. I'm sure if we read into that, we will probably understand what she was trying to say."

"No, no." Kabonn sighed. "It's always been like this. She leaves me alone for cycles, ignores my requests, and when she eventually decides to commune with me and 'help', it's nonsense like this. Always with things bursting into flame..." He shook his head. "I had hoped this time, perhaps, things would be different. It *started* nicely."

"She does this often? Sets things on fire?" Piria asked.

"Oh, every time." Kabonn said. "At least, the ten times in my life when she actually answered an appeal. The first time scared me out of my skin. I was eight. Half the house burned down."

"Hmm," Akteron grunted, lowering his hand at last, satisfied that the damage hadn't been too extensive. "Well, I'm sorry for...whatever that was." Then he gestured to the tangle of alleys again. "Vision aside, though, if you say the thief ran out of the stone and carried on that direction, that's as good a start as any. And Piria has some material she'd like to analyse, now." He turned to the curator. "I think at this point, we'll head back to the Bureau and consider what we have, then plan our next steps. We'll be in touch at once via Riallo if there is any news."

Kabonn nodded, shaking off his vision-related disappointment before that familiar, warm grin returned. He set the spent metal ingots back into his belt and extended a hand to Piria. "It has been a pleasure, Ms. Kii, Mr. Uusei. A true pleasure. Yes, please let me know as soon as you find anything. I eagerly await your insights, and...I apologise that I was unable to be of more service."

Akteron shook his hand in turn. "You've been very helpful, actually."

"Kind of you to say, lad. Would you like me to call a coach?"

"No, I think we're both up for a stroll." He glanced at Piria, who nodded in agreement.

"Splendid. Oh, and Mr. Uusei..." Leaning over and voice dropping to a whisper, the curator's smile faltered. "I suppose I don't need to say it, but you, as a fellow countryman, surely know what's really at stake, here..." Akteron could almost smell his nerves as the man went on. "I don't mean my pride. I mean our *history*, and very possibly, the peace of our two nations. Naturally, I fear for the wellbeing of the relics, but I fear for the wellbeing of that peace far more. So I beg you. Be swift."

For a moment, the pair met eyes, and Akteron was shocked at the distress he saw.

Bouncing on his heels, the curator then stuffed his hands into his donvul pockets and began wandering back towards the museum's entrance. "Please, do keep me abreast of all developments!" he called after them, smile reinstated.

Akteron waved in acknowledgement, and the three parted ways.

———■———

"You *are* lucky, Ro," Piria said, fidgeting with leaves on a flower stalk.

The pair were reclining on a park bench and the sun was parting for another day, a few, thin clouds flushing a fervent orange beyond the great canopy.

Their intention hadn't really been to return to the Bureau. That was just official puffery Akteron had become used to dousing clients with when he needed time to think. Instead, they had wandered to the park.

Before them now, Torril City inhabitants meandered the winding, pebbled paths through carefully placed stones and greenery, some with leggy birds trailing behind, or smaller breeds resting on their shoulders.

A cluster of youths sat on circular benches, chatting and enjoying the last few warm days of the cycle.

"I realise," Akteron replied. "I just don't like drawing attention to it. It's awkward. I'd rather people weren't privy."

"That would mean never petitioning Kandaar in front of anyone," Piria said, "which is silly. Why not take advantage of it? Use it? Certain organisations in Torril are built on good weldings and strong Sharak, you know."

Akteron shrugged. "I'm aware. But I didn't do anything for this. I never worked for it, never asked for it. It's just the way things are."

"So, you won't seize this amazing advantage to give yourself a boost because it's not earned? That's admirable, I suppose."

"...but?"

"But do you realise how dumb that is? How rare it is to have what you have? Most people would *kill* for a welding like yours. A Sharak like Kandaar."

"Kandaar is wonderful," Akteron said. "I am thankful for him. I just don't like using him like that."

Piria made a quiet sound. "You aren't *using* him...that's not how Sharak work. What you have is a partnership that's *functional*," she repeated. "It's pointless to feel guilty about that."

Tossing the stripped flower stalk to the grass, Piria chuckled and gazed across the park. "You didn't see how Kabonn was looking at you when Kandaar showed us that shadow. You didn't see his eyes, Ro. He was amazed. As if he was seeing what *could* be done for the first time."

"*Ugh.* That makes me feel far worse," Akteron said. "That's exactly what I mean. So many people go their whole lives not having...not *knowing* what a good welding is or what Sharak can do. And then I come along and rub it in their faces. What right do I have to do that?"

The scant, wispy clouds were red, now. Like trails of fire leading across the powdery sky.

Piria sighed. "I guess that's a point." She leaned against him, resting her head on his shoulder. "I can tell you though, that not many people think that way. Personally, I've never believed it's all just chance, either."

"Oh? What, then?" Akteron asked.

Piria shrugged. "Well, for a long time, wasn't it established and 'true' that weldings were tied to intelligence? Now we know that's nonsense. And if that can be wrong, who knows what else is? I don't believe Sharak are assigned to us by the gods, let's say that much. Nor that their strength is influenced by the 'phases of the moons'..."

Akteron chuckled. "So, the whole Paramallion and thousands of cycles of doctrine are wrong?"

"*Pshh...*" Piria hissed, eyes flicking about warily and her voice dropping to a whisper. "That's a strong word. I just feel like they've leapt to a few too many...*unsubstantiated conclusions*, that's all. I don't think they, or anyone, has figured it out properly, yet."

"But you have a hypothesis..."

A pteranar nearby began calling its evening song in the quiet, dusky air. It was a complicated cry, rising and falling to end in a trilling, ringing tone that echoed and hushed that laughing cluster of youths, nearby.

Akteron watched as the first stars of the night blinked into being through an opening in the canopy.

"Alright. Imagine a pair of meteors whizzing through space," Piria said, pulling Akteron down until they were both almost lying on the bench. She pointed through another hole, to a spot of evening sky.

"Both of these meteors are separate. Flying far away from each other. No relation. Not from the same place or source. Simple, so far?"

Akteron laughed. "Very."

"Now, imagine that at some point, these two meteors collide with each other." She clapped her hands together softly to illustrate the event. "Random? Or not?"

"Random." Akteron said. "It has to be random."

"Why?"

"Well, for a start, they're just two dead objects, flying through space. There's only two options. Option one, they fly on forever. Option two is that at some point, they hit something."

"But they hit each other."

"Well, yes." Akteron wrinkled his brow. "But for those two that hit each other, there are billions — *trillions*, of others that didn't. The fact that they're similar objects doesn't really mean anything, just that we *saw* two similar objects colliding. What we *didn't* see were the countless others, and that makes it seem that the one *we* saw happened for a reason. We assign the event meaning because that's what we want to see."

"Well put." Piria grinned. "Have I really had that much of an effect, on you?"

Akteron chuckled.

"Alright," Piria continued. "So, you're saying that perhaps it's observation *itself* that gives this illusion of meaning?"

"...yes." he replied carefully. "I mean, our brains are wired to recognise patterns. But this one would be a false-positive. The collisions are random."

"Alright. What if I then said that both meteors had been launched by an intelligent power, with the *express intent* that they'd collide."

"Hey, that's not fair..."

"Why?"

"Because-..." Akteron faltered. "You can't add things afterwards."

"Just because you didn't know about it, doesn't make it unfair. It just means I had more knowledge than you."

"That *is* unfair."

"Alright. It's unfair. It doesn't change the fact that these two, seemingly random objects and their seemingly random collision is actually anything but."

"So, you say there *is* a meaning behind our weldings?"

"No, I'm not saying that, necessarily. Not *meaning*. Though... perhaps *intent*."

"Well, that's almost the same thing. You're still saying that there's some conscious mechanism, behind it all."

She shrugged.

"The Paramallion insists Sharak are a divine gift," Akteron added, "but maybe it's just how nature works? Different things attract one another all the time in nature. Nectar attracts insects. Trees attract birds. Alcohol attracts sailors…"

Piria gave an amused grunt, before eyeing him sideways. "That's it, though. That is *exactly* what I'm getting at. Somehow, attraction *is* involved. There's some kind of synchronous-…ugh." She flicked a piece of stone off the bench, beside her. "Never mind. I don't want to bore you. It's nothing we need to talk about, now."

"No, it is important. I know you've been researching it."

Piria lifted one brow.

"It's what you've been researching since before we met," Akteron went on, "I've seen the stacks of texts in your office. I clean the house, remember, and that door is always ajar. If anyone else saw how many books you have…those piles of paper…"

"I *told* you, don't clean The Cave!" Piria said. "I like it messy. I know where everything is."

"But it was *soo* messy," Akteron groaned.

A light chuckle. "Honestly, if you hadn't cleaned it, I'd never have found that old ring of my mother's…" Piria trailed off and a small silence fell, before she picked up her words again. "And that research isn't super secret. Not to you, anyway, or I'd have hidden all that in my super secret hiding spot."

Akteron smiled but his mind was still working through her question. "Who hasn't pondered weldings, now and then?" he admitted. "How and why Sharak bond with us, and what it means? We still know so little about it, even after all this time. Isn't that odd?"

"They don't seem to want us knowing about it…" Piria said quietly.

The pair allowed that to sit, watching as a flock of larger birds soared above them in a circular formation. They were heading the direction of the Seat and probably roosted around there.

"You know what else is fascinating?" Akteron said, at last.

"Dinner tonight. It's going to be like nothing you've ever eaten. Like a meal fit for the Great Chair or a banquet for the gods, themselves! Though, I still need to go and buy those garinians...I hope Kello hasn't sold out already."

"Well, then," Piria said, sitting upright. "I mean, it *is* on the way. And we do need good food for all the difficult thinking ahead. We have to find some leads for this case."

Akteron nodded. "Undoubtedly. And wine. Wine will help, as well." He stood and extended a hand, and Piria grabbed it, allowing herself to be pulled to her feet.

"Cheese is also like wine...in that it's helpful," she added.

"The most helpful," he concurred, and the two set off toward the docks.

CHAPTER FIVE
WINE, SUSPECTS, CONFUSION

A pair of candles burned low on the windowsill.

"So, we have a few possibilities, then," Akteron said, eyes tracking a paper lantern on the ceiling as a breeze prodded it in ponderous arcs.

Lying flat-backed on the carpet in her apartment, he and Piria had listened to the settling city through an open window, sunset passing while the city's avifauna sang goodnight. The ruckus was so loud it threatened to dislodge masonry but finally, stillness had fallen. Now, there remained just the occasional, chirping lizard, the clatter of shopfronts being locked for the night, and the odd coach rattling past in the temperate dusk.

Piria's apartment was tucked off the main streets, nestled in 'Copperbelly Snicket', a curving laneway which terminated in a round dead-end — perhaps the reason for the name. It was just one of many such lanes which, on street-level, contained the workshops and metal supply stores comprising the Molten Quarter, and Akteron loved it here.

He loved the quiet, for metalworking was neither a business which ran after dark, nor an attractor for throngs of people. He loved that, set back as it was, it provided a refuge from the bustling thoroughfares and teeming city squares, the perfume which often drifted in from a creeping flower on the outside wall, and also that it looked down onto a café, whose activity provided a pleasant buzz in the daylight hours.

"I'm still a fan of the first option," Piria said.

"That the thief was a nobody? I'm not ruling it out. But the others are also viable. I mean, an antiquities dealer would go crazy for artefacts of this value and the leg-up they'd provide."

"Risky, though, pitting themselves against two powerful states just for a leg-up."

"Some criminals thrive on crazy. And I don't doubt the shadow-market knows how to handle high-priority goods discreetly."

"Is Tagill a suspect, then?" Piria asked.

"Unlikely, but I think we should question him all the same. He's been caught selling at the shadow-market before and even if he's not the thief, he's bound to know something. That lot always have an ear to the ground. This is a serious theft and they'd all have heard about it by now."

"Mmm," Piria said, tapping her finger against her wine glass. "I do also like the idea of a contracted thug, though."

Akteron grinned.

"He's desperate, he's dirty. He loves taking on the jobs for the thrill, more than the charge. He'll bargain with his employer, too. Why take the agreed upon price after all he's been through?"

"What's his name?" Akteron asked.

"Grubaal," she said immediately. "Grew up in the Soldiers' Quarter. Kicked out of a rough household young and joined the wrong crowd. Learned to work a sly-deal like a second tongue. He applied and never got into the Bureau of Security but his hands are calloused, anyway, not just from working at the forges, but from practising in secret with a pike he stole."

"I'm sure many fine members of society grew up in the Soldiers' Quarter," Akteron said.

"Sure they did. But not Grubaal...he's dangerous and shifty, through and through. Tricked the Seat themselves out of a stockpile of ingots."

Akteron laughed, sitting up. "I kind of like this guy."

Piria chuckled, but then went quiet.

"What is it with you and the Seat, anyway?" she asked.

Akteron cocked his head. "What do you mean?"

"Come on, Ro. I hear it. That trace of scepticism, the thin coating of aggression whenever you speak about the Bureau or the Seat. You need to be careful with all that..."

"I don't know what you're talking about," he said. "I love the Seat."

"See? That's it. Right there."

"What? I mean it. They're the protectors of Tarma. They hold this city together with a firm, uncompromising grip. They pay me. What's not to love?"

Piria sighed and sat up. "I'm getting more cheese."

She stood and wandered over to the table, where a knife and a half-block of Kal Brioran Green sat on a cutting board beside a slowly melting wedge of aged, Harbour Rund.

"You'll have bad dreams if you eat any more," Akteron warned.

Piria ignored him.

"Alright, so, who else have we got?" she asked, leaning against the wall beside the window, pressing the small piece of cheese she'd cut as if it were a stub of rubber.

"Well, I also liked your idea of a high-family pulling the job," Akteron said. "It makes sense, I suppose. They have an object taken from them, they want it back. Simple motives are often the ones that click."

"No, it doesn't fit," Piria said. "The collar might have been appropriated from the Parsaan estate, but that doesn't explain the other two objects."

"True. But maybe-...maybe it's payback?" Akteron said, then

sighed. "*Ugh.* We need more to go on. This speculating is pointless until we really *know* something about this thief."

"We *do* know something," Piria said.

"Right," Akteron agreed. "We know he was average height, average build. Longish hair. Donvul looked thin and kind of loose. So it was cheap, then. Or old. We couldn't see his pants, nor boots. Nor his ingot-belt." He grunted lightly. "Honestly, it's all a bit useless."

"If he even *had* an ingot-belt..." Piria added and popped that piece of cheese into her mouth. "I thought his donvul looked thicker, too. Woollen, maybe."

"Still doesn't really help," Akteron said. "The clothing was probably a disguise. I mean, the first thing criminals learn is that a Sharak is going to show your deed to the Bureau pretty soon after it's done."

Piria nodded, chewing as she thought. Then she knocked absently on the window sill. "I say we head back to the Bureau tomorrow, get you charged back up, then head back to the museum."

"Aw, I'm not going through that paperwork-headache, again. And what for, exactly?"

"We could ask Kandaar to reveal some more details. I'd like to be certain about those things. If the guy had a belt, for example. And what he had in his pockets..."

Akteron shook his head. "Kandaar really doesn't like being pestered about the same things. I don't want to annoy him...and the window for the vision will have reached its limit by then."

"The limit differs from Sharak to Sharak." Piria waved off the concern. "He'll be able to see *something*, I know it. And, have you ever *really* annoyed him?"

"Yes, actually," Akteron replied, and the odd way he said it gave Piria pause. She didn't follow that point any further.

Sighing, she went to cut some more cheese. "Maybe you're right. Maybe we need to look elsewhere. I have that residue to analyse, anyway. That's got to tell us something. And you have a couple other shadow-market contacts like Tagill, don't you?"

Akteron gave an unsure nod. "Not sure if anyone *but* Tagill will be any good on this."

"Alright. Well, like you said, we ask him to keep an ear to the ground, anyway. If anything resembling our objects pop up, then we'll know–"

– *tingatinnggg!* –

The doorbell. Its chime was quiet and innocent despite the late hour, but Akteron sat upright.

"Hmm," Piria grunted, setting the cheese-knife down and crossing the room. "Late, for a caller."

With some effort — and a little woozily due to the wine — Akteron stood and walked to the window, leaning out to peer into the street below.

"Message runner…" he said.

Piria pulled the entrance catch and a moment later they could hear the front door closing, followed by quick footsteps on the staircase leading up to her apartment. Piria opened the door and Akteron then watched as a red-cheeked, pimpled youth appeared, atop his head, a flat, red cap, and in his hand, a letter.

"Evening, Miss," he panted, checking the name-tag beside the door before presenting it. Once in her grip, he bent to catch his breath.

Prying open the small, wax sealed envelope, Piria withdrew a square note.

"From the Bureau," she told Akteron, her brow creasing as she scanned the few lines written there and read aloud.

"To all staff: Due to a disturbance and effective immediately, we urge all citizens to avoid the Official Quarter unless absolutely necessary. Reports detail mass confusion and rioting. Bureau officers and residents of the area appear incapacitated, using garbled, unintelligible speech, and in many cases are presenting unruly and hazardous behaviour."

Akteron shot her a worried glance.

"Thank you," Piria told the runner, holding an ingot out to him. He nodded, withdrawing his own, and they pressed the metals together briefly before he disappeared down the stairs. She closed the door.

"Garbled, unintelligible speech?"

"The bell..." Akteron uttered. "*Great Lights,* the thief *used* it! He must have. We need to get over there, now."

Piria was already pulling on an evening donvul.

"What if he rings the bell again while we're there, though?" she asked as Akteron downed a glass of water and leapt to grab his own from the back of a chair. "We don't want the same thing to happen to us. I don't fancy spending the rest of my life unable to speak."

"Kabonn said the effect is short-term," Akteron replied, pocketing a small notepad and pen from a side-table. "Though I don't know what his definition of 'short-term' is...perhaps we should organise a place to meet tomorrow, just in case. If anything happens, let's meet at The Huntress." He thought for a moment, scrunching up his forehead. "And let's each bring a book. Then we can point at words if we need to communicate."

"I'm not sure that's how it works. We'll just have to play it by ear–" Piria also hesitated. "Or another way."

Flicking the lantern off, she followed Akteron out the door.

———◼———

Tanaar Street was in chaos when Piria and Akteron stepped from their coach to find the populace going mad.

"I hope you don't mind if I get going..." said their cabbie, an older, jowled man with thick lips, as he ducked a bottle that sailed over his head and smashed on the sidewalk. "Feels a little,

I dunno. Unsafe?"

"Here." Piria quickly held up an ingot to pay him, and the coach was soon parting a mass of shouting inhabitants to pull off, again.

They had asked to be dropped outside Sekiir's Eatery, a landmark of the old Official Quarter and one of Akteron's favourite restaurants. Yet, as Akteron stepped aside to dodge a man running and wielding a loose cobblestone, he wondered how wise that choice had been.

Scattered mobs stormed about, some looting, some drawn together as if for protection, and the area was a mess. A number of street lanterns had been downed, flickering fragments of their disengaged, lumstone cores lying on the cobbles or in the dirt of overturned planter-boxes. And not far away, Akteron could see a damaged fountain spraying water into the night air.

Sekiir's hadn't fared well, either. Built into the still-recognisable former entrance of a Bureau — a solid and imposing building used until the Seat's sweeping new towers had been completed — the restaurant's doors had been barricaded. The front window was gone, and the agent of destruction — a stone cap from one of the official avenue's numerous stele — lay inside atop the litter of shards and overturned furniture.

Why looters would want to get into a restaurant that badly was beyond him. The food *was* mouthwatering, but honestly, it was the atmosphere that drew him back each time...

"Watch it!" Piria yanked him backwards by the shoulder as another coach flew by, only to peal around the next corner and out of sight.

Regaining his balance, Akteron stared down at his donvul, wide-eyed. "That maniac clipped one of my buttons clean off!"

Piria turned to inspect the patch of fabric, from which threads hung like the roots of some plucked vegetable.

"Lucky it wasn't your nose..."

That was a point, and despite his annoyance, Akteron gave her a smirk. "Maybe we should use the sidewalk?"

"Safety first…"

The pair stepped off the road and began walking the stretch, eyes scanning the surroundings warily, Akteron's fingers lingering on those loose threads as if holding a wound closed.

It soon became apparent that while many had taken to violence or opportunism in this confusion, there was another dimension at play here. In the doorway of an abandoned shop, a well-dressed lady growled at a large quill on the ground. A mere jump from her, two men stood facing each other on the sidewalk, one smiling and waving a plant frond about as the second clapped and bared his teeth. And not far from them, a small girl perhaps six cycles old crouched and barked into the gutter while rubbing the tail of her long, braided hair into a puddle.

Beyond all this, flames curled out of a building's smashed windows and lapped at the white stonework and Akteron hoped to the Winds the place had been evacuated.

"*Great Lights…*" he muttered, absorbing this nightmare.

"Hey, look." Piria had sighted something across the avenue. "A Sec Bureau coach…"

Akteron saw it. Parked tidily and in a kind of sphere of calm, the vehicle was intact, though its doors were open and its cabin, empty.

"Officers gone," Piria went on. "That note from the Seat said they'd been incapacitated."

"…but due to the bell, or the aftermath?" Akteron asked.

The pair stepped between two planters to allow a small mob to blunder past, all babbling, laughing, one even squawking.

"Who knows. But I don't blame the officers for leaving the scene, either way."

"No. I mean, how do you handle something like this?" Akteron turned his eyes to Piria, avoiding the sight of a young man hammering a wall nearby in frustration. "In any case, I think we can confirm that this was our relic."

She nodded.

"It took the populace here completely unawares," Piria said as they walked. "And they don't realise it will wear off. And how could they? They wouldn't have a clue why this happened. Oh, it must be awful..."

A spooked pterenar dodged past them, its heavy, clawed feet clacking on the pave-stones and its large, thrashing wings barely missing two figures who stood under a nearby streetlamp.

Older, wrinkled and still in their robes, the pair appeared to be scholars and stared at books in their hands, and contrary to the scattered, panicked mass around them, they appeared oddly calm.

As Akteron watched, the closest of the two, a woman, looked up and crossed her eyes, then proceeded to say something in utter gibberish.

The man, bearded and spectacled, crinkled his brow together, laughed, and spouted further garbled nothings, at which point the woman jumped on one foot, prompting the man to whirl his hands in circles.

That done, they both looked down at the books, again.

"Well, I think we can rule the book idea out," Piria said.

Both she and Akteron then leapt as a man burst from an alley and darted towards them. Delivering a string of pleading grunts and squeaks, he then gave a small curtsy and fell silent.

"Whoa, there," Akteron said, raising his hands as if talking to a spooked pterenar. "I know this is difficult–"

The man merely stared at the motions before, with a pained giggle, he darted back into the alley.

"It's as if..." Akteron began, watching him go, "as if even simple things, even simple gestures–...oh!" Suddenly, he turned to Piria. "Ri, what if...what if the bell doesn't just confound *literal* tongues?"

Piria's cocked her head for a moment. "What do you mean-..." Her eyes then widened as well. "Oh, of course, of course! It confuses *all* tongues! The written word. Gestures. Expressions. Everything! *All* kinds of communication."

Akteron nodded. "That's why this is so out of control. I imagined that even without spoken language, people could still communicate *somehow*. I couldn't see how this object could have caused the disasters Kabonn spoke of. But now..." He took a deep breath and gazed about. "That's why this is such a mess. This is why the relic is so dangerous."

"But it's all so *unnecessary*. So...*mean*," Piria added, dodging a combative young couple who grappled, struggled, then stumbled into a planter box together. "And why would *anyone* ever ring this thing?"

"Well..." Akteron nodded. "Perhaps that's the point. That the perpetrator doesn't do it knowingly?"

Piria picked up the thread. "*Ah*, that's good. Kabonn did say it's a weapon. But it's a weapon made to *deceive*. A poisoned-pie, of sorts."

"Right. Intended to be found or seized in victory, perhaps. Or gifted to an enemy. And based on its fine workmanship and appearance, the receiver would no doubt be one of high-status."

"Who would cripple their own army."

"Or send their own populace into chaos," Akteron said, realising something, "the Day of Blood is only said to have become a massacre because the tide of battle changed unexpectedly, at the last moment..."

Turning a corner, he digested the implications of all this with an uncomfortable nod.

In this next avenue, agitation and despair filled the night as people flocked, ran, hopped, and rolled about.

"But even if all this is true," he continued, "there has to be a way to avoid its effects, right? A way to reverse it or some way to negate it? I mean, if this thing was carried into battle, imagine it being struck accidentally by your own forces, in the wrong place, at the wrong time."

Piria took a breath. "I think right now we need to focus on two more pressing questions. Namely, what's going to happen here? And, where is the thing now?"

Akteron hummed. "Yes. Well, if what Kabonn said about the effects is also true and the people here can just survive for a while, they *should* return to their senses and everything will be fine...cleanup aside." He shot a doubtful glance at a burning park bench. "As to where the bell is *now*. You're right, that's the greater concern. I mean, ringing it here in the Official Quarter where the most common objects lying about are books and quills is one thing. But if it were rung again, say, in the Soldiers' Quarter..."

Piria winced and opened her mouth to add something, then halted mid-stride. "Hey, have you noticed things have calmed down?"

True enough. As they'd been walking, the street before them had gone eerily quiet, just one or two lonely souls wandering and babbling to themselves under the flickering streetlights.

"Odd..." he said, glancing to the previous street where that burning house and bench still bathed the street in orange, and cast jittering shadows across its surrounding structures.

"Not really," Piria replied, pivoting sharply to march back towards it.

The change in trajectory was so sudden that Akteron almost kept walking without her.

"Erm, why not?" he then said, jogging back to her side.

"Because it tells us something import–"

Mid-sentence, the window of a building nearby exploded in a shower of glass, a vase sailing out to hit the street with a heavy – *CLESSHH!* –

Garbled yells followed from inside the dwelling, but Piria didn't even break stride.

"Something important?" Akteron prompted her, brows knitting together. "What does it tell us?"

"Think about it. Bells make sounds."

"I think we can both agree on that, yes. And let's not play the 'I know something you don't know,' game again. Out with it."

Piria smiled as she strode on. "Sound carries a certain distance, but falls off with exponential decay after that, right?"

"Sure..."

"Which means the chime could be heard only within a certain range..."

Akteron suddenly understood. "Oh! Brilliant! You think we can find the epicentre?"

"I don't see why not. The more panic we see, the closer we should be to the place it was struck—"

Just then, a familiar voice called out from behind them.

"Oi, you two!"

Surprised, Akteron turned to see the coach driver from that morning approaching down the rubble-strewn sidewalk.

"Erm, good evening."

"Not really, skipper," the man answered, running a hand along his outstretched arm in Torrilian greeting and nodding to Akteron's orange donvul. "Thought I recognised them fancy stitches. You're the two from the museum this morning, ain't you? Eighth of a chip?"

"That was us, yes," Akteron answered. "Can we help you with something?"

"Not me, skipper. You two'll need help, though, if you're plannin' on wanderin' that way. City's gone mad, y'see?"

Piria cocked an eyebrow. "Yes, that's actually why we're here. Do you live in the area?"

"Sure do," he said, tilting his head. "Just round the corner, alley on the left. Can't go home at the moment though, because my buildin's teeming with lunatics."

"I don't think they're *lunatics*," Akteron said, shooting an unsure glance at the broken vase and the fire still leaping from those windows. "Say, would I be right in thinking you just got home from work?"

"That'd be right," the driver said. "Found the place a complete, stinkin' mess, too. One neighbour throwin' books out his window and howlin' like a marsh-beak, the other singing backwards."

"That must have been a shock. What time do you think that was, exactly? When you came home, I mean."

"Well, it must've been…'bout an hour ago," the driver answered, scratching at the driver's cap he still wore, despite being off duty.

"An hour," Piria muttered. "Good. The person who informed the Bureau couldn't have been here when it happened or they'd have been confounded. So, it must have happened just before that…I'd say two hours ago, at most."

Realising the driver was staring at them suspiciously, Akteron then said. "Oh, right. Introductions. I'm Akteron, this is Piria. Bureau of Security."

Piria flashed him a cynical glance.

The driver didn't question it. "Dinill," he said with a nod. "So, you know what the heck is happenin' here, then?"

"We're trying to figure that out," Akteron replied. "And as it happens, it'd be most helpful if you could tell us what you saw when you got home."

"Like I said. Madhouse," Dinill answered.

"Do you mean everywhere? All through the area?"

"I did go lookin' for anyone who could tell me what in the wastes was goin' on," Dinill said. "I know these streets better'n anyone." He shook his head. "But right across, from Coneer Avenue through Subuur Street, all of 'em. Crazy."

"All that way?" Piria nodded back towards Sekiir's.

"All that way. Nobody spoke a damned word I could understand. Like the city had been taken o'er by Kal Briorans.

And people were fightin', cryin'. Never seen anythin' like it..."

"That's a good, eight-block stretch," Akteron muttered.

Beside him, he saw Piria reach into a planter box and run her finger through the dirt.

Akteron cocked an eyebrow but glanced back to the buildings around them. "How is it possible that such a small bell could be heard across that distance?" Then, he turned back to Dinill. "And after those streets, did you go any further?"

"Nope."

"Why?"

"Well, I finally found someone who could talk, didn't I?"

Akteron started. "You *did*?"

"Sure. Accusin' me of lyin'?"

"No, I'm just surprised. Where did you find this person?"

"End of Subuur Street. Young woman peerin' out of her window, golden hair, bright little bird on her shoulder. She was right troubled, as I was. Said she saw it happen. Saw it all start after the evenin' temple song."

"Hah! Spot on with your time estimate, Ri," Akteron said over his shoulder. "The temple song was two hours ago. And Dinill, this woman was troubled, but not *confounded*, is that right?"

"Seemed to speak the same language, skipper..."

Akteron turned to find Piria grinning.

"We have enough points," she said, gesturing to a circle she'd drawn, with a number of dots and lines running through it. "If we consider Tanaar Street, where we were dropped off"— she pointed at both points —"and how things are here, where it all seems calm. We add what Dinill said about Subuur Street...and Coneer Avenue..." Akteron watched as she poked one last point into the makeshift diagram. "Then triangulation can give us an approximate centre. We're likely at the edges, now. At one extreme of it all."

"In which case," Akteron turned to Dinill. "Dinill, What's between here and the city wall, in that direction." He pointed down the street, towards the chaotic noises they'd come from. "Do you know the alleys in there?"

"'Course I do," Dinill said, puffing his chest up as if insulted. "In the middle, there, that'd be Dagger's Clutch."

"That's it. The epicentre is there," Akteron said.

"Rough corner, that..."

"And what better place for a thief to hide?" Piria added. "Dinill, would you mind leading the way?"

"To Dagger's Clutch? Sure, why not? Night can't get any worse. But let's make it quick...what with all these lunatics are runnin' about."

"They're just confused," Akteron said. "They'll return to their senses in a few hours...we hope."

Dinill *PSHH*ed through his teeth, then nodded towards the street with the burning house. "If you say so...that's the way we need to go, then."

"After you."

The three set off at a cracking pace.

CHAPTER SIX
DAGGER'S CLUTCH

The alleys were murky tunnels filled with the haunting echoes of bell-induced chaos as Akteron, Piria and Dinill edged along, towards what they hoped was the source of it all.

Their feet crunched in gritty puddles as small creatures scuttled about, unseen in the darkness. It all held a distinctly unwelcoming air, as if they were disturbing some slumbering malevolence whose eyes watched from every unseen corner and crevice.

"Almost there," Dinill assured them in a low voice and Akteron let out a quiet sigh.

He had, in honesty, been hesitant to plunge into this labyrinth with a man who seemed to know this dubious area a little *too* well...but as they'd trodden further he had rationalised that, if Dinill wanted to rob or kill them, he could have dropped his helpful guise long ago and been done with it. Ten minutes later and without a knife in his gut, Akteron was satisfied that the man was genuinely trying to assist.

That did nothing to distract from the unease he felt. For this place was eerie. Pervading the air were utters, sobs and cries which drifted through the night, echoing as if this place were a canyon in some dusky, spirit realm.

"When *will* it wear off?" Piria asked quietly as she hopped a pile of jagged wood, barely visible in the murk.

"Kabonn didn't know exactly," Akteron muttered back, "but he was adamant that the effects only last a short while. Whether that means an hour, a day, or a span, I don't know. I doubt he did, either. He said that knowledge of the bell is all taken from old fragments of manuscripts–"

"Shh!" Dinill hushed them.

Akteron continued in a whisper. "The Day of Blood was only taught to us in school because of the political implications. The bell was only mentioned briefly, from what I recall."

Piria made a low noise as they took a corner and street lanterns came into view, ahead.

Dinill stopped and turned to the pair.

"Not much point, me going further," he uttered. "This is the heart of the place. But guard yer ingot-belt, skipper. Quick hands about. And don' speak to anyone unless you're ready for a good scuffle."

"I don't think we could even if we wanted to," Akteron replied, drawing an ingot and holding it out to Dinill.

"Kind of ya." The driver waved it off. "But I'm not interested in charge this time, just give me some peace 'o mind so I can sleep. 'aight?"

Akteron nodded, replacing the token and pulling his donvul over the belt to hide it.

"Should we put a ward on, though?" Piria asked. "I have enough for a simple repelling-hex. You do, too."

Akteron looked uncertain. "I'm going to try and spare all the charge I can, for now. Who knows what's waiting for us?"

Exchanging a quick gesture of thanks with Dinill, Akteron and Piria trod into Dagger's Clutch.

It was a small, dingy square, reached via one of a series of twisting alleys that all branched out from its heart. There, an empty fountain stood, its stones darkened with soot and grime and onto which all the buildings stared down, as if in mourning.

"Lovely aesthetic they have, here," Piria said as a babbling shadow flitted across an alleyway opposite them.

"I am seriously uncomfortable," Akteron replied, turning to check the lanes behind them. All appeared empty, Dinill already having gone. "But...who knows? Maybe our thief and the bell are still here."

As if to test that, Piria prodded a small pile of junk with her foot, perhaps hoping the bell might fall out. She didn't seem to be anywhere near as unsettled as Akteron was as she sauntered to and fro, checking an empty planter box, the front of a boarded-up tavern, a pile of rotten crates, then each of the alleyway entrances in turn.

A cold breeze blew through the square and Akteron shivered, putting his hands in his pockets and trying to imagine how this place might look in the daylight...

Nope. It would still be awful.

"Well, what do you think?" Piria said, turning to face him. "If you had just stolen a bunch of precious artefacts, why bring them here? And what might make you set one off?"

Akteron peered at the front of a nearby shop, its door nailed fast with blackened timbers.

"I think if he wanted to pawn it, he's about ten cycles too late..." he said.

Piria nodded. "I considered that, too, but I doubt transactions go on in the stores, here..." She glanced into one of the dark alleys.

"True. So, perhaps he *was* meeting a buyer and it went awry?"

Piria tilted her head. "Possible."

"The bell gets set off by mistake in a scuffle. Or maybe the buyer wanted a test-run?" he elaborated and Piria chuckled, the sound lightening the mood greatly.

"While we're guessing," she said, "it's also possible that he rang it himself by accident...unaware of what it did."

"Ah. Still sticking to your 'smash and grab' hypothesis." Akteron pulled at a faded, weathered poster until it began peeling from the wall. "No, I have a little more faith in our rogue. I don't think this was an accident." He turned to face the square. "I have a feeling he came here for a reason. Actually, I'm sure of it."

"Ah, right. You think he has some grand purpose, with all of this," Piria said. "A lofty goal, more important than simply making a profit?"

"Hey, let's give him the benefit of the–" Akteron stopped talking and cocked one brow. "Wait. A lofty goal..."

Slowly, he tilted his head upwards.

"I was just teasing. Testing your assumptions." Piria shrugged, before catching his stare. "Hey, are you alright?"

"Yes..." he said. "And better yet, I think I might know what happened, here."

Surveying a nearby building, he then began marching towards its flanking alley. Piria only caught up with him as he plunged into one of the more shadowy lanes and reached out to shake an old drainpipe.

"Ro?"

"Hang on," he replied, grabbing a couple of outcropping bricks only to find them crumbling beneath his grip. "Nope...not there."

Glancing down the wall, he shook his head and returned to the square.

"Come on, now *you're* doing it," Piria prompted. "The 'I know something you don't know,' game."

Akteron's reply was simply to point upwards as he hopped into another alley.

"Yep. It's a lovely building..." she said to its boarded-up front doors. Akteron didn't hear her sarcasm.

"Bam!" he announced, gesturing triumphantly to a window. "Here we are!"

Its insides were barely visible in the murk, but tossing a fragment of stone through the gaping frame, it clattered to rest inside, confirming that there was, at least, a floor.

"You can't be thinking of–" Piria began as Akteron leapt up and vanished inside.

A moment later, his feet found purchase. The floorboards bounced and groaned at each movement, definitely rotten, and one of them gave a loud crack as Piria's feet landed next to his.

"I could try petitioning Lathiik for some light," she whispered, the words echoing in a short silence.

"It's alright," Akteron replied, reaching into one of his pockets and withdrawing a small, rough-edged object whose softly glowing, yellow core spilled light enough to carve through the gloom.

Piria gave a grunt, Akteron unable to tell if the tone was impressed or critical.

"You stole government property?"

"Hey, *I* didn't knock that lantern over," he replied, waving the shard about. "A useless, shattered lumstone just lying in the dirt? The Seat won't miss it."

Her unease was almost audible in the darkness.

"Oh, we'll be fine. Let's just hope it lasts long enough to get us where we need to go, though."

"...and that would be?"

Akteron nodded to the other side of the room, and in the faint light from the lumstone shard, Piria saw the staircase.

———◼———

It took three flights of rickety stairs for the pair to emerge into Torril's temperate, evening air again.

Here, above the tangled alleys of Dagger's Clutch but below Torril's endless canopy, they found a terrace spanning the rooftop. One which provided a vantage of the whole, sprawling, messy quarter.

"It has to be said," Akteron began, following the low railing, "that if I were a thief looking to ring a bell, and if I wanted it to be heard far and wide, I'd bring it here."

He reached the end and peered down at the square and its forlorn fountain. Night had long since fallen but in every direction a messy crop of structures could still be seen, lit by the glow from streets below.

"The sound would certainly carry, at this height," Piria agreed. "I can't think of a better place. The problem is *proving* it was here. And working out where it went, next." She turned to face him. "So, should we petition Kandaar? See if he can show us anything?"

Akteron shifted on his feet.

He was aware that so many petitions in one day was presumptuous, and that chances of Kandaar assisting diminished with each request. What if he needed something else — *really* needed something — before the night was out? If Kandaar refused to answer when things were dire...

Briefly, a memory flashed through his mind of a small, moonlit room, furniture toppled and his and Ren's belongings, strewn about...

If that happened again–

But he couldn't return to that place, now.

"I mean, again, I *can* try asking Lathiik," Piria added, her tone betraying a distinct lack of optimism.

Akteron shook himself. "Whatsay we use our own eyes before we bother them?" he suggested.

Piria didn't press the issue.

Running a hand along the railing beside him, Akteron tried to ignore the sounds of bell-induced chaos still evident through the endless gauze of hanging vines, surrounding them. He tried to ignore the shouts, the bangs and wails, and focused instead on a visual.

Turning to look back at the door they'd come through, he plotted the thief's movements in his mind. Tried to imagine the squat figure emerging through that door, just as they had, and trudging over to this same railing. How he'd gazed down onto that same square.

Still brandishing his lumstone shard, Akteron crouched and passed its light over the brickwork. Then the low wall. Then back over the ground near his feet. And there, mid swipe, he paused.

"Ri, *look*..."

Piria crouched down beside him.

"That hole?" she asked.

"An impact-divot," Akteron confirmed, leaning closer. "Not deep, but it's definitely from something heavy. And definitely recent, look at the little chunks of stone lying around it. Even light rain would have washed them away. Most importantly, though..."

"The mark seems to have a slight curve to it," Piria finished for him. "From the bell's lip? You think he dropped it?"

Akteron pressed his lips together for a moment. "Seems awfully clumsy, doesn't it?"

Tracing the divot with a finger, he then swept the shard about and narrowed his eyes.

"There's more," he said, scrutinising what appeared to be a number of small pellets, and plucking a few from the ground, he stood and rolled them around in his palm. "What do you make of them? You grind up stones for a living, don't you?"

Piria huffed, likely at the brazen over-simplification of her field of expertise, then pulled a pair of gloves on to give a closer examination. "May I...?"

Akteron nodded and she took one in her fingers. "Slightly transparent...and scuffed...they *might* be some kind of precious stone." She held it close to the lumstone. "No, not gemstones. Too foggy. Not weighty enough." Then she squeezed it. "And they're slightly malleable..."

Shrugging, she took a small phial from one of her pockets and deposited the granules Akteron handed over. "Well, just more to test, I suppose."

Akteron nodded, and dusted off his hands. "Alright. So let's say the guy comes up here, bell in-tow. He brings it over to the edge, maybe he rings it, then drops it. Or maybe he drops it before he rings it? Either way, it hits the ground. The thing I want to know, is *why*?"

"I'd find it pretty awkward, holding up a solid metal bell that size and trying to strike it at the same time."

"Fair point," Akteron returned to the rail and ran the stone along its lip. "Or he might just have stupid-fingers."

"He might have-...*oh*, wait, Ro!" Piria tapped his shoulder. "Bring the light back this way."

He did.

"Down there, in the gutter." Piria pointed. "Something caught the light...*there*!"

Carefully, Piria steadied herself and reached over the railing. Her fingers barely reached the object but when she finally drew back and stood again, her eyes were wide.

"An *arrow*?"

It was, and as she turned it in hand, Akteron could see that its head was a kind of white, polished stone which reflected their lumstone's light cleanly.

"Lying atop the leaf litter..." he muttered, glancing into the canopy from which leaves were slowly spiralling down to pepper the rooftop and fill the gutter. "So, it must have been recently fired."

"At him?" Piria mused. "Now *there's* a good reason to drop a bell."

"Maybe." Akteron turned to gaze at the surrounding buildings. "But look around. This place is a blind spot, no windows look onto it." He glanced back to the gutter. "Seeing as we found it in this gutter, it would also have to have been fired from the adjacent rooftop, perhaps from...*there*, between those brick outcrops."

Studying the chimneys atop the next building, Piria gave an agreeable nod. "Possible. But if we go with all that, then there's the question of why someone would be on this rooftop with a bow and arrow in the first place?"

Akteron shook his head vaguely. "Beats me. What if our answer is at the end of these rooftops, though?"

"You know I don't like feelings and intuitive leaps..."

"Every leap is intuitive. And I'm all ears if you have a better proposal. We can't just ignore this thing." He waggled the arrow and Piria's eyes grew a little distant.

Ugh. Akteron always felt dread at those stares. It usually meant she was about to tear a hole in whatever he'd just uttered with a burst of logic.

But this time, she didn't. After a moment's hesitation, Piria simply crinkled her nose. "Alright. Let's try an intuitive leap."

———◼———

– *SKETUSH* –

The feeling of puddled, gravelled ground met Akteron's feet again and withdrawing his lumstone shard, he discovered it had finally run out of charge.

"Fine timing," Piria remarked, dropping down behind him.

"Perfect." Akteron cast it aside.

It hadn't been difficult to find a way across the rooftops, all the buildings in the Clutch so tightly packed that a leap usually sufficed. And there seemed only one real route to follow as the pair crossed planks, skirted ledges, and clambered over the spines of buildings until the lofty obstacle course ended. On the final rooftop, Akteron had found the vines, and the fact that these had been corded into a rope, fastened, and hung over the edge of the building left little doubt as to their purpose.

Now, back on the ground, however, the way forward was not so clear.

"It's like we've landed in a coal mine..." he muttered, trying to peer ahead. Only the vague impression of walls filled his periphery but trying to rely on sound, instead, he found that in all directions but one, a closeness filled the night.

"This way," he said, trusting intuition and trying hard to ignore the whispers he swore he heard behind them.

A few more crunching, squelching footsteps, and both sighed to see the alley leading to a lumstone-lit street, ahead.

"I have to be honest," Akteron began, "I am kind of thrilled this wasn't the base for a gang of knife-wielding miscreants."

"Knife-wielding miscreants?"

"You know. The type that say, 'hand over tha' ingot belt or oy'll stick ya...'"

Piria scoffed. "Why do I get the impression you've never been held-up, before?"

They hopped a mouldering crate, a number of tiny creatures scattering into the night.

"I don't need experience. I'm good at imagining."

Piria gave a huff. "Well, we still have plenty of time in these alleys for that to change."

"And on that note, let's agree that if anything happens, I get to die first. I don't want to have to watch you get chopped up."

"Aw. You're sweet when you're afraid."

The two reached the street and Akteron took the less-lit direction, figuring that fewer lanterns equalled a greater chance of finding their skulking quarry.

Apart from their lonely footsteps, it was silent. Coaches had no chance of driving here, peppered as the stretch was with potholes and undulating lumps of cobbles. Oh, and the enormous beige trunk which thrust from the ground, ahead, completely blocking the way.

Pulling a leaf from her donvul, Piria shook out her hair as Akteron took everything in. The looming tree and the dilapidated buildings around them.

"I...recognise this place, from a lecture I attended," he uttered, passing under the street lantern they'd seen from the alley, and whose lonely light broke the otherwise tenebrous stretch. "This is the old Official Quarter. It must be. Look at the seals on the stele." He gestured to a squat, blackened stone pillar beside the street. "The whole quarter was completely ruined during the Krio uprising, almost a hundred cycles ago."

Piria caught up with him as he moved. "That was a *century* ago?"

"Give or take. And once it was over, the Seat wanted to project a new image. To assure people it had changed..."

"But they never bothered to repair all this?" She gazed at an empty building, its gaping windows like deadened eyes tracking them in the night. The architecture was definitely Torrilian, fashioned in the familiar, terraced design so common back then, but its once-white stonework was now charred and its balconies, barren, all traces of the former overflowing greenery, gone.

"It was deemed too much effort," Akteron explained. "The construction was too resilient to knock down and the resources to repair it all, too scarce. So, the city deemed it a write-off and focus simply shifted elsewhere. The surrounding quarters eventually grew larger, blocking the entrances and throughways, and the place became a refuge for squatters and anyone looking to evade the system."

A night-bird's lonely song echoed down from the canopy to the stone world, below.

"So what you're saying is, it's a perfect hideout," Piria said. "Do you think the thief might live here?"

Akteron was considering the idea when the pained sound of

someone wheezing caught both their ears.

Raising a finger, he gestured to a nearby alley and a second later, the pair had sidled up to the entrance.

"Come on, then. Give it up!" a gruff, nasal voice said from inside.

Peeking around the stonework, Akteron found a dead-end bathed in the dim glow of another lantern. There, two men — their arm-wraps indicating affiliation with some gang — had forced a third, oddly pale-skinned young man up against a wall and were threatening him at knifepoint.

Accompanying the two assailants was a pterenar, young, plucky and irritable looking. It stood taller than Akteron, its short beak purposefully serrated and sharpened, and there was a leaden look in its eyes.

"Ro," Piria whispered urgently at the sight.

Then, the pale young man attempted to run, and made it a whole two steps before being grappled and shoved back to the wall again with a grunt.

"You're out of your element here, kid. It's the bracelet or your life. Now take it off," the nasal voiced man prompted anew, the second poking their captive with the knife-tip.

"*We need to help,*" Piria whispered, and without waiting for Akteron's answer, strode into the alley brandishing her badge. "Bureau of Security!"

Despite the unease in his gut, Akteron stepped out behind her. He had hoped to formulate some kind of plan but Piria seemed to have done so on her own.

Well, whatever advantage she might have expected, it did not materialise.

Without blinking, the first, unarmed thug made a series of soft whistling, clicking sounds and at once, the bird pivoted its head to fasten its gaze upon her. Head feathers fanning out, it chuttered in a telling sign of aggravation and Akteron groaned inwardly.

Pterenars were docile enough in the wild, but when trained and commanded, they could be ferocious. Finding out just what they could do to people was not on Akteron's list of priorities tonight, and he was just reaching out to grab his partner's shoulder when a brick fell painfully onto his own.

"Ow!"

He was spun about to find it was no brick but some monolith of a man's hand, which had clamped onto him and held fast.

"No fast stuff. Mitts where I can see 'em," the giant rumbled through his beard.

"Right, yes," Akteron muttered back, raising both hands and wincing as he was then forcibly turned back to face the scene.

"The Bureau?" The nasal man now scoffed. "Not likely. Now, stop where you are and ingot-belts, off. Both of you. Come on. We ain't got all night."

Huh. Akteron had to raise an eyebrow at the accuracy of his earlier imitation, though Piria didn't notice.

Hearing the thug's words, she had instead cocked her head and muttered, "All night..." Then, she brightened. "Oh! Yes, this is perfect! Contradictory data!"

Akteron shot her an anxious glance, trying to unpick the obvious ruse and hoping she knew what she was doing. In his experience, trying to distract thugs was never very productive.

The nasal man raised his knife and spoke over it. "I said, *ingot-belts. Now.*"

"Sure, sure," Piria began to take hers off, beaming. "But tell me, why aren't you all confounded?"

Akteron gave a crestfallen sigh.

Wonderful. Piria wasn't going to plead for their lives. She was going to disarm and quiz them, instead...

"I'm not...*what*, now?" The nasal man asked, thrown off by the question as she carried out his command. "Listen, just shut your mouth and–"

"Confounded. You know, unable to communicate?" Piria cut

in. "Were you not affected at all? How long have you gents been in Dagger's Clutch, tonight?" She turned to the giant holding Akteron, ignoring the nasal man who appeared to be the ringleader.

But it was a new voice who answered.

"They just got here," the pale captive said, still up against the wall.

"Oi!" the knife-wielding thug warned him. "Speak again and you'll get some new holes!"

"He's right," the slab behind Akteron then said. "We ain't been here long. Thought we'd take advantage of some trouble we got wind of—"

"*Kessik, Bollan,* shut up!" Nasal Man hissed.

Nearby, the pterenar gave a drawn-out warning noise from deep in its throat and shifted on its feet, but Piria simply gave an affectionate sigh.

"Aw, hello sweetheart," she said, stepping over to it. "What are you doing out here at this hour?"

Making a series of clicks, herself, Akteron was then astonished to see the bird fold its plume of feathers back up and give her a searching, sideways glance, before it leaned down and allowed her to stroke its neck.

It was so distracting that Akteron didn't see the man with the knife until it was too late. He approached around the bird's other side, and as Piria spoke on it was clear that she hadn't noticed, either.

"Really, there's no point in being—" she had just started saying, when the man leapt forward and drove the knife directly into her gut.

– *BZZZZZAT!* –

"*AGH!*" at once, he yelped and leapt back, dropping the blade and shaking his hand as it began to smoke.

"Kessik, you scungy *moron*," the ringleader said. "They're protected, 'course! Look at their clothes..." He smiled coldly at

Piria, who seemed completely unharmed. "But now you're defenceless and I'm done asking nicely. So, let's get real, here."

Piria wasn't listening. With a thoughtful air, she dug around calmly for something in her donvul pocket and a second later, Akteron watched her don the gloves she'd worn earlier. He then heard the soft *POCK!* of a stopper being uncorked.

Pouring something onto one of her palms, Piria waited until her smoking-handed assailant bent to grab his dagger. She waited until he straightened again. Then, she blew a fine powder directly into his face.

The man gave a stunned splutter, snarled, then lifted his knife as if to strike again — before he stopped.

A blank look overcame his face as he twitched his nose, and Akteron saw his skin begin to shift in the low light. Like someone pulling a sock over a melon, it seemed to tighten, drawing the man's features smooth, his nose and mouth taut, and his eyebrows high.

Realising this, the man screamed, his weapon dropped a second time as he reached up to paw at his tightening skin. It was obviously painful and even the pterenar backed away with an uncertain chuttering until at last, when the man's facial features were elongated impossibly, that pain seemed to subside and his breathing calmed.

An uneasy sigh came through his harrowing, enormous smile. But it wasn't over.

Before everyone's eyes, that tight skin began to shift the opposite direction. The man cried out anew as wrinkles formed and his cheeks drooped, his whole face sagging like a wet garment on a doorknob.

Piria, brow still furrowed, leant to study the effects as he moaned in dismay and felt over his warped visage.

"*Always* something else," she uttered, dusting off her gloves. "Last time *bruised* skin, this time, too *much* skin..."

A few paces away, sensing that their muggers were focused on

Piria and sufficiently sidetracked, Akteron used his chance. With a violent twist, he tore free of the giant's grip–

"OW!"

Except he didn't. The man just gripped him harder, iron fingers digging into flesh and locking him in place.

"Easy there, skinny," he rumbled, causing Akteron to bristle. He was *athletic*, not *skinny*!

Then, there was fire.

It began as a bright, snaking arm of flame in the shadowy depths of the dead-end and trailed across the ground. Barely a breath later, it had reached the ringleader, upon whom it exploded.

"*AGH! Kessik! Bollan! Put it out!*" the man shrieked, hair and clothes suddenly alight. Staggering backwards, he tried to smack at the licking, dancing flames and when that failed, he dropped to the ground and began rolling about.

The giant threw Akteron aside and ran to assist, his heavy footfalls thudding over the cobbles as another arm of fire swept through the night. It caught him mid-stride and burst into a ball of sparks like the first, but the effect wasn't as dramatic. When it subsided, the lug merely stood there, stunned, but fine. Except for a fire in his beard, which he batted irritably.

"*KESSIK!*" his leader called for his last crony, still thrashing on the cobbles. But Kessik was useless, now, his new excess of skin and drooping features obscuring his vision. Moaning, he stumbled past Akteron and Piria, hands drawn up over his face, and fled. The pterenar joined in the din, squawking in panic before taking off at his heels.

It was only after Akteron had stood and begun dusting himself off that he noticed a faint, orange twinkle at the back of the alley...

"*Ro!*" Piria launched and bundled him out of the way as that twinkle became a final trail of flame. It roared past them in pursuit of the droopy-faced thug but much to Akteron's aggravation, missed him, hitting a stone bench instead where it also exploded into sparks.

It didn't matter. The trio of crooks had taken their cue. Groaning, bumbling, and trailing smoke, they staggered off into the shadowy streets.

Piria gave Akteron a hand and helped him to his feet.

"Sorry..." she said, "I thought she was firing at us."

"*She?*" Akteron asked, as a small figure strode out of the shadows.

She was tiny and dressed in curious garments, a pair of triangular spectacles atop her curved nose magnifying beady eyes, and around her wrinkled face, vibrant, red hair ran in a thick braid over one shoulder. As she waggled one hand to cool it off, she eyed Akteron and Piria.

"*Rotten-roots*...what a start to the evening," she said, removing a small tin from one of her pockets. Opening it, she held it out to the pair. "First everyone goes insane, next, hoodlums start causing mayhem right on our doorstep..."

In the dim light, Akteron could see the tin was full of flavour-coals.

"Erm...not for me," he said over a residual, adrenaline-fuelled shudder. "Never liked the taste."

When Piria also declined, the woman simply shrugged, taking one for herself before gesturing to the blackened bench across the way. "Those numbskulls are lucky I had a new recruit watching the entrance, tonight. If Gindon had been on duty, I dare say they'd all by dead..."

"'New recruit?' Do you mean the young man they were hustling?" Akteron asked, only now noticing the pale youth was gone. "You know him?"

The woman nodded as she chewed, and a second later, wisps of scented smoke began curling from her lips. "I'd have come up to greet you earlier," she explained, "but I had an unexpected meeting. Timing is everything, isn't it?"

Akteron glanced unsurely at Piria.

He'd noticed that this woman had been staring intently at them ever since she'd arrived. Or more specifically, at their mouths.

"I think we're both thankful you showed up at all," Piria said, dusting off her trousers and removing her gloves. "I was out of ideas and if you hadn't intervened–"

"They'd probably have gutted you all, stolen your belts and other valuables, and left you to die," the woman finished.

Akteron gave an uncomfortable noise and peered briefly at the streak of charcoal those flames had left on the cobbles.

He understood why the Seat fought so hard to project that appearance of Torril as the urban idyll. But now and then, something like this shook that vision. Now and then, it became obvious that even they couldn't stop cracks from appearing in their perfectly polished glass.

"Nice work, with that powder-trick," he then said, turning to Piria. "Lucky they weren't confounded, either, or your nonsense-talk wouldn't have distracted them."

"Nonsense-talk?" Piria asked, checking her ingots were still in place. "I was asking serious questions. But yes, it was lucky. There'd have been no way to deal with that if they'd been uncommunicative like those back at Sekiir's."

"Oh, there are always ways to communicate," the older woman said.

Akteron shook his head. "On any normal day, I might agree. But not tonight. This is different."

The woman eyed him wryly through her spectacles. "Communication is more than just words, dear. More than writing, or gestures, fluttering an eyelid or puffing up one's chest..."

"Yes, but it's impossible to–"

"Nothing is impossible." She waved his comment off. "So, a few people forget how to waggle their tongue the right way.

What of it? They haven't forgotten the far more important form of communication we're all schooled in until the day we die."

An expectant silence.

"Nature's," she then said. "Doesn't she communicate with us with every breeze? Every scent? And even the confounded understand her messages just fine, I assure you. They understand her laws and words, even if theirs have turned to goop." She pocketed her tin of flavour-coals and gestured back towards Dagger's Clutch. "All those poor folks made stupid by this bell. You don't see them leaping off houses or drowning themselves. Why?"

Akteron considered that.

"Because they still hear nature," she explained. "You want to get a message across? Learn from her. Use her language." She cocked an eyebrow at Piria. "Or bladeshroom and scarlet-bud powder..."

Piria gave an appreciative grunt.

"Wait, you know about the *bell*?" Akteron asked, his face lighting up.

"Come," the woman urged them, turning back into the alley. "Answers when we get there."

"Answers-? Who *are* you?"

She didn't respond, and Piria had already turned to follow in this stranger's footsteps when Akteron tapped her arm.

"Ri," he whispered. "We're not just going to trust her like that, surely?"

"I don't see why not..."

"Erm, how about *because we know nothing about her and she almost killed us*? And what are the odds she's actually able to help?"

"You're still treating this like a chance encounter, aren't you..."

"Of course. What else could it be?"

With a shrug, Piria turned away and Akteron sighed as a word bubbled to mind.

"Right...meteors."

———————■———————

Akteron shivered. He held himself for warmth as the red-braided woman turned a wheel affixed to a heavy, metal door, first one way, then the other. Next, she pressed a large button by the doorknob. And then she waited.

"When *did* you put that hex on yourself?" Akteron whispered.

"Just after the vine-rope," Piria replied. "I wanted to put one on you as well, but Lathiik didn't answer the second time and then we got distracted..."

Akteron grunted, thankful that the knife had been thrust her way and not his, in that case.

"And the powder? That was...interesting."

"A side project. It's a work in progress," she answered.

"Oh, it looks perfectly dangerous. I'd bottle it and sell it tomorrow. We can't be the only ones to get mugged around here—"

"It's supposed to be a skin treatment."

Akteron's mouth opened once or twice, wordlessly. "Ah. Maybe it needs a little work, then."

The house they'd been ushered into after that had been completely bare. No furniture, no carpet, windows boarded up, only a dim lantern and a lone figure, inside. Taller even than Akteron and with a pale, moonlight-complexion, this man seemed to be guarding a door, arms folded, a wild glint in his eyes and dressed in...well, honestly it had looked like leaves and vines. It had been hard to tell in the gloom. As with the old woman, however, a faint whiff of familiarity had danced just outside Akteron's thoughts at the sight of him.

Through the door, a winding descent took them deep underground, ending where they now stood before a large, round, metal door. Exactly *how* far down they were, Akteron couldn't figure. All he knew was that his shirt and donvul were no longer enough to stop him shivering.

The woman turned to them.

"Just one thing," she said, face serious, "if you're cosy with any timberjacks, hunters or trappers, keep your *own* traps shut down here, got it?"

The pair nodded.

With a deep, metallic – *CATUNK!* – that door then swung open.

"Great Wastes..." Akteron muttered.

Sweet, warm air flooded into the antechamber as a grand, subterranean tunnel was revealed, chiselled out of the living rock and sweeping ahead into a blur of greenery.

It seemed to Akteron almost like some dreamlike interpretation of the Clutch — though this place was much livelier. From hollowed dwellings which formed the walls, people peered to observe the newcomers, while at Akteron's feet, a smooth, earthen road was filled with meandering figures and carts and crossed by intersecting tunnels.

But the biggest difference was the greenery. Billowing shrubs, phosphorescent ferns and nighttime blooms, even full *trees* burst from the mossy ground, their leaves and buds imparting a mix of fragrances while lumstone-lanterns shed mellow spheres of light.

Against all this, pale figures clad in plantstuff tended vegetation. Watering, clipping, or gathering. Some worked the soil and others seemed to stare reverently at bushes, pruned into various forms.

Unfamiliar as it all was, though, there was another reason this space felt so strange.

Nobody was speaking. As far as Akteron could tell, every

person here was going about their business wordlessly.

"Come on, one foot after the other. No time to dally," Red-Braid called over her shoulder, breaking the silence.

Akteron and Piria hurried to keep pace.

"I can't usually tell an obelisk from a streetlamp..." Piria spoke under her breath, once that door was no longer visible behind them, "but this place is old, isn't it?"

Akteron nodded. "Not just old. It seems ancient..."

"As in, 'before we met' ancient, or older?"

Akteron gave an amused grunt and shook his head. "Hard to say, exactly, but from what I can see, I'd put it all at...well, I wrote a paper on Idma Temples in the second-age, and those oldest structures bore carvings just like these..."

This was to say nothing of those distinctly *un-Torrilian* figurines hidden in nooks and fissures in the stonework, nor of the distinctive architecture all around them, with its curves and bevelled edges. But he was content to walk and observe as their world became one of gentle light and hushed silence, as sculpted plants, curious masonry, and unusual people swept by, all creating a sense that they were treading somewhere sacred.

Reality only called Akteron back as the passage widened into a great garden which filled an immense cavern.

Countless gem lights lit the space, set atop squat plinths or into tree-trunk hollows, while above, giant stalactites hung, visible between a tangle of hanging vines.

"A city under a city...a jungle under a jungle," Piria uttered as they trod a bridge over a gurgling stream.

Not long afterwards, their crunching footsteps were stifled by a waterfall thundering from the cavern walls. Still, the path meandered, through swathes of dense, humid vegetation and tended, secluded glades in which Akteron and Piria glimpsed birds, fish, and on one occasion, a formidable-looking lizard slumbering on a boulder. Then, at last, they found themselves confronting an elegant stone pavilion — the apparent centrepiece of this underground domain.

Atop its wide stairs stood a pale-skinned woman, who bowed and parted a series of thick curtains to allow them to pass.

"Welcome," she said in a voice like an autumnal breeze. It was the first utterance any of the inhabitants had made, thus far, and Akteron entered to find their guide waiting for them. Only once those curtains had closed again did she speak.

"I guess I owe you both an explanation."

"That would be nice," Piria said.

"Not that we didn't appreciate your assistance, up above," Akteron added, quickly, "but Piria and I are actually on business for the Bureau, and we really can't afford to get, erm-... derailed."

"I'm aware of your business," the woman said, eyes twinkling. "And trust me, you're going to want to hear this." She held up a hand to them and looked to one of the pale men nearby. "Fermilan, is she back, yet?"

The man nodded and in the abundance of light, here, Akteron noticed the tattoos lining his pale skin. As if the artist had tried to trace every branching vein...

"Fetch her, would you?"

Bowing, the young man vanished through the curtains and Red-Braid turned back to her guests.

"Would you mind first explaining where we are?" Piria now asked, glancing around.

"You're in the '*old city*,'" the woman said with a chuckle. "Though, it's probably known more specifically to your academics as–"

"*Kivadra...*" Akteron muttered. "As in, ancient Kivadra — from the stories? The city that was here before Torril?"

The woman watched his lips form the words through those spectacles. "Very good...the city that *was*, and still *is* here," she said with a nod. "Well, partially. We're still digging it out."

"The stories say Kivadra was totally destroyed."

"No," Red corrected him, "*buried*. Kivadra was *buried* under the sands."

"*...when the desert threw its arms to the south, reaching for the city it could not have,*" Akteron added, only now realising the implications of a story he'd heard in childhood. "It was *buried...*"

The woman smiled. "An admirer of history?"

"Ugh. Don't get him started," Piria groaned. "Most days all he talks about is potsherds and pretimes. It's exhausting."

"Perhaps," the lady said, "but we mustn't forget the past or others will remember it for us, and trust me when I tell you, they won't do as good a job as you'd hope."

Piria accepted this with a nod.

"Which leads me to the next question," Akteron said. "Does the Seat know about this place?"

"The right people in the Seat, yes."

"The right–" Piria had just begun to say, as the curtains behind the redheaded woman ruffled and parted.

Another short woman entered the pavilion.

Dressed like their guide, in feathered garments and a matching, wooden necklace — its centrepiece a flat, aqua stone — Akteron noticed that their similarity stretched further than clothing and height. They also shared the same slightness. That same, curving smile and button nose, and those same, twinkling eyes.

The two women embraced briefly before the newcomer turned to the visitors and now, Akteron cocked an eyebrow.

"Oh, boy," he said, those threads of familiarity weaving together, at last.

"*Erm, isn't that the woman from the docks,*" Piria whispered out the side of her mouth, "*the woman you arrested?*"

"Akteron Uusei Nisbri," this woman said, eyeing him up and down, "it has been a while. I hope this meeting will be more pleasant than our last."

CHAPTER SEVEN
THE CASE AT MILLET DOCKS

Ikta, the familiar stranger, had been businesslike in her manner.

After a brusque introduction and a flurry of hand gestures, a squadron of silent figures had sprung into motion to arrange the sunken centre of the pavilion. Luxuriant cushions were strewn about and small tables were placed and furnished which jugs of water, bowls of fruit, and fragrant cups of tea.

Not a word was exchanged with the two guests during all this and yet, as these pale-skinned men and women bustled about, Akteron noticed that many of them shared those same, snaking tattoos. More disturbing still, they seemed not just to be *wearing* that leafy, floral garb. A surreptitious inspection of one woman's arm revealed not a *bracelet*, as he'd supposed, but a small cluster of greenery growing from her skin...

He shivered at the sight, but the discomfort faded a moment later as he and Piria were ushered down to that pillowy landscape, their hosts on the opposing side of the ring.

The two older women took their teacups in hand. Piria and Akteron did the same, and it was only after a salvo of sips had passed that Red-Braid finally broke the silence.

"*Great Wastes,* this is more awkward than a Kal Brioran baby-naming ceremony. Speak, would you, Ikta?"

Ikta had been eying Piria over her cup but now, with an amused grunt, she turned her gaze to Akteron. "It's not often we meet with Torrilians," she began, "rarer still that we welcome them into our enclave...but circumstances change, so here we are."

Noting that — despite the pleasant warmth down here — Akteron was rubbing his hands together, a stranger handed him a light shawl and Ikta waited as he gratefully wrapped it around his shoulders.

"Rama, my sister, had an interesting visit, earlier this evening," Ikta then continued, nodding gently to Red-Braid. "One of our scouts up at Dagger's Clutch abandoned his watch to deliver an urgent message. Said the Torrilians up there had gone mad."

Red-Braid, or *Rama*, threw a grape into her mouth and took over. "And before you think us daft, we know that neighbourhoods up there aren't prone to descending into mania at a breeze." She searched the bowl for another. "Torrilians are impulsive, ignorant, negligent, and their fashion choices are terrible, but they're not *that* strange..."

"Alright, pause. I need some notation, here," Piria spoke up, waving heat from her tea. "You refer to Torrilians as if you're something separate...but who exactly are *you* all and what are you doing, excavating these ruins? And why don't you want the Seat to know about all this?"

"And what about Torrilian fashion is terrible?" Akteron added, straightening his donvul.

Rama looked to her auburn-haired sister, who turned a wry smile on Akteron. "Perhaps *you'd* like to explain to your partner who we are, Akteron?"

The young man shifted and muttered something into his cup.

"What's wrong? Afraid you don't have the whole story?" She waited a moment. "Well, at least you've learned a lesson, then."

"Akteron told me he arrested you at the docks," Piria prompted. "Something about spreading a dangerous, magickal contagion?"

"It wasn't them," Akteron said. "We were mistaken, that night. The real perpetrators got away."

Piria crinkled her brow. "I don't understand."

"The whole sting was a mess," Akteron said, taking a deep breath and peering into his cup. "It started when an anonymous informant contacted the head of security with a tipoff. According to him, a group of malcontents were meeting at the docks. A group the Bureau had been after for some time. Back then, I was trying out for a potential position at the Bureau and Riallo was still a field agent. He told me he wanted me there for the training, but I realised later he really wanted Kandaar nearby when they made their arrest..."

———■———

"Easy, Akteron. Slow down," Riallo whispered, motioning for Akteron to stay back as a number of Security Bureau grunts crept down the gangway onto the main dock. "Let the team go in, first."

Akteron waited, eyes trained on the black-clad unit and their silken movements as they padded through the shadows. Beyond them, he could just discern The Noble, a small, three-masted frigate at anchor and bobbing in the calm of night. Its hull reflected the faintest light from the dock's sparse gem-lanterns but its masts were only visible against the tenebrous cast above when they ticked in front of stars, for both moons were absent, tonight. That made it the perfect night for a getaway — and the perfect night to be caught.

Standing there, Akteron felt a slight thrill welling up inside him. A warmth at the knowledge that his team were closing in on their unsuspecting quarry and that some good might really be done, here.

"Remember, their specialty is deception," Riallo warned, nodding at the cluster of shadowy figures by the frigate. "Whisper are trained not to look threatening, to blend in. It's what makes them so tricky to nab. This all looks like a standard ploy."

– KTUNK! –

Akteron's ears caught the sound before he saw it. The shadows by the Noble were flinging grappling hooks skyward, the metal flutes making purchase on the vessel's siding.

"They're boarding her..." Akteron uttered, watching the figures begin to climb.

Riallo nodded, holding a steadying hand out to still his partner. "Don't worry, we have this. Just don't engage them directly. And for goodness sake, if you see any kind of dust, don't let it get into your lungs..."

Akteron nodded, hoping he'd have the mindset to remember that if things spiralled out of hand. He tugged absently on the fabric mask he wore and tried to focus his breathing. It was a warm night but he was pretty sure he wasn't sweating because of that.

Seeking reassurance, his fingers ran over his holstered stunshot, then his ingot-belt, thanking Sevellan nothing had fallen out on the dash here...

All the while, his eyes tracked the Bureau team before him. Six figures, barely visible as they moved low and silent to spread out around the handful of malcontents.

Within moments, the first climbing figure disappeared over the rail, and the Bureau readied to engage. Only then did a peppering of doubt nibble at Akteron's conscience.

"This doesn't seem right..." he uttered.

"What do you mean?" Riallo uttered back, eyes fixed on the

scene.

"Why aren't they using any light? Why are they scaling the sides?"

The officer shrugged. "Darkness is their style. But more likely, they're trying to make a stealthy getaway, perhaps after getting word we were coming."

"But if this is their ship, surely they'd use the gangplank... wouldn't they?"

Any answer Riallo might have made was lost in a sudden shout as the Security Bureau grunts engaged. Brief, muffled noises of struggle punctuated the night in the form of yells, footsteps, and the – *PECK!* – of stunshots. At the same time, a number of torches flared to being from the water, Riallo's second unit having approached by boat. Within moments, two of the shadowy gang were arrested and on the ground, and Akteron watched as a third struggled briefly, before being bundled down and handcuffed.

He heard a few strained grumbles but other than that, the Whisper members didn't really react. Nor did they fight back.

Another – *PECK!* – and the remaining figure scaling the ship's hull released the rope and fell, telling Akteron the small pellet had met its mark. The unconscious figure was caught by a Bureau operative and lowered to the ground, then handcuffed beside the other four.

"Alright, then. That's our cue," Riallo said, smile evident even though Akteron couldn't see his face.

Riallo moved, and he followed.

It seemed this would be a simple success, tonight, and Akteron was surprised at how smoothly it had gone. He'd never expected Whisper to be so bungling and benign, and he'd certainly expected some kind of altercation. But all that would only serve to make this look very good on the report. Not just for Riallo and himself, but the whole team. Perhaps this would be the–

"Wait..." Akteron hissed, halting on the spot as he saw something shift in the darkness. Something huge, right beside the handcuffed Whisper disciples on the dock.

"Riallo, stop!"

It was the Noble.

In the dim flicker of the gemlights, the ship's hulking form somehow rose up, then fell back, and as it hit the water a wave exploded upwards. The impact carried such tremendous force that a score of the dock's huge planks were loosed and Security Bureau operatives were swept clean off the platform, vanishing into the dark swell.

Grabbing hold of a thick hawser, Akteron's barely managed to hook arms with Riallo as a wall of water met them head-on, the surge knocking them off their feet. Receiving a shot of salty brine up his nose, he managed to hold on until, spluttering, soaked, but still on the dock, the water subsided.

Quickly, the pair regained their footing just in time to watch a second phase begin.

In the air above their remaining agents, a fizzing announced a shower of sparks. Innocuous at first, this quickly gained intensity until sparks began raining down onto stunned heads with hot crackles. The Bureau unit leapt about, trying to avoid the singing, burning deluge, one agent attempting to flee along the dock only to be struck on the head. His cry was muffled as he dove into the sea.

Of course, this panic was exactly what the handcuffed quartet of Whisper disciples needed. Untouched by the wave and the ensuing rain of stars, they began to leap to their feet and dash for freedom.

"Intervention," Riallo said, spinning to Akteron before the night could turn to the Bureau's disadvantage. "Now. Quickly, or we'll lose them all!"

Akteron had already closed his eyes. "Ath viraan, Kandaar," he whispered, and a coolness fell in the air around him. "*Sweet fishbowl...*"

Before missions, agents in Akteron's position were routinely told to think out petitions for various, undesirable situations. Even the most diligently planned stings could spiral off-course at any moment, after all, and *nexers* like him with strong weldings and capable Sharak were always brought along to wrench the operation back into line, if and when that happened.

Although Bureau policy and Seat law forbade petitions which brought harm against another human — and Sharak ignored such requests, anyway — Akteron knew there were many other ways to settle an unruly crowd. This particular petition had cost nine whole ingots. But as the coolness in the air around Akteron lifted, he felt Kandaar's focus turn from him towards the ship.

A breath or two passed as nothing happened. Then, one of Whisper's fleeing, handcuffed disciples wavered, slowed, and sank to his knees. The next collapsed suddenly like a dropped sack of tubers and in the flickering torchlight, the regrouping Bureau unit spectated as thin, visible bubbles formed around the gang's heads.

Riallo turned and gave Akteron a sideways glance. "What are you doing to them?"

By the time the officer had turned back to the scene, all four handcuffed felons were on the ground, and it didn't much longer before each seemed to visibly slacken, their chests rising and falling calmly, their encircled-heads lolling about. One even began to giggle.

"The bubbles," Akteron explained. "They're infused with sweet air."

"Sweet air?"

Akteron nodded. "Nitrous oxide, like physicians use. Harmless enough, but a good way to make our targets more, erm-... *manageable.*"

Riallo gave an appreciative hum as one felon gave an inebriated *whoop!* And whoever had petitioned that spark-shower and churning water obviously hadn't expected the play, either, for within moments the heaving sea had settled and the fire-shower ceased.

The potential disaster had been brought to order.

Sopping and dazed, the two inundated Bureau members clambered back onto the dock from the water, while another duo approached from the gloom further down the pier. When all were accounted for, their unit leader gave a signal and the Bureau moved onto the boat.

◼

"We found the crates in the hold, as our source had tipped off," Akteron explained to Piria. "And inside them, the flowers which Whisper had sent those poor Seat members. They were all laced with a magickal toxicant, apparently ready to be shipped off to new targets. But it became clear later that night that those we'd arrested had nothing to do with it."

"So, what *were* you doing at the docks, then?" Piria asked, turning to Ikta, and the older lady put down her teacup.

"Akteron's explanation, that these flowers were laced with magickal toxicant, is not the entire truth."

"I was merely simplifying," Akteron said.

"Still, the whole truth was more disturbing," Ikta went on, "for the flowers were not just laced, but *corrupted*, their stamens altered to *produce* this toxic pollen upon maturation." She waited as one of the pale figures refilled her tea, then took the cup again. "When someone tampers with nature like that, it's only a matter of time before we feel the disturbance. That time, the signal was strong, indeed."

"But in *order* to alter a species like that..." Piria whispered, almost to herself, "you'd need an *extraordinary* charge, more than any ingot-belt could hold. Not only that, but toxicological skills, botanical skills, a welding of improbable magnitude..."

"Yes. And the Bureau still don't know how Whisper pulled that off," Akteron told her. "But the whole thing was clearly part of a bigger plan. A few span earlier, a rumour had been spread that the Seat was forcing non-Torrilian high officials to leave the city. That these officials could either leave of their own volition or be removed forcefully." He shook his head. "The Seat denied any such plans, of course, and knew the lie was cooked up by Whisper to exacerbate tensions. But it worked. Specific targets in the Seat received these flowers and were poisoned, and for a while nobody knew why they were getting sick, why their skin was going white and their eyes, red. People believed the rumours. A newspaper almost published a story saying the Seat *really did* want to oust non-Torrilians from the city before, luckily, the Bureau took steps to clear the air. It still almost came to a riot..."

"Torrilian issues weren't our concern," Ikta said, "but otherwise, we were there for the same reason you were. We wanted to destroy this repulsive creation and stop whoever was behind it."

Piria turned to Akteron. "So, it was all just a case of mistaken identity?"

He nodded, but Piria furrowed her brow, again. "Once again, then...who *are* you?"

Ikta smiled. "No point in keeping that a secret. *We* are the Doraun," she said, and made a gesture around the pavilion — not just gesture to the silent, pale sentinels standing at attention and drifting about, Akteron felt, but to the cavern in which it stood, the entire cave complex. "We are the last, fading breath of an order, older than Torril, itself."

At those words, Akteron began making sense of that reverent feeling which had twined its way through him, and it appeared Piria was beginning to feel it, as well.

"Akteron mentioned that you were a shaman…"

"No. Not exactly, but I see the convenience in assigning such a label," Ikta said. "The Bureau likes labels and files. Things it can sort. Traits it can use to identify. But I dare say they have no proper description for what we are."

"And you say you *felt* the disturbance when those flowers were altered…" Piria continued.

Red-Braid pointed at Piria as if she'd hit the mark. "Right. And *that's* where all this gets interesting."

With a flourish of her hand, two of the younger Doraun crouching in the pavilion leapt to their feet and uncovered what appeared a large wooden bowl on a back table. This, they carried with careful steps into the central pit, setting it before the guests.

As that happened, Akteron couldn't help taking the chance to examine the greenery which sprouted from these attendants' skin. The young man, who couldn't have been older than his twentieth cycle, had a whole *vine* which extended from one shoulder to his lower back, while the young woman, about the same age, had flowers blooming across her cheeks. It was at once somehow beautiful and unsettling, and Akteron was unable to suppress a wince.

"Come and look," Ikta said, rising to stand before the wooden bowl.

Even on her feet, it only came to her middle. A couple of the buttons on her vest -TACK-ed against it softly and Akteron wondered how Sendil would handle making such unique, wilderness-inspired garb. The average clothier would have no end of trouble with the intricate stitching, that bark-like collar and the interwoven foliage, but surely Sendil could handle it. Perhaps he could even refine that loose sleeving-…

"She is awake," Rama muttered to her sister, and Akteron refocused.

Reaching over the bowl, the two sisters appeared to feel

around in the air. Their fingers swept about and seemed to brush over something Akteron couldn't see. A moment later, they began to draw that invisible something upwards with gentle, scooping motions, and the bowl's mossy, inner coating began to glimmer.

Akteron felt Piria nudge him, and following her gaze, noticed with a slight start that both Ikta and Rama's eyes had changed. No more did they resemble the colour of a dark, shaded grove. Instead, they had shifted to match the fervent, luminous insides of the bowl.

"Though the peoples of Torril, and Kriolar, and the other modern lands have all diverged from the first path," Ikta said, eyes staring into nothing, "welding with Sharak and ignoring the ancient ways, the Doraun have protected and maintained, keeping another channel open for thousands of cycles."

Out of the bowl, a head-sized sphere of liquid now began to rise up, tendrils extending and waving from its surface only to sink and vanish, again. It reminded Akteron of the sea anemones he'd often find on the beach as a boy and oddly, he had the sense that this watery form was also alive...

"Ages ago, this path was far more common," Ikta went on, "and provided a link stronger even than Sharak, with which one could access forces more raw. More pure."

Rama turned to her guests, now, those intense, verdant eyes, unsettling. "Reach in and hear the Rootmind, Akteron, Piria," she instructed them.

"What?"

"Reach in," Ikta reiterated.

The pair shared an unsure glance.

"*Quickly*," Rama wheezed, her voice no longer cool and collected.

Lifting their hands, Piria and Akteron both watched with concern as their fingers neared that watery form and the tendrils began to turn and feel out for their skin, to stretch and seek the contact being offered to them. Moving their fingers closer still, the tendrils made a final stretch, and then wrapped tight. They were cold, and there was a sharp, electric tingle which ran up Akteron's arm at the contact. It ran along his spine and into his mind–

And then Akteron was weightless.

He gasped as a shadow, larger than the city of Torril itself swept past behind him, and saw that he was no longer in the pavilion of the Doraun. He was somewhere else, amongst clouds of purple, blue, teal forming an endless, tumbling mass in every direction.

Piria was no longer beside him, either, and yet he *could* hear her breathing and muttering as that shadow darted past again, its vague form rippling through the clouds in an immense blur–

"The Rootmind has sensed you," Ikta's voice met Akteron's mind as he floated in this strange world. "Allow it to tether, allow it to know you."

Akteron now realised that there was no single shape drifting about him, but numerous shapes, all enormous. Tendrils, or perhaps *roots*, both nearby and waving in the distance. Rising, falling, searching, as those in the watery shape had done.

Right before him, one smaller tendril rose, but kept space between them and as Akteron's fear mingled with curiosity, he saw it reacting to both. When he grew unsure, it drifted away, but when the desire to know it bloomed within him it approached and gently, slowly, wrapped itself about his torso.

The sensation was like nothing Akteron had ever experienced. A ripple of understanding, beneath which lay power, and vulnerability, and complexity. For a few, short moments he was connected to a vast consciousness, an ancient presence which parted the shroud of his human mind and allowed him to peer into its deep, almost limitless ocean of existence.

But Akteron quickly realised that the entity was holding back. It was trying to be gentle, he sensed, with the tiny, delicate form in its grasp, though it could not completely hide the dazzling power pulsing inside itself. Like the starry sky, Akteron felt the sprawl of its reach and a billion, tiny dots of awareness. There was no malignancy, there, though there was...*distrust*. There was also hope, and joy, shining beneath the surface. And sadness, and pain, and something else...

Whatever that last, obscured facet was, the entity longed to share it and Akteron realised it was refusing to do so, perhaps for his own protection.

Akteron willed it to show him.

Still, it held back. Pulsing. Shielding him.

Akteron then *urged* it to show him.

Don't worry, he thought. *I can understand. Show me what you're hiding.*

For a mere heartbeat, a jolt of panic and urgency like white, hot fire, coursed through his body and Akteron gasped, finding himself standing in the pavilion once more, sweat running down his forehead and Piria blinking beside him as both withdrew their hands.

The sisters' eyes had returned to their original, dark shade of green and Ikta nodded, seeing Akteron's shocked expression while he returned from his stupor.

A lightheadedness forced the young man to stagger backwards before he bent to steady his breathing.

"We felt it, as well," Ikta told him. "All of it. It is not common that the Rootmind shares such strong emotions, but that may be why you are both here."

"What was it..." Akteron asked, gripping one wrist as if that surge of hot panic had burned him. "How can something like that exist?"

"Whatever do you mean?" Ikta asked, eying him. "How could it *not* exist? How would *we* exist, without it?"

"I think I understand," Piria then spoke between breaths, and narrowed her eyes in thought. "Ro, what we just felt. What we saw." She turned to him. "It was the consciousness of — the *mind* of nature, itself. Wasn't it?"

Rama nodded. "In a manner of speaking."

"And you are all entangled with it. The Rootmind, somehow," Piria continued, "that's why you can sense when there's a problem."

"We Doraun are not *entirely* human," Ikta admitted. "And to forge a connection with nature is not like welding a Sharak. We continue this tradition because without us, there is no finger on nature's pulse, no voice for humans to hear. If nature then cried out, how would we know? Who would come to its aid? It alone cannot fight back against the faster and constantly changing force of human toil. It needs a hand, an arm...an *army* on its side."

As his breathing steadied, Akteron now found the mist of confusion fading. "The waves at the dock. The sparks, the fire, in the alley, above...I wondered how you managed such powerful petitions so quickly, and what kind of ingot-belt you wore. But you're not petitioning..."

Ikta bent to one side, then the other, showing that in fact, she wore no ingot-belt.

"You don't need a Sharak or charge," Piria finished for Akteron, eyes going wide. "It's all elemental magick. You're calling on nature..."

"Oh, we pay another price," Rama said, eyes hinting just for a second at some distant pain. "It's certainly not just sunshine and free hexes, around here. We dedicate our lives and are repaid for that. Still, many who spend cycle upon cycle to attain a link never make it. Nature's requirements are too severe for some to handle."

Akteron glanced at the pale, young man standing in the shadows with the vine growing across his back. At his malnourished appearance, that pale skin. The lad was shaking, he now saw, despite holding his posture, and his breathing seemed a little erratic. He was suffering.

"You literally merge with flora," he said. "You allow it into your body..."

"So, then what about that vision?" Piria asked. "Akteron said you faked a vision, that night–"

"No, I didn't," Akteron cut in pointedly. "I *said* that the vision failed. That somehow, Ikta had influenced or blocked it."

Ikta laughed. "I did no such things. The Bureau tried to identify my Sharak with a petition and presumably, all they saw was a blur of leaves and flower petals. They assumed I had some magnificent welding defending me."

Piria gave a light huff of amusement. "When, in fact, they were simply seeing your *true* welding..."

"Enough about all that," Rama said, waving the comment off. "We didn't bring you here to give you a treatise on Doraunic lore. And we're going to need payment in advance before we go further, too. We need your *word*."

Piria looked up from whatever deep thought had occupied her. "Sorry, what word? What payment?"

Ikta took a deep breath. "It is custom. You *have* seen our enclave, learned knowledge kept hidden for over a thousand cycles. You know our identities, not to mention you touched the mind of nature." She leaned forward and fixed the two with a grim stare. "The Doraun's survival is dependent on secrecy. Officially, this place doesn't exist and if it were to be discovered, that would be the end of us. The Seat would snuff it out like a Formation Day candle. So, to show your mettle, you're going to have to bind yourself to us, and to that secret."

"If you wish to leave, alive, that is," Rama added.

Piria bristled. "You might have specified that before bringing us here."

Rama turned to the fruit bowl beside her. "I told you it would be worth your while, didn't I?"

"Is it? I don't mean to be rude, but I'm still not clear what we're getting from all this." Akteron said.

"Let's clarify something else," Rama continued, ignoring him. "That jolt you just felt? Oh, it was shocking enough, I'm sure. But that was a mere *whisper* compared to what we felt when all this began. A scream, a howl...deafening." She shook her head. "The Rootmind has sensed something coming. Something with the potential to injure nature, itself. It took span upon span to determine what kind of 'something' we were looking at, but today another tile in that mosaic clicked into place."

"Go on," Akteron said.

"Interpreting the Rootmind is tricky," Ikta took over, "but no matter how many times we talk to it, we're being handed the same concepts. What we can now say for certain is threefold. First, there is a shadow, interfering. Then, two seekers who can soothe. And finally, a sharp, black stone, of which death is covetous."

Piria sat up and turned to Akteron. "A sharp, black stone?"

"The blade..." Akteron uttered.

"Most likely, the blade," Rama affirmed. "We figured the blade stolen from the Museum and now, due to the Rootmind's insistence on talking to you both, that seems rather certain."

"*Of which death is covetous*', though?" Akteron asked.

"Even nature is prone to a little drama, now and then," Rama said with a shrug.

"Is it prone to prophesying, too?" Piria said with a touch of annoyance. "Because this sounds a lot like a prophecy and I will tell you now, I really don't have time for those..."

"Good. Me neither. They're garbage," Rama then told her. "But this is no prophecy. Picture it more as *pieces of probability*, which the Rootmind sensed. Pieces in play right now, which are leading towards something predictable. It's not about seeing hoozy-goozy visions in a bowl of scented water, but adding factors *together* to see a probable outcome. Like watching someone push a glass towards the edge of a table. You'd be able to predict the outcome there, wouldn't you?"

Piria tilted her head in acceptance. "Sure."

"But step back, a second," Akteron said, rubbing his eyes to alleviate a lingering discomfort from that vision. "That's another question. How do you know all about the theft?"

Ikta grinned. "Oh, kiddo, we have eyes everywhere. One of our brethren guards the enclave entrance near the museum and she–"

"Not important!" Rama interrupted. "The point is this blade. *That's* what you two are hunting, is it not?"

Akteron nodded.

"Good, and you need to retrieve it. *That's* the take-home, here. Because apparently if you don't, we all experience a *ripple*."

"A ripple..." Piria repeated.

"Mmm, we weren't sure about that one, either," Rama said. "But from what our interpreters can determine, it's not a 'drip on a calm pond' scenario, more a convulsion of order, at which point life itself is sucked from the continent."

Silence.

"And you learned this...from the Rootmind? You trust what it says?"

Rama laughed. "Do we trust the Rootmind?" Even a few of the silent figures standing around the room let a chuckle go at that, and Rama waited for the noise to settle. "That's a good one. But yes, implicitly. And think of 'it' less like a single entity, more like billions of entities all linked together."

Akteron nodded, seeing those dots of awareness, again. They were all...plants? People? Animals? Who knew? And whatever lay at their core, whatever connected them all was deeply troubled by...

"The Umbral Blade," he uttered. "How? How could it be capable of–"

"No idea," Rama finished for him. "But it doesn't matter. All that matters is that you find it, secure it, and make sure it's not in the hands of whoever this 'shadow' is."

"It's the thief," Akteron said, almost to himself. "We saw how callous he was with that bell. No wonder the Rootmind can see where this is all leading."

Piria shot him a look. "We don't know that for sure," she said. "What if the 'shadow' is a metaphor for something else? What if it's a misinterpretation?"

Akteron shook his head. "You saw the vision Kandaar made for us at the museum. He used literal shadow to create it..."

"Alright, alright." Piria closed her eyes for a moment. "Fine. So, we have to find the Umbral Blade. Great. We knew that already, even without ripples and threats to the safety of the continent." She turned to Akteron. "Just remember, there's another threat to the continent on the way if we don't find the other two objects, too. We are on a case, here, and not for the Doraun or the Rootmind, important though their input is." She raised her hands. "No offence."

Taking a deep breath, Akteron had to agree. "You're right. Madame Ikta, Madame Rama, thank you for your help, really, it's been, erm-...enlightening. But we can't do anything if we stay here, so what word do we have to give before we can leave? We'll find the blade, but this bell is still a threat, too, and who knows where that collar is..."

"Oh, you daft dears," Rama said, popping another grape in her mouth. "Haven't you figured it out, yet? We have the bell, of course."

———■———

It was a simple enough deal. Two promises. Two pledges, in return for a relic.

The first, of course, was a pledge to recover the blade, and was agreed to as Rama led the four down the overgrown, stone path outside the pavilion. Thereafter came a promise to keep the Doraun enclave in the strictest confidence.

Beyond the small, subterranean forest and its glowing, swaying lanterns, the four at last arrived at a cleft in the bedrock walls, inside which four guards stood watch over a pedestal. Soldiers, Akteron noted, in a kind of metal and bark armour and bearing wooden spears whose tips glinted softly. At a nod from Rama these men stood down, uncrossed their spears, and allowed ingress, but Akteron barely noticed. His eyes were fastened onto the item they guarded.

The Bell of Tongues, radiant in the gemstone lantern-light.

There was its lustrous, curved-metal body, the exotic detailing on the bottom lip and top ring, just as Kabonn's drawing had shown.

"...and if you break this covenant," Rama finished, stepping over to the relic, "we *will* know, and you agree that your body will transform into a cold, gooey mulch, becoming non-sentient, organic matter. *Compost*, if you like."

Akteron's eyes widened. "*Compost*? That's a bit much, isn't it?"

"Alternatively, we could send assassins to kill you."

Akteron didn't find either outcome particularly appealing.

"I'm still a bit unclear on one thing," Piria said, peering at the bell's decorations. "You didn't explain how you came into possession of it."

"As I said earlier, our Dagger's Clutch scout brought it in. Your thief dropped it and fled as soon as he'd rung it."

"So, he *did* drop it," Akteron muttered, a satisfied grin appearing.

"Possibly confounded," Piria added. "He accidentally affected himself and ran off in confusion..."

"Oh! That's a good point," Akteron then added. "Your scout, wasn't she confounded by the sound?"

Rama sighed. "I hope you're more observant than *this* on your casework," she said. "You have noticed that everyone here is deaf, right?"

Akteron nodded slowly, his mouth opening and cheeks reddening beneath his dark complexion.

Rama chuckled. "You didn't think I'd been watching those lips of yours just because they were pretty, did you?"

Akteron gazed quickly at the guards, at Ikta, and then Rama. "That's...another requirement of the Rootmind?"

She shrugged.

"Hold on," Piria interrupted, "so your scout actually *witnessed* the bell being struck?"

"Oh, the whole thing," Rama said. "Your thief seemed to know exactly what he was doing, climbing to the terrace of old Twurgy's Tavern and giving it a good slug. Vanra was only a stone's throw away, on watch atop the adjoining rooftop. Soon as she saw the effects that thing had on the locals, below, she fired an arrow, a glancing blow, nothing fatal, to stop it going any further. It was she who brought the bell in."

Piria brightened, spinning to Akteron. "Ro. That means she got a good look at the thief!"

"In all his seedy glory," Rama confirmed.

"*Perfect!*" Akteron whispered.

"Is there a chance we can talk to Vanra," Piria now asked. "She'd be the best lead we've found."

"Sure. Once you both stop screwing around and agree to the damned covenant." Rama nodded impatiently to the Bell. "So? What'll it be?"

———◼———

Getting the Bell of Tongues out of the enclave, through

Dagger's Clutch, into a coach, and back to the Bureau of Security had been an exercise in patience, and was only made more difficult by the bluster and temperate rain which had picked up while they'd been underground.

Bent double over the relic, Akteron had used his own donvul as a protective wrapping and by the time they were safely in a coach and clattering down the main avenue again, the garment — one of his favourite weaves — was soaked, stretched, and torn. A sacrifice, but one which Akteron considered noble.

Still, that hadn't been the hardest part. No, the hardest part had been the *temptation*.

The whole way to the Bureau, Piria had eyed the bundle in Akteron's arms as if it were some new pet she was dying to play with, and the curiosity had been infectious. Several times, Akteron had batted her hands away, only to relent at last and lift the donvul, allowing them both a proper, close inspection. Then, Piria had muttered quiet desires to hear what it sounded like in person, to unlock its secrets and reveal how it functioned...

Truthfully, Akteron had to admit that as alluring and mysterious as the bell was, it was neither as big, nor heavy, nor sinister-looking as he'd expected. Quite the opposite. Its complex beauty was unassuming and unique, and that such horrible power could be contained in something like that simply made it all the more dangerous...

They'd passed Sekiir's Eatery, its windows already boarded up. And the fire down the road had been extinguished, too, leaving blackened windows to stare out as if in a traumatised stupor. But all the previously chaotic roamers were absent, and hopefully back to normal.

Clattering along the cobbles, the only other sounds had been the dark-hour songbirds and the rustle of the endless canopy, above, and Akteron held the bell tightly the whole way to the Security Bureau's night-door where, after a round of paperwork, the relic was at last taken from them and secured somewhere deep in their vaults.

When the pair arrived at Piria's apartment again, they debriefed again over cheese and a glass of wine, musing all the while about the Doraun's subterranean world — Akteron reasoning that discussion with each other hadn't been forbidden — and about their unlikely success. They then lay on Piria's floor, excited chatter sparking on through the night until at last, exhausted, both retired.

Just before falling asleep, though, Akteron smiled.

One item was already theirs. Two more remained. And now, they knew what he looked like.

PART TWO

———————— ▪ ————————

Dear Ren,

Yes, I finally picked up a pen again. Sorry it's been so long.

I don't want to bore you with business but I've landed my biggest gig, so far. You'll think it's boring, so I'm not even going to tell you what it is, but it feels like progress. It also makes moving to Torril feel more worthwhile. Oh, and best of all, if I crack this one it'll be a big step towards getting that clearance badge. Imagine! After all these cycles, finally being able to choose my own gigs! To have access to the Case Archives...

The point is, today we ended up in a place that reminded me of that festival at the Satholan Gardens. Remember the lanterns strung up in the trees? It was like that. And I still laugh, you know, picturing you struggling along with those shoulder-buckets. It was funny, I don't care what you say. But why did you take part in that game, knowing it was too much for you? ~~I guess you overestimated yourself and leapt in headfirst and maybe that the reason things worked and didn't work out but why do you always have to~~

Sorry. Ignore that. I know it's easy to criticise with the benefit of hindsight.

Wishing you were here. Please write back.

Love,

-Akteron

———————————————

CHAPTER EIGHT
FRESH AIR, FRESHLEAF, FRESH NEWS

– KADUUNK! –

Akteron felt the stone walls vibrate from where he stood, wrapped in an apron and frying mushrooms in Piria's kitchen.

A moment later and proceeded by mumblings, Piria herself trudged in, darkening the mood in the sunlit space as if she'd pulled a thundercloud behind her. Apparently her morning dose of fresh air had gone sour and from the look on her face, Akteron could guess why.

He turned back to the mushrooms lest they shrivel and pretended he hadn't noticed, the steam curling about his head.

"Your tongue is going to crackle when you taste these."

Oh, yes. Adding that crushed gelsi-root had been a good decision. It was filling the house with that incredible aroma which usually brought Piria running.

She hadn't even noticed it, yet.

Eyes locked on the pan, Akteron held a glass of fresh juice her way.

Still no response. Just that odd, mumbly-breathing thing she did when she was working through inner-turmoil. And glancing over his shoulder, Akteron also saw that surely enough, she was doing that thing with her face, again. Jaw clenching, lips wiggling as if they were churning words about. She plodded to the window and settled her face a mere hair from the glass and Akteron hoped this wasn't like last time...

"Go on, then," he prompted.

"He has a new cart," she said, planting her hands on the sill.

Akteron moved the mushrooms from the heat and took the juice to her.

"You know he's a buffoon, Ri. Don't let it get to you." He set the juice down beside her hand and leant against the wall, untying his apron. "He's a showman, that's it. You've got more skill in your left nostril than he has in that entire, tacky wagon."

"He has *six* new powders..."

"Wow. Six." Akteron sounded thoughtful. "I bet none of them turn someone's face into a soggy bread-loaf, though..."

Piria gave a light snort and Akteron was relieved that it held a flake of amusement. It told him this wasn't like last time. Thankfully.

Piria drummed lightly on the sill with one balled fist. "How does everyone believe his *slop*? A powder to repair glass...sure, reasonable enough. But a powder to strengthen *petitions*? A powder to speak to the *dead*? Please..."

"They'll discover he's a fraud soon enough. I mean, the name alone...*Tyroli Bomballion*? Even if he is from Saj Minoor, that sounds about as legitimate as a warm-tack snowstorm."

"He tells them it's up to *their inner-will*. That *trust in oneself* is what makes his *'fabulous creations'* work, so if one doesn't, it's because *you* didn't believe strongly enough. It's clever. It's evil."

"'Evil' might be going a little far. It's absolutely crafty and dishonest, though." Absently, Akteron took her drink and began sipping. "Honestly, Ri, forget him. When you decide to put your own stuff out there again, you can show people what a pulvichist can really do. You're a lot smarter, with a boatload more creativity."

"...even if that were true, it doesn't seem to be enough in this

136

game."

"Ah...well, you're also a lot prettier than he is."

She laughed, and that dark cloud she'd dragged in began to dissipate. The mottled sunlight on the floor-tiles also seemed to brighten a little and Akteron sighed, inwardly. Very few things tilted Piria's even keel, and seeing her *angry* was rare as a golden beak. Her emotions were usually so tamped down he wondered at times if she actually had any.

"You're right," she said, relaxing those crinkled brows. "You are right, of course." Then, reaching down for that glass, she found it gone and Akteron received a flick on the shoulder.

"Ah, sorry." He pulled himself from the wall, plucked his own glass from the table, and set it in her hand. Only then did Piria glance at the two, neatly set places there. At the flowers in the centre of the table. And only then did she seem to smell that sautéed gelsi-root and allow herself a deep breath.

"If I had any interest in settling down," she said, "you really would be a contender."

Akteron raised his eyebrows while spooning mushrooms onto their plates beside mixed, seasoned vegetables and steaming sweet-rice.

"I would?" he said. "Well, Miss Kii, I'm honoured to be in the race. And curious to know who the competition is."

She smiled.

"Oh, come on."

"No. I don't think I'm ready to share that. And aren't you the one who always says, 'mystery is the spice of life'?"

Akteron feigned shock. "Yes, but if there *is* someone, you *must* tell me, my satin-cheeked, silken-haired, sunbloom-scented paramour..." Placing the pan in the sink, he then stepped to open the window and spoke over his shoulder. "I'd rather we end our lust-laced dalliance on a civil note, rather than me finding a foreign donvul in the wash, one morning..."

Piria snorted as he returned to the table. "I'll be sure to

introduce you to Mr. Imaginary as soon as he blinks into existence, then. But honestly, you know I'll never find someone who can cook like this."

"Any other answer and I'd have laced your next meal with alkamium."

"No, that's not...how alkamium works."

The pair took their seats.

Piria then shook her head, apparently in self-reflection. "What am I doing, getting all heated up? I'm fine. It's just that-...ugh, he really knows how to drive that spike in. Even if what he says and sells turns out to be rot, in the end."

"I know, Ri."

The faucet dripped in the sink behind the pair.

"But speaking of things ringing," Akteron went on, "are you ready to see Riallo's face when we walk in that office door? I mean, we *found* it."

"I know. He's going to leap through the ceiling. It's barely been a full day since we got the case."

"Right? I can already hear that dopey giggle."

Piria took a bite of the rice and Akteron went quiet, just observing for a moment. He knew she was a proponent of delayed gratification, so it was always interesting to see what Piria loaded onto her fork *last* at mealtimes.

"And after that? What do we do, then? We need to have something to tell him..." she said while chewing.

"Yes. Well, I thought about that, last night," Akteron replied, stabbing a pair of larger, oily fungi.

"I thought I heard you writing."

Akteron stopped stabbing, his fork hovering briefly as his gaze melted through his plate, and behind them, the faucet dripped again.

"Don't worry, you didn't wake me," Piria added. "I was already up and saw the light under the door, and that nib you use is scratchy."

Akteron's eyes studied the pile of vegetables, steam rising softly past his hand. "I haven't written to him in ages," he said. "I don't know why. I suppose there just wasn't much exciting to talk about. It's been over three span..."

"Oh, Ren won't care. He knows you're busy. And if I were him, I'd be happy to get any word at all, after what he..."

Akteron didn't notice her trail off. He was too busy staring at those vegetables and mulling over Kriolar and the memory which had caused his fork to still. Strange, how speaking Ren's name could do that, sometimes.

A breeze rustled the plants by the open window and the shutters clacked softly against the stonework before he began hunting mushrooms again. When he glanced up to meet Piria's eyes again, his face was free of concern.

"Anyway. After Riallo," he said, "I think it's time we got in touch with Tagill."

Piria nodded. "I was going to suggest the same. Hopefully, he'll know something."

"He hasn't let me down, yet."

"But he's going to want payment, right?"

Akteron nodded. "I know exactly what Tagill wants. We'll stop at the market on the way."

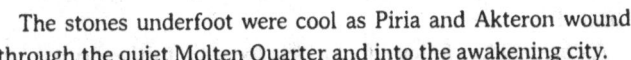

The stones underfoot were cool as Piria and Akteron wound through the quiet Molten Quarter and into the awakening city.

Above, Torril's canopy was alive with a million voices sharing their morning songs and a warm breeze rustled the spiked fronds lining the avenues. Such sweet air, here in the jungle, when nature exhaled in the dawn hours and flowers opened in the pillared light from above. Akteron found it enlivening, so vastly different from the dry, dusty heat he'd grown up with in Kriolar.

Avoiding the route which led past Tyroli's new wagon — as Akteron wished to avoid confrontation, today — he and Piria soon found a coach on the main street and it wasn't much longer before the cleanly paved entrance ramp to the Bureau's gaping maw was underfoot.

It was all pristine, as ever. No seedpods lying about. No leaf-litter gathering. Everything was shaped. Tidy. Trimmed. Just how the Seat wanted it. And ascending the main stairs, Akteron didn't find it surprising that the polished stone halls and gleaming bannisters gave no indication of the derelict, old Official Quarter and its seedy back alleys. Nor that the Seat left it, mud-encrusted and mouldering, despite clearly having the resources to do otherwise. It was too easy to throw a thick weave over things that didn't add further lustre to their veneer, he supposed, only to return later, tear down and pummel and press things into a new, desired form—

Hmm. Akteron pulled himself up, noticing that 'scepticism' Piria had mentioned.

Passing down the arcade of lilac banners and the battery of treated, wooden doors, the two at last reached Riallo's office.

The official's blue eyes were already glistening with pride as they entered.

"You two!" he exclaimed, lifting the veil from the item on his desk. "My agents! This is truly first class. First class! I can't imagine how you managed it. Oh, Kabonn is going to be thrilled!"

A dopey giggle followed and Piria loosed a furtive grin at her partner.

"Hey, this is why you picked us for the job," Akteron said. "You wanted the best."

Riallo didn't stop smiling but shook his head. "You can boast when you've found all three relics, top-shot. Until then, let's just say you're doing well, and I'm surprised."

Akteron's confident smile faltered. "Surprised? Erm-...but you're right, we shouldn't celebrate just yet. Not until we check it. I mean, it could be a different bell, for all we know. We weren't brave enough to give it a smack and find out."

"I bet. But we've already sent a runner, so Kabonn should be here to assess the piece any minute." Gently, Riallo tilted the object to one side, then the other. "As for the likelihood of it being a 'different bell', Kabonn mentioned all museum items have a catalogue number, somewhere..." A coloured marking Akteron had noticed in the coach came into view on the bell's rim. "There, you see?"

"Certainly makes identification easier."

"It does," Riallo replied, peering further about the object. "But there's another which only shows up under a certain lens, too." At last, he carefully set it down again and turned to his agents. "In any case, time to spill the grain. How on Aliru *did* you retrieve it so quickly?"

"Oh, now." Akteron raised a finger. "For *that,* we are going to need some freshleaf."

It didn't take long for one of Riallo's aides to bustle into the room bearing a tray of steaming cups. And once each had been set down, Piria and Akteron launched into their retelling of the events at the Official Quarter, Dagger's Clutch, and the chaos surrounding the evening.

The tale was augmented by the resident birds of Riallo's windowsill, who added an occasional, excitable, '*Aark!* Good work!' or, 'You're late!' or, 'Get it done!' — phrases clearly learned through prolonged and close proximity to Bureau tedium. And these interruptions, plus the pair's evasion of specifics in order to keep their promise, made the retelling decidedly clunky. A few of Akteron's bolder fabrications even drew crisp winces from Piria, who seemed averse to inventing an entire tavern, for example, outside which they had brawled with drunken sailors until a grouchy captain had scared them off with bad breath, alone.

Yet, Akteron knew it was necessary, not only to explain the large bruise which that iron-like choke hold had left on his neck. But also, of course, to explain the recovery of the bell, found on that rooftop in this version of events.

"A messy night," Riallo had remarked, eyebrows raised as the tale drew to a close. "Be sure to add all that to the report. And let's hope your impeccable luck holds up."

Wait...luck?

Akteron winced, realising only now that this modified account also vaporised most of their investigative efforts. That was a blunder, indeed.

Relinquishing some pride was better than 'transforming into gooey mulch', or whatever Rama had threatened, however. And Akteron was more concerned with how he was going to remember the tale they'd just whizzled up, later.

"Odd, though," Riallo said, tracing the metallic dome's contours and decoration with his eyes. "It certainly doesn't *look* dangerous, does it?"

"Not really," Piria agreed. "Our angle is that it's better viewed as a weapon. Hard to see what kind of utility it would serve, otherwise."

"Well, it's certainly not for waking the town."

"Unless you really hate the town."

Akteron snorted. "And it's certainly capable of doing that, if last night is any indication. By the way, any news from the Official Quarter? It seemed as though things had settled down, when we drove past at about moon-zenith. There was a lot of damage on Tanaar Street outside Sekiir's, though, and I imagine there were residents wanting an explanation."

"Sure were," Riallo said, turning to his agent and letting a breath out through his teeth. "The Seat dispatched criers this morning to make statements in all the main squares. Official story is that the 'disturbance' was caused by a bungled, cooperative petition, and that it's been managed."

Akteron nodded, aware that such explanations were easy to concoct and impossible to prove. Probably standard operation for the Seat. Absently, he wondered how many times it might have been deployed to cover up other 'disturbances' in the past.

"They made no mention of potentially deadly items stolen from the museum, as we agreed." Riallo added with a shrug. "And for now, that'll have to suffice. Keeping all this hushed is still paramount, especially after a demonstration of these relics' abilities."

"Was anyone hurt?"

"Depends on how you define 'hurt'. The infirmary was flooded with citizens, though few had significant injuries."

"Injuries aren't always physical," Piria said.

"Correct. And a good deal of patients did believe they'd gone mad. More than a couple of relationships ended. A handful of youngens came out of it not wanting to go home, again. Others lost all their valuables, or their pets, or their faiths..."

Akteron shrugged. "It could all have been a lot worse. We were lucky things went the way they did."

Riallo shrugged back. "Better still if it hadn't happened at all..."

Their teapot was empty by now, and Riallo was just beginning to reach for a small bell when without a knock, the door burst open and Kabonn Saal Nisbri burst in, eyes desperate and sweat glistening on his red cheeks.

Riallo, Akteron and Piria all leapt in their seats and Akteron's cup pitched into his lap.

"Mr. Saal–" One of Riallo's aides also leapt to her feet but Kabonn's prodigious midsection drove her aside, a smile the size of Inran Bay forming as his gaze met the item atop Riallo's desk.

"There she is!" he cried, arms out. "There she is! Ah, the flock was torn apart at her disappearance but one by one, my chicks return to the nest!"

"It's alright, Kina. Let's let protocol slide on this one." Riallo told the aide, who withdrew.

Standing, Akteron attempted to pad up the stain on his pants with a napkin before finding a pair of arms flung about him.

"You wonderful boy! Wonderful!" the curator literally cried, tears running down his face. "And you, marvellous, genius girl!" He turned to advance on her but Piria backed away, rounding her chair.

"They made quick work of it, Mr. Saal," Riallo said, distracting Kabonn by gesturing to the item. "Like I said. These two are the best we could have picked."

"Indeed, indeed!" The curator took a deep breath and tried to regain his composure. "And I just knew that a fellow countryman would handle things swiftly, properly, or I never would have insisted on a Krio taking the case!"

Akteron almost found a prideful grin on his lips before he blinked. "Wait, what? You requested that a Krio national took the case?" He turned to Riallo. "Why?"

"Why?" Kabonn asked back with a chuckle. "Isn't it obvious? I already told you at the museum, lad! Surely you wondered why no grand, official task-force was organised to raid the city? I wanted things kept quiet! A small operation, led by someone who would understand my perspective."

Riallo cleared his throat and spoke quickly. "All reasonable. So, curator, we should discuss the verification of–"

"Hang on," Akteron broke in, still trying to absorb what he'd just heard and turning to his superior. "You were *told* to hire us? I thought you'd 'pulled strings on this one'? That you'd done a mound of paperwork to make this happen?"

"Oh, I don't doubt that!" said Kabonn. "But Mr. Palaman didn't really have a choice, my boy. The Bureau couldn't afford to ignore my request. Too much on the line."

"I did have a–....hold on." In the crossfire, Riallo raised a hand.

"Listen, Akteron, I would have put you on this case, anyhow. Really."

Akteron didn't reply immediately, though reddening cheeks spoke for him. "It's fine," he muttered, trying to shake off the small betrayal, and for the next few moments an awkward silence settled.

It wasn't just that Riallo hadn't been honest with him. Akteron understood that his superior was often compelled to acquiesce to loftier forces and that he was rarely at liberty to discuss the reasons. But he might have let *something* slip, rather than leading Akteron to believe his competence had won him this investigation...

And even overlooking that, it was the *implications* of this particular decision which Riallo hadn't seemed to grasp.

If Akteron succeeded, the Bureau would take the credit as expected...things would end in Kal Brioran wine and fine garments in the museum's exhibition hall.

But if Akteron failed...

An expendable, foreign detective on a case of national importance? A detective who had formerly worked for Kriolar's own Bureau of Security and who had grown up through the Krio Rebellion, ten cycles earlier? *Gods.* He almost snorted at their good fortune, the outcome as clear as Riallo's glass paperweight. Losing his career would be the least of his concerns, for Akteron realised now that the Bureau had the perfect scapegoat on which to pin it all...

Briefly, he wondered if that had been what Riallo whispered to Nomos before this case had begun? How easy it would be to manage, if things went sideways–

He shook himself.

No. Riallo wouldn't do that. Not to Akteron. *Great Wastes*, he had to start keeping this scepticism in check, or it might transmute into paranoia...

Turning to the curator, Akteron took a deep breath. Kabonn

was still studying the relic and seemed not to have noticed the tension.

"Truly," the man said, "I can't say how thrilled I am to see her, safe from shadow market and crucible! You and Ms. Kii are already proving an excellent decision."

"I'm glad to hear it," Akteron replied. "But there are still two other items out there somewhere, curator. They don't have any telltale effects we can track down and they're smaller. More easily concealed."

"Oh, I have the *utmost* faith in you both!"

Wiping his hands on his trousers, Kabonn now reached into a pocket in his tightly stretched vest and withdrew a small ring of metal, inside which a polished, gemstone disc hung, suspended in the centre. "Not that I think it's necessary..." he said, crouching to eye the bell while raising that ring to look through it. "But let us just be *sure*...that what we have, here is-...*ah!* There! Yes, this is the true bell, as I'd assumed."

Akteron nodded, realising that he'd just found the hidden mark Riallo had mentioned. That had been simple, at least.

Re-pocketing the glass, Kabonn straightened and turned to the young detective. "And as to your earlier comment," he said, "do you and Miss. Kii have any idea whither the dastardly brigand might have absconded? Or any threads to wind together at this prosperous juncture?"

"We do have a potential lead," Akteron replied. "And we finally have a description of the thief, too. Though, I'm afraid we can't share many details."

Kabonn chuckled. "Oh! Quite so, quite so! My apologies, lad, I won't press and pry into your workings."

Riallo cocked his head. "A description of the thief?"

"Oh, yes," Piria began. "We were getting to that, before..." She bucked her head towards Kabonn, who had already turned to fuss over the bell, again. "So, if you're sure you want to be underwhelmed..."

Riallo whipped out a pad. "As sure as the sky in Torril is green, Miss Kii. Shoot. What can you tell me?"

"Well, he's male, as we suspected from the museum vision. Now, we also know he's around his thirtieth cycle. Our witness said he had a large, beak-like nose and thick eyebrows, one of which, his left, appeared half-burnt off. Probably weighs as much as I do, and about my height, too."

Riallo scribbled away as Akteron wandered over and helped himself to the tea-service by the wall, remembering what else Vanra, the Doraun scout, had told them. "At the time he was seen, he was wearing a mid-weave donvul. Patchy, older, and too large for him." He turned to lean on the sideboard. "The colour was unfortunately too hard to discern in the dark. Footwear and trousers seemed standard. Any ingot-belt was equally impossible to make out, and might have been concealed."

Riallo nodded, repeating what he'd heard under his breath.

"True," he then said with a final *TWIP!* of his pen, "it's nothing groundbreaking, but that eyebrow bit might well produce a hit. I'll have a team start a search in the Identificary and will send a runner tonight if anything comes up." He glanced to Piria. "To your address, again?"

Piria nodded, and Riallo hadn't even pocketed his pad before all four of them caught the unmistakable rhythm of footsteps pounding down the carpeted hall, outside. Again, Kina sprang to the ready and even braced herself against the door before a rapid knock sounded through it.

Riallo nodded, she opened it, and a young messenger strode in and stood at attention.

"Officer Palaman? Urgent news from the Krio consulate," she announced, brandishing a letter.

With a worried glance, Riallo took it, muttering, *"Here we go..."* and by the time the message was out of its envelope, the runner was gone again.

The officer didn't bother to keep the contents to himself.

"His Grace, Zikaron Feriin Tesbri, Krio Ambassador to Torril City, Silent-Speaker, Second-Official to Kriolar's Bureau of Antiquities, has been informed that a recent theft of Krio national heritage was knowingly concealed from His Grace, and demands a formal explanation and immediate action on part of the Torril City Bureau of Security, culminating in the restoration of both objects within three days, failing which, His Grace must declare this an act of hostility against Kriolar, noting that such actions can only be seen as an attempt to erase remaining Krio history and national pride. Torrilian honour and mutual amity rest on your response."

Pressing his lips together, Riallo folded the note again and for some reason, three sets of eyes locked onto Akteron.

"Oh dear," Kabonn said, blotting his forehead with a handkerchief. "That's a far worse reaction than I'd imagined."

"Aark!" A bird squawked from the windowsill. *"Get it done!"*

CHAPTER NINE
TAGILL'S TIPS

"BAAAP! BAA-BAAAP!"

A trio of coastal brigarees circled above the cobbled laneway in the afternoon sun, their calls piercing the air over the rustle of leaves.

At times, whorls of them circled listlessly over the city's seaside quarters and docks but most often, they could be seen drifting over boats at sea, annoying fisherman to no end while attempting to steal a catch.

And *by Fulbiscan's flaming hair*! Akteron was reminded why seafarers dreaded forgetting ear-mitts. Why boats often sent up sparkbangs to drive them away. He felt for the dogged, toiling sods who couldn't rid themselves of the pests until their catch was hauled in, and who had to deal with this *fracas* for hours on end.

Honestly, the Bell of Tongues might just be preferable...

Lifting his gaze, Akteron found a sea-breeze rippling the canopy and creating a vast, inverted ocean of waves, above. Up there, higher still than the brigarees, the city's avifauna were singing their own song as they settled for the day, preferring the sturdy, ancient boughs of Torril over the rippling blue expanse.

Unfazed by the ruckus, Piria leaned against warm brickwork still radiating heat from the day, beside a towering pair of locked warehouse doors.

"Kandaar did deliver the signal, didn't he?" she asked, flicking a leaf in her fingers.

Akteron had started to wonder the same thing but knew what he'd felt, earlier. He couldn't mistake the coolness which had descended around him. The gentle prodding in his mind.

He pursed his lips and kept pacing. "He did. And he received a signal back from Silvaatra while we were at the market. I'm sure I felt it…just as I arrived at Lomi's stall and you were looking at gem-lamps."

– KATACK! –

A large seedpod from some feathery squabble above whooshed past his ear and cracked to the ground.

Akteron didn't notice.

"He's usually very punctual, though. And if there *had* been a problem, surely I wouldn't have received a signal back."

Perhaps. But it was getting late.

Through that salty breeze, which carried with it the waft of fish and wet timber, the distant – *TANGG!* – of the afternoon bell had been pealing. Now, its last note left a lingering echo in the air.

"And you're sure Tagill knows what the signal means…"

"Of course. He was the one who came up with it."

Piria grunted and Akteron couldn't help sensing that despite that easy pose, she was nervous.

"Technically, he's not late. We're just early," he said. "He'll come."

"BAAAP! BAAP!"

Ah. Those birds weren't just circling over the warehouses, Akteron realised, but himself and Piria. Shooting them a dusty look, he held out his empty hands.

"I don't have any fish, you cretins!"

Looking back to his partner, he then saw she'd stopped flicking and started picking that leaf apart, instead. It was time to address the problem, head-on.

"You seem worried, Ri," he started. "It's not necessary. Tagill's past sounds more nefarious than it is. His life is a fascinating story. You'll like him."

"I'm sure I will," she replied, dropping the shredded leaf only to start fidgeting with the sleeve of her donvul. "It's just that thieves just aren't exactly the most reliable types, and it's hard to verify anything you manage to squeeze out. Makes the data unreliable..."

From the doors beside her, a metallic – *KITUUNK!* – then sounded and one ground open with rusty reluctance.

A wrinkled, stubbled, and lopsided face appeared from the strip of shadow within, one eye closed and a wry grin below it.

"*Former* thief," the stranger corrected her in a gravelly voice. "And I feel my data is reliable enough."

Piria's face reddened slightly as Akteron strode forwards.

"Tagill," he announced, brushing a hand along his arm.

"Yeah, yeah, good to see you, too, kid. Now, get inside before I petition lightning for those brigarees."

Akteron glanced over his shoulder. "Glad I don't live here. They're magnificently annoying."

"Oh, you've no idea. What I wouldn't give to tie one to each of my enemies' backs..."

The three passed through that gap in the doors and into the warehouse, and at once, the temperature dropped. A musty, damp cool enveloped them, the smell of fish actually stronger, inside.

Bolting the doors, Tagill pivoted to his guests, levelling an expectant stare at Akteron. "So? Want to introduce us, already?"

"This is my partner, Piria," he explained. "I couldn't relate much in the signal or I'd have told you she was coming."

Tagill looked her up and down, face growing slightly wistful as he scrutinised her kinked locks. "Red hair," he remarked. "Always reminds me of sunrise at sea."

"You're a sailor, then?" Piria said.

Tagill chuckled as he swung back around and lead them towards a small stair which descended into the warehouse proper.

"Never sailed a ship in my life," he replied, taking each step carefully, almost as if one leg wasn't cooperating. "But some experiences leave impressions."

Spread out in the space below, Piria and Akteron could see an expansive floor studded with huge, open-lidded vats, rippling inside like satin under rows of hanging gem-lanterns. They were full of water. Salt-water, if the smell was any indication.

"You aren't limping," Akteron noted, following the shorter, older man down. "I take it Kollis finally finished the leg-brace?"

"Sure did," Tagill grunted, "and I feel more cramped than ever. If it weren't for the pain, I'd ditch the thing and live with the dud limb, useless as it makes me."

"What happened?" Piria asked, as the three met the floor.

Tagill ambled into the shadows nearby and tugged on a pair of gloves. "A lifetime of pilfering," he replied. "Seems you never *get* without *losing,* in return. That's the Balance, for ya..." He then re-emerged holding a small wooden bucket, inside which Piria could see a glittering pile of dried fish. With the bucket's handle settled into the crook of his arm, he plodded past her towards the first of those squat vats. "Can't really complain, though. I've had more luck than most, my whole life. Stupid not to expect it to run out, at some point. To pay the price..."

Digging for a handful of fish, Tagill flung them into the dark water and continued on, mumbling, "A price for everything. Never get something for nothing..."

Following along, Akteron took a moment to peer into the first vat. It only came up to his middle and as they walked by, he caught the pastel, moonlight glimmer which began within. First, the water began to burble and shift as a luminous smear grew. Then there were two smears, which began circling and sliding over one another. Finally, a pair of glowing tentacles broke the surface, plucking a few floating fish with incredible dexterity and dragging them down.

"What are these things, again?" Akteron asked as the pair caught up to Tagill, already two vats ahead.

"Multipods," their guide replied, casting fish into the next tank before stopping to observe the creatures under the water. "And this lot are almost ready to go. Always sad, this time of cycle. I've looked after 'em since they were this big." He held out an open hand.

"And...where do they go?" Piria asked as another trio of slender tentacles rose out of the water to pick their selection of fish.

"To the ocean, 'course," Tagill replied, turning to continue. "They're the best brine-fungus hunters around. Let a pair go at night, and *WHSSSH!*, they'll beeline for the first big colony they smell."

Piria spun to observe all the rows of vats around them, probably considering the scale of this venture.

"But why do you need multipods?" she asked. "Can't sailors find the fungus without them?"

"Brine fungus only rises to the surface at night," Akteron explained. "Difficult to see, unless you have a glowing arrow pointing the way..."

"That's it," Tagill confirmed, adding, "no better way to find it. No better multipods for the job, either. Mine are the finest around. Grow the biggest. Glow the brightest. And I train 'em to recognise the best fungus, too."

Akteron gave a light huff of amusement. It seemed Tagill couldn't resist playing salesman, even when he didn't have any real customers around. But Akteron knew the man could talk a pterenar into buying snow-boots.

"But keeping them in here must be uncomfortable for them, right?" Piria asked. "The vats don't quite look big enough..."

"Not anymore." Tagill shrugged. "Lots of room when they first hatched, though. Last few span is when they grow the fastest. They'll be back in the ocean, soon enough. Lots of room, there."

"They're beautiful," Akteron said, watching luminous tentacles under the water refracting through the ripples, the colour a muted blend of blue and silver.

"Sure are. No idea what makes 'em light up, either, but as long as they keep doing it, they're welcome in my barrels."

"It's chemical bioluminescence," Piria said, peering at the row of dark vats before them as they wandered further. "Two chemicals, to be exact, which mix to create the effect. But it's not certain why that happens. Why they do it."

"For hunting?" Akteron suggested.

"It wouldn't make sense to make yourself so visible," Piria answered. "That'd only scare off their prey. It's probably a signal of their emotional state, like how tikkils change colour. Or maybe it's so that multipods can find each other?"

"I'll take your word for it," Tagill said, turning into the second row of vats which led back towards the front of the warehouse. "But, now, you aren't really here to discuss multipods. I know you don't send signals lightly. So, what's the problem?" He continued casting fish into the murky waters as they walked and talked.

Akteron cleared his throat. "We need your help."

Tagill laughed, stilled his wandering and turned at last to regard Akteron. "In all my cycles, I've been given that line so often my donvuls could be woven from it. 'Course you need help. Everyone does. What with?"

"We're trying to track down some stolen goods."

"Mmhmm."

"We thought maybe you'd caught a whisper or two," Piria continued. "Due to the items' nature, the theft isn't being publicised, but we're pretty sure word would be floating around, anyway."

Tagill's eyes twinkled. "Three items?"

Piria nodded.

"Stolen from a certain museum?"

"That's them."

Tagill rubbed his chin. "Well, now. First up, if I *had* heard of any such objects, I'd be remiss not to revisit my earlier point..."

"Something for nothing?" Akteron said, knowing where this was heading.

Tagill gave a modest shrug.

"Now, really," Akteron said. "Would I have visited you without bringing a gift?"

The wrinkled, lopsided face of Tagill's had just one symmetrical part, his thin-lipped mouth, and at this statement, it opened into a toothy grin. "Garinians? From Tenolar?"

"Best mushrooms of the season. I cooked some up this morning and the caps are firm. They've held moisture well throughout shipping. They're perfect raw or to fry, and they'll go even better with some Kal Brioran Stout..."

Tagill raised the eyebrow of his good eye.

"Yep." Akteron nodded. "It's all being delivered this evening. Should be here at final bell."

Tagill was about to laugh when that grin faltered. "You've outdone yourself, kid," he said softly, clapping a hand on Akteron's shoulder, and something flickered in his eyes which Piria seemed to catch, as well. A kind of distant pain being remembered under that shifty, rascal's guise. It was the look of someone whose own shadow seemed to chase him. Which clung like the cold and wouldn't allow itself to be shaken off, no matter if he stepped into warmth.

"I'll pay you for the ale," he said. "Whatever it's worth."

"No, that's not-...I'm paying *you*. For the help," Akteron replied.

"Let me pay, all the same."

"It's just ale, Tag. Take it. I told Piria earlier that you've never let me down and I have a good feeling about this time, too. It's the least I can do."

"But I don't-...always a catch," Tagill muttered, "some other condition..."

"Tagill." Akteron ducked in front of the man's good eye to get his attention. "You're not in that world, anymore. Not now. I don't attach strings or run cons. And in exchange for your help, I'm giving you a bloody keg of ale."

For a brief second, Piria's red hair flashed in a stream of afternoon light from the window and this seemed to snap Tagill from whichever reverie he'd fallen into. Akteron watched as the man's past released him from its chokehold and that haunted look evaporated.

"Right..." he muttered, finding his voice. "Right. Well, word did reach me that there's a market tonight. At the Holes, outside town. Mmm. Second market in two nights, which is rare, and the big three sellers will all be there. Geltak. Komod. And, of course, Bozik." He turned to Piria and added, "To that lot, Bozik is known better as 'Snaptooth'."

Watching Piria shift on her feet, Akteron had to admit, the name made him uncomfortable, too. He wasn't dying to know its origin.

"Now," Tagill went on, "the only times the big three return for a second night in a row is when one of 'em has gotten their paws on something big — something unique. That much is clear."

A tentacle in the vat beside them rose to the surface, plucking the last fish out of sight and vanishing with a – *SCHLUP!* –

Tagill didn't even blink.

"And then, in comes one of my kids this morning, bringing a rumour that one of the three landed whatever it is, last night. You can be sure all three will be at the market when that moon comes up."

Akteron gave an appreciative grunt. "Our thief *has* been busy."

"You don't know which of the three sellers it was, do you?" Piria asked.

Tagill shook his head. "That's part of their play. All three of 'em will say they're the one who has it, now."

She wrinkled her nose. "Why would they do that? Won't it become clear which two are lying?"

"Not really, no. By now, most people in that scene know there were items stolen from that museum. Maybe each of the three really does have one."

"Not possible," Akteron said. "We already recovered one of the artefacts, last night."

"Ah. Well, that still leaves two." Tagill scratched his chin. "And to answer your question, this lot have a kind of 'agreement'. Each of 'em knows the others' business, more or less. Each of 'em knows when one of 'em lands a big piece. So, when one sounds the horn, the others do, too. Generates more interest, that way. Lures in more buyers. It's a game, y'see. An' they have better chances at hawking something of value if none of the customers know which of 'em has the goods, or what they're supposed to be nettin'."

"But we do know what we want to net..."

"Well, don't mention that," Tagill warned. "That'll sound suspicious. Better to play ignorant. To be a bit aloof."

"I take it that means you won't be coming with us," Piria said.

"No chance," Tagill replied, shaking his head. "I'm done with that lot an' their cut-throat plodguffery."

At that, he took a step back and gave both Piria and Akteron another examination. "Which leads me to my next point. I figure you want to get in and out, alive. Right? Well, you won't get two steps into the Holes like *that*. No way. You both look like you just came from a Seat lunch."

Ah.

Looking down at his own thick, finely-woven donvul, his clean boots and pressed trousers and that finely crafted ingot-belt, Akteron knew the winkled old fellow was right.

Tagill was a boon on cases like this. His eyes and ears seemed tuned to catch mannerisms and turns of phrase which gave folks like Piria and Akteron — folks from more 'respectable' circles — away at a glance, and his mind was a compendium of skullduggery, compiled over long cycles in dusty tavern basements and dripping service-tunnels. Tagill knew how each tiny gesture or utterance could make or break a deal and what each variation on a scowl or grin could hide.

But Akteron had also known Tagill long enough to guess that all this left marks which he himself wasn't prepared to bear.

And now, as they stood there beside writhing beasts in great vats in this cavernous warehouse, Akteron realised that he also wasn't helping the situation. Here was Tagill, after all, building a reputable name for himself in far less dubious spheres. Trying to distance himself from that shifting, misty world, those faces. From his former self.

He'd told Akteron as much last time they'd met and now, with a pang of guilt, Akteron realised why the mention of favours had caused that momentary rupture.

"So, you're saying we go in different clothing." Piria broke his thoughts.

"Aye. You'll need a change of rags, at the very least," Tagill confirmed, "but equally important is the change to all this." He gestured to the rest of her, but seeing confusion on her face, realised he'd have to clarify. "You can't go in as yourselves. No good."

Akteron nodded. "Understood. And that point we'll still have to figure out. But I already know just how to solve the first."

"Here's a third point," Piria added. "Where is this market? I've never heard of 'The Holes', nor any other markets outside town."

"Ah. If you head over to the western docks at around moon-centre tonight," Tagill explained, "you should be on time. From the docks, walk southwards along the beach until you find a ramp fixed into the cliffs. It's not lit or marked, so it'll be tough to make out, but when you notice a rock in the shallows that looks like the Seat tower, you're in the right spot. Follow the ramp up. It'll lead you right to the entrance."

"Great. And once we arrive, we beeline for the big three and try to scope out their wares before the place gets busy," Akteron suggested.

Tagill shook his head. "The big three won't sell the items straight away, if they have 'em. They'll wait until there's significant patronage, until the word's well and truly gone around. They want interest to build so they can get the best price, 'course."

"And what if you're wrong?" Piria asked. "What if a buyer nabs it, early on?"

Tagill shrugged. "Could happen. I'm just sayin' what I know is likely."

"We only have one chance," Piria told Akteron with furrowed brows. "If they actually have the blade and we miss it..." she trailed off, and Akteron knew she was thinking about the Doraun's promise.

Or was she thinking about the Krio ambassador's threat? Or the potential turmoil facing Torril and Kriolar? Or Kabonn's heart breaking as they announced they'd failed?

Mentally ticking all of the above, he met Tagill's eyes again. "I trust what you've told us, but Piria's right. If we mess this up, there's more than a couple of missing artefacts to worry about. I'm going to send a runner to Riallo, tell him what's happening tonight and that we might need backup."

Tagill held a hand up, the other still clutching his bucket. "Do whatever you like. Just keep my name out of it." Reaching the last vat in the row, he upended it to dump a final pair of dead-eyed fish into the dark water. They were quickly snatched by more tentacles and pulled out of view. "A protective hex would be a good move, and don't worry *too* much. You both seem sharp enough, they'll never see you coming..."

Tilting his head, he then added, "Then again, if anyone *does* find out who you are, for the love of Kal Brioran Green, run fast."

CHAPTER TEN
A DOUBLE PROBLEM PROBLEM

"I'll just go as myself," Piria said, brushing a green frond aside as the pair strode the lane around Riol Park.

A near-deafening clamour of birdcalls was needling the air as the sun tucked itself beneath the horizon, but thankfully, a wall of vegetation ringing the park muffled it enough to make conversation possible.

That wall needed trimming, Akteron thought. It was testing the park's iron fence, lengthy green arms reaching across the sidewalk like desperate captives straining through bars, eager to burst free and invade the rest of the city, but behind it, the hum of voices could also be heard as groups gathered on the grass, listening to the evening serenade and watching the light fade. A daily ritual, of sorts.

"Tagill was adamant we not do that," Akteron replied, "and really, I trust him on this."

"I know, but trust or no trust, you go in character, I'll...just have to go as myself."

"Have to? I don't see what the problem is. It's just a little theatre, a one hour performance free from script and director. And then we're done." He hopped a large root bursting through the pavement at his feet. "Didn't you ever have theatre class at the Idmaion?"

Piria remained silent.

"Ri, it'll be fun. Truly. Just imagine you're—" he stopped himself before he uttered the name *Tyroli* and made a fatal mistake. "...Gruubal. Your trickster who grew up in the Soldiers' Quarter. Remember? How did you describe him, again?"

Piria sighed, but broke a small grin. "Desperate. Dirty," she said. "Works a sly deal like a second-tongue."

"That's it!" Akteron said, giving a little in-stride hop. "Why not?"

Piria shook her head. "No. Look, you play Gruubal. Just let me — I'll...I can't right now." And she pressed her lips together.

Though tempting, Akteron ignored the impulse to nudge her further. "That's progress, I suppose," he muttered, and gestured to the other side of the road. "Let's take the lanes. The Main Market will be chaos this close to closing."

Giving a pair of clattering coaches a wide berth, they crossed over.

Akteron's observation proved prescient, for each trading day as the light melted away and the market concluded, all those stalls and bodies had to disperse. They filtered out into the surrounding streets like blood filling the veins of a sleeping limb and for a good hour the area would be a mess. Already, carts and tradespeople were appearing, sacks or wares slung over their shoulders, and navigating that was about as appealing to Akteron as chewing pebbles.

The two hopped the curb, veering into a lane where the low afternoon sun ran gleaming fingers of light along the rooftops.

"I'd say we still have about four hours until moon-centre," Akteron estimated. "Plenty of time to organise our tactics before the Holes gets going. And to flesh out some of Gruubal's mannerisms."

"If you're really keen to test yourself, you could also go as Beldunn..." Piria said, bucking her head towards an elegantly painted sign above a small restaurant.

In curly, golden letters, it read, "AGIIL'S FINE FARE."

Ah. That restaurant.

Odd, Akteron thought, that memories could sting but then leave a lingering feeling behind. Like a pleasant aroma.

There, in the austere, candlelit innards of Agiil's, tables adorned with crisp white cloth and polished silverware would be ready for the night's well-to-do guests. Akteron knew they would be served equally fine fare in unsatisfying, pretentious little piles, barely enough for a tikkil's blip of an appetite.

He let out a quiet *humph*, feigning offence and looking her up and down. "Beldunn! A low blow from Ms. Kii."

They drew on and left the eatery behind. Then, his face grew thoughtful.

"But, using past trauma as creative fuel isn't altogether a bad idea, actually..."

"I wouldn't say you were *traumatised* by him," Piria replied. "He was just a crummy roommate. We've all had one."

Akteron narrowly avoided a lady bustling past in the opposite direction before muttering, "He was a disaster."

"He ate your cheese and drank your wine...that was bad, not a *disaster*."

There was so much more Akteron had failed to explain. But he worded his reply carefully.

"Cleaning up after him I could bare. Cooking for him without ever getting a word of thanks was manageable. Him accidentally locking me out every second day I learned to live with...but he also ruined my *clothes*..." He gave an exaggerated shudder.

"He was a *bit* of a disaster," Piria admitted.

Akteron was content to accept that, but in reality, that first tack had been almost unbearable. Half a cycle of wondering if it had been the right choice to leave Kriolar with nothing but an ingot-belt and a back-sack. To start over in a city where not one person knew his name, leaving the place and people he knew so well, and the security there, and dive into a culture which differed in so many ways.

That, of course, was without the unfortunate pairing — and Beldunn had done more than just ruin Akteron's clothes. That would have annoyed Akteron enough, but later...the simmering flicker of contempt in his eyes, its ignition into violence.

Akteron kept those parts shelved and out of sight.

No, it had not been the fresh-aired, petal-feted introduction to Torril City he'd imagined, yet who hadn't misjudged the odd character, once or twice? He'd needed a place to live and had paid for the rash decision of snatching the first offer which floated his way.

In retrospect, Akteron was capable of seeing the upside of it all, too, for without his former roommate's scummy habits and the tense atmosphere to drive him out that night, he would never have met Piria back there, at Agiil's Eatery.

That had truly been the break in the clouds he'd been waiting for.

"I wonder if they changed their rampillion recipe after that night?" Akteron asked, and Piria gave a snort.

"I doubt it. Persuading that chef was about as futile as telling two non-ullaminar base metals to adhere."

"Right?" Akteron pretended he knew what that meant. "I don't understand, though. One customer telling you you're cooking them wrong, you can ignore. But four? It's the most basic rule, you *never* salt rampillions. Surest way to ruin the flavour."

"If I hadn't eaten them almost every span as a child, I might not have known to agree with that. But once you've had good rampillions..."

Akteron smirked. "We'll make a chef out of you, yet."

"I am a chef," Piria stated seriously. "I just don't cook food."

Huh. True enough. Pulvichemy was pretty similar to cooking, when he considered it. The ingredients were just more chemical and the preparation, *far* more precise. Still, without being able to eat the final result...

Nope. He wouldn't have the patience.

The pair peeled off Agiil's lane and entered another which skirted the Main Market. At once, the clatter of stalls being packed up, of wagon-wheels on cobbles, of shouts and then the afternoon bell grew louder.

If Akteron were capable of ignoring the crowd, he knew this would be the best time to snare a deal. Now, when sellers were desperate to rid themselves of their swiftly deteriorating produce. But he couldn't ignore the crowd. He could almost *feel* them converging on him, a mass of people. Too many people in one place, and him at the centre-...

He stifled a shudder as they ducked into the next alley.

Glancing to Piria, he found that her lips were no longer pressed together and decided to prod again, just a little.

"So, what's bothering you, then? First Tagill's and now here. I mean, if anyone could cause a fear of dressing up, it'd be Sendil. But I have a feeling it's not him that's irking you. You've been off all afternoon, so out with it."

"Oh, no, it's not him," Piria said quietly, clearly trying to brush the prodding away. "It's nothing."

"You realise that 'it's nothing' *always* means something," he replied, "and I'm not going to spend the evening with you simmering away beside me while our lives are on the line. We need to be as sharp as Tagill expected us to be."

"I'm not *simmering*. I'm-...*ugh*."

Akteron cocked an eyebrow. "That tells me very little."

"It's just that-..." she began. "Fine. I'm stuck. Still stuck on how he did it. I can't work it out, and I certainly can't come up with *another whole persona* while this is pinging around, in there!"

Ah, of course. Piria's fabled, 'Double Problem Problem.'

Akteron had recognised her annoyed and thinky face the

moment they'd left the docks — the face she used when a solution was circling outside her field of view, evading capture and impeding her internal calculations. Whenever she encountered such looming, insurmountable problems, Piria seemed unable to negotiate with them. Helpless, as they seized her cognitive powers and made tackling others impossible.

It was understandable. The problems Piria contended with sat far beyond Akteron's own abilities and he had no qualms letting them remain her problems, alone. This time, though, he felt he knew exactly what she was about to say, and the reason was simple. That same little splinter had been digging itself into his own mind since the previous day.

"Which part are you stuck on in particular, then? Because I'm still baffled by all of it," he said.

Piria nodded back and they took a corner, spooking two pterenars who chuttered at the interruption before lowering their heads to resume pecking at the ground.

"The difficulty is...well, firstly, how the thief got through those blocks of stone."

"...and I assume your tests didn't shed any light on things?" Akteron asked.

Piria seemed confused.

"That residue you found on the museum wall," he clarified. "I wasn't the only one of us up late, last night. I heard you clinking about in The Cave."

"Ah." Piria nodded, but her brow only knotted further. *Darnit.* No. It turns out the residue didn't say much. I don't even know if it was deposited during the theft. There were traces of kusamium in it...basically an additive or modifier...but kusamium is everywhere. It has a thousand different applications and a thousand different effects when combined with other reagents."

"Why didn't you mention this at the Bureau?"

"Because I have no idea what it means," she said. "It's like trying to analyse a breeze. It's there and you can measure it, but trying to assign it significance..."

"Hmm."

She sighed. "And that's not even the *main* issue. The main issue is that *nothing* is adding up! Take the hammer. I assume he petitioned for some kind of hex to strengthen its blows. Right? Enough to shatter those protective wards..."

The conversation faltered as they passed an older lady with soil-covered hands, bent over and sorting vegetables into two baskets on her doorstep.

At the sight of the colourful tubers in those trugs, Akteron's mind immediately leapt to the dinner they wouldn't be eating, tonight, and his stomach gave a small, acknowledging grumble.

"...but he *must* have petitioned something for those stone blocks, too," Piria continued once the lady was out of earshot again. "That's a minimum of *two* petitions, which, depending on their nature and my reckoning, doesn't check out."

Akteron gave a thoughtful hum. "It flicked through my mind, as well, that he petitioned a passthrough for the stone."

"Of course, it's obvious." She clenched one fist as if attempting to choke the answer out of the problem. "But it doesn't work. I mean, there's a reason would-be criminals find any other way of breaking into target locales."

"...and avoid using Third-Level Manipulations to do so," Akteron muttered, recalling the chart he'd memorised back at the Idmaion.

Beginning before a child even welded with their Sharak, all citizens were made familiar with the petitioning, and this instruction began with the basics. How to commune with Sharak. What common, everyday petitions were. What Sharak were capable and incapable of.

Later, as a child's relationship with their Sharak grew more complex and the possible dangers needed to be addressed, so, too, did these lessons grow in complexity. The various levels of

'*Manipulation*' were the first category of petitions which all students of the Idmaion needed to master to gain their first ingots at the official examinations.

And there was a good reason neither of them had seriously suggested a passthrough petition as the solution.

"Going in would have left him without enough charge to get out, again," Akteron said.

"Right. The thief would have been stranded on the wrong side of the stone, *inside* the museum, and still needing charge not only to do...whatever he did to that hammer, but also to leave, again. Three petitions. All of them at least third-level." Piria gave a doubtful huff. "If a passthrough to get you through a window pane costs five to eight ingots, then a slab of *granite*, a full dash thick...?"

"He'd need half the city's ingot-belts to pull it off," Akteron calculated roughly as savoury smells from last-meal preparations in the houses around them began to waft through the air.

"And again, that's just to get *in*," Piria reiterated. "So, how in the Blue Robes' best biddings did he do it? I just can't crack this..."

"Let's also not forget that from the vision, it didn't look like he made any petitions inside the museum," Akteron pointed out, recalling that shadowy figure beelining for the cases and the way it had struck the glass almost at once.

"I *know*," Piria growled.

Leaping a substantial pile of bird-dung not yet cleared away by the street-keepers, Akteron then narrowed his own eyes. "Well...perhaps he had–"

"Don't say it."

"...another ingot-belt. Or twenty?" Akteron winced.

"Yes. Setting off every detector in the city," Piria finished with a shake of her head. "And inviting the most horrific penalties the Seat has." She snorted, again. "Come on. It was you who told me when I first came on board–"

"It's *never* another ingot-belt," Akteron repeated. "I was just kidding."

Funny, Riallo had told *him* that when he'd first started with the Bureau.

And he was only half-kidding.

Sure, the solution was about as feasible as a pterenar taking flight, but…what *if*? What if the city's detectors didn't work, or the buzz of forty or fifty full ingots didn't make the air ripple around whoever had managed to break one of Tarma's most concrete laws? What would it be possible to petition, then?

He grunted. Piria's frustration was almost making the air ripple, as it was. Here was the young scientist who spent days at a time, eyes fastened onto enlargement-glasses under which she combined minute amounts of powder together, noting reactions and results with mechanical precision. Who could lose herself in pages of numerical problems and forget to eat until Akteron knocked — almost to her irritation — bearing food, and to remind her she needed to remain alive in order to solve them.

No wonder this was consuming her. It was one of her thought experiments come to life. Acted out before her eyes. But she couldn't resolve the math.

Still, that's what she'd asked for when they had first teamed up, wasn't it? The promise of unique puzzles? The opportunities for oblique thinking? A chance to put her pulvichemy to use?

"A group petition would have been detected too, I suppose," he tried again.

Piria nodded.

"Well, then…maybe he finally persuaded a Sharak to perform teleportation?"

Piria's "*Hah!*" echoed down the street. "Ready the history books, then."

Yes. A foolish suggestion.

Although Piria herself had once told him that *any* potential solution to a problem was worth pursuing, it was true that most outlandish ideas had already *been* pursued, tested, and condemned as nonsense. Teleportation was one such petition. Apparently, it just couldn't happen.

They emerged at last into Lusiin Street, a wide, older looking stretch, coated in the usual white Torrilian stone and dotted with overflowing planter boxes. It swept off in a curve, as if built expressly to encircle a truly gargantuan tree trunk which loomed behind Lusiin Street's low-rise constructions.

Known as *Kubkub* or, 'The Great Grandfather', this tree was one of Torril's famous landmarks and a remarkable sight for visitors, its trunk larger than some city blocks. It erupted from the city in majestic enormity only to vanish into the green world, high above, and as Akteron glimpsed it this evening, an image of that strange realm the Rootmind had shown him flashed into his memory. The feeling of floating and of roots entangling him. The pinprick connections to immeasurable points of consciousness...

Just then, a lamplighter scurried by, pausing ahead to ignite an old-fashioned lantern. The flicker drew Akteron's attention back to where, small and barely visible in the failing light, an unobtrusive sign hung.

The store below it was far too bland in appearance for the colourful personality who owned it, and how Sendil would love to paint the façade in some gaudy colour scheme! Or hammer signs all the way down the avenue, to break the mould and make sure his workshop was known about from end to end of town! But things in Torril were too tightly controlled for that.

Finding his lips pressed together, Akteron realised he was nervous.

It wasn't from any attempt to secure the latest, beak's-edge item of fashion, tonight, or banter about new imports or weaves, of course. But because this visit was the beginning of something dangerous. Tonight, Akteron was walking freely into the whetted teeth of Torril's shadowy underworld, a place he had never really been and which offered only the unknowable...

"Alright," he said to distract himself, and gestured ahead. "You had better pack down all your deeper 'thoughtenings' now, or we'll have a repeat of last time."

Piria took a deep breath. "Blue Robes forbid. I'll keep things light, I promise. I'll just pretend to be stupid, again. I'd rather he didn't notice me at all than corner me with his divine pfaffle."

"Sendil will only talk about his beliefs if you push him like you did. It was your fault."

"It's *not* my fault he believes in giant, omnipotent spectres."

"Weren't you the one who gave me a speech on 'divine' intervention yesterday? You're saying you don't believe in *any* of that?"

"What?" She frowned for a moment, before almost laughing. "Oh, you mean the meteor speech? *Great Wastes,* no! That's not what I meant."

"An unseen hand, guiding things we can't comprehend? Wasn't that the gist of it?"

Piria shook her head. "No, *no!* Alright, let me clarify," she told him, suddenly quite serious. "I do not believe"— she dropped her voice to a whisper —"in '*The Divinities*'. Or, any of that *garp* the Paramallion peddles!"

Despite her low voice being easily lost in the evening din, Akteron sent a nervous glance about them.

"If true *divinities* existed," she continued, "surely, they wouldn't be so uni-functional. Not to mention cruel and-...and *irrational.* Surgannith would have done something about those awful droughts, being a god of rain, right? Kelenn wouldn't allow babies to get diseases...or maybe he'd have made gorin-fruits edible."

Akteron didn't answer.

"Come on!" She insisted. "*If* any of them really existed, surely, these beings would actually *do* something useful or logical, now and then! Show themselves or communicate to us all, rather than only to a few, weirdly dressed, fanatical citizens through those ridiculous, wooden boards." She paused a moment. "Also, really? A god of *alcohol*? What is that about?"

"Felebol is strange..." Akteron admitted.

"That's what I meant with the meteors. I don't discount the idea of other *beings* out there. Intelligent beings like Sharak, who influence things, let's say, and outside our level of awareness. We know that there's a Rootmind now, and that's a perfect example. But let's call it what it is, 'intervention from another party,' maybe, and not, 'divine intervention!' The Paramallion do not get to stamp the term 'divinity' on forces we don't understand. Nor their seal on the entirety of the universe's mysteries, claiming ownership and knowledge of everything..."

"Reasonable enough," Akteron said. He could appreciate her viewpoint. "Well, you certainly don't have to pretend to be stupid."

She shot him a dark look.

"No! Erm, that's not what I-...I mean you don't have to *pretend anything*," he corrected. "Just be yourself with Sendil, is what I'm saying. And don't mention–"

"Apostasy, or logic, or reason," she ended the sentence for him.

"Sure. Those things."

"Fine. Well, if I'm not pretending"— a sly smirk bloomed on her face as a lady pushing two wheeled crates forced them aside for a moment —"then you shouldn't, either."

Akteron cocked his head.

"Oh, no...don't play innocent." She said with a smirk. "You know precisely what I'm talking about."

"I have absolutely no idea *what* you mean," he replied, though his tone betrayed that he had, perhaps, an inkling.

Piria put on a deep voice. "'What a *sublime* weave, Sendil! It must have been so difficult, sourcing such fine Kal Brioran cotton! Even the Seat's robes don't look this good! Look at these overlocks!'" She puffed up her chest and put her hands to her face in mock awe at each line.

"I appreciate his work, is all..." Akteron could feel his cheeks warming.

"Bollocks. You appreciate the attention and the free garb."

"Hey, I fail to see how any of that is my fault. The man basically throws clothes at me."

"Yes. Because he loves your face," Piria said, chuckling. "You're shameless, using your looks on him. It's sneaky and bad. You're a bad person." She then gave him a hip-bump and his face reddened further.

"Absolute nonsense," he muttered. "I'm sure he treats all his customers the same way."

———■———

"*Ak! Ter! On!* My *favourite* man! *Woolala!*" Sendil exclaimed, running a hand through the air to follow the angles of Akteron's chin. "I mean, what can I say? The *skin*, the *stubble*, the *jawline!* Not to mention these *shoulders! Rawrr!*"

The finely clad, grey-haired man stepped back, lifted one hand and supported it with the other, then proceeded to devour Akteron from head to toe with his eyes. "I'd have an artist paint you in everything I make," he said, adjusting the donvul and shoulder-piece he'd assaulted Akteron with. "If this city's artists weren't so flagrantly usurious! But having you wear me around the city will suffice...as long as you tell everyone who the master behind the look is, of course! And I do mean loud! And! Clear!"

"Oh, I do. You really are the best clothier in Torril," Akteron told him, giving a reactionary wince, for Piria's impressions of him might have been a little *too* accurate.

Nearby, Piria herself stood with crossed arms and regarded this display in cool silence, and Akteron worried if that sly smirk would become a permanent fixture.

"Oh! You are too much!" Sendil said with a giggle. Not one hair in his smartly combed plume jiggled out of place. He then twirled to a nearby garment-stand and began flicking pieces aside in turn. "So, tell me, tell me. What else will it be, today? Mauve—? *Blue!* Yes! Cornee feathers are *in* right now! In, in, in! Look, here…aren't they *delicious*?"

Akteron's grin faltered at last, and he lifted the donvul slowly over his head. "Sendil, these are all excellent creations, as always. Truly. And I'd love to wear a bunch of them right now. But—"

"Don't! Don't say it!" The clothier beamed, spinning back to Akteron with a piercing, searching stare. "You're after something more…*distinctive*! The chef's finest! The piece to show off these classic, *heroic* proportions!" There was a small, silent moment as he fanned both hands across Akteron's shoulders, again.

Akteron cleared his throat. "No, not that. I mean, yes, I *would* love something unique. That is, not now—"

Piria sighed, knowing Akteron was struggling.

"Sendil," she interrupted, stepping forward, "we need your help with something urgent."

The man spun and blinked as if realising she was there for the first time, and his face flashed shock. "Why, *madame*, of course! I am here to provide anything I can, especially to my most loyal customer and his most remarkable friend! Simply tell me what you both require and Kuuthera and I will make it so!" He gestured to the air as if his Sharak were floating there and listening to the exchange. Perhaps she was.

"Right," Piria began. "Well, fair warning, it's going to be a bit of a challenge for you—"

"I love a challenge…" Sendil muttered, eyes growing

determined.

"Because our job is to disguise ourselves."

"A disguise..." He cocked an eyebrow.

"And to blend in as best we can."

"The very best blend..."

"As criminals," she finished.

There was a lengthy pause as Sendil's mouth dropped. It hung a moment, as if detached from his face and Akteron could hear the stately clock behind the counter tick slowly, before the clothier's eyes flickered with devilish glee.

"As *criminals*...!" he whispered, slapping his hands together and spinning from the pair to scurry through the back door of his showroom.

"Sendil?" Piria called after him.

"Criminals!" Sendil's muffled voice called back. "It's as if the Divinities themselves had intervened and brought you to me! Such *luck*!"

Piria rolled her eyes at Akteron as he laid the thick belt, finely woven donvul and shoulder-piece on the countertop, brushing down his shirt and retrieving his own donvul from a nearby stool.

"How I have *longed* to tackle such an unusual, unique, precarious request!" Sendil was babbling through that door, deep within a jungle of boxes and clothing racks. "How *marvellous*!"

Akteron had to admit, he was curious to see how Sendil would handle that request.

"Yes, as Piria mentioned," he called into that room, trying to clarify, "we need to blend in at the Holes, a rather dangerous underground market, tonight, and host to a very shady crowd. And whatever you dress us in needs a certain, extra touch, too... apologies that this is all so 'last-minute'–"

"Akteron! No fuss, no *fuss*! Don't lose one hair off that *gorgeous* head!" the man called from the back room. "I have just the thing for you both! I know *exactly* what you need!"

The pair shared an unsure glance as he re-emerged from the back room at last, bearing two teetering boxes and a bundle of sewing equipment. Setting it all on a low bench, Sendil swept to the door of the shop and drew the blinds. Then, he turned back to his guests.

"And might I just tell you, now, you will not just blend in, tonight. No, no. You will be the most dastardly pair these holes have ever seen!"

CHAPTER ELEVEN
THE HOLES

Crickets were humming from the clifftops as Aliru's larger moon, Kara, and its red, satellite meteor neared their zenith for the night. Kara's smaller sister, Tria, never as dramatic nor as bright, lagged behind as ever, but presently the two moons would fly together and bathe the beach in a lustrous, silver glow.

The celestial twins were only really visible here on the coast, where Torril's canopy capitulated to open sky and where two lone figures now crunched a rhythm along the shelly, sandy stretch.

Perhaps the two were alone because this coastline was so knotty to reach, but no doubt in ten cycles or so — if trade kept booming and the city continued to expand — this pristine shoreline would be sacrificed to extend the western docks, and ships would pull in here to load and offload cargo from Saj Minoor, Kal Brior, Kriolar and Tenolar.

"Think of it this way," Akteron muttered, tugging at his new, oddly constructed garment's neckline again, "at least we didn't have to pay for it all."

"Oh, no," Piria replied, struggling with each sandy step in the tall, side-stitched boots she now wore, "we're paying. With dignity. And potentially, our lives."

A small silence fell.

"There wasn't really much choice."

"There were bins in the alley beside Sendil's. That was a choice."

"It was not," Akteron grumbled, noticing that his trousers were slipping ever so slowly down, again. Sendil had insisted that they were to be worn 'low', but surely he couldn't have meant half way down his thighs.

If he secured the trousers to this unusual donvul with the buttons on its lower hem, which he assumed was the idea, then the trousers might stay up. But then his ankles were exposed, right up to his calves.

Either far too short, or far too low. Those were the only two serviceable modes, apparently.

"We look like the buccaneers who robbed a soot factory..." Piria then mumbled, and Akteron couldn't disagree.

At any rate, she didn't look like the Piria he knew. That straight-edged, quietly-spoken pulvichist who abhorred any attempt at augmenting her appearance. He'd never seen her wearing earrings, or makeup, or any colours louder than her coral hair. Yet tonight, that hair had been combed back and was held in place by a thin, angled headband, Sendil assuring them it made her more 'edgy' and less 'cute'.

She'd taken that as a compliment, despite Akteron feeling Sendil hadn't meant it as such.

Contrary to her protests, the clothier had also applied makeup to 'emphasise her features', and fitted her with dark gloves reaching almost to her elbows. They matched a sweeping, sleeveless, black coat — black being the theme of the evening, apparently — which attached around the neck and which fell just short of dragging in the sand. It left her shoulders bare and exposed, but completed the 'look'.

True. She did look formidable, Akteron was in no position to debate that.

On the other hand, for the first time in his life, Akteron felt that Sendil's efforts had ended in acute disaster. The coat he wore had a collar which flared up around his head, and not only did this 'lizard's frill' totally obscured his view if he tried to look backwards, but there seemed no way to detach it. The shoulders ended in architecturally hard corners, and the piece wasn't one, continuous garment as his normal donvul was. Rather, like Piria's, it was a series of parts which overlapped like scales across the front and back. This was all to say nothing of the metal studs and buttons everywhere, though at least Akteron had lucked some input, there...

It was not the kind of fashion Akteron would have chosen to exude 'mood and menace.' And he doubted the clothier's assurance that they would fit in tonight, for the simple fact that Sendil hadn't seemed to have the faintest idea what the Holes were.

But it was too late to turn back, now...

"Ro, look," Piria said, motioning towards a vague, diagonal smudge on the cliffside. "That must be the ramp."

Akteron followed the line while reminding himself again that it was Piria beside him, then turned to the water's edge, where he spotted a stone rising from the gentle swell, slender and egg-shaped. A fair, natural representation of the Seat's tower.

"*Just as Tagill said,*" he muttered.

They altered course and headed towards the cliffs.

"That's one point for him, then," Piria said.

"I told you, he's never let me down. And he was right about the western docks."

"Barely. He could have given us an easier route."

Akteron leapt a stone. "You think there's an easier way?"

"There has to be. We haven't seen one other soul since we passed Durgy's Alehouse back there, and it wouldn't be much of a market if everyone had to run this gauntlet to get there."

She did have a point. But so far, following Tagill's instructions, they'd found things precisely as he'd described. At the western wharves, they'd avoided the wandering deckhands and the ever-watchful harbourmaster to wiggle through the fence beside Durgy's.

Overcoming a grove of spike palms, a wonderland of boulders, and a number of soft, shifting dunes, their feet had then finally met beach. After that, jungle-choked cliffs had run the whole way from the city's edge.

Now, they were approaching the firths, a series of inlets which formed Torril's south-eastern limits and where, presumably, the Holes lay.

Piria must be right, then. There must be another route, for how else were goods and stalls transported to and fro?

"Perhaps Tagill was giving us a 'back door'? A quieter way, so we'd avoid the clientele?" he suggested.

"Or perhaps it's been so long since he was here, things have changed..."

Akteron liked his suggestion, more.

Trudging their way to the wooden incline, a number of small crustaceans scuttled across the sand for refuge.

"Up we go, then." Akteron's eyes drifted up the narrow ramp. "And let's just hope...this stays where it's fastened."

He now saw there was no barrier. No footholds, either. Just wooden planks forming a ramp and fixed in place by large, horizontal piles rammed into the cliffside. Ahead, sections of the ramp seemed to sag unsettlingly, perhaps where a pile or two had rotted away.

With nerves fluttering, Akteron reached out with one foot and tested the nearest board — first prodding, then stepping, then jumping with his whole weight.

"And?" Piria asked.

"It seems...reassuringly stable."

"Well, thank Zoilla for that."

They began the incline.

"You *would* thank a mathematician," Akteron mumbled, leaning towards the cliff-face instinctively as he moved.

"She wasn't *just* a mathematician, she was a genius. One of her earlier projects was creating formulae to calculate tensile forces which, coincidentally, explain how this ramp is anchored in place."

"Oh. Lovely. Let's talk about something else, please."

"Sure," she said, and Akteron heard her gasp as her foot met a particularly wobbly board, though she recovered quickly. "How about our chances of retrieving the collar or the blade, tonight?"

He gave an uncertain hum but decided not to talk about anything, after all. The walkway had slowly grown...well, *tiltier,* and any feeling of stability was dissolving as more and more loose or missing boards broke the stretch.

With cautious movements and half-held breaths, however, they trod ever upwards, until the ramp began to curve around the cliff's sweeping face and into the first of the firths.

At once, that whisper of wind they'd felt on the beach gave way to mighty gusts and alarmingly, Akteron found his frill-like collar catching them and batting him about. A few steps further and the situation was made even worse by a rocky outcrop and a trio of missing planks.

It took both hands to grip and manoeuvre around the outcrop, Akteron's donvul catching on a small, dead shrub and almost ripping before he managed to pick it free.

"Honestly," he said, "I think it's likely that Tagill–"

"*BEKAA-KAKA-KAA!*"

Right beside his face, a seabird burst out of a cavity and Akteron leapt, stumbling towards the edge of the ramp.

For a moment he seemed suspended, teetering in the air without a handhold in reach before Piria struck out with surprising speed, grabbing the sleeve of his coat and yanking him firmly back towards the cliff.

Akteron's eyes stayed wide as cartwheels and it took a moment of silence and a number of deep breaths through his nose before he recovered his ability to speak.

"You-...just saved my life."

"We're not *that* far up," she tried to comfort him. But gazing off the edge, Akteron saw that she was wrong. They were barely half-way up the incline but already higher than Piria's apartment building. Below, there was only a carpet of rocks.

"I will cook for you. Anything you like," he said at last. "Anything...anytime...never a problem..."

"I hope you realise I will drag that debt out for a long time to come," she replied. "Come on, keep moving."

Akteron's guess, that the beach had been a 'back door' of sorts, turned out to be correct. The narrow plank-way had terminated not far around the cliffs with a ladder, at the top of which they'd found an overgrown path which led them, at last, to the entrance of the Holes.

There, crouching in the dark and peering through the bladed fronds of a squat palm, however, both he and Piria began to realise how precarious this situation was truly about to become, and why this place was named as it was.

Access to the Holes was gained via a bridge and guarded by a man who looked like he juggled boulders for a living. The brute seemed to be greeting everyone who arrived with a challenge, after which the visitor could cross the span, dangling high over the firth's heaving waters and leading to a gigantic, rock pillar.

This was just the first of many pillars rising from the sea, all lit with flickering torches ringing their crowns like swarms of night-bugs. Between each, Akteron could also see bridges threaded about like a vast web, their drooping lengths already bouncing and swaying with market-goers.

These visitors were wandering not between stalls, as Akteron had expected, but caves, chiselled into the stone uprights.

"Well. This complicates things..." Piria muttered, pulling back from their cover-palm and watching as a shifty-looking pair of guests emerged from a nearby path, approached the watchman, and received their challenge.

"Tagill didn't mention anything about this..." Akteron said.

"As I said, maybe he hasn't been here for a while."

"Well, I'm sure it's simple enough. We just have to stick to our parts, like we planned on the way...right?"

Piria gave an almost inaudible grumble.

"Does that mean you're ready?"

"Nope."

Akteron loosed a sympathetic look. "Just...try and keep the theft out of mind, for now. We'll figure it out later. We will. Right now we need to keep our minds on this and this only."

Piria gave him a slow nod, though in her eyes he could see the unmistakable flicker of uncertainty.

"Do you think...that runner delivered your message to Riallo?" she then asked.

"I don't know. And if he did, anyone he sends as backup won't be visible, that's for sure. Hopefully, though, they'll be nearby."

"And the signal is one shot into the air?"

"That's it," Akteron confirmed. "Just petition Lathiik for one big spark, upwards from your position if you need to. And remember...treat this like what it is"— he gestured to the flickering, suspended torches —"just another market...right?"

To say she looked unconvinced wouldn't have done her facial expression justice.

Still, when Akteron stood, she did, too.

———■———

Follok's night had been boring as an empty hold.

Most nights were, here at the bridges, but tonight his partner was absent again and nights like these always stank. Hours upon hours with only the wind to talk to as the murk descended and expelled even murkier characters from that path out of the jungle.

At least those damned birds had shut up, now, though.

Stretching his trunk-like limbs and with a yawn, Follock glanced up at the barrier of green which began nearby, and from which they'd tweeted their faces off for the last three hours. At least here on the cliff he could see the stars.

Stupid city-folk...choosing to grow up and live their lives without ever knowing that glittering expanse, above. Without knowing what they were missing. City folk had no idea how to chart a course, nor follow the wind, nor read that great dome.

He scratched his bearded chin and grunted.

Wet Deaths, what he wouldn't do to be at sea...

It was hard to say he missed the spray of salty air because being next to the ocean, there was no shortage of that. But being on *land* was just...different. The ground was unsettlingly still. Even after all these cycles he expected it to shift and tilt, especially when he could hear those waves crashing about in the bay, below.

He lowered his eyes to that jungle path again and took a long, deep breath.

Boring. Boring. Boring.

He'd just have to count on the visitors to the Holes livening things up, tonight, though so far it had been the usual, dull assortment. A couple of ragged loxers, their sallow faces full of that hollow, empty-eyed glee the drug delivered. He'd turned one away, already, but the others had still been capable of speech and in their stupor they often spent more than their even-headed counterparts did, so sellers welcomed them.

Then, there were the more well-to-do clientele, faces obscured with shawls or masks, and pouches of gemstones or reagents for trade hanging at their waists. Objects at this market often cost more than one belt's worth of charge, after all, and carrying something else of value was always a wise decision.

The foreigners were the worst, though.

Follock almost chuckled at the thought. It *was* a little rich from him, seeing as he was from Tenolar, but at least he could speak the language, here. At least he knew the customs and dressed like a real person-...

Speaking of which.

Ugh. Great, leaden depths, here was a pair, now — probably from Kal Brior if that ridiculous collar and that coat were any indication — here to pluck what they could for their pleasure gardens or galleries back home.

Follock narrowed his eyes as they emerged from the bushes.

Hmm. Alright, maybe not Kal Brioran. Though whatever style *that* was, it sure wasn't Torrilian...

Plucking a flaming torch, he held it up and peered at the newcomers, emerging into the orange ball of light it threw across the jungle's edge.

"Where did you two come from, then?" he asked the taller one — a man with a ridiculous collar.

"Torril," the man growled back, stepping over a mossy log.

Follock rolled his eyes and stepped towards them. "You don't say...I meant, why didn't you take the path?" He gestured with the torch to the dusty track ending before him.

"Lost it..." the man replied, motioning towards the jungle. "Torch went out. Saw your light & followed that, instead."

That gravelly voice of his didn't seem quite to match his appearance, but it wasn't the strangest voice Follock had heard in his time, here — and at least the pair weren't bearing weapons, as far as he could see.

Standing back, Follock relaxed a little. "Easy 'nough to do," he rumbled, ramming the torch back into ground from which he'd plucked it. "Had two visitors visit the water, last span, instead of the bridges." He waved one meaty paw at the cliffside not far from where he stood. "They didn't stick to the path, neither. Or maybe they were more interested in fish than goods..."

"We are most very interest-ed in goods," the woman piped up. "The goods over there. In the mark-et."

Huh? Interest-ed...? Mark-et...? What on Aliru was that accent?

The utterance caused the tall man with the stupid collar to study her, and an odd look crossed his face. Of...fear, maybe? Was he afraid of her? These two *were* strange, no doubt about it...

"Most visitors are here for the mark-*et*..." Follock said back, eyeing the woman more closely, her pale skin and pointy cheekbones, the intense, blue, unblinking stare. She was jittering, slightly.

Ah. So that was it. Probably another one on lox. And *darnit,* the jittery ones were usually the violent ones. The ones between fixes. The regular addicts who turned up here were tricky enough but for some reason, this one seemed wilder still, with that severe jacket, those metal studs and slicked back hair.

Ignoring all that, he nodded to their waists. "Hope those ingots are charged up, tonight. Though you know petitions are–"

"We know much and the ingots are charg-ed full! Full!" the woman almost shouted and Follock held up his hands.

Ugh. He didn't want to get stabbed again, tonight. He wasn't getting paid enough for that. And beaks in the night! This one looked ready to tear the wings off a pterenar with her teeth, which she'd now bared.

"Right," he said. "No need to get worked up. I'm supposed to ask questions...part of the job."

"Your job to ask...my job to tell...we all have jobs. Jobs to tell and ask..." she muttered, still staring at him.

Follock cleared his throat. "Right...you both know the rules, then?" And he turned to the man to avoid that disconcerting stare. "No weapons or petitions, inside. No touchin' the merchandise unless a seller offers. No *loxin'*"— the woman twitched —"and of course...no jumpin' on the bridges."

The tall man raised an eyebrow.

"Safety first." Follock shrugged.

The man huffed in annoyance. "Anything *else*?"

Follock could have asked more questions. He was supposed to check everyone who came out of that jungle path in case the Seat came sniffing about, as they sometimes did. But these two looked so unlike the crisply dressed city guard it almost made him laugh. Plus, the odds of the city sending only two guards were remote. They always sent a small army when they wanted something.

As three more figures began emerging from the jungle behind them, therefore, Follock merely stepped aside and gestured to the span, keen to get these two weirdos and their flashy, idiotic-looking garments out of his sight.

He was glad when they took his invitation and said nothing more.

Watching them leave his bloom of torchlight and cross the bridge, though, he couldn't help but let out a snicker.

Damned foreigners...

"Brilliant. That did the trick," Akteron whispered to Piria as they trod across the first bridge into the Holes. Though the span bounced with a satisfying elasticity and each board *was* reassuringly hard, the rope-barrier was cause for concern, giving small creaks at every movement.

"It wasn't so difficult, really," she whispered back. "Though I think I'll drop the accent..."

"What was your inspiration?"

"A drunk who used to throw garbage at people from the corner of my street," she replied at once. "Prickly old thing. The amount of times I'd take an early walk and find trash slung at me...and she was especially partial to sardines."

"Charming. Memorable."

She smirked, despite her nerves. "That sort of thing tends to stick with you."

He smirked back. "How punny."

"The important thing was that it got us past Tiny, I guess."

"...and that's fine," he said. "We don't need to overdo it. The goal is to find what we're after and be forgettable."

"No easy feat when looking like the town fool..."

"Town *fools*."

Piria chuckled. Another good sign.

Still, Akteron couldn't dispel his own nervousness. As much as he trusted Piria and no matter her performance, their risk of being discovered was significant and he didn't want to discover the penalty for being caught conning a bunch of crooks...

Cool, evening gusts seemed to draw them onwards, towards the first of the enormous rock-pillars, where visitors wandered a torchlit platform encircling the rock like a ring on a finger, ducking in and out of those caves hewn out of the living rock.

Each cave was no doubt filled with various wares, but now, Akteron could also see that each was painted in a different pattern, the first smucked with blue and white stripes, the second with patterned, red squares.

The reason seemed simple enough, for it would make each stall distinct and ease navigation in this lofty, disorienting world, he supposed.

The bridge joggled underfoot and pressing up to the rope barrier, Akteron allowed a pair of oncoming visitors to pass.

He was reminded again that beneath his feet and the

walkway's thin, uneven planks, dark waters churned and as if to prove the point, right then a wave smashed into the next pinnacle's foundations. There was a thunderous roar and a faint, salty plume met Akteron's face. Then, the wave continued through the firth, hitting each of the other pillars in turn with a series of muffled booms.

And here he was, entrusting his life to this tiny span of rope and wood...

Looking up, Akteron let out a nervous breath and resumed his inspection of the pillars as they began moving, again. In the dim combination of moonlight and torchlight, the edifices were clear enough, most sculpted by time and the elements into rounded uprights, crowned with trees and vegetation. Flat sides here and there suggested that calvings had taken place, however, and that even these stoic uprights were slowly, inevitably vanishing into the sea.

Another wave smashed into the pillar ahead, and Akteron felt the bridge shudder.

"Why didn't we just have the Bureau raid the place, again?" Piria whispered, offering a blessed distraction.

"Too risky," Akteron replied. "Just one glimpse of an official uniform or badge...or even a rumour that something was happening...and we'd lose what we came for. Those relics would vanish quicker than a shadow in the dark."

"Hmm." Piria understood the dilemma, then. "So, once again, Bozik, Komod, and Geltak are the targets..."

"Right."

"And each seller as likely as the others to have...the things we're looking for."

"A bit of a shot in the dark, I know," Akteron said. "The first challenge will really be to weed out the right seller from the duds."

"Sounds fun."

"Yes, I suppose it could be. So, whatsay we take it in turns?

We each get a shot at questioning a seller, and the winner gets the third?"

"...which won't be necessary," Piria muttered, "because if we don't have luck with the first two, the third seller has to be the one with the artefacts. Then it's down to us to-...well, buy them, I suppose. Though I'm not entirely comfortable with that."

"Ah," Akteron said, ignoring a muffled cracking sound and shifting to another board, "yes, well, I've had a think about that part, too."

Piria raised an eyebrow. "The fact that we'll basically be funding the criminal underworld if we purchase anything, here?"

"Yes," Akteron replied, lowering his voice again. "Don't worry, though. We won't be *purchasing* any artefacts. Let's just say the Bureau prefers other procedures in situations like this."

"And when were you planning to enlighten me on these 'procedures'?"

"Erm-...on the job, of course. In the moment. Best time to learn."

Piria gave a small, concerned hum. "Strange as it may seem," she said, "I can't read your mind. So, especially on cases like these, I need to know the *general* play, at least. I thought we were going to try and haggle for whatever we find?"

"We are. It's just that if we aren't successful, we take a more direct approach..."

Piria seemed to understand. "We're going to steal from the thieves."

"Let's use another term for the transaction."

"Re-acquire?"

"That'll do." He gave her an apologetic glance. "I'll try not to keep secrets, in future."

They reached the end of the bridge and stepped onto that circular walkway, and Akteron gave a relieved sigh. At last, a floor which didn't bend and sway under their feet.

"Next question," he whispered to her between passing buyers, "which of the three do we locate, first?"

Piria took a deep breath and eyed the bank of cave-stalls leading in both directions. "How about whoever's closest?"

He nodded, then drew a hand across his face. "Logical. Let's *characterise*, then."

"Who you tellin' to characterise?" Piria growled, suddenly all cold belligerence.

"Nice..."

They pushed into the crowd and at once, Akteron was astounded at the clientele, for what an exotic smattering of faces flowed around them!

There, a heavily perfumed man wandered past, head shaved clean on the sides and a thin, aqua mantle fastened to his shoulders. He didn't have that small row of vertical lines — or *kavs* — over his eyebrow as Akteron did, but he didn't need them to be recognisable as Krio. The clothing and hair styling of Akteron's homeland was distinct enough.

Next and accompanying this man were two women, apparently from Kal Brior, with thick jewellery glinting on their wrists, necks and ankles and telltale metal beads hanging from their clothing. Their skin, smooth as spread butter and dyed with floral decorations were typical. Kal Brioran women were known for spending a great deal of wealth and time on beautification.

But others were harder for Akteron to place. As they wove through a light crowd perusing and haggling, he failed to recognise certain weaves or styles of headdress, and realised how little he had actually travelled in his life.

Certainly, moving from Kriolar to Torril was nothing to shake a feather at, but there was so much more out there, and this market seemed to demonstrate that more than even the streets of Torril...

More people came and went. A tall lady with a black and gold dress had leant to inspect a box of luminescent mushrooms, a wooden neck-circlet arcing over her scalp and terminating at a point on her forehead. Next, two short, stout men growled to one another as they bumbled along, sacks slung over their shoulders. Their bare torsos were emblazoned with tattooed patterns, though their arms were covered by long sleeves attached to shoulder-rings.

Ahead were sailors from Saj Minoor in unfashionable, one-piece uniforms, and everywhere else he could see Torrillians in radiant, feathered garments, all drifting in and out of the lantern-light at this strange, nocturnal bazaar, all searching.

"The problem is," Akteron whispered as Piria suddenly pushed past him, "where to start...we can't just go and–"

Piria didn't hear him. For some reason, she had started shifting people out of her way and beelined for the nearest stall — a vendor of metal piercings, as it happened — and even before Akteron had sidled up beside her, she was rapping harshly on the counter and seemed to have gained crazy eyes...

"Oy!" she blurted at the stall-keep, who turned from whatever he'd busied himself with to eye her with annoyance. He was a sinewy, younger man with a shaved head, who had apparently stuck himself with one of every item he sold.

Akteron supposed Piria was taking the first turn at questioning, then.

"Lookin' for Komod. *Kom-od*," Piria told him, leaning on the bench with one arm and clenching a hand over and over. "Where's Komod at?" Under her breath she added, "*Where, where, wheeerree?*"

Coolly, the shopkeep looked her up and down, various metallic fixings jangling from his ears, nose, and eyebrows. Then, casually, he slung a small rag over his shoulder and opened his mouth to reveal a row of filed, jagged teeth.

Akteron made an awkward gurgle.

"Who wants to know?"

"Me. I wanna know. Got some business to do..." Piria didn't miss a beat and inhaled with a strange, laboured sound. "Gotta speak to Komod now. You speak, I speak...we gotta speak." She clenched her fists again and widened her eyes further, fixing him with an unblinking, birdlike stare.

He stared back and when she didn't look away, he even began to smile. "And who are *you* exactly, Scales? Sure you don't need some piercings, to go with that jacket? They'd suit you..."

Ugh. Another salesman like Tagill and-...wait, was he *hitting* on her?

Oh, no. Not right now. Leaning forward, Akteron formed his best snarl and spoke in that low growl. "*Scales* and I got urgent business with Komod. Need to find him *now* — or someone's fingers are gonna get separated from their hands..."

A thoughtful grunt, and the man took a step back, though he didn't seem too perturbed. "You're in luck then," he said. "I'm Komod."

"Hah!" Piria exclaimed.

Akteron, however, wasn't buying it.

"Prove it."

Eyes narrowing, the man leant forwards. "Been running this stall for twenty cycles, me and my old man," he said, "and ain't nobody ever asked me to do that. I've worked metal my whole life, making items you won't find elsewhere in the Holes. Or in Torril. Goods designed to...encourage people to cooperate, or else to teach 'em a lesson."

He grabbed the rag hanging over his shoulder and began polishing a metal...*claw?* on the counter as he went on.

"Nobody else can forge like I do. Here are pieces that'll never rust or tarnish. A nail, three dashes long and so strong it'll never bend or break...or an ingot that'll hold its charge ten times longer than that Seat junk." He nodded to Piria's ingot-belt and Akteron barely refrained from blurting, *"But that's illegal!"*

"What about selling things made long ago," he asked instead.

"Things that have seen many owners, already?"

"I got some high-quality, petition-moulded items, here. This used to be a spoon. Now it's a spork." The man gestured to the item. "This metal glove? Well guess what, it used to be a bowl..."

Akteron gave a huff at the not-so-impressive, not-so-old wares. "No antiques, then?"

The salesman remained silent.

"You're not Komod."

In character, Piria drew her nails across the counter and gave a low growl, face darkening.

"'Course I'm not," the man replied, flicking that rag back over his shoulder. "Worth a try, though."

"Alright. Then tell us...*tell us* where to go. *Now*..." Piria said.

"*Pff!* Why should I?"

"Because if you don't–"

"*Hey*," Akteron growled, raising his hands to calm them both. "Ease up. No need to let this get messy." His hand then met the countertop with a slight – *KTINK* – and when he withdrew it, a thumb-sized, oval chip of metal lay there, decorated with a fine script. "A metal seal, from one of the older, high families of Kriolar," he said. "Excellent workmanship and a rare inscription. A valuable trinket to the right seller, and it's yours...*if* you're willing to help us find our way."

The metal-studded merchant plucked the tiny object up and held it to the light, inspecting it closely. He tapped it on the bench, then weighed it in his hand. "Might be worth something if I melt it down, I 'spose." He grunted, gesturing flippantly with one hand. "White cave in the next pillar, few stalls from the bridge-way. Now, I got real business to do, so get lost." That hand brushed them away.

Turning to leave, Akteron was surprised to see Piria blow a kiss over her shoulder, and even more surprised to hear a gruff chuckle in response. The pair dodged a lady who powered past with a number of menials, speaking again only when they were out of earshot.

"Aren't those seals valuable?" Piria asked.

"Not really." Akteron jingled his pocket. "Put your hand in the sand down in Kriolar and you'll come up with a palmful. I'm just glad I thought to bring some."

"Me, too."

"We still weren't quite as forgettable as I'd have liked, though. And by the way, what in the Great Wastes was *that,* at the end, there?"

"Hmm? Oh, I'm developing my character."

"By blowing kisses..."

"Sure." She shrugged, eyes avoiding his. "What? He was cute."

Akteron had to blink to keep his own eyes in his head, at that. "I have *never* heard you say that about *anyone.* Save the odd, deceased author."

"Yes, I know. It's just...the eyes. They were just so *blue.* And it didn't hinder the plan."

"True, and true...even if I wasn't *so* keen on the filed teeth. Or the attitude. I mean, he was an eleven on the too-cocky scale. Though...he did make one good point"— he made a clunky, deliberate inspection of her face —"a nice, big nose-spike would really suit you."

It wasn't possible for Piria to hide a smile as the pair then found themselves confronting two bridges, each leading off towards a separate pillar.

"Alright," she said. "Left or right?"

Akteron squinted through the night at the former. "Depends if that looks like a white cave to you...over there."

Piria followed his finger. "It could be anything, for all I can tell in this light."

"Good enough."

He led the way across another, bouncing bridge, gripping its salt-encrusted rope-barriers so hard he might have squeezed them clean, and as violent gusts met them side on, the whole span rocked. Above the sound of crashing waves, Akteron could hear also the ropes creaking as if tightening. Tightening. Threatening to snap...

He kept his gaze locked onto the torchlight, ahead.

"What's odd, though," Piria said, "is that it doesn't look that different to your regular market, does it? What about all this is so illegal?"

"I suppose you were so lost in your performance," Akteron muttered, "or those bedtime eyes, that you failed to hear he was selling boosted ingots?"

"Well, sure. There was that."

"...each of which would be punishable with a cycle's hard labour."

"Yes, yes. But boosting ingots is hardly a serious crime."

"Erm, *excuse* me?" Akteron said, face flashing real shock. "Are you *my* Piria? Did you just mutter something that could almost maybe possibly be classified as *anti-Seat*?"

Piria snorted. "Oh please. How dangerous is having charge that doesn't deplete within a couple of span, after all? Even I've worked out formulae to allow longer term charge storage. Not that I'd ever actually *create* them."

"And the claw?"

"I saw the claw," Piria said, giving him a dry look. "I'm not blind. It might be for...decoration."

Akteron snorted. "What about the Bureau-issue killshots on the shelves at the back? The garrotte-wires, artfully organised by length and thickness?"

She gave an acceptant head-bob. "Alright, I missed those."

"All things to consider when vetting a future partner..."

Moments later, hands sticky with damp salt and hair tousled by the wind, the pair reached the next pillar and it became clear that, had Piria waited a moment longer to raise her doubts over the moral flavour of the Holes, the row of wares which now slid into view would have made the decision clear as a warm-tack sky.

"Oh, no..."

Hearing her whisper, Akteron turned and found several young-looking pterenars, hunched and cawing quietly within the confines of rusty, narrow cages. Interspersed were larger birds which stood, blank-eyed and giving their bars slow, defeated pecks, while behind the counter sat still more cages containing rarer breeds.

None had room even to spread their wings, most looked to be losing their brilliant plumage, and the stench of rotten straw and bird leavings was like a shovel to the nose.

But Piria wasn't even looking at the cages. Her eyes were leaping around a series of glass boxes set triumphantly on the counter, inside which hatchlings of various species sat in decorative arrangements, posed upon branches, or peeking out from foliage or from hollowed-out shells. A sign before them stated, "FROZEN BEAUTY - A TRUE AND UNIQUE RARITY FOR YOUR HOME!"

"Chrono-apathy..." Piria uttered. "They've been stuck in place. They're frozen..."

And so they were, beautiful wings held aloft or their mouths open in silent calls, indefinitely.

Akteron wasn't sure how it was done, exactly. Official physicians sometimes employed a similar method after accidents, when time was needed to keep someone stable as they were transported. But it cost a grievous amount of charge and worse, Akteron knew that the individual in stasis remained aware the whole time. The petition only affected the movement of tissues and cells — not thought, not consciousness. That meant the creatures in these glass cases and in their fanciful poses were alive. They were aware. But they were unable to move, and they would remain so until the petition wore off and they re-animated, only to die from mouldy insides or dust in their lungs or stomachs, cycles later.

Akteron let a breath through his lips.

Caging the fauna in Torril was forbidden as it was, but petitioning to freeze a life-form in time...

Casting a glance at Piria, Akteron could almost hear her thoughts. He'd seen her notebooks, brimming with powder recipes, mathematical formulae and theories — but most striking were the loving sketches of Torril's abundant avifauna.

The only option right now, however, was to turn and leave the awful sight behind.

This, they did, moving on while Akteron hoped the pained scowl Piria wore might just be mistaken for her character. But any lingering frivolity the two might have drawn from tonight's venture had drained away, now.

"Maybe we *should* call for the Bureau to close it down tonight," Piria whispered through her teeth as the white cave drew closer. "Maybe they can burn the whole place to the water–"

"Keep focused," was all Akteron said in reply, pushing past two older men with silver bands around their wrists.

"It's monstrous," she replied.

"I know. But keep focused."

Laying a hand on her shoulder, Akteron gave it a gentle squeeze–

Just as a voice nearby caught their ears. "Ah! *There* you are! You two've been lookin' for something particular, as I hear it..."

The pair spun to see a grinning, older man at a stall of assorted, mechanical curios. The cave itself had been painted a deep blue and the owner had a ponytail to match, its hue impossibly vibrant down to the roots, suggesting he'd petitioned the alteration. A bit of a waste, Akteron thought. Though, if the gent wanted to make an impression, an impression he'd made.

Donned in fine enough clothing — all tailored but not over the top — Akteron then saw that almost every inch of the outfit was smeared with grease.

"Not interested," he growled, turning away.

"Oh, but *my, my,* would you really have come all this way simply to give up what you came here *for*?" The seller continued before he could escape. "Surely, you know I craft and collect the finest mechanical wonders this side of the Glassy Sea, nay, in all the corners of Aliru!"

Akteron rolled his eyes. He'd heard this one already, tonight.

"And that being the case, I can only guess that you two are here for an especially *rare* piece..."

Hmm.

Akteron paused and shared a look with Piria.

"Oh, yes." The man bounced on his feet, taking pleasure in the reaction his words had caused. "I knew it. You won't find many sellers here more in the know than I am."

"And you are?" Piria asked, and the man gave a small bow.

"Geltak, at your service."

CHAPTER TWELVE
DIMSKULL'S DISCOVERY

His blue hair was full and his rough, sun-wrinkled skin showed his cycles, well enough. Despite his advanced age, though, Geltak's entire, skinny being seemed to emanate a jittery energy. The grin stretching from cheek to cheek on his round face was a grin, Akteron felt, of a man whose game had been perfected to such a degree that finding new ways to play was the only real joy, now.

"'Matter of fact," Akteron said in tonight's gravelled baritone, stepping closer. "Maybe I am looking for something rare."

Geltak clapped. "Well, how about that? But like I said, I may have been tipped off in advance..."

Without warning, Piria stalked to the counter and put her crazy-eyes on, again. "Who told you? *Who?*"

Geltak gave a chuckle. "Oh, when a pair like you come to the Holes, word gets around!"

As with Prongface, back there, Geltak didn't seem the least bit phased by Piria's performance and though this was worrying, Akteron realised it also wasn't surprising. Playing a leering lunatic in a place where thieves and crooks routinely met to hurl skills at one another — and where the sellers themselves, no doubt, concocted personas for themselves — could only end in immunity to such tactics, really.

And indeed, as a performance could go two ways, Akteron was

inclined to think Geltak's words pure garp, just then.

Sure, people had seen them tonight and sure, he and Piria might have made an impression, but nobody knew what they were *really* here to do, and there had certainly been no time for Prongface to spread any word.

Beaks, though. The man had conviction...so much so that Akteron almost believed it.

The trio's discussion faltered as another customer sauntered past and eyed Geltak's wares.

"Let's get to the interesting part," Akteron growled once she'd gone. "A rare find? What of it? And how recent. We talkin' the last day or so?"

"I might just be," Geltak leaned forward with a conspiratorial air. "Doubtless, you've caught whisper of a certain object or two, recently released from confinement and ready to find a new home with a discerning buyer?"

Piria rotated her head to Akteron slowly and levelled an unsettling leer. "*Dimskull*," she hissed. "He might have one! *He might!*"

Oh, shoot...

In the frantic preparation and journey here, they'd somehow forgotten to give themselves new names, hadn't they? But *Dimskull*?

He eyed her back and growled, "Patience, *Gumpina*...let me handle this."

Piria gave the slightest narrowing of her eyes and turned away, sputtering in frustration. Perhaps it was even *real* frustration. Akteron wasn't sure.

"My partner speaks too openly," he then told Geltak. "No nuance."

"Ah! But we needn't speak in riddles," Geltak answered. "Tell me, if what you seek is in my possession and if I were willing to part with it, tonight, what price are you willing to pay for a relic with such a storied past? And I don't mean to be indelicate, but you do understand *the price*, don't you? Not merely charge nor baubles, for *this* item..."

The young agent eyed the salesman carefully.

Interesting.

Geltak was speaking as if there were only one object and that was important. But it was also important for the man to remain unsure of Akteron's knowledge. If Akteron slipped-up or made any mention of the relics — the descriptions of which were still unknown to the public — well, that would be the end of this evening's attempt, and possibly the end of more than that.

Akteron kept his expression flat. "I do know the price. I know it's important."

"Oh, not just *important*," Geltak cast a look about as if hidden eyes were observing them from the crags of the pillar, and that grin faded. "Let me be more direct — this item is unique and worthy of secrecy beyond normal bounds. By now, the noses of every officer and agent of the Bureau will be tracking its scent, I assure you..."

Huh. How true that was.

"So," Geltak continued, "while I do love making a sale, and oh, do I love that...I cannot, out of respect for my customers, out of *honour*, put them in harm's way, unwarned! It is my duty not just to sell, but to protect their well-being. You understand..."

Akteron raised an eyebrow. "Considerate of you. What kind of protection?"

"In this case"— Geltak leant even closer, and dropped his voice even lower —"*advice*. About how much *caution* this item merits, even after the conclusion of our business."

Yes, yes, that point is clear, Akteron thought. Yet despite the babble, he also felt this was all promising.

"So, if you remain adamant in procuring said valuable," Geltak continued, searching Akteron's face for confirmation, "then perhaps we can begin with...a *viewing*?"

"I was about to ask." Akteron grunted. "Let's see it."

That wide grin stretched across Geltak's face again, and as he bent behind his counter Akteron felt a prickle of excitement. Perhaps it would be that easy? Perhaps Geltak did have the blade, or the collar, or both?

"Long have I waited for such a piece to come into my possession," the salesman uttered and the sound of keys jangling were heard, followed by the – *KITICK!* – of a small lock being opened. "You see, it just so happens that, during the course of my many expeditions to procure valuables, I have chanced the acquaintance of one or two very interesting contacts…"

As Geltak talked, Akteron caught Piria in his peripheral vision scanning Geltak's collection of curious. Possibly trying to determine if anything else of interest lay amongst the vast sea of trinkets and gadgets.

"…and moreover, he travels across the vast tracts of Aliru in search of true beauty, *true* rarity!" Geltak continued. "What luck, then, when occasionally such rarity comes into my possession, here at home! Such a boon for my clients!"

Finally, he stood again — clearly having drawn all this out to augment the drama — and proceeded to set down a small, cloth covered bundle. Gripping the corners of the cloth and waiting for the right moment to whip it away, Akteron tried to place the shape underneath.

"Now, *this* particular piece has belonged to many a grand personality," Geltak announced, "and I dare say, the tradition of its noble ownership will continue with you. Still, I must repeat, you are not the only interested party, tonight, and I cannot guarantee the item will remain here for long with all the attention swirling around it. So, should you find it to your taste, I urge you to be swift with your purchase!"

He whipped back the cloth.

Now, a small, golden casket with a tented lid was revealed, which Geltak carefully opened.

"No, don't say it!" Geltak held up a finger "I know! *Exquisite,* isn't she! Who could fathom such workmanship? Clearly, an extraordinary music box! This remarkable object hails from across the Glassy Sea, once the proud centrepiece of the noble family of Gurr'teth's receiving-parlour."

Akteron inhaled through his nose.

Blasted Sands. This was a bust. Geltak didn't have any of the relics, after all...

Swiftly as possible and without showing anything on his face, Akteron ticked over possibilities in his mind while the wily, old con explained the history of this 'royal' bosh — likely snatched from some wealthy traveller's pack-wagon on the road to Kriolar.

Tagill *had* mentioned that if one of these three made a find, all of them claimed to have whatever that object was — an 'agreement', of sorts, for mutual benefit. It didn't mean they were partners, nor that they were working together, and Geltak's exploits here only proved that fact. He was acting in accordance with Tagill's script precisely, trying to make a sale from another's boon.

Well, now Akteron needed an out. Something quick and simple.

"...and it plays that melody on *three, separate* combs! Really, an exquisite piece and for obvious reasons, only a true fit for those fanciful, foreign nobles or indeed, a most savvy collector..."

Geltak was now positively humming over the relic, pointing out every minute detail and benefit of his merchandise.

Akteron glanced to Piria. She glanced back. He bucked his head. She nodded.

"Hey! *Hey!* I wanna set *fire* to something...!" she then hissed, sweeping towards the counter just as Geltak finished winding the music box for a demonstration. The older man lifted his eyes.

Huh. A simple, 'not interested,' would have sufficed. But, why not? Akteron could work with this.

"Fire. Fire. *Fire*," she repeated under her breath.

"Again?" Akteron growled, rolling his eyes. "No. No fire. Not here."

"*Fiiire.*" She stomped in place like a petulant child and Geltak, his much-trumpeted music box still in hand, now drew it back protectively.

"Been less than a span," Akteron muttered. "Wasn't it enough, incinerating that ship?"

"No. It wasn't," she said while eyeing shelves and items in Geltak's stall. The merchant glancing from Akteron to Piria and back, again.

"And what happens if this place goes up? Huh? Look at it"— Akteron tapped the platform under them with one foot —"all wood, won't be pretty."

"*Pretty–*"

"*No.*" Akteron said again, then turned to the stall-keep and gestured back the way they'd come. "That first bridge the only way out of here, then? What happens if it's...out of order? Everyone get stuck here?"

The wide-faced seller's attention was now firmly fixed on the pair before him, and–

Ah! Finally, a disconcerted look! They'd cracked that seller's mask, just a little.

"There is...another way out," the man said slowly, bucking his head over one shoulder. "The supplies bridge. Impractical, but possible..."

Then, as that grin vanished, a realisation seemed to dawn.

"*Blasted Sands,* you're not interested in my wares, are you? You're-...*Bozik* sent you? Didn't he? *Didn't he?* I told him, I'm staying off that pillar! I never wanted to set-up there!" Geltak backed up from the counter a little. "I want nothing to do with it!"

Taken off-guard, Akteron blinked.

This was unexpected...

Then, he shook his head. "Bozik didn't send us," he muttered. Geltak, however, eyed him warily before snapping the lid of the music box shut.

"Nonsense! If he didn't, then-...*oh!* That *darned, connundling, meddling–!*" Taking a breath to regain his composure, the merchant stepped back towards Akteron and raised a finger. "You listen *closely*, I don't know what you're all planning, but you tell Komod to leave me out of it all. I will not dance to her tune! I will not!"

A tense heartbeat passed as Piria and Akteron both processed that statement. Realising he'd wasted a chance to learn more about Bozik, Akteron then latched onto this new lead.

"Well. That's disappointing," he said. "You know that's not what she wants to hear..."

"I know damned well it's not what she wants to hear! But it's useless to prod me any further. My part is done, you hear? I sold what I sold, and it's out of my hands. What she or any other customer does after a transaction is completed is totally up to them."

"Then what are you disagreeing with, again?"

"You know damned-...alright. It's very simple," Geltak hissed back. "When I hear a bad proposal, I reject it, just like any other level-minded idiot. So, if Komod wants to level the playing field, then that's up to her–"

He paused mid-word as a new customer — a pale, sallow-looking Teno man — approached the table.

"Go, now," Geltak then whispered. "Both of you, and forget all of this. We never had this discussion..." Pasting a smile over his discontent, he stepped back from the counter to greet his new customer.

"Sure you don't want to cooperate? Specify exactly what you don't agree with? There's still room to negotiate," Akteron whispered back, hoping to prod some final admission from the merchant. He wanted to find out exactly what Komod had proposed...what she'd bought from this blue-haired tinkerer... had it been one of the relics?

But Geltak simply pressed his lips together.

Darnit. He'd clammed up.

"Geltak, right?" the Teno man now asked.

"That's the name!" Geltak chirped as if nothing had happened. The new grin which slicked his face seemed decidedly forced, though. "Ah! At last, you arrive! I was told you'd be here earlier!"

Akteron gritted his teeth. "I guess we're done, here," he growled. "Might want to keep that supplies bridge in mind. Just in case this one does her thing again, tonight."

"*Fiire,*" Piria added, staring a nearby torch down hungrily.

Geltak didn't turn away from his new customer, but blotted his forehead with the back of his sleeve, despite the evening's cool breeze.

"Come on, Gumpina."

Taking Piria by the shoulders, Akteron guided her from the stall, the pair continuing around the sweep of the platform until they were out of earshot.

"I think we can cross Geltak off the list," he then said.

"Right. He's out," Piria agreed, switching from a manic ramble back into Gumpina's swaggering stride. She was really getting the hang of all this. "If he had a relic, I see no reason why he'd hide it from potential buyers."

"Nor why he'd make things up about the other two sellers."

"Unless he wanted to dissuade us from going to them."

Akteron creased his brow. "Sure. But I'm not sure he's that phenomenal an actor...that nervous sweat looked real. I just wish we'd been able to figure out what had spooked him."

"Let's get Komod to fill in the blanks," Piria suggested. "She's the next closest."

Akteron looked at his feet as they moved. "He didn't seem like such a bad guy, did he? A formidable salesman's tongue, but otherwise...I mean, I didn't see any garrotte-wires, this time."

Piria dodged an elderly man with a mouth full of gold-teeth struggling with a wheeled-cart. "Neither. And I was looking. Just a bunch of polished doo-dads."

True enough. Geltak's wares had seemed just what he'd said they were — mechanical gadgets and gizmos. That music box was a fine example but there had also been clocks, scales, typing machines, even an astrolabe adorning his shelves. Nothing had looked too dangerous.

The pair skirted a stall selling what appeared to be poisons and came another with stacks of books. Next, they approached one laden with beakers, phials and tools for chemistry and pulvichemy, and Akteron wondered if they would have to make a stop.

But Piria didn't even blink at it. She didn't break stride.

"I wonder what his story is?" she then uttered. "How Geltak ended up here?"

Akteron shook his head, keeping his voice as low as hers. "No idea. I mean, just because this place is known for shady dealings, that doesn't mean everyone here is shady. Some might just be trying to earn a living. Trying to sell what they can outside the Seat's restrictions. That'd be my guess for Geltak. And don't tell me some of those restrictions aren't ridiculous."

Piria refrained from answering as they passed another stall which demonstrated his point.

"Look," Akteron pointed. "Glowing asrelia flowers...only outlawed because the Seat finds them 'odd'. It's just a simple luminescence petition."

"Not even," Piria added. "You can get that effect with a certain pulvichemical mixture...though it hasn't been proven safe, yet, either." She frowned through her character's scowl. "Ro, I know what I said, earlier. But don't you figure the Seat makes these decisions to make Torril safer? To protect people?"

"I think the Seat routinely makes decisions to reach their own ends. To enhance their own standing and cement their hold, regardless of the impact on the people."

"...so, without them people would be better off, is that it?"

"Likely."

Piria grunted. "This isn't about Torril and Kriolar. You know that, right? Not everything is. There are good people working in the Seat, and painting them all with the same brush is-...it's not fair."

"Sure it is. The Seat treats everyone else the same way, after all."

Perhaps noting his stubborn tone, Piria let that sit as they passed under some more crackling torches.

"I don't know the whole story," she then added, "but it must feel awful to have the weight of distrust dragging you down, all the time...wouldn't it be easier to allow yourself to believe in them, now? Just a little? Doesn't the Seat seem to be trying to make things right, again?"

Akteron shrugged. "Distrusting something makes it harder to get hurt or betrayed by, I suppose. The Seat may have opened the borders again, stopped the propaganda. They may be trying to convince everyone that Torril and Kriolar are united and peaceful, but let's not pretend they aren't still in control. Any peace is only valid so long as the weaker party agrees to forget what happened. To smile and obey. Isn't it?"

Piria's silence said it was likely she hadn't heard the situation spoken of like that, before.

Akteron really couldn't blame her. She'd grown up here, in Torril, in the safety and order of the largest and most sophisticated city in Tarma, most of whose inhabitants had never visited Kriolar or Tenolar or Nen Kimiin, and never would. In Torril, distraction was ample, enough to keep one's eyes and mind far from the distant problems of other cities which carried on in the background, largely unseen and unheard from. With only scant lines of communication open and some curation, no matter how intelligent one was — and Piria was surely one of the brightest people Akteron knew — Torrilians only ever heard what the Seat wanted them to hear.

So how *could* the average citizen know what it was like in Kriolar? How could they know what had happened, there? What was still happening?

"Well, let's agree on one thing, at least," Piria muttered after a moment, "regardless of how nice Geltak *seemed*, who knows who he actually is. It's logical that his line of work would make acting the meek and kindly shopkeep attractive. A person like that would be far more effective at selling than a scheming plotster whom people distrust, after all. Less threat equals more sales..."

Sure. Akteron could agree with that.

The pair stepped aside as a bickering pair of bearded, tattooed men rumbled past, both holding a wooden trunk between them. Then, at last, they bent to pass under a rough-barked, u-shaped bough sprouting from the rock. When they straightened again, a scene both satisfying and worrying confronted them. For there, gaping like a scute-giant's open mouth was a whitewashed cave, the same hollow they'd seen from the first of the stone uprights.

It was definitely their target stall, that much was evident from a sign written in bold characters which stated, "KOMOD'S ANTIQUE METALWARE, TOOLS, BOOKS, & SCROLLS". But a big problem then became evident.

"Nobody home," Akteron muttered, conjuring Dimskull's growling baritone again as they neared.

Indeed, the pair were confronted only by an empty shell of a shop. Devoid of wares or owner and with just three, lonely tables ringing the space, it looked to have been closed recently. A pair of oil-lanterns still flickered on the rock walls.

"But how could Komod be gone?" he asked, peeping into the space to be sure. "I thought all three were here, tonight."

"They are," a husky voice replied, causing him and Piria to jump.

Turning, the two now found an older woman, bent over a pair of carrying sacks nearby and stuffing what appeared a donvul inside. She'd been so far back into the shadowed corner they'd missed her entirely.

"One of them has given up, though, and is heading to Bozik's," she said, drawing its string tight, straightening and — after some effort — hefting the sack over one shoulder.

"Given up?" Akteron asked.

"Sure. It's what you do when you know you're beaten and don't want things to get embarrassing."

Beside him, Piria was eying the woman suspiciously, perhaps worried that she'd been caught out while speaking as Piria, rather than *Gumpina*, and wondering if she should keep up the act.

The momentary uncertainty vanished quickly, however, Akteron watching as Piria's straight-shouldered posture melted into a skulking hunch and her expression soured. A subtle change, to be sure, like water evaporating from a damp stone, and if he hadn't been watching for it, there was scant chance he would have noticed.

"How?" Piria then asked. "How are you 'beaten'?"

He had to admit, this was impressive, especially for someone who was averse to this whole charade, tonight. Suddenly, he was accompanied by that incendiary rogue, again, rather than his closest friend.

The stall-keep, meanwhile — whom Akteron could only assume was Komod — took a deep breath, sack over her shoulder, and regarded these newcomers just as carefully.

Her slender arms were encircled with large, coloured bracelets and she had a thick puff of hair, a billow of silver like a cloud which framed her face. She was certainly older and yet, like geltak, the way she spoke, the way she held herself, and the twinkle in her eyes gave her the spritely aura of someone half her age.

"Ah..." she said. "Well, that's how it usually works, isn't it? On nights like this, it's usually only a matter of time 'til the buyers get wise and the game is ruined for the others." Now came a sigh. "I can't really complain. I've had my time being the seller with the luck. And I *did* get a couple good sales in, tonight. But I'm done...time to go have some fun."

"Fun? Watching Bozik make a sale?" Akteron asked.

"Of course. Why not? It'll be a blast," Komod replied, and those words allowed the pair a brief glimpse behind those twinkling eyes to something else. Something not so wholesome. "You wanna be part of the proceedings, then one of you can bring that other sack. That'll speed things up. The other one, put those lanterns out. Quickly, now. We don't want to miss anything."

That was all the incentive the pair needed to leap into action, Piria grabbing the surprisingly heavy sack while Akteron used a steel cap-staff to stifle the few lantern flames flickering in the cave. All the while, Komod observed them from the platform.

"I suppose you two are here for the 'big item' as well, then?"

"Might be," Akteron grumbled as Komod began plodding towards a nearby bridge, and a slight narrowing of Piria's eyes confirmed what Akteron had heard.

'The big item.' Meaning, just one.

"Well, good luck," the seller told them over her shoulder. "You've got yourselves a contest, tonight. It seems — at least from what I hear — like some of Torril's shiniest and finest have turned up." She then snorted. "*Why?* I don't know. The thing seems useless enough, but I suppose it has a story and that's all that seems to matter to some of these wealthy idiots. Practicality only seems to be of value to those with less."

"*Ignorant fools!*" Piria hissed in agreement.

"Wait." Akteron stepped onto the span behind their new

acquaintance. "You know what it is?"

Yikes...he'd almost forgotten how unstable and neck-pricklingly precarious these bridges felt.

Komod chortled. "Of course I do!"

"But I thought that was part of the arrangement? That none of you knew what the others had?"

"*Arrangement?*" Now, Komod shook her head with a, "*PFF!*", their combined steps causing the bridge to bounce. "Oh, you think you know how things work around here, huh?"

Behind the two, Piria could be heard, panting with some effort to shift the sack on her shoulder. Doing so, a metallic jangling came from inside.

"Don't drop that!" the woman snapped. "If the pieces in there break, it'll be your life...and mine."

Piria winced, adjusting her grip, and as Komod continued across the bridge before them another large wave crashed into the pillar. This time, the span really vibrated at the impact.

With a brief mutter to herself, the merchant then spoke aloud again, almost wistfully. "Let me tell you something. I've been here long as these bridges have," She glanced up to regard the stars. "Hard to believe, I suppose. But amusing, that some of the antiques I sell nowadays were new when I started!"

Akteron believed her, though he wasn't sure how that was possible. Either these bridges weren't that old, or she was ancient.

"And in all that time," she went on, "the rules have been clear. We own this place. We three. Geltak controls the first two pillars. The next two are mine. Bozik controls the last three. We keep things in order, make sure dues are paid, keep the bridges up and strong, and any seller here who doesn't respect that doesn't have a future at the Holes..." she gave a light snort. "Far worse, though, is when one of us three *doesn't* respect the rules. That's when there's blood..."

Akteron considered that as he watched her out of the corner

of his eyes, those colourful bracelets clacking together while she hauled her sack.

"I guess that doesn't happen, often," he prompted.

"Hasn't for a good while."

"So, about this evening's item..."

Now, Komod gave him a sideways grin.

"Nice try, darlin'," she said. "But you'll have to wait along with all the other schmucks to find that out."

"Wouldn't you say," Akteron said, motioning to the sacks, "we're helping you out with this? Not asking for much in return, except a little tidbit. Least you could do to thank us, really."

"You helped of your own choice, I only promised to get you to him," Komod said, dodging a broken plank, "*...idiots should have fixed that.*" Then, she looked up again. "I don't remember offering anything else. I might have given you some charge at the end out of the goodness of my heart, but now I'm changing my mind."

"We're full, anyway," Akteron said, patting his belt. "I'd much rather know what Bozik got his hands on."

"Too big a price." Komod replied, waving the request off again. "And it's mighty bold to ask for something that important from someone who bargains for a living...even if you had something better to offer than carrying a sack."

"Right. I see," Akteron then said airily, giving a sigh and stopping in place. "Then, Gumpina, would you be so kind as to drop that sack over the edge?"

Piria stopped trudging along and without questioning it, started to swing the sack over her shoulder.

"Hey, *whoa!* Let's not be stupid, now," Komod snapped, pivoting to face them. "Keep moving, we're almost there."

Akteron crossed his arms. "I don't see why we should. We don't even know what's in there. It's not important to us."

The look in Komod's eyes said it was very important to her, though.

Piria was still frozen mid-gesture but hadn't yet shifted the sack from her back. She seemed to be waiting for someone to tell her what to do and Akteron appreciated the way she was making her eyes and nose twitch. It really sold that whole 'unhinged' thing.

Komod, in turn, was scrutinising Akteron with what appeared barely disguised frustration, probably calculating some odds. Firstly, of them actually doing what he said and dropping the sack. Next, of how she'd haul both sacks the rest of the span by herself...

The outcome seemed clear enough.

"*Ugh.* Alright. Fine." she relented. "Bargaining *is* what the Holes is all about, after all. Though, you've been warned, I can only tell you what I know." She took a deep breath as if the next sentence had caused her physical effort. "It's a piece from a theft. From a museum–"

"No good. We know that, already."

"Well then I can't help you!" Komod snapped, and a moment later, having cleared her throat. "Because...truth be told, I lied. I have no idea what it is."

"Another lie."

"It's not!" Komod's eyes flashed to Piria in case her hands began releasing the burden she carried. "Look, rumour had it that three relics from one of the bigger exhibits were nabbed, and damned if I know which exhibit that was. All I know is they're all one-of-a-kind items. A stone knife, some fancy collar, and a mask..."

Akteron almost opened his mouth to correct her before reminding himself to watch his tongue. Komod's eyes had returned to his and were locked on rather intensely, and he realised this could still be a trick, that Komod might be testing him to see what he knew.

"Happened yesterday morning, from what I heard. Then, last night, Bozik gets a visit at his stall," Komod went on. "Of course,

Geltak was desperate to find out what the stupid thing was, because somehow he got wind that it was mechanical and that's his thing. No doubt you know that already, though."

Akteron nodded.

"Hmm. Well, sometimes we bargain with each other when there's an item another knows more about, for obvious reasons. No good hawking something we're not ready to story, after all."

Interesting. By that description, it was very likely the item they would find here tonight was the collar. That was the only relic close to having 'mechanical' qualities.

"But none of that matters, now," Komod then said, re-hefting her sack. "I told him to forget it and I did, too. I had no interest in doubling-up with Geltak, this time and Bozik wasn't playing by the rules...no surprise there, really. But if making threats and throwing his weight around is how he wants to handle things, then he can deal with the consequences..."

"Anything else?" Akteron asked.

"Oh, by *Fulbiscan's flaming*–" Komod began to protest when, to her horror, Piria hefted the sack off her back and held it out over the drop.

"Nothing! No more! That's it!" she gasped. "Honest to the *Blue Robes*, I haven't got any more for you!"

Another gust of salty air drifted over the three and Komod's billow of hair seemed more bedraggled than before while, in the dim light, Akteron tried to read her eyes.

Really, she didn't really have any reason to lie. The risk of losing this sack was too great, apparently. And she did seem legitimately nettled at Bozik, so there was no reason to help him out with secrecy. Especially when it sounded like their arrangement had been dishonoured.

"So, how did the relic find its way to Bozik?" Akteron asked.

"The same way every damned thing does," Komod said hotly. "Dropped right into his greasy hands. Almost handed over, without even a decent haggling!"

"You're saying someone just *gave* it to him?" Akteron growled.

This drew a half exasperated, half disbelieving snort.

"Of course not. Nothing is *given* in this life, hun...but like I said, stranger comes into the market last night and suddenly, from what one of his grunts tells me, Bozik had the thing for a pittance. That's how it went."

Akteron filed that away for later consideration.

"And who sold the relic to him? What'd he look like?"

Komod seemed to mull this over for a moment before, in her eyes and deep below that twinkle, something happened. It passed like the shadow beneath water, but that was all it took for Akteron to suspect he'd asked too much.

"No idea." Komod said, eyeing him carefully. "But let's be frank, something about it all just wasn't right." She straightened, hefting her sack again. "Now, if you're done interrogatin' me, let's all just...play nice, here." She gestured to the other sack and a moment passed without words.

Then, Akteron nodded to Piria.

With an acidic grumble, Piria slung it over her shoulders again. Komod immediately seemed to relax.

They covered the last half of the bridge at Komod's plodding pace while a pair of night silks overhead broke the silence with their lonely, whistled calls, and as the next and final pillar in the formation neared, they found its suspended platform bustling with stall-goers. Almost as if people *smelled* a rare sale in the air, over here.

This last, stone pinnacle was thicker than its sisters and peppered with fewer hollows. Still, as Akteron glanced up to survey it, his eyes couldn't help falling onto a small, oddly-shaped...*thing*, suspended over the wandering buyers. He'd seen another similar to this on a previous pillar but had mistakenly thought it a torch-holder.

"Is that—"

"A petition tocsin." Komod finished for him. "Things are

hanging everywhere, now. A really big, damned nuisance. Next thing you know, he'll be putting up street lanterns throughout the Holes." Two visitors approached along the bridge but Komod simply kept walking, parting them with just a stare. "After that trouble we had a couple of cycles back, though, I guess he figured tocsins were the only solution."

"What do the tocsins do?"

"You'll find out pretty quickly if you try to petition anything, here," Komod answered. "Tip from me. Don't do that."

"Tocsins are usually designed to mark out the petitioner in some way..." Piria thought aloud.

Komod shook her head as she ambled along. "These do far worse."

Akteron waited for her to elaborate but the elderly woman did not oblige. She seemed to be growing tired and as the whistles of the night silks faded, her laboured breathing was all that accompanied them in those final paces to the end of the bridge.

At last, with the more stable feeling platform beneath their feet, Komod proceeded to whistle into a crowd of people from which, a moment later, a boy no older than his twelfth cycle wiggled out.

"Well, look who decided to report for duty..." Komod said to him. "Didn't feel like meeting me at my stall, or what?"

The lad was well-dressed but grubby all over, his cheeks blackened with grease or soot, and he looked to Komod with expectant eyes, but said nothing.

"Never mind, we'll talk about keeping our word, later..." Komod then turned to Piria. "He'll take that, hun."

Piria removed the sack again and carefully, the older woman slung it over the boy's back. How he carried it was anyone's guess, but Piria's eyes widened as the youth hefted it with ease and managed to stay firm under its weight.

"Well, despite your scaring my brains out with your little prank, it was good of you to help," Komod now told the pair, adding with some obvious reluctance, "I'm heading left, here. You two will want to head right"— she pointed along the platform —"and keep going until you reach the bend. Follow the scaffold around, past the two big idiots, and you'll find the last idiot. Can't miss him. Just sniff the air for self-importance."

"Kind of you," Akteron said, with less growl than he'd intended. "And...sorry about your bad luck with the relic."

Komod eyed him, again.

"Don't thank me, yet, hun," she said. "He's a monumental prick." Then, she gave a kind of sigh, almost as if she didn't want to. "Look, you both. Not that I'm judging and not that it's *aaany* of my business...but I can't help but sense you're not really, erm, whatever all this is," She waved at the pair.

Akteron stiffened.

"Mmhmm," Komod confirmed. "I can smell the effort oozing out of you like kekkrion sap, and I see through that phoney scowl like it were newglass, missy." The look she cast at Piria was almost sympathetic and caused Piria's cheeks to redden slightly under her makeup. "It's all in the eyes." Komod then whispered, hand circling in the air to illustrate the point.

To her credit and despite the critique, though, Piria's cold expression didn't crack. She didn't morph back into herself and once again, Akteron wondered if it were actual, true annoyance or just her characterisation.

"Now," Komod went on, "maybe you *are* traders from afar. We certainly get our share of them." With a conspiratorial air, she then leant towards them and lowered her voice. "But, more likely, and let's not waste time debating it, you're from a more... *official* source."

Akteron was ready to bolt back across that bridge at the utterance, carrying Piria with him if he had to. He shifted on his feet, but it didn't seem to be Komod's intention to ensnare them. She didn't call for anyone or set off any alarms.

"Why would it matter to a pair of shadester quickfingers like yourselves who sold Bozik the relic, after all?" she asked.

Darnit. Akteron knew he'd said too much.

"So, I won't guess what you're up to, tonight, but here's a little word from that bad person who, for once, is trying to do a little good. Don't bother. Turn around and get out of here, because there'll be other, badder people than you in these caves, tonight, and regardless of whatever Bozik's dangling, I'd hate for that pretty face to get all messed up over it."

Akteron realised she was looking at him.

Piria gave an amused snort.

But...*Blasted Sands.* Caught out for the second time, tonight? That wasn't encouraging.

Not to be put off, though, Akteron took a deep breath. They were here for a reason, and damn anyone who tried to stop them, after all this.

"We still have to go in there."

Komod grunted. "Your choice. Just don't say I didn't warn you."

Without another word, she and her young ward then turned and plodded off around the platform, leaving the pair amongst the excited bustle of buyers and the calls of stall-owners.

Piria let a strange breath out through her teeth.

"Something about all this tastes...off."

Akteron nodded. "I know. I'm feeling that, too."

"We missed our chance with Geltak, but we really should have pressed her more and tried to find out how Bozik works, at least, before rushing in blind. *Ugh.* This is all too *unstructured.* Too uncertain! I can almost feel our chances getting slimmer by the moment."

"No, our chances are still fine," Akteron insisted. "We've found our target. We just have to stick to the plan. We're here and we're close. I can feel it. We just have to keep playing our parts and see if we can snag this thing, then we get out of here."

Piria nodded. "And about that plan...you're sure that when we find the relic, you can secure it?"

It took Akteron just a moment to reply. Just a heartbeat. Yet even then he knew that his hesitation had been too long.

Sometimes, a flickering gaze or a stalled breath is all it takes for the truth to be loosed into the air, and there it hangs, glimmering for all to see.

Worry flashed across Piria's face.

"I am," Akteron said, all the same. More to convince himself, perhaps. And Piria gave him a slow nod in return.

She trusted him.

"So, shall we?" she asked.

Re-setting their faces into their tailor-made scowls, the pair then took off along the platform, to their last stall of the evening.

CHAPTER THIRTEEN
LAKALAK

"Your ingot belts," a grey-eyed, hook-nosed man instructed Piria, his face indifferent from routine.

She obliged, removing her belt and handing it over without fuss, but Akteron felt decidedly uncomfortable as he did the same. One's ingot-belt was like-…like underwear, after all. You didn't just take it off and hand it around. That was improper. It was *wrong*…

Still, there was nothing for it. Disarming — both magickally and otherwise — was the only condition of entry to the auction, so obey this rule, they would.

Yes. An auction. This was to be no trestle-tabled, quick-tongued haggling. Bozik had certain decorum in place for this evening and he wasn't playing around. Clearly defined steps had been set in place and designed, Akteron imagined, to ensure that only serious buyers were taking part.

Removing their ingot-belts, the next step in the process was a little more hands-on and Piria's appreciation there was clear to see.

"Oi, watch it!" she snapped, mouth drawing into a snarl as the doorman roughly spun and patted her down.

At last, the gent eyed her severe coat top to bottom, then straightened and waved her through a doorway.

Grumbling, Piria — as *Gumpina* — took only a few paces

before turning to wait for Akteron.

The procedure began anew, and as those gloved hands began patting his shoulders, Akteron felt his nerves rising.

He tried to push them down but for the first time, tonight, the reality of how truly and completely helpless they would be if discovered made itself apparent. There was nowhere to run, here, and nowhere to hide, and he wasn't merely thinking of the insides of this pillar. Out on the platforms things weren't much better, unless he was ready to take the highest dive of his life into a chaos of roiling water...

Well, anxiety won't help anything, he thought.

He needed to remain cool-headed, now more than ever.

This is just another, ordinary sting. Just another, ordinary job. Just you and Piria trying to put things right. It'll be fine.

Unlike all the other stalls, the pair had arrived to find Bozik's cave unpainted. Within its raw, calcareous walls stood shelves and tables, each crammed with old jars, bowls, and decorative weapons. But the main oddity had been a small, curtained door in the back wall into which, now and then, an occasional visitor had slipped.

With the well-founded inkling that the wiry, sour-faced salesman was far too apathetic to be their fabled, final seller, Bozik, Akteron had enquired where 'the *real* goods' were and much to his satisfaction, had been silently waved through it.

A small, twisting passage had then funnelled them into this antechamber, musty-smelling and barely lit, where the pat-down was taking place.

"Weapons?" the man grouched, his body odour anything but subtle as he slapped along Akteron's arms.

Akteron shook his head.

The man then bent to check his ankles, anyway, and Akteron endured it patiently.

"Your discs," the man told the pair, at last, handing Akteron and then Piria a small sack. Jiggling it, a lacquer-like clacking could be heard from inside.

The pair didn't ask why they would need a sack of discs and the grunt didn't care to explain. Satisfied that the pair's ingot-belts were safely stored in a locked trunk and no weapons were to be seen, he quickly waved them onwards.

From the antechamber, the murmur of conversation had already been evident — a dampened, constant hum bouncing off the stonework. It now grew in volume as the pair entered the heart of this place to find a dimly lit, formally furnished chamber.

A smattering of eccentrically clad people flowed slowly around a raised, presentational case, here, adorned with a cloth to obscure whatever lay inside. Others stood in tight clusters, holding delicate glasses and chatting in low voices, and before they became entangled, Akteron took an opportunity to scope things out.

The place was circular. Low ceiling. Two exits, including the passage they'd come in by, and another which led out the back of the chamber. No windows, of course. And seeing as he was more than familiar with reading ancient structures — having grown up playing in the bones of Kriolar's old quarter long before his studies at Kriolar's educaria — he read this place two ways. *Old,* if the walls, smoothed, discoloured, glossy from countless, oily hands said anything. But also *modified,* according to the crisp doorframes, squared ceiling, and stone torch-mounts.

The renovator hadn't been shy about adding an element of drama, either. Ridges of shining, cerulean tile-work ran like conduits across the walls and framed the occasional carving, hung with torches to cast theatrical shadows.

Tasteful, but showy.

There was definitely a kind of inflated self-importance behind all this, dying to be acknowledged. Just as Komod had implied...

Akteron's eyes came to rest on three tall cabinets along the back wall.

Each showcased a lone treasure, each was lit with its own, meticulously placed gem-light, and the items glittered and shone in just the right ways.

First was a series of golden, tribal armbands. Most likely from Nen Kimiin, Akteron reckoned. The adjacent case housed a set of jewels on a fabric pillow, tilted to show off the delicate chain, arranged into the shape of a serpent. The last contained a series of what appeared emerald cylinder seals.

Akteron dreaded to imagine the price of any one of these rarities. Each would have been more than comfortable in one of Kabonn's exhibits. Or the palace treasury in Kal Brior.

Of course, that final, lone display case he'd seen upon entering stood in the centre of the room, too. But due to the guests milling about, it was difficult to approach.

Ah, but then there were the guests, themselves.

That initial inspection had made Akteron feel extremely out of place, for what he'd *expected* tonight were crummy thugs, each bickering and snapping over whichever glinting treasure was on offer. A wild miscalculation. The scene before them was closer to savouries at a Seat soirée. All that was missing was–

"Excuse me, sir."

Akteron glanced up to see he was being offered a drink by a waiter. Clad in stiff, pressed whites, the man stifled a twitching eyebrow while surveying Akteron's collar but Akteron ignored him, lifting a glass filled with something sparkling and yellow.

The waiter then turned, keeping his expression tamped down even once he sighted Gumpina.

Her reaction was less subtle, nose crinkling at the sight of his combed and greased-up hair. Still, her character wasn't one to turn down a free nip, apparently.

Gripping the delicate flute in her fist, Piria watched the waiter waft off through the crowd before she spoke out the side of her mouth.

"Right. Who are our candidates? Which one is Bozik?"

"No idea…" Akteron replied, still establishing the options.

A mere pace away was a tall man in a form-fitting, silver coat, sauntering like a tar-flow around that central case. Beard tied into a thick cord and held together with a fine, wooden clasp, his hands were fixed behind his back as he spoke quietly to a tall, sleek woman.

This woman's eyes were obscured behind a mask, her mouth drawn into a thin line, and the black dress she had donned was ornamented with extremely rare, green cachak feathers. A pretty thing which would have cost more than a few ingot-belts.

Moreover…something about her was familiar, too, Akteron felt. Something about those lips, which curled into a vague grin as the bearded man spoke in her ear. Something about the eyes he could make out, glittering under that mask…

"*There*," Piria muttered with a nod, pulling his attention towards a smaller, squatter gent engaging two ladies. Both were Torrilian, if their feather-adorned wrists and hair were any indication. "I'll bet my gloves that's him."

Hmm.

Well, the squat fellow *did* look sophisticated enough, grey hair tidily swept to one side. A salesperson's grin was evident on his face as he regaled some story and drew a chuckle from his audience, and the fine cloak he wore was some newfangled weave which shimmered in the low lighting.

And yet…

"No. Not showy enough," Akteron whispered. "He doesn't match the fixtures. All that snooffery in the entrance and in here…my mark is on Bozik being someone who stands out like those pillowed jewels, over there."

Piria now seemed to notice their surroundings for the first time, and gave a thoughtful hum.

"But Komod was spot-on," Akteron then noted. "This lot look like they only dine off platinum plates." He squinted a little.

"Even if most of them are artisans or traders, they're clearly a cut above. Look, there." He gave a subtle nod towards a broad-shouldered, scar-faced man standing alone at the back of the chamber. "That one is a master-metalsmith. See the emblem clips on his jacket? Must be one of the most sought-after in Torril to have earned that many..."

Piria nodded to a woman in the middle of the room, also masked like Feather-Dress was. "I recognise that one, beside the central case. It's Tizuun Nooma Kasbri," she whispered. "I'm sure of it. One of Torril's finest mechaneers. She invented the lock-cases and seal tubes the Seat uses. I'd *die* to see inside her workshop. Though...I'd never have expected to see her, here."

"All stiff competition, that much is certain," Akteron answered, taking a sip of his drink at last and–

Beaks in the night! He almost coughed it back up, wondering if he'd just swigged lamp-lighting fluid. The stuff burned like a Tenolar pepper! Even if it did leave a pleasant, citrous aftertaste...

"Hmm," Piria said, eyeing him, then her own, red drink. "Mine tastes like gorin-fruit. Not much better."

Since the pair had arrived, they'd been drifting slowly around the perimeter of the chamber. Now, as one, final individual arrived, a small bell was waggled by the waiter and the doors were quietly closed.

"Dear guests," the waiter said. "Your attention, please, as your host joins us for tonight's auction."

Perhaps it was the way that murmur ebbed and made the room feel smaller all of a sudden, the absence of sound causing the stone to press in on Akteron, but once again, he had to swallow down that biting, nagging sense of dread which had slowly been building since they'd come here.

This was what you expected, he thought, *things will work out. Stick to the plan and remember who you're supposed to be.*

Guests shifted to one side of the room, and now, at the

waiter's direction, the second door at the rear opened and a young man strode in, making for the centre of the room.

"Good evening, good evening, to you all!" he said, each movement tracked by all the eyes present, some of which had widened a little at his appearance, for–

This was Bozik?

Akteron gazed through a gap in the guests while the young man took position before those glass cabinets, and finding a good-enough slice through which could see, almost snorted.

Their host was a *kid!* And one who surely hadn't seen more than eighteen cycles.

Well, at least Akteron's earlier speculation seemed to have been on the mark. He'd known Bozik would be dressed to make an impression, and this young man was dressed immaculately. Sendil himself would have gaped at the smart coat fitted to his shoulders. That perfect silhouette. And the complex weave, more visible around the cuffs and neckband in which what appeared silver thread was sewn.

Also, was it Akteron's imagination, or–...

He shifted to another gap to see the whole garment.

No. There was no mistake about it, the piece was a replica *Kusman,* high-class garb worn by the nobles of ancient Kesh. Up one side ran the distinctive, red buttons. And that squat, flat collar was undeniably lifted from those past designs. Further, while the lad's hair was styled in modern, Torrilian fashion, Akteron noticed the sides and sideburns were shaved with geometric shapes. Just as the ancient Keshians had once done.

He stifled an amused huff. Was it arrogance, or mere eccentricity which led such a young fellow to emulate the ancients, like that?

Either way, things started to make a little more sense, now. The puffery and obsession to detail in this place...it was all in agreement with its owner.

Facing his guests with the air of calm control, Bozik's wrinkleless features were devoid of expression in the dim light. His icy blue eyes studied each visitor over his nose and didn't glint with exuberance or mirth. They seemed to contain more seriousness than a Seat clerk's.

But on purpose, Akteron knew. This was all intentional. This was all about proving something.

Bozik allowed a few seconds of muffled chatter before raising a hand, at which the low whispers faded.

"Let's get the obvious out of the way first, shall we?" he said. "I am Bozik, and not Bozik the elder, of course, whom some of you might have known as 'Snaptooth', but his successor." Placing his hands behind his back, he nodded to the cavern around them. "The operation of this enterprise, and his good name, have been entrusted to me as a promise. To uphold a level of care and diligence which *you*, our loyal and distinguished customers, have come to expect. So that you may continue to benefit from our most *exceptional* services."

Ugh. He even *sounded* like a Seat official...

"And while things may *look* a little different, now, the items we procure and sell to you are far beyond anything we have offered, before." Bozik now motioned to the glass cases around him. "No doubt some of you have already had time this evening to peruse a few, new additions to our catalogue. These exquisite armbands from Nen Kimiin and dated to before the eruption of Mount Kansarogod, for example." He let his palm guide his guests' eyes to the next cabinet. "Or these transfixing jewels, once conjured for the High-Jekan of Saj Minoor..." He allowed himself a slight smirk. "Priceless, really. And yet, I have no doubt that someone here will also conjure a price I'll be unable to resist."

A light chuckle filled the room and Akteron blinked, having joined in. He had to remind himself that this was a place outside the law. A place where Aliru's past — items thieved and wrested from their original homes and doubtless through bloodshed —

were being sold off by a youth barely old enough to have filled his ingot-belt. And to a group of smarmy, over-dressed criminals...

A prickle ran over his skin.

"But of course the *real* reason you are all here tonight is clearer than Kara and Tria," Bozik continued, "and I know you are all anxious to move on to that *most peculiar* find. Indeed, it is the reason I called tonight's auction in the first place."

The young man stepped forwards to that central case, and as he did the crowd seemed to draw backwards from it. Only then did Akteron and Piria have a clear view of its insides.

At once, Akteron knew that they stood a mere two paces from the second relic. Inside atop a small cushion lay an item under a small square of silk, and its outline was unmistakable.

Gildran's Collar.

Reaching out, it seemed as if Bozik were about to open the case and retrieve it, before he stopped. "Oh, but those of you familiar with my auctions will know there is *one* thing I *love* to do before a sale such as this..."

Drama. Always with the drama, Akteron thought.

Admittedly, anticipation was causing him to sweat under his dark coat, and he was not alone. Beside him, Piria was battling her own nerves, if her jaw muscles tensing and relaxing over and over were any sign. He almost wished they could just flash their Bureau-cards and be done with it all. But the suspicion that they wouldn't survive ten-seconds after doing so was not something he was willing to prove.

"You will recall receiving a small pouch upon entry, tonight," Bozik said. "And in my constant quest to make your experiences here as memorable as possible, I call on you all to indulge me by playing a short game."

Akteron gripped his pouch in one hand, inside which he could feel those lacquered chips.

"I love to meet and get to know my buyers, and I guarantee

this diversion will take no more than a few laughs, or possibly, another drink." Bozik stepped back from the podium. "Please be so kind as to open your pouches and inspect the contents."

The waiter swooshed by Akteron again bearing a tray and paused, as if reading his mind. Nodding, the young Krio set his mostly-full glass atop the tray — inebriation just another complication he really didn't need right now — and the beverage was whisked out of sight.

Piria shot him a concerned look as she opened her own pouch to withdraw one of eight discs, holding it between her fingers. A small, black token, with a coloured centre. In her case, green.

"It's a simple enough concept," Bozik continued. "A game of knowledge, or *historical trivia*, if you will...at the end of which, the winner will gain a special advantage for the ensuing auction."

A murmur seeped into the room and Akteron's ears pricked up, a slight glimmer of hope blooming inside him.

Historical trivia...by Felebol's Flask! Perhaps this could actually work to his advantage!

"Yes," Bozik spoke above the hum, "at auction's end, the victor will wield the power to purchase the item at the final price, regardless of who placed the final bid. A kind of game I think makes everything a little more...*exciting*." Bozik paused until satisfied that his guests had familiarised themselves with their chips. "The game is played as follows. Firstly, take one of your discs and place it in your pocket, this ensures we don't get mixed up when the game comes to an end. You cannot use this disc for play."

Akteron and Piria did as instructed, each placing one chip in a trouser pocket.

"Now," Bozik said. "The interesting part."

The youth seemed truly to have come alive, now. His eyes twinkled with a barely contained exuberance and Akteron found that oddly reassuring, for it told him Bozik *could* actually emote.

Now, their host motioned to another waiter standing stiffly against the back wall, the latter nodding and bending to retrieve something.

"In ancient Kesh," Bozik explained, taking the object carefully in his hands, "where games were the most highly valued facet of society, one in particular was loved by rich and poor, alike. And as luck would have it, this game survived the Keshian civilisation's collapse and is still played to this day all across Tarma. In their time, it was called *Sekanna*. We call it: *Lakalak*."

Lakalak! Akteron almost laughed.

How many days had he spent playing that very game as a youth? How many nights had he and his rat-pack of friends watched from the sidelines as their parents bet, and won, and lost...?

Too many to count.

Picking up a fine-looking, earthen pot, its neck adorned with seashells and its lip flashing gold, Bozik displayed it to his audience. Around the vessel's torso, a number of triangular tokens dangled on strings, clacking at every movement. It was a fine piece, and Akteron knew its purpose. While he'd always played with a simple, wooden bowl and coloured rocks in his youth, he imagined that fine vessels and discs like this were common in more sophisticated circles.

"Lakalak follows a simple rhythm of question and answer," Bozik explained. "I will ask a question, and whoever answers it correctly earns points. At the end, these points will be tallied and the player with the most, wins. Clear? Simple?"

Glancing around the room, Akteron watched various guests nod, some weighing their pouches absently while others flipped discs through their fingers.

Not the metalsmith, though. He had drawn his expression into a toxic glower and looked ready to throw his sack of discs through the display case.

"The uniqueness of Lakalak," Bozik continued, "is that

players are told the nature of the question *before* they answer. Thus, the more knowledgeable you feel about the topic at hand, the more discs you should deposit into this pot. When the time comes to answer, the person who wagered the most discs answers first."

"What is the purpose of this?" the metalsmith suddenly barked, his low rumble filling the chamber. "Some of us have no patience for children's games and want to see an auction…"

Ah. There it was. This one clearly favoured business over amusement. But Akteron had already known that from the man's expression, a perpetual glower formed by grizzled creases.

"Oh, of course, you needn't!" Bozik said, turning and giving a respectful nod to the man. "*Any* who wish to forego this little game may do so."

In response and with a flick of his wrist, the metalsmith thus let his sack of discs fly. They struck the waiter holding the drink tray in the neck with a – *KATACK!* – and the man gave a peep of surprise. The smith then leaned back against the chamber wall and crossed his arms.

"For those who *do* wish to participate, however," Bozik added, "a warning."

Akteron knew what was coming next, the final, crucial detail of *Lakalak*.

"Should you answer a question *incorrectly*, or should someone answer correctly *before you*, you will lose any discs wagered. Your true goal is thus to gauge your perceived skills carefully. Be bold, but be *prudent*, for losing a large bet will leave you deprived of discs to wager on future questions."

"And if one does not wager *any* discs?" that tall lady in the black, feather-trimmed dress spoke up, eyeing Bozik with intrigue.

"A fine question, madame," Bozik said, handing the pot back to his attendant. "Anyone who refrains from wagering *any* discs has forfeited the game. Thus, if you would like to play, you *must* wager at least *one* disc each question."

"I see," the lady gazed back to the pouch in her gloved hand.

"And...well, whatsay you, Gusaan?" Bozik then added, glancing to the attendant holding the pot. "This seems a sharper crowd than usual..."

Gusaan remained silent, probably sensing the rhetorical question, and Bozik turned back to his guests.

"Yes. I think our game tonight will be played by Krio rules. This means the *final, third* round will net the winner double points."

Krio rules?

Akteron approved. This slight modification was a fateful catch and a rule which tripped most beginners up. But it would certainly make things interesting.

"Of course, all of this is useless without knowing the *stakes*, dear guests," Bozik said. "So, to help any others decide if they should partake, or not, allow me at last to introduce you to what you are all playing for this evening. Our guest of honour!"

Gusaan was at the ready with a small key, and now turned to open a small lock on the glass case. Carefully, Bozik then tilted the opened panel, reached inside and took hold of the silk cloth. He drew it away to reveal the glittering metal of Gildran's Collar.

And Akteron almost grinned.

"Magnificent, isn't she?" Bozik then commented, setting a loving stare upon the ring of metalwork.

Akteron had to agree. It was exactly what he had imagined from that old sketch Kabonn had shown them, and was every bit as beautiful as the Bell of Tongues.

Masterfully fashioned, each segment was fitted together perfectly and decorated with fine, patterned etchings. All except the frontmost face, which Akteron could now see bore a closed eye, each eyelash painstakingly incised.

Though tarnished and scratched, the item seemed to gleam with some inner lustre and even the metalsmith against the wall perked up at the sight, eyes flashing interest before melting into that grey glare again. Perhaps he'd regretted flinging that sack away — and then remembered he didn't like games.

"That's it!" Bozik announced, closing the case again and opening his hands to his guests, that salesman's smile spreading across his stubble-free face.

"Let's begin."

CHAPTER FOURTEEN
A BOZIK-BRAND BLOWOUT

Honestly, Bozik's smile gave Akteron the creeps.

It wasn't dissimilar to the perpetual grin knifebeaks wore and to take the similarity further, this young man's ice-blue eyes also shone with a cold hunger.

But worrying about that would be a foolish move right now. Instead, Akteron turned to gauge his competition for the evening.

First in the lineup was the dumpy gentleman who they'd seen telling jokes, earlier. He didn't look like much of a threat, all smiles and animated gestures, but beside him was that sleek, masked woman in the green-feathered dress, whose dour face spoke of control. She was accompanied by the man with the corded beard and perhaps they were a couple, for Akteron hadn't seen them separate since the evening began.

Last in the row was an older lady with a puffy, purple shawl, bringing the number of playing guests to six, and gazing down this line, Akteron wished he'd slept more. A foggy mind wasn't ideal when the success of this case rested on a game of mental acuity, after all. And how frustrating it was once again, to be right *there*, a mere hop from the object he and Piria sought but powerless to retrieve it.

The far more troubling thought, however, was another guest winning and spiriting it off into the night.

Well, Akteron supposed he would just have to win, instead. All he had to do was best a bunch of strangers, after all. Strangers whose skills and knowledge were as opaque as the stones he stood upon...

He shifted uneasily as a bubbly, older voice caught his ears.

"S'pose I should inquire if you're any good at history, seeing as we're playing for keeps, here!"

It was that squat, smiley gent beside Piria, and though his attention was fixed on the collar in the case, the way he leant made it clear she was the target of the engagement. "I'm something of a pundit in the art of telling stories, myself, though mine have more to do with *current* affairs..."

His bald head glinted under the gem-lights like the object before them as he finally glanced at Piria, his grin revealing perfect, too-white teeth.

Piria's return-glance was cold enough to turn a rockshell inside-out.

Muttering something inaudible, the man promptly turned away.

"So? What are we doing?" she then whispered to Akteron.

"This is a chance to get our hands on the thing without a fuss..." he whispered back. "I say we play the game..."

"Is that wise?"

"It's the only option I can see that doesn't end in a mess, at this point."

"Hmm. I wish we'd known what we were walking into," she replied, adding, "I feel like we're standing on those bridges, again."

Akteron winced a little at the words, for he knew exactly what she meant.

- TING-TING-TINNNGGG! -

The attendant's bell stifled all chatter and Bozik clapped, surveying the small group before him.

"Six players. Marvellous." He glanced to the other crowd, who had become a temporary audience for this odd diversion. "Are you all well served?"

"Get on with it..." the metalsmith growled back, a fresh drink in hand.

"As you command." Bozik bowed. "The topic for this first question, then. And players, please have your discs at the ready. Remember also that speaking after this point will forfeit participation."

Akteron's discs were between his fingers in one stack, and taking a deep breath, he allowed the slightly dusty, perfume-filled air to calm his nerves.

"Our first question is about Torril City's *birdlife*. Yes, the avifauna of this wonderful, green city of ours. That will be question number *one!*"

That seemed a straightforward enough topic.

Akteron absently counted out four of the thin, lacquer tokens, even running his finger down the stack and separating them before he stopped.

Stupid...

It *had* been over ten cycles, and he had almost forgotten how this game was played. Flashing through his childhood and teenage cycles, he now recalled that it was usually a mistake to bet big on the first question. He'd seen a lot of games lost that way.

Although...sometimes betting big up front had worked out, too, hadn't it?

Ugh. It suddenly dawned on him that he'd never actually been any good at this game. He had nice memories, sure, but actually, hadn't Sabekan always beaten him? That grubby-faced little snot—

Focus, he told himself. *Just hit this carefully...no big bets up front.*

Deep in thought and too distracted with figuring out his first move, Akteron had failed to notice the glint in his partner's eyes.

The way she'd perked up at the words 'birdlife' and 'avifauna'. The speed at which her fingers had sifted out the five tokens, and the determination in her azure eyes.

It wasn't until the attendant came past, jiggling the collection pot and behind those clacking, wooden triangles that he heard her bet being deposited and widened his eyes.

But there was nothing for it. Akteron couldn't have warned her. He just had to trust that nobody was more knowledgeable on this topic than Piria, now.

"Don't reach into the pot."

The attendant was speaking to him.

Akteron realised he'd been staring at the vessel as it hovered before him and obliging, now, let his single disc loose.

The attendant withdrew to tally them and a moment later, Bozik had the floor, again.

"Differing wagers, all around. Though, two of you seem especially keen to answer!"

Gusaan, the attendant, had spread the tokens out on the glass case's top, and gazing thoughtfully between the sorted piles, Bozik selected and plucked up a single disc. "Who owns the purple-centres, then?"

The broad-shouldered man with the corded beard and silver coat raised his own token. "I do."

"You wagered all seven of your tokens, the highest wager in this round. So, you may answer first." Bozik set the chip back down and straightened his posture. "And here is your question: In ancient times and before the Great Pterenar which nowadays adorns our ingots, another bird claimed the prestigious title of 'symbol of Torril City', seen on ingots and official seals. Which bird was it?"

The man grunted in amusement. "That would be the now-extinct, Red-Crowned Cachak."

Beside Akteron, Piria cursed through her teeth.

Of course the man was a blasted bird-expert. Perhaps they

might have deduced that from his partner's spectacularly plumed dress.

"Correct!" Bozik said, scooping the purple-centred tokens up and returning them to Cord-Beard's waiting hands. "An easy first-round!"

The remaining discs were swept into a sack and removed from play.

Good that you played it safe, Akteron thought, six discs still in hand.

Piria held just two, however, which meant she was effectively out of the game already.

"Let's move on," Bozik said, holding up two fingers. "Our next question will be about world history. Yes. A question about the general history of Aliru. That will be question number two."

Now, it was Akteron's ears which pricked up.

Great Wastes! This is what he'd been waiting for! The chance to bet big.

Already, important dates and names of foreign lands and rulers were firing through his mind as he took his six remaining discs in hand.

Peering down the line of guests, he then tried to determine his most likely combatant.

Beside him, Piria was trying and failing to hide her disappointment, while the squat man beside her was biting his lip and staring at the collar. It didn't look likely for either of them. That sleek, masked lady's mouth was flat and un-telling as ever, though. And then there was Cord-Beard, grinning like an idiot, wager well-concealed in his fists.

Damnit...him again.

A big bet would improve Akteron's chances of answering first. So, he settled on five discs.

Then changed his mind.

Not five. A wiser number to play — to leave him with two for the final question — was *four*. Wasn't it? Or, perhaps he should split his remaining chips into two equal bets, just in case?

Creasing his brow, Akteron began to recount his wager when suddenly, the attendant was before him.

"Sir?"

Akteron dropped three discs into the pot.

As for Piria, only one of her remaining pair was deposited before the process continued down the line.

"Another interesting round, it seems," Bozik said, once the counts were before him. "And seeing as two of you wagered four discs, I will let luck choose our first player…" Shaking two in his hands, he drew one at random. "It seems we are beginning once more with you, sir." He held up a purple-centred disc, nodding to the man with the beard.

Akteron let a tense breath out, knowing the man's answer might still be wrong…

"As we are all taught," Bozik began the second question, "the ages of Aliru are based on the recurring emergence of the Silver Ones, who have appeared at regular intervals throughout history. Your second question is, therefore, which age are we currently in, *and* in which cycle did this age begin?"

Akteron almost leapt for joy, now, as Cord-Beard hesitated and shifted on his feet. One of the man's hands seemed to be squeezing his remaining three tokens hard, if his white knuckles were any indication.

"We are currently in the ninth-age," the man said, certain enough of that, then slowed, "and this age began in cycle four-thousand, nine-hundred and ninety-one…"

Bozik set the disc back on the glass case with a – *KATACK* –

"I'm afraid that is incorrect," he stated.

The bearded man giving a strange, guttural sound in annoyance, stretched his neck, then shook himself off.

Akteron gave a quiet sigh.

"We now move to the next and equal wager…" Bozik continued. "Who has the red-centred discs?"

"That would be I," the lady with the billowing, purple shawl at the end of the line said, raising another chip to prove it.

"Excellent. Please go ahead, madame."

"We are in the ninth-age," she repeated, "but it began in four-thousand, one-hundred and *eighty*-one."

Well, this one knew her history. Clenching his jaw, Akteron clicked his tongue perhaps a little too loudly, for at the sound, Bozik gave an expectant smile, rocking briefly onto the balls of his feet and back again.

"Just out of curiosity," he said, "did any other players have the same date, in mind?"

Akteron gave a small nod and received a thoughtful glance from the seller.

"Well, I hate to say it," Bozik went on, "but fortune really does favour those who bet big."

The onlooking guests gave a soft chuckle.

"Madame, you are correct."

As Bozik then scooped up her four tokens and handed them back, Akteron felt hopelessness spreading through him. A cloud of doubt, stifling any flicker of hope he'd clung to.

A movement beside him then drew his eye and turning, he saw Piria step forward. Clacking her final token onto the glass case with a grunt, she then abandoned the line, retreating to the shadows by the back wall.

"I take it you are leaving the contest, madame?" Bozik asked.

Piria merely growled in response, before casting a feral look at the other guests, a couple of whom raised eyebrows and looked away quickly.

"Too bad. But perhaps you'll have better luck during the auction."

Attention returned to the centre of the room.

"What a fitting way to lead us into our final question!" Bozik continued. "Which is, of course, about our guest of honour, here." He nodded to the collar.

*Of course...*Akteron thought, staring blankly at that gleaming metal. He should have seen that coming. Yet, the outcome was now clear. The end of Lakalak was always the same. Everyone would bet all their remaining chips on this question and that would leave him near the bottom of the pile.

Hopeless.

Unlike Piria, though, who knew her odds and didn't want to embarrass herself with a foolish hope, Akteron stood fast. He wanted to see this through.

When the rattling pot came by, he dropped his last discs inside and then balled his empty fists, casting all worries about this game aside and turning them to an alternate plan.

He recalled the passage they'd entered through...the guards at their posts by the stall, outside...the grunt in the antechamber and the two attendants, in here. And Bozik, himself.

And let's not forget the other guests, who will doubtless try to interfere...

He relaxed one fist only to clench it, again.

It had to be done at the perfect moment, when whoever won that collar dropped their guard, when the last thing they expected was an ambush...

"Duplicate wagers all around!" Bozik announced, staring at the discs before him as the attendant sorted them, and Akteron glanced at the ground, heart beating like a blacksmith's hammer.

Then, again out of the corner of his eye, Akteron caught sight of Piria doing a strange little...foot shuffle. Almost like she were dancing. But no, it was too erratic. There was no rhythm. Akteron looked back to Bozik, who had just picked a disc at random.

"Ah! For the first time, tonight," he said, "we begin with another guest." He gave a curt nod to the lady in the purple shawl. "Madame, your question is this. When this collar was first unearthed, what did the discovers famously claim its purpose was?"

Akteron turned to face the elegant lady, clearly readying her answer. Under her mask, Akteron could see she was squinting, slightly.

Yet then, a grin.

"As I recall, the collar last belonged to Kinetheron, founder of Torril City, and was worn at the most formal of ceremonies."

Bozik tilted his head. "A prestige-piece, then?"

The woman gave a gentle nod.

"I'm afraid that answer is incorrect, madame. I thank you for playing."

With another nod, she withdrew from the line, and Akteron gave an inward snort. She'd had no idea, just spouting the first line she'd thought up.

Either way, here it was. Doubtless, it was Cord-Beard's turn, again.

"Which brings us to the next, equal wager. I believe you had the yellow-centred discs, sir?" Bozik turned to the squat man now beside Akteron, who gave a surprised grunt as if he'd expected to be a silent participant for the whole night. Akteron shared the surprise, and realised right then that he had miscalculated.

He'd *miscalculated*...

Cord-Beard hadn't enough discs left for the largest bid, which left–

"It has no purpose, other than being a handsome piece of jewellery," the man spoke over Akteron's thoughts. "There was no statement other than that."

Still grinning, Bozik gave a quiet grunt. "Ah, but if that were the case," he remarked, "I would not have gone to such lengths to present this sparkling piece with such finesse, tonight, would I? I am afraid that answer is incorrect, sir. Thank you for playing."

A quiet chuckle came from the small audience and within Akteron, that tiny bloom of warmth started to flicker. The frustrating flicker of hope, again.

But Cord-Beard still had that smug grin pasted across his jaw and Akteron figured there was no way he or another guest would answer incorrectly, now. Purple-shawl and Squat-man had thrown their last chances away and yet, remaining was a group who were clearly very well versed in their history, their crafts, and their relicry.

"An aqua-centred disc..."

Akteron's breath caught as Bozik turned to him.

"Since you are the only unidentified colour remaining, sir," Bozik said, giving Akteron's lizard-like cowl a once-over. "It seems this is your moment to reclaim some ground." He then swept a hand in invitation. "If you please..."

Akteron's heart was pounding. He was sweating. This was it. *Now, think, damnit! What do you remember from those sketches... from what Kabonn said?*

Akteron cleared his throat and readied his grating baritone, determined to remain in character and not let his nerves run him off-track.

"It's rumoured that the collar has a lost twin," he explained, just as someone sneezed, loudly, "and that using both, one could see through the eyes of whoever wore the other."

Luckily, the sneeze hadn't interrupted his answer. Even so, there was a brief moment in which he thought he'd answered incorrectly, for Bozik's eyebrows rose faintly, his mouth opening just a sliver before that grin flashed back into place.

"Correct!" he said. "That is indeed correct, and I must congratulate you on your knowledge of relics, and of history... all of you!" He swept a hand through the air along his line of players.

Inside, Akteron sighed. It was done. This ridiculous game was done and he didn't know why he'd become so worked up. Now that it was over, though, he allowed himself a deep breath. A moment to calm down and perhaps stop himself sweating through his coat.

"Ladies and gentlemen, just one moment," Bozik muttered, reading the tally his attendant had held up before him, "as I check the scores, here...and, *oh*! A very interesting result, indeed."

The metalsmith leaning against the far wall let out an exasperated groan. "Get *on* with it, boy!"

Huh. Apparently, the smith had clearly enjoyed the drink service during the game for his cheeks had taken on a rich, red colour. Akteron hadn't thought a man that heavy could be affected by one glass of anything, but he understood. He'd tasted that red stuff, too, and it had almost blown his frill off. The warmth spreading over his own cheeks was the result of just one sip.

Bozik had ignored the interruption, nodding to Gusaan who withdrew the tally, again. "First, an honourable mention." He turned to address Purple-shawl. "Madame, your total was four. Nicely played."

She returned that familiar, precise nod.

Bozik then turned to Cord-Beard. "But your total is six, master ornithologist. A fine game, indeed."

The man's face did not change, for clearly, he already knew where this was heading.

"Which means," Bozik said, now pointing his gaze towards Akteron. "That your three-disc wager in the last round — worth double, let us not forget — has resulted in a tie!"

Huh?

Akteron started. Stupidly, he'd forgotten about the double-point rule completely.

"To break it," Bozik continued, "I will ask an additional question and this time, the first to answer correctly wins. Understood?" With a click, one of Bozik's attendants then approached and the pair entered a quiet discussion.

To Akteron's surprise, the bearded man took the opportunity

to stride across the room, stopping a mere arm's length away.

"You can still scurry back to whichever boat you were cast off," he said under his breath. "No need to embarrass yourself like your partner did. Neither of you belong here, and I'm taking that collar home..."

Right. Suddenly, this one seemed less an ornithologist, more like the guests Akteron had earlier assumed would be here. Still, as his pulse quickened, Akteron reminded himself that this was simply a ploy. It was just an attempt at working him up so he'd be unable to think clearly.

Sniffing the air, he crinkled his nose. "I never realised cachak dung was used in cologne. I had wondered what the stench in here was..."

The man's face twitched and he leaned a little closer. "You both think you can just saunter in here and steal Torril's history? No way. Our property stays in Torril, well out of reach of those dirty, foreign fingers."

Akteron almost sighed, itching to correct the gent and point out that the collar was actually from ancient Kesh, currently belonged to Kriolar, and was only on *loan* to Torril.

Before he could open his mouth, however, the man snorted.

"Aah," he said, inspecting the dashed kavs above Akteron's eyebrow. "So that's why you think you smell filth, everywhere. You're used to it from down in Kriolar."

Now, Akteron felt heat flood over his face.

"Pity that place is falling to pieces. But maybe you should try another rebellion? You all seem desperate for more humiliation and maybe this time, you'll finally realise your only national talent is tilling dirt."

Akteron balled a fist—

"Gentlemen!" Bozik announced, turning back to them and oblivious to the exchange. "We have agreed on a question!"

He met their eyes to secure their attention.

"And the question is this..."

Though Akteron's heart continued pounding under his coat and his fist remained clenched tight, his focus was now razor-sharp.

"In the inter-nation skirmishes of ten-cycles ago between Torril City and our neighbours to the south, which Krio leader successfully hid the statue of Ukatamon the Enlightened, protecting it from harm–?"

"It was no leader," Akteron replied at once. "The statue was removed by a simple miller's daughter, who kept it in her family home until the fighting ceased."

Bozik made a sweeping gesture towards Akteron. "Fabulous! A round of applause, please, for the winning gentleman!"

Clapping filled the chamber and Cord-Beard flashed his teeth, stepping backwards. But even while retreating, everything about his face spoke of danger.

It didn't matter. Akteron had done it.

"Now," Bozik continued over the noise, "I would like to invite our winner to a short, private discussion. Sir?"

Akteron nodded.

Bozik turned to the remaining guests. "Please enjoy yourselves. We won't be long."

The two groups in the room began to disperse as Akteron trod after Bozik towards the second door, noticing that his heart hadn't slowed and that his hands were now ice-cold. Half way there, Piria slid into stride beside him, her face betraying concern.

"I hope you don't mind if my partner joins us," Akteron said to the young seller as the three reached the entrance.

"I'd be disappointed if she didn't," Bozik replied, and they entered another passageway, leaving the relic chamber behind.

———■———

"So many guests from so many different locales present, tonight!" Bozik told the pair as he set a triplet of small glasses on a fine, wooden sideboard. "The turnout was far better than I expected for such a spontaneous event."

It had taken a good while for Akteron to calm himself after the interaction with Cord-Beard but some quiet, deep breathing and a little thought experiment in which he'd petitioned Kandaar to set the man on fire had been sufficient.

Now, they stood in a half storage-chamber, half sitting-room affair, the latter expressing that typical, Bozik-sheen. Lantern-light played off craggy walls and ancient wall-carvings, mounted around a lounge and fervent, red rug.

The other half of the room housed stacks of wooden boxes and shelves, crammed with objects bearing labels, some curiously encircled with chains.

"Of course, that's what anyone in my position dreams of," Bozik continued, pouring a light, purple liquid into each glass in turn, before plucking them up. "Attention, and competition. It's the only way to work."

Akteron and Piria took their small vitrics — each containing barely more than a mouthful — and were motioned to sit. They did, while Bozik placed his own glass down and brushed down his classical, Keshian coat. Then, he sat with them.

"Before we broach any other topic, however, you must tell me whence you both hail, for these garments are making me positively *burst* with curiosity..."

Well, now, Akteron thought. *Finally, it's time for the real game...*

"Few are familiar with my homeland," he explained, his face exuding a hint of mystery. "And fewer still know our name. We're a proud people, but we are not many."

Bozik crossed one leg and, still eyeing Akteron, circled his glass-lip with one finger. "Just so," he said. "Then I hope I don't cause any offence by asking where this homeland is, and what it is named?"

"Sanas, on the western coast of Tarma. The wildest seas of Aliru make landfall where our city stands," Akteron answered, taking on a proud, pensive tone and looking briefly into the carpet as if remembering the crashing waves and raging winds of that imaginary city.

"And do your people often visit Torril?" Bozik asked. "I regret to admit, I have never met anyone from Sanas, before, and am one of those ignorant of the name and, presumably, your customs. You also perform a kav ceremony, though, as in Kriolar?" He nodded to Akteron's eyebrow.

"We do," Akteron answered. "And we engage in business across all of Tarma. Though, Torril City has now become an important focus for us. We have established a good base here."

"Trade, then," Bozik prompted.

Akteron nodded once. "Our less liberal traders deal in the usual goods. Metal ores, fine timbers, and, of course, our famed Sanasian house-slippers. The most comfortable in Aliru."

"I don't doubt it." Bozik took a sip of his drink. "And...the more liberal traders? Like yourself, perhaps? What do they deal in?"

Akteron gave a knowing smile. He'd seen Bozik pull a number of them tonight and felt he'd mastered the art through observation, alone. "My partner and I," he began, "are sourcing unique objects for a purpose which, regretfully, we cannot share."

Bozik raised a hand. "I see, and forgive my intrusion. I simply like to familiarise myself with buyers, especially buyers who seem to share my love of the past." Standing again, he walked back to that sideboard and without hesitation, drained the little glass of its burning contents, setting it down with a soft – tek –

Leaning against the sideboard, he then peered thoughtfully at the roof and Akteron had to wonder if somehow, this young man had actually stolen the spirit of some elder, Keshian noble and stuffed it under his teenager's skin. No youth Akteron knew carried himself with such a confident, established air, nor spoke of the past as if he'd actually been there. They didn't lean on sideboards or sell antiquities while enjoying a snifter of lantern-fluid...

Still, Bozik's claim to 'love' history couldn't be that sincere, since he had so little trouble auctioning it off.

"It's a curious thing, this business," Bozik said. "My predecessor used to tell me that selling antiquities was like selling people a limb they didn't know was missing. A sentiment which I can admit has merit. But where he spent his life trying to discover the best way to hawk his various valuables, I seemed to come upon a better solution without much effort."

Akteron found a waft of the liquor he held meeting his nose and jerked back a little, setting the glass on the side table.

"How hard to realise can it be, after all? You simply have to make people *want* to *want*," he said. "It's not a case of showing something off, then starting a free-for-all. Beaks in the night, how crude, no wonder nine out of ten stalls fail within the first few cycles—"

Bozik was halted mid-explanation by the sound of plodding footsteps and panting, which broke the silence from the second of this chamber's two passages.

Glancing towards the noise and that patient smile growing thin, the teen watched as a scrawny man entered, removed his small cap and wiped his forehead. Deep, blue rings hung under his eyes, and Akteron noticed that not only was one of his hands bandaged, but that two fingers also seemed to be missing...

"So sorry for the interruption, sir," this man said, "but your payment from Komod has arrived. She wanted me to say thank you-....I mean, she wanted me to thank you, from her."

"Clarify at once."

The man straightened and gave a nervous shrug. "She said to thank you for showing such honesty in your dealings, lately. That was the only message, sir."

"Nuisance of a woman...doubtless another bribe," Bozik muttered as he ran a hand through his hair, again. "What is it, then? And where did you put it?"

"Not certain...what it is. It's in the back chamber, though," the man panted. "Doz and I lifted it inside, just now. Heavy as a block of night-iron, it is..."

"Well? Can you not bring it here? You know deliveries can't stand in the sea-air!"

The man looked momentarily pained but Bozik brushed him away with a simple, "See it done!"

The man stood on, glancing unsurely at Akteron and Piria for a moment, almost as if he wanted to say something more.

"*Bugger off, Pon,*" Bozik repeated.

Cap still in hand, the man did so and Bozik gave a sigh before returning attention to his guests.

"*Blasted lot of-*...where was I?"

"Showing off..." Akteron said.

"Yes. Right." Bozik cleared his throat and stood straight again. "It's not about just showing something off, but *preparation*. No matter what you're doing, in life, you need to think things out properly. In advance. Otherwise, who knows what slip-ups you'll make?" He returned to his pacing, but something in that utterance set Akteron on edge.

"Most importantly, you need to know those you are engaging with. Who *are* they? What do they want to hear? What do they want to *want*? And more importantly, what are they *hiding*? You can see it in their faces and gestures, clear as a lumstone in the dark if you know what to look for..."

The youth grew more animated as he met Akteron with a cold, blue gaze, and it was only then Akteron turned and caught sight of Piria.

For just a heartbeat he was confused, for gone was Gumpina's cruel, cold grimace. Gone was that crazed confidence and the accompanying glare, and in their place was just Piria, and fear.

She was staring at the floor with trembling fingers and at first, Akteron wasn't entirely certain why.

"Let's have a final, *secret* round of Lakalak," Bozik then said, ceasing that pacing to swivel and face his guests. "How about it?"

As the youth then held up a finger, the soft shuffle of feet betrayed someone approaching from behind Akteron. Someone who came to a stop so close that Akteron could feel heat on his neck. He knew then why Piria was concerned, of course. But he didn't bother turning, for her expression told him enough not to move.

"Your single question is this..." Bozik's eyes flicked between the seated pair. "What allows someone to spend their life selling illegal treasures, and never have so much as a *finger* set upon them by the authorities?"

Turning his head slightly, Akteron caught the second figure behind Piria, dressed in the same, grey gear which Bozik's security guard in the first chamber had been.

"*No*...how about this one?" Bozik said with that thoughtful air. "How could two traders from a city whose name I've never heard, show up at an auction bursting with facts about a stolen relic which nobody should possibly know?"

Piria hadn't looked up from her glass as Akteron suddenly found two hands yanking him out of his seat.

"The answer to the first question is simple," Bozik began.

Piria averted her eyes as Akteron was spun around, a fist the size of an ale-flagon driven into his stomach. It swept the wind from his lungs and he doubled over, gasping, knocking his small glass from the side table where it smashed on the floor.

Bozik watched on without emotion.

"*Fear,*" is all he said.

Breathless, Akteron's head was now guided downwards by two hands, where a knee connected sharply with his face.

There was an audible – *KNACK!* – followed by a metallic

feeling spreading through his skull and a ringing which filled his ears, and Akteron gasped as the pain raced down his spine.

"You are possibly the worst detectives I've ever seen," Bozik said, leaning down to his captive, "bounding in here, dressed like that and thinking, what-...that you can blend in with me and my guests?" He almost laughed. "Do you have any *idea* who these people even are?"

Akteron's neck was still in a vice-grip of cold fingers, blood pouring from his broken nose. The pain was almost unbearable. But Bozik didn't order any other point to be made. Not now, at least.

The youth gave a disbelieving huff and straightened, again. "The man whom I allowed you to best tonight, with a question I knew only a Bureau agent could answer"— he returned to his sideboard, pouring himself another drink —"one of Torril's greatest metalsmiths. He creates the finest and most expensive weapons in Tarma. Yes, weapons. *Illegal* weapons! Beaks in the night! Don't tell the Seat!" He wiggled his fingers in ridicule. "His patrons are foreign nobility. Empresses. *Kings!*"

Breathing through his teeth, Akteron made a momentary attempt to straighten but that grip on his neck simply tightened.

He remained in place.

"The lady with the mask and the feathered dress?" Bozik then snorted, taking a sip of his newly poured drink. "To her enemies, she's known as *The Dusk Warden*. Half the city is pressed to her feet, shackled under the weight of a thousand secrets all of which could turn the Seat inside-out in a day."

From the corner of his eye, Akteron saw Piria being held in place, as well, a grunt's hands affixed to her shoulders. Her eyes were shut and Akteron didn't blame her. He wanted to close his, too, but knew that would only cause him to focus on the pain rather than the floor beneath his head and the gluggy puddle of crimson, there.

"These people are far beyond you." Bozik said. "*I* am far

beyond you."

The sounds of exertion and scuffling footsteps were now echoing from the corridor out of which Pon, the tired-eyed fellow, had earlier scuttled. As if two people were nearing and heaving something immense between them.

Akteron didn't struggle, simply staring at that growing puddle.

"Now, you may well wonder why I'm bothering with all this." Bozik took another sip of his drink. "But you see, since I came into possession of the collar yesterday evening, I've had all manner of 'experts' scurrying in here to tell me what they knew about it. All for a fee, as you can imagine. And so many differing details!" He shook his head. "What I needed was corroboration. And I thought to myself, 'how best to get it'?" Turning to Akteron, he noticed the young agent's distant gaze. "Don't drift off, now. I'm still speaking." He reached out and gave Akteron's nose a squeeze.

Through clenched teeth, Akteron screamed but the grunt held him fast.

"So rude, the older generation, these days," Bozik wiped the blood off his fingers with a handkerchief. "Anyway, the solution was simple. I knew the Bureau would spare no time hunting these items down and naturally, any agents on this case would also have been briefed on them...probably by the curator, himself." He chuckled. "So, I organised the auction, open to all, and with a little game which any agent from the Bureau would naturally play if they wanted to recover the item. You lot always try the road of least resistance before reaching for your little stunshots, after all. And all this was done in the hopes of confirming a crucial question about the collar, which now, I have! It has a twin!" He clapped in satisfaction. "So, now, as a final show of respect, there's just one more thing I'd like you to tell me."

He leaned down towards Akteron's ear.

"The name of your contact," he said quietly. "Who is the skulking little snitch that tipped off the Bureau I was in possession of the collar?"

Akteron gritted his teeth.

No chance. He was *not* going to do that. Tagill deserved the chance to put this world behind him...

At that moment, Bozik's two menials entered the chamber, panting and carrying what, from the corner of Akteron's eyes, appeared to be a mounted globe.

"Oh, a meteosphere?" Bozik turned to them. "Lovely. Set it down, there."

"Sir, are you...sure you want it in here?" Pon dared, bow-legged as he carried the object to the location Bozik had indicated. "It makes a rather irritating noise–"

"*Pon,*" Bozik said through his teeth. "I am aware of the noises meteospheres emit. It turned on while you were lugging it about, no doubt. Now, set it on the floor and get out. I have guests." He gestured to Akteron and Piria.

Pon gave a nervous series of nods as the pair carefully lowered their burden, then half-ran out the door.

At that moment, the meteosphere did make a subtle buzzing noise. A low, warm hum which filled the space, and Bozik waited for it to finish before he muttered, "Damaged, of course... Korlon, make a note to send it for repair."

The man holding Akteron in place gave a grunt in confirmation.

"Anyway, lest we drift too far off-course...that contact. I need a name, now."

So easily...Akteron found himself thinking.

Bozik had seen through their ploy so *easily*, and it made Akteron cringe. Sure, he'd seen something in Bozik's piercing eyes which had unnerved him, at the start. Something which had warned that there was more to this kid than met the eye. But Akteron kicked himself mentally for not heeding that warning.

For not reading the signs and taking any of this seriously. He'd treated it like a game, and worse, he'd dragged Piria along with him.

He was always so confident that things would work out, and she'd trusted him...

And now...

Why were those words boring into him, so deeply? Was he truly a bad detective?

"Alright. Here's the honest truth," Bozik pressed. "I always get what I want, one way or another, so that leaves us at a rather clear juncture." He spread his hands before him. "It's an easy choice. You tell me who this contact is, and I spare you both further pain." He glanced to Piria. "How about poison? Quick, painless, always pleasant for everyone?" He turned back to Akteron and shrugged. "Or I have you both tied by the ankles and lowered into the swell." A nod towards the floor and he gave a mock wince. "But be quick. I do have an auction to begin and-...and what *is* that smell?"

Cutting himself off, Bozik gazed about.

There *was* an unusual smell. Somehow acrid and metallic, wafting through the air.

It was Piria who answered.

"*Magamium,*" she whispered, Akteron turning to find her wide-eyed. "It's magamium..."

"But, surely–"

"*Great Sands...*Ro, that's it," Piria went on, her face, white. "Komod put a bomb in the metcosphere. That's why that sack was so heavy...why she said not to drop it!"

Bozik was glancing between the two with disbelief. "A dismal attempt. Not even creative. I see through such–"

"*Shut it!*" Piria cut him off. "Listen, inside the sphere there's a Paran-Mechanism. Komod bought it from Geltak, that's why he was so edgy...she's hooked it up with phials inside the sphere, all on a timer. And if I'm right and it *is* a magamium-bomb, then just before it goes off it's going to start sparking..."

Bozik narrowed his eyes trying to see through the lie, even though uncertainty flashed across in his expression. "Nonsense. If that's true it'd blow the whole firth. It'd disintegrate this and all the other pillars, including hers. She wouldn't be that stupid."

Spitting blood, Akteron then widened his eyes. "*Oh, Gods,* Ri, that's what she meant by, 'I'm done here!' She didn't mean *tonight*, she meant at the Holes, for good!"

He glanced to Bozik.

"She told us you'd broken the rules. That there'd be blood..."

Bozik's stepped forward, hand raised to strike Akteron when suddenly, the meteosphere began sparking.

"*Great Teloran's Tits...*" he uttered.

"Let me go," Akteron said, then. "Let me go, I can stop it!"

Bozik glanced at Akteron's face and for the first time, Akteron saw the meagre cycles in the youth's eyes. He saw fear under those blue irises — and the reflection of sparks, arcing from that globe as the meteosphere began to hum again.

"They're not important," Bozik yelled to the grunts holding the pair. "Get to the auction chamber, now! Get the relics!"

Akteron and Piria were thrown to the floor at once, the men fleeing down the passage towards the auction-chamber. Bozik followed in their wake after snatching up some small items from a shelf, nearby.

"Ro!" Piria was on her feet at once, speaking over the ever-growing hum and the snapping of some electrical energy being loosed from the device. "It doesn't matter if we run...he's right, this thing is going to take out the entire firth."

"No it's not," Akteron said, running one hand down his coat while peering into the air. "Ath viraan, Kandaar..."

He couldn't tell if the air cooled or not because just then, heat started pouring from that machine.

"*Kandaar!*" he tried again.

It didn't seem there was any response. He spoke on, anyway.

"I don't know if you can hear me, but we need help... anything you can do to stop this explosion. Dampen it or contain it...I offer you every ingot I have." He ran his hands down his coat, touching each of the metal studs, one after the other. "*Please, Kandaar...*"

Still, no response, and Akteron let out a dismayed groan.

"Ro..." Piria said.

Looking up, he took her hand and they ran, leaving the humming, sparking machine behind. Akteron brushed his hands along the studs on his coat the whole way back to the auction chamber and entering the lantern-lit space, they could see that while the relics were still in place, everyone had fled, except–

Oh, by Sevellan...

There in the centre stood the young seller, alone and making exasperated grunts as he struck the display cases with a server's tray, trying in vain to get to the emerald seals, within.

"Kid!" Akteron called, spitting more blood. "*What in the-...* leave them and get out of here!"

Racing over, Akteron grappled the youth by the arms just as a vibration began in the stonework. "*Leave them!*"

He hauled Bozik backwards.

"LET ME GO!" the young man called back, breaking free, when–

– KATASSHH! –

Both men wheeled to see that Piria had pushed the central display case over and was grabbing the collar from the shards of glass as showers of chalky powder began falling from the ceiling. At that moment, the hum from the last doorway also changed pitch...

It took no more than a few heartbeats before Akteron, Piria and Bozik burst from the tunnels onto the platforms of the Holes, again.

The platforms were devoid of wandering souls, now, only a

few panicked figures fleeing across the nearest bridge as a deafening siren pealed through the night.

The petition tocsin above them had activated and as Akteron watched, it began to illuminate, almost as if charging itself up–

"It'll blast us all to bits! Get back!" Bozik shoved him aside and lifted one of his wrists, and rotating a bracelet, there, the tocsin gave a strange noise, its glow fading.

The young man didn't pause, bolting wordlessly for the bridge after the fleeing patrons, Akteron and Piria at his heels and all three soon out on the span.

"The bomb should have gone off, by now!" Piria yelled above the ceaseless vibrations now causing the bridge to quiver and rocks to rain down from the pillar's vegetation-covered crown.

Akteron's fingers were still brushing the ingots on his coat as he ran, eyes widening as he felt the lack of charge in one after another...

"Kandaar," he yelled back. "He's holding it off!"

"But for how lo–"

An explosion behind them ripped through the night, flinging all three onto their faces.

With a deafening boom, the pillar's upper half blasted clear off the base, becoming a cloud of shattered rock. There was a sound like a titan's bones snapping as the rest of the edifice then fractured into gigantic shards, each collapsing slowly into the sea.

Akteron hadn't registered the bridge breaking apart and the three of them dropping through the air, for one of those flying rocks struck him on the forehead, but Piria and Bozik screamed all the way into the blackness, below.

CHAPTER FIFTEEN
AGAINST THE WALL

Akteron awoke to hear waves lapping at a pebbled shore. He was lying on his back, shivering under bright moonlight with Piria and Bozik standing over him, and his head ached as if someone had been dancing on it.

Slowly and through dazed blinks, he saw Piria, who gave a heavy sigh and collapsed to the ground, holding her forehead and panting for some reason.

Bozik's only reaction was to turn away, blank-faced, though he too was panting. Akteron couldn't be sure why.

"What-..." he managed through the cold. "Ri...where are we?"

Lifting her head from her hands, she reached out to grip his shoulder reassuringly. "Still in the firth," she explained between breaths. "A small pocket beach...under the cliffs...we had to swim, and you..."

Akteron raised a hand to his head and winced — not because of his nose, but because he'd fingered a lump the size of a pterenar egg near his temple.

"*Achh-...damnit!*"

"You were...struck as we fell," Piria said. "Not sure what it was. We only...just got you ashore. Damned clothing didn't make it easy. I almost went under with you...but somehow your coat came free as we towed you along. Bozik guided us here."

"I'm sorry..." Akteron uttered.

Piria almost laughed. "You have nothing to...be sorry for. If Kandaar hadn't held off that explosion so long." She shook her head. "We both owe you our lives."

"Kandaar..." Akteron muttered, and began feeling about on his person but, as Piria had said, his coat and ingots were gone.

Still, how many ingots had Kandaar accepted to stifle that bomb? Surely, not all of them, for Akteron had touched them erratically, at best. He couldn't be sure if his fingers had even found them all.

It didn't change the fact that Kandaar had answered the petition. He'd saved their lives–

"That *shellbitten nut!*" Bozik sputtered now, as Akteron finally sat up and followed the young man's gaze into the firth.

The young man's pillar was no more. Only a sad pile of rocks remained, jutting up just above the angry waves which surged about in the bay. The other pillars surrounding it were still mostly intact, but many of their platforms and bridges dangled like an old official's jewellery down their sides. The one closest to Bozik's was missing a huge chunk from its base, now — no doubt shaken loose in the explosion — and a lump of rock in the water nearby said where it had landed.

"She actually tried to kill me!" Bozik said, turning and rubbing his face with one hand. "That bloody lunatic–!"

"Do you blame her?" Piria snapped, and Bozik straightened as if slapped in the face.

"You broke the rules...threatened her and Geltak. You tipped the Balance and didn't expect things to tilt back, in return? In a place full of thieves, murderers and crooks?"

The lad opened his mouth but no words came. Instead, he glanced back to his ruined base.

In the chaos, he'd been relieved of his stylish, Keshian coat and was now stranded in a basic ensemble. Combined with his dripping hair and pained expression, it made him look more like a child than ever.

"I'm going to need that collar back," he said all the same, turning and straightening those sopping garments in an absurd gesture.

"Erm, no," Piria replied. She shifted on the ground, picking a rock out from under her.

"I *said,* hand over the collar."

Bozik stuck out a hand.

"I bet it's a strange feeling, to have lost everything," Akteron muttered, causing the young man's eyes to narrow.

"I didn't lose *everything*, you idiot. I wouldn't be so stupid to keep all my valuables in one place..."

"Oh, that's wise." Akteron spat and casually rubbed something from his eye. "I suppose you'd like to keep things that way, too. Fair assumption?"

"What on *Aliru*-...are you trying to *bribe* me?"

Good. From that venomous tone, Akteron imagined Bozik didn't take part in exchanges like this very often. He usually ran the show, after all. He held all the chips and called all the plays.

But his grunts weren't here, anymore. He was alone and defenceless...and not just that, for if Akteron's eyes were working correctly, he was in more than a spot of trouble.

"I just mean, it would be unfortunate if you lost whatever you had left, as well," Akteron continued, each word causing his jaw agony.

"Threaten me again–" Bozik started, peering about and selecting a rock which he plucked up.

"Oh, put it down." Piria gave a tired sigh. "Listen to what he's saying."

"Why? Why would I do that?"

"Because," Akteron explained, "in less than five minutes, a Bureau support team will be on this little beach to get us out of here"— he looked Bozik in the eyes —"and that leaves us at a rather clear juncture..."

Bozik's face twitched at the mimicry. The hand holding that

rock twitched, too. But he was listening.

"Firstly," Akteron told him, "you're not walking out of this with the collar. It's over. The relic is going back to the museum. But if you play nicely and don't kick up a fuss, you can at least walk away with your freedom...plus whatever other valuables you've stashed away." He shrugged. "The other option is, we tell our chums up there exactly who you are." Holding out both his hands, he pretended to weigh the choice. "While it's not really the Bureau's style to dangle people into the firth, I imagine a long time in a small, cold cell wouldn't be to your taste, either."

At that, Bozik turned his head skyward and caught sight of the gem-light torches sweeping over the cliffs.

Search calls had started echoing over the waves and signal lanterns were fanning out from that first bridge onto the remaining platforms. Riallo had come, as Akteron had prayed he would, and the Security Bureau's team had been deployed.

"Why would I trust anything you say?" Bozik asked, his eyes jumping between the pair. "You've lied all night...what guarantee could you possibly give me that you'll get me out of this and let me go..."

"Listen, Boz," Piria now said, getting to her feet, and the young man seemed set to interrupt before she cut him off. "Unflattering as it will sound to you, and as horrid a brat as you might be...you're not our business. We don't care about how you spend your time and who you swindle. We're only after these relics. Our job is to get them back to our client, and that's it. So, you either play our game, now, or try to swim somewhere else and find another way up."

Glancing at those surging waves out in the bay, the fire finally left Bozik's eyes. He turned and reluctantly dropped the stone and when he spoke again, it was almost between his teeth.

"*Fine.* And the second point? What do you want?"

"Information," Akteron said at once, trying to sit up. "Tell us who sold you the collar. We need to know what he looked like, where he came from, and when he showed up…" He then gave a hollow smile. "And do be thorough, please."

With a disbelieving huff, which then melted into an infuriated groan, Bozik relented.

"He showed up just before closing, yesterday," he grumbled, massaging his forehead. "Average looking, except that one of his eyebrows was half-gone. Looked burnt-off."

Akteron glanced to Piria and met her eyes. This was the same guy Vanra saw in the Clutch, no doubt about it.

"A drifter, if ever I've seen one," Bozik said. "Shorter than you and with a pretty slight frame. He had an odd stink about him, too. A kind of damp, sour smell which I couldn't place. Needless to say, none of my usual clients smell like that. Good thing it started raining just when he arrived, because he needed a good soaking…"

Akteron cocked an eyebrow. "Go on…"

Bozik took a deep breath before doing as he was told. "A scar. He had one on his face. Just there." He pointed to his own jawline. "And then there was the way he spoke…" he trailed off as if searching for the words.

"He had an accent?" Piria tried to assist.

"No," Bozik replied. "He just didn't speak like anyone I've ever haggled with, before."

Akteron and Piria shared a glance. Komod had touched on this, earlier.

"So? What did he say?"

"It wasn't *what* he said…" Bozik took a second to consider. "Sure, I mean, it was that, too. At first, he put the usual spin on things. Said he'd sell the collar though it *pained* him to do so, *blah, blah, blah.* He was clearly trying to sound as if he were really attached. As if it were the most valuable possession in his life, and that he wanted a good price for it, but"— the lad shook his head —"when it came to the price, so meagre was the ask I thought the item must be a fake."

"How did you discover it wasn't?"

"My appraiser, Gusaan..." With a faint gasp, Bozik now glanced towards the collapsed pillar as if remembering the wellbeing of his staff for the first time. "He...he spotted the signs that marked it as legitimate. Something about how the details were etched, that the edges were tarnished and about the 'eccentricity' of the clasps. Gusaan can spot a fake from two pillars away. He knew it was real in a heartbeat."

"I don't see what's so strange about all this," Piria said. "It sounds like the thief had no experience selling, which makes sense, and that he was trying to sound knowledgable to get a better price."

"But that's just *it*," Bozik replied. "He played the game at first, yes, but when I suggested a price, ludicrous as it was, he didn't even blink. He almost threw the thing at me."

"As if he were eager to get rid of it, you mean?" Akteron asked. "Also not surprising. We expected him to get rid of these things as quickly as possible."

Bozik furrowed his brow. "Like I said, that's not it. Believe me, I've seen desperation many times"— Akteron believed him — "and this was something else. It was as if he were trying to lose the item quickly, but...not for any real *gain*. It didn't make sense."

"Well, I don't know how far we can read into that. The point is, he got paid, and you got a bargain. Or, *would have,* if we hadn't shown up..."

Bozik didn't reply to that.

"The question, now," Akteron went on, "is where he went after the firths. It's been a whole day, he could have hopped a wagon and arrived in Kriolar by now..."

"He's a local," Bozik then said over his shoulder. He had turned to gaze out into the bay again, and was regarding that group of Bureau agents up on the pillars as they surveyed the broken bridges, platforms, and flashed their gem-lanterns about.

"Local accent, local clothing. And he's still got more relics to hawk. If he's not a complete dunce, he'll know there's no better place. Your thief is still in Torril."

Akteron grunted, about to add somewhat smugly that they'd already retrieved another of the relics, but reckoned it was probably a good idea not to explain case details to one of the city's shadiest crooks.

Instead, as he watched Bozik standing there, sopping wet, helpless, the lad's business in literal ruins and running a hand through his hair, again, Akteron sighed.

"What was he like? Your predecessor."

With unexpected calm, Bozik now turned to face him and settled on a nearby boulder. "Smarter than I am," he said bitterly. "He ran that stall for over thirty cycles. Longer than I've been alive. *Pff*...I've had it less than six span and now it's underwater in a billion pieces, along with some of Aliru's most sublime treasures..."

In the trailing silence, Piria shifted, causing a small pebble-slide.

"He taught you about the trade?" Akteron pressed, feeling silence more dangerous than talk, at this point.

"He taught me everything."

"You didn't take his name on, though. His pseudonym, *Snaptooth*."

Bozik snorted. "Why would I?"

"I'm sure you've snapped a few teeth in your time," Piria suggested.

Bozik shook his head, again, the dim light revealing a wistful look. "That name meant so much to people. It scared them. But it was no more than a joke, as most things were to Kosur. It was his own tooth that snapped one day, while he was trying to lift a metal idol down off a shelf."

Akteron almost chuckled, but even this caused a fresh surge of pain. He groaned and shut his eyes for a moment, and when he opened them again, found Bozik's gaze had settled on him. Sitting there, on that boulder, the youth's eyes caught the moonlight and for a second revealed a flash of...*something*, inside. Perhaps it had been regret. Akteron didn't have time to ponder for just then, a loud – *SKETUSHHH!* – sounded out and an intense flash of white flooded the small, pebble-beach.

Turning, Akteron saw Piria with a finger pressed to one of the metal rivets on her coat. Above her, a pellet of white light was rocketing into the sky and in response, a few of the gem-lanterns on the pillars immediately turned to shine in their direction.

Bozik gave a small, appreciative hum. "Weaving your ingots into your coats. That's a new one."

"Ready to get out of here?" Piria asked, stepping over to Akteron and offering a hand.

On his feet again a moment later, Akteron heard a shout from the cliffs, above. It was quiet and indistinct, but presently a pair of ropes unrolled through the night air and slapped against the cliff-face.

"Riallo recognised the signal," she said, turning back to Akteron, "but he won't know we're three, and it'll be impossible to yell over the wind and waves–"

Gauging the height of the cliffs, Akteron's world suddenly tilted, his hearing becoming muffled, and he knocked against her, blurry-eyed.

"*Damnit,*" she muttered with concern. "No way you can climb four-storeys, like this."

A tense moment then passed before she turned to Bozik.

"We're going to have to tie him and haul him up..."

The lad was watching her warily, as if expecting the next line.

"...but we only have two lines, so-...*ugh,* as stupid as this sounds, *you're* going first, and I'm going to trust you to do the right thing." Taking a step towards him, she then lifted a finger and levelled it at his chest. "Just let it be known that if you *try* anything...*anything*, I will hunt you down and rip every single part of you that can be ripped into *very. Small. Pieces.*"

Bozik didn't flinch. Smoothing down his soaked shirt, he stepped past her to the cliff-face, grabbed the first rope, and began climbing. Piria's gaze remained on him for a moment, cold and intense, before she muttered again and began tying a loop for Akteron's foot in the second rope.

Akteron simply waited, watching the surroundings wobbling, the sounds of shouting and the sea filling his ears and mind. He wasn't sure exactly how *long* he and Piria waited on that pebbled beach, but the next thing he knew, he was being lifted into the air and she was climbing that first rope, beside him.

Gripping his rescue line with one hand, foot in that loop, he used his free hand to avoid being grated along the cliff-face and gradually, slowly, he found himself being lifted out of the firth.

At the top, gripped by reassuring hands and hauled back from the ledge, Akteron was set on his feet again by a pair of dark-clad men. They led him unsteadily through some dense foliage before a familiar voice broke the silence.

"You two are beyond lucky." A lumstone-torch flashed through the surrounding greenery, and a relieved-looking Riallo emerged. "I was sure you'd gone down in that blast. Sure as the sky in Torril is green."

He stepped out and actually hugged Akteron, but the agent merely freed himself to turn about, searching.

There was Piria, beside him and wiping her forehead with one arm, *but–*

"Where...is he?" Akteron asked.

"Who?" Riallo replied, eyeing his agent with concern.

Dense foliage blurred around them as lights lit up fronds and mossy rocks and tree-trunks and figures moving about.

Yet there was no sign of–

"Me. And I'm here." Bozik's voice met their ears.

Akteron pivoted to see the young man leaning against a tree in the dark, and Piria had to steady him as he swayed dangerously.

"Could you give us a moment, Riallo?" Akteron slurred.

"You need medical assistance..." Riallo told him.

"Just a *moment*."

Reluctantly, Riallo stepped back and engaged himself with a pair of agents who had just come crashing through the brush, leaving Akteron, in Piria's assistive grip, to approached the youth.

"You didn't run," he said, keeping his voice low.

"I thought you might have a change of heart about the collar," Bozik replied, nodding to Piria's damp coat, inside which a ring-like bulge was still evident. Akteron couldn't miss hearing the sarcasm in his voice.

"That was decent of you," Piria then told him. "Helping drag Ro to shore, down there."

Bozik pushed himself off the tree trunk. "Are we done?"

"Listen, Bozik...or whatever your...real name is," Akteron said, trying to hide the look in his eyes from Piria though she must have seen it, for she narrowed her own and studied him.

Akteron ignored her. He tried not to let the sudden flush of anguish cloud his mind because beneath the wavering visions and echoing noises around them, he knew this was a chance — his *chance* — to right something.

"You're still young," he said through a slow blink. "You have so much opportunity...but this path that you're on, it's...a dark one, and who knows if tonight was the worst of it?" He raised a hand as if to excuse himself, for his mouth wasn't quite forming words the way he wanted it to. Still, this had to be said. It *had* to be said. "Take this chance...why not change things? You can. Most people can't, but you can...so, why not take your life in another direction?"

For a moment there was silence, and Piria had to shift her feet to keep holding Akteron up while Bozik observed the unsteady agent over his nose.

Then, with a huff, that arrogant air from the Holes reappeared.

"A life for a life," he said. "That's all this was."

With a final grin, Bozik turned and vanished into the jungle.

PART THREE

Dear Ren,

I know...second letter in two days, and fair warning — I might be concussed. But this case seems to have no end of nostalgia to spoon out. Tonight, it was a person who reminded me of you. The confidence was definitely there. So was the taste in expensive clothing. And like you, he also seems trapped. Like he's fallen into a deep tangle of something he can't quite wrest himself out of...which might already own him. Maybe the right decisions can help him tear free, or maybe it's too late. I only know it's not my place to solve his problems. In the end, all we can do is contend with ourselves, our own choices, our own paths, right?

I still wonder if it was right to move up here. Sometimes I feel I'm betraying you all. Sometimes I wonder if I've lost sight. But honestly, working cases for the Seat in Torril is much like it was in Kriolar — just with more trees around. And if I focus on my work, I tend not to lose myself in the past. Ironic, I suppose.

Anyway. I'm not daft. I know you're not going to write back and I sometimes feel stupid for keeping this up. Perhaps I'm doing it more for myself than for us. Still, I have this absurd hope inside that you'll read these words and somehow explain everything, someday.

Love always,

-Akteron

CHAPTER SIXTEEN
MIX-24B

Piria fanned the cup in her hand as she read over an old notebook on the living room table. She was surprised at how different her handwriting had looked only a few cycles ago. How that rolling cursive had completely morphed into the tight blocks of capitals she used today — except for in some of the formulae, of course, where a lowercase letter made all the difference.

Thinking back, she remembered making that choice, scribbling away in the wee hours as an idea had bloomed and deciding that capitals were better for clarity. To be sure nothing she wrote could be misunderstood.

There was a messy, first attempt on this page. And she'd obviously been excited about something because the letters had been smudged by her scribbling hand before the ink had dried.

Oh, yes. She thought, reading down a list of quantities. *That powder.*

The one she'd come up with to test if food was stale. It was a deviously complex formula and hadn't really worked, in the end. Well, not on food. An innocent kitchen spoon had received a dusting as she'd been cleaning up that day, and to her surprise, the powder had reacted with a dramatic plume of sparks. A fivespan of tweaking later — plus one work-desk charred to cinders — Piria was finally able to narrow down the main, reactive component and determine that the mix might have applications in testing the degradation of metal. Not altogether useful, really, seeing as rust and corrosion were visible to the naked eye.

Taking a sip of her tea, she burned her lip and resumed fanning.

Discovering this dusty softcover hadn't been intentional. It had been down beside her side-table and she'd only just spied the corner while sliding a box of old, cold-tack clothes from under the bed. It must have fallen down there a couple of cycles ago. And seeing as these test-sentences were on the last, inked page, perhaps it had been on that very night–

"You're up-...*ugh,* early." Akteron's low voice met her ears and looking up, Piria saw him emerging unsteadily from his bedroom like a lost child might stumble through city streets.

His face was partitioned by the bandage over his nose and he was clearly expending effort not to rub the raised, purple bump under his hairline — though his fingers were lingering in dangerous proximity to it.

Dressed only in sleeping-trousers, Piria could also see other bruises, cuts and scrapes on his torso as he made unsteadily for the kitchen.

"A blackbeak decided to take up residence on the building opposite at sunrise," she said. "Male, I think — couldn't see any red in the plumage. Surprised it didn't wake you."

"Am I awake? I feel like I'm wading through sand."

"You're concussed," Piria replied, standing to follow him. "Nothing too dangerous, but the physicians still warned to go easy, today. Riallo needs us to go into the Bureau to confirm the find with Kabonn, but otherwise...I'm not sure if we can do much, with you like this."

Setting a mug on the countertop, Akteron began poking about, presumably for the tea leaves. "I'll be fine. It's really not that bad in moments when the floor stops tilting."

"...if you say so."

"Well, it's not like we can just stop," he added, "there's only two days left before the exhibit opens, isn't there?"

"I'm more worried about the Krio ambassador, to be honest."

"Me too." Akteron nodded, shifting cans aside and squinting at various labels. "I can't believe he's threatening to go to the press..."

Piria slid a squat tin over to him. "There's the freshleaf."

"Brilliant."

A moment later, he was ambling back towards the sofa, steaming cup in hand and monitoring each step like his own feet might attack him.

By Sevellan, he'd taken a beating. But that look in his eyes...it wasn't quite *weariness,* and it wasn't from the excitement and injuries he'd sustained at the Holes, either. Piria knew that look. The distant, contemplative calm.

"You were up in the night, again," she said, watching him settle awkwardly on the sofa and lean back with a groan. "Writing?"

He didn't answer, setting the mug atop his leg.

"That's the second letter in two days," she continued. "Might want to give him time to answer the first, hmm?"

"I just wanted to keep him informed about...all the action lately," Akteron trailed off, closing his eyes and rubbing them. "*Ugh.* You're probably right."

Piria took another, more cautious sip.

Ah. Finally, it was cool enough.

"I just feel it's better not to seem...desperate."

Akteron seemed to consider that for a moment before, sitting up and apparently also finding his tea too hot, he placed the mug on the table and slapped his leg.

"Right," he began. "So, what do we know?"

Piria didn't understand how he did that. How he could change gears so quickly. How one topic could just be...dropped...and another begun without bringing it to a satisfying conclusion.

When Akteron had first moved in she'd found this frustrating, but four cycles later and it was expected behaviour. She was used to it. And she could see the utility, for it did free the mind to chase other lines of enquiry. In any case, she'd noticed Akteron dropped the subject far more easily when it was about Rennik...

"We know a little," she replied, readying herself with a deep breath and figuring that when he wanted to talk about that, he would. "Enough to review..."

"Great." Akteron then gave her a sideways glance. "But just to check that my brain is still working, mind if I start?"

Not such a bad idea...

Piria signalled for him to take the lead.

"How about we attack the timing, first," he said. "We have a few key moments, now, which we can string together to build a movement-map. The first being the theft, of course. At the museum, two days ago and in the early hours of morning. Accurate?"

"Sounds like you're still sentient."

"Next would be the ringing of the bell at Dagger's Clutch that evening, at which point he's shot at and injured by Vanra." To Piria's amusement, he fired off an invisible arrow, adding a small *'pwing!'* "The thief then makes his way to the Holes and hawks the collar to Bozik."

"Which leaves the question of that gap," Piria began. "Between the theft and ringing the bell at the Clutch. What did he do all day?"

Akteron gave a nod. "And where did he go after the Holes? And does he still have the blade? Or did he already get rid of it in the gap, beforehand?"

A moment then passed without comment and inside, Piria could feel uncertainty prickling her again. Getting to her feet, she plucked up her mug and wandered to the window.

"I hate to admit this, but the more I consider it, the more I feel you were right," she said.

"About what?"

"The break-in. The whole thing. Given this guy's behaviour, I just can't escape the notion that premeditation was involved."

Akteron grinned. "I knew you'd come around."

"That gap in time is just another example." She turned to face him. "I mean...what stopped him from ringing the bell straight away? Right after the theft?"

Akteron peered into his steaming mug. "As I see it," he said, "he wanted to maximise the effects. So, the bell was stolen and taken into the middle of a shifty neighbourhood at a time when the most people would be in the area, right when they're coming home from work. He then strikes it from a *rooftop,* whose location was tucked well out of sight but which *guaranteed* the sound reaching the busy thoroughfares nearby."

"Sure," Piria said. "But all that still doesn't explain *why.* Why was it done?"

Akteron shrugged.

Huh. At least her confusion was shared, then.

Piria routinely avoided basing conclusions off *feelings* or *hunches.* Doing so went against everything she knew, after all — everything she'd taught herself about reaching verifiable solutions or predictable results. Solutions were reached through hard math. Through formula and calculation, adding and subtracting elements, and by testing the results again and again.

And before Akteron, she'd thought that the only way to tackle problems.

But working with him had proven that...well, that *other* way had some merit, too. That an inkling from within was sometimes beneficial. Not enough to solve a case, perhaps, but enough to reach the next position on the board. Cracking cases with Akteron was, with startling frequency, a shot in the dark, but Piria now had to admit that speculation had utility. Hunches could help one find unusual and unexpected possibilities. So, now and then, she allowed herself to run with it. To speculate a little.

Here came the next question, already, rolling off her tongue.

"So, can we figure out that 'why'?" She leaned against the sill. "What benefit would there be in causing a panic? And why in the Official Quarter, specifically? And what's the benefit of doing so, only to ditch the object, afterwards?"

"Well, it's likely that he dropped it involuntarily. I mean, we know Vanra fired a warning shot and the arrow caught him on the arm." Akteron's distant stare said he was picturing events as he spoke. "Shocked, or injured, or both, he then fled the scene, leaving the relic behind, which Vanra collects and takes to Ikta and Rama. As for the rest...well, what *could* the possibilities be?" He now shifted to stretch his legs out on the sofa, then started a tally on his fingers.

And there it was.

Piria leant back, watching and listening to him *inkling* it out.

"Maybe our thief just went home after the theft? Kept low? Slept? Then woke in the evening and went out to cause some havoc." He tilted a hand in the air. "Or perhaps it was all a distraction technique? Diverting our attention from something else? Or maybe it was revenge? He knew someone in the area who needed a good confounding?"

Hmm. Revenge.

See? Piria wouldn't have thought of–

"Wait...*confounding*," Piria cut her own thoughts off.

"Right," Akteron said. "Perhaps he had an enemy in the Clutch. Wanted to make the evening unpleasant. Who knows?"

"No, not that," Piria narrowed her eyes. "*Confounding*. Ro, we've overlooked something."

"What's that?"

She put her mug down. "How did the thief do this without confounding himself?"

Akteron cocked an eyebrow. "Huh."

Piria nodded slowly. "Vanra didn't mention him acting like the other confounded people we saw, and he escaped just fine. She said he even swore while doing so..."

"Well, as she was deaf and was unaffected, maybe he just petitioned to be temporarily deaf, too?"

"Easy enough to do..." Piria agreed. "But that just leads to the next point. How did the thief even know what the bell was capable of? How did he know it *could* confound people?"

Akteron pursed his lips for a moment, then seemed to come to a solution. "The placards in the museum," he then announced. "He could have read about it during the robbery."

Piria closed her eyes and remembered the scene. The way it had felt, standing in that echoing hall and how it must have looked, when all the lights were off.

"No...I didn't see him read anything during that vision," she said. "And I read the placards, myself, while we were inspecting the break-in. The items were storied in the usual, romantic museum vernacular, but there was no mention of the bell being able to confound people."

She set her tea down.

"Kabonn himself said the bell had never been tested, and while there was a brief appearance in Idmaion curriculum, even *you* didn't know what it did. So, what are the odds that a lowly thief...presumably without your grip on history...could?"

Akteron levelled a stare at the table before him, some wheels clearly turning in that banged-up head of his again. "That bit is tricky to answer," he said slowly. "*Although...*"

A sudden intensity filled his eyes.

"*Hah*! That's it, Ri! That's the proof! Whoever this guy was, the simple fact that he was *aware* of the bell's function means he knew something before the theft!"

"It makes sense..." she uttered. "So, it *was* premeditated. He knew what he was stealing, after all."

"And if that's true," Akteron went on, "odds are the rest was thought out, as well. The ringing of the bell. The sale of the collar. Whatever he's doing now."

Piria nodded. "If that's true, though, then he certainly went to great lengths to make it look spontaneous."

"To throw us off, no doubt. And he did a good job." Akteron tilted his head in thought. "While, ironically, highlighting how odd it all is. I mean, it's a bit strange that such a momentous theft looked no more difficult than a stroll through the market. The guy smashed into those cases as if they were made of wet paper. He passed through that wall as if it wasn't there."

As if it wasn't there...

Piria gave a thoughtful hum in agreement, picking up her tea and stirring it again...

Until a spark of possibility stilled her fingers.

"Are you...alright?" she heard Akteron ask, but without answering, Piria set her tea down again and took off across the living room.

She couldn't lose sight of that spark...

"Ri?" Akteron called from behind her.

Opening the door to The Cave, Piria snapped on a lantern and a moment later, was busily rifling through papers in her desk drawer, eyes flashing across titles, formulae, charts and scribbles.

When had it been? Two cycles ago? Three?

It was at the end of the first warm tack, she remembered that much...

"Water: Cooling. Water: Boiling. Paint: Simple Green..."

Pages upon pages of notes passed under finger. Research. Cycles of work.

Not there.

She slammed the drawer shut and opened the next.

"Should...I be worried?" Akteron began, appearing in the doorway only to find a hand silencing him. Piria needed to remember the title. It was on the tip of her tongue — but what had she *named* it?

"*Snap Fire...Cumulative Dust...*" Was it under D? Maybe she'd done that thing she sometimes did, and had come up with a nonsense word for it-...*ah!*

Suddenly, her fingers locked onto a small series of papers tacked together along their margin.

"Gem-Aid!" Piria said, spinning around. "Akteron! *Gem-Aid!* Here, look..."

She smoothed the trio of pages onto her desk in a line, and pointed to the first. "A couple of cycles ago, I made an unexpected discovery."

The sheet she was pointing out still carried that blurred smudge where the water had spilled, that night...

"I created a powder, and it could have had great potential for jewellers. Could have made gem-shaping a pinch." She gave a chuckle. "The components were mostly crystalline-reactive, but included some metallic derivatives. A pinch of magamium and a few non-oxidising types."

Stepping from the desk and not checking if Akteron had understood, Piria then turned to her 'phialing-cabinet'. Running her fingers along the hundreds of small, glass vessels, it took a few breaths before those fingers hit one labelled 'Mix-24B', inside of which was a small palmful of light, creamy-looking powder.

She pocketed it while, behind her, Akteron perused the math on the first page with a blank stare, clearly trying to decode her scribblings.

"So...it was some kind of bonding agent?" he asked.

"Much more interesting than that."

Piria now crouched to dig through a wooden crate on the floor filled with rocky fragments. It was a mess, in there. She'd never bothered to sort things out properly and the little labels she'd stuck to various samples now littered the bottom of the box.

Still, a moment later, she'd grasped all she needed.

Thunking a book-sized slab of white stone onto the workbench, Akteron winced, taking a hand to his head.

"Sorry," Piria muttered.

He waved her on.

"The process was simple," she obliged, sliding an empty, metal bowl from a shelf and grabbing a second phial from a collection. "Applying my formula to certain stones, one could avoid cumbersome, specialist gem-shaping tools and save days of work. It would allow a jeweller to use a common kitchen knife, had they wanted to, and get the job done in minutes."

"A kitchen knife to slice gemstones?"

"Right!" she nodded, cleaning out the bowl with a rag.

"Are you saying the thief cut through the museum wall?"

"No..."

Grabbing a grubby, half full glass of water, she dunked a dropper in and filled it. Next, opening the two phials, she tipped a small mound of powder into that bowl from each.

"The way of triggering the reaction was the trick. You see, for the powder to work, you have to pass charge through it...and that's inefficient, as you can imagine."

Beside her, Akteron gave a sage nod.

"Charge is like *white-energy*. You know, like lightning. It can only pass through conductive materials."

Adding the water, Piria stirred, whereafter the substance in the bowl took on a strange, glittery appearance and became smooth and viscous.

"So, instead of powder–"

"You made lizard spit," Akteron said.

She chuckled. "There is a resemblance. But that's what allows you to apply the charge." Pouring the paste onto the slab of white rock before her, Piria slid an ingot from her belt.

"I'm confused, though," Akteron said, peering over her shoulder. "That isn't a gemstone..."

"No, it's not. But full disclosure, I'm testing two new assumptions right now."

Lowering that ingot towards the workbench, she made contact with the paste, which issued a small crackle. Then, both she and Akteron witnessed the odd reaction, discovered all those cycles ago. Or, a similar one, for if Piria hadn't botched her internal math, there would be a very interesting difference to come...

"The first assumption is about the components my formula reacts to," she went on. "Because my records indicate it only reacted with certain gems. Amethyst, citrine, prasiolite, carnelian..."

At first, the paste just seemed to bubble. It appeared just as it had when she'd last tested it and as Piria watched, she scoffed at her own lack of imagination.

"I never made the leap," she said. "I assumed only *gemstones* were affected and didn't consider the wider implications..."

Akteron was watching her eyes, as if trying to glean answers based on her expressions. "What's the second assumption?" he then asked as the next phase began.

"That a new ingredient I just added will dramatically augment the reaction-...*yes!* That's it!" Piria cried, almost leaping as the stone began to deform in the centre.

"I...still don't understand," Akteron said, hand hovering by the lump on his head. "Is it easier to cut, now?"

"No! Not at all!" Piria brushed her hair back behind one ear, trying to calm herself enough to explain. "Alright. Remember that residue? From the museum wall?"

Akteron nodded as, before their eyes, that deformation in the slab grew deeper, deeper, until it met the underside of the stone and swiftly formed a hole. Then, finally, he seemed to have pieced together what he was seeing.

"Nine Gods, Ri..."

"When we inspected the scene," Piria went on excitedly, "such a reaction didn't even occur to me because I'd never considered adding kusamium. But even then, recall that I said I thought the powder only reacted to gemstones? Because of that, I couldn't imagine it would affect *this* type of stone."

"Which is...?"

Piria beamed. "It's *granite*. But granite is a composite stone! It's composed of feldspar, mica, and *quartz*. In ordinary circumstances, around thirty-percent."

"...and the whole museum is made of granite blocks," Akteron finished for her, those green eyes sparkling now, and as lively as she'd ever seen. "Ri, you did it. You just discovered how the thief got in! He used this tunnelling paste..."

"Still sentient," she told him, grinning. "I should have seen it earlier. I just wasn't using my brain." She then added a thoughtful mumble. "*It also means the concentration needed for the reaction on granite is far higher...*"

"Incredible!" Akteron gave a celebratory clap before his smile faltered. "But, hang on. If it creates a hole, why didn't we see one at the museum?"

"Ah," Piria said, the sample before them still changing. "Well that's the beauty of it. The stone's molecules aren't *gone*, they just get displaced. Shifted aside for a while. Their original structure remains largely intact, though." She tilted her head, thinking of an appropriate comparison. "Imagine a bowl full of a gelatinous substance. Now imagine you drop a stone into it. The gel is parted as the stone passes through, and that hole stays open for a little while but eventually seals itself up, again. It's a similar process, here."

Indeed, on the workbench before them, the stone was slowly sealing itself back up. As if molten in structure, that hole was shrinking away, closing to leave the rock in its original shape.

"As if nothing ever happened," Akteron muttered, now having forgotten the lump on his head. "And how long does it last? The hole, I mean."

Piria shrugged. "In my tests, temperature seemed to affect the resealing speed. Colder temperatures extended the duration. A chilly morning and enough paste, and it could stay open for... *mmm*, thirty-seconds or so?"

Akteron's eyes grew thoughtful before her he turned to meet her eyes. "That timeframe matches what we saw in the vision." Then, he slapped his knee. "*Yes! And that's* why the vision was so odd! Kandaar couldn't show us a hole, because the real wall-block was in the way. So, it just *appeared* the thief had walked through the solid wall!" He turned back to the sample. "It all fits!"

"Mostly," Piria added. "There are still two problems. Firstly, this powder is *unconscionably* expensive to make. That's part of the reason I ditched the research. I mean, this phial alone would be prohibitive, but the quantity needed to get through a solid, monolithic slab like that? It'd be worth more than this building."

Seeming to weigh this, Akteron tilted his head. "Still, not an *impossible* hurdle..."

"Not if he stole the reagents, I suppose," Piria said. "But then he'd also have to come by a decent amount of Razakium, the stockpiling of which is controlled in Torril." She shook her head. "Then, there's the second problem."

Staring at the papers on her workbench, Akteron's brow furrowed, apparently already having worked out what that problem might be.

"Of *course*..." he muttered. "How on *Aliru* did the thief know about your formula?"

Piria gave a grunted agreement. "This research was never published. Largely because it was a mistake. But while it's not *unthinkable* someone else stumbled on the same solution, it's *very* unlikely."

"Unless our thief is a master pulchivist, too," Akteron said with a light huff of disbelief. He then stepped back from the table to think. Or perhaps the light was hurting his eyes. Piria couldn't be sure.

"I know you like to run solo ordinarily." He nodded towards the papers. "But did you happen to show *anyone* else this research? Do you remember?"

Piria didn't have to think very hard on that. At once, a face and a memory floated to greet her. "As a matter of fact, I do," she said. "Kialla. An old friend of my mother's, also a pulchivist. She was kind of a mentor to me and I used to send her research to verify."

Akteron nodded. "And you sent this to her?"

"One of the only things she never got back to me about."

"Well," Akteron said. "We know our next stop, then."

– TUMTUMTUM –

Piria rapped on the door a second time.

This early in the morning, few people were drifting up and down Kaluur Street's wide sidewalk and sunlight still cut through the canopy at a low angle.

"I *know* this is the right address," Piria said, then lowered her voice. "I just hope she hasn't...you know..."

"What? Gone to meet Great Kendara?" Akteron added in a whisper. "Kialla wasn't *that* old? Was she?"

"Around seventy five, if my dates are any good-...*ah,* hold on, I hear something."

It was the faint clopping of footsteps behind the door which caught Piria's ear, growing steadily louder and ending with a series of metallic clicks. Then, a pair of steely eyes could be seen, peering through a crack.

They landed first on Akteron and his bandage-covered face, and narrowed. A second later, they shifted and found Piria, and widened again.

"Well, if it isn't–" the door swung open to reveal a svelte, elderly woman wrapped in a bathing-robe, her feet stuffed into wooden clogs which put her almost at eye-level with Akteron.

"Piria? My *Pestle*? Oh, by *Sevellan's Lost Ledgers*!"

"Hi, Ki," Piria said, finding herself engulfed in a tight hug and giving a tolerant smile as she was shaken about.

Kialla had always enjoyed a good hug.

Piria had never been so partial.

"My stars, come inside," the older woman exclaimed, ushering the pair in. "Come, come and sit and bring your man, and–" she suddenly seemed to realise what she was wearing. "Oh, Blasted Sands, let me get changed."

"Don't be silly," Piria replied. "We can come back–"

"No! No!" The woman was already vanishing into a room nearby. "Just a moment!"

As soon as she was out of sight, Akteron leaned over. "*Pestle?*" he whispered.

Piria leant back. "Oh. Ki told me once that I'd get so lost grinding and crushing powders, that I'd always forget to clean and store the pestle, afterwards. She figured if she tacked the word onto me, maybe I'd remember...and it kind of stuck."

Akteron chuckled as she then turned to gaze about the space, surprised to notice for the first time how modest Kialla's little apartment really was, especially for a former professor of the educaria.

Not one cushion seemed to have been shifted since Piria had last been here, either. There were the same sketches of colleagues, students and friends hanging on the walls — still none of family. The same plain, glass vase stood underneath them on the same bamboo side-table. And as when Piria had last been here, the soft scent of burnt incense-sticks filled the air, covering the damp, sweet smell of bird litter.

So, Serotonin was probably still alive, then. Hiding under the sofa, perhaps. The little sneaker had always been skittish with visitors. Piria wondered if he was moulting into his cold-tack plumage, yet...

Overall, the ambiance and quiet brought back memories of long, studious nights. Candles burning low. Tea at sunrise and a sore hand from writing for hours on end. This place had been a second home to Piria for a good while.

"What can I get you both?" Kialla reappeared in a fine but understated donvul and trousers, though she still wore the clogs. Tokking across the room, she began swinging cupboards open.

"Tea? Juice? For the gent I have-...well, what time is it?" She froze mid-rifle to check the clock, then peered at Akteron over her nose. "Oh, we only live once. Something strong?"

"Not for me, thanks," Akteron answered.

"Turns down a drink before midday bell?" Kialla turned to Piria, wiggling her head. "He might be a keeper."

"He's not my-...we're not together, Ki," Piria explained.

Kialla made a sceptical appraisal of them both. "You aren't together?"

"No, I mean, we live together, and he's my partner–"

"So you *are* together."

"No, not like that," Piria said, growing a little flustered. "Listen, I'm sorry to visit out of the blue like this but unfortunately, this isn't just a social call. We're on a case for the, erm-...Bureau of Security."

Kialla cocked her head. "The *Bureau of*-? Oh, don't tell me you've signed on with *that* lot?"

"Yes. No. Kind of," Piria stammered, trying to collect her thoughts. She took a breath. "I'm a *consultant*. Akteron is a *detective*." She motioned Akteron to step forward. "And we're *working* together on a case."

Kialla's face had soured a little, and she now looked Akteron up and down, eyes lingering on that bandage.

"Ah-ha..."

"We're investigating on behalf of the Torril City Museum," Akteron explained. "They had a break-in, recently, and a number of relics were stolen."

"Hmm. And by, '*on behalf of*', I'm to understand that..."

"Oh, I'm independent. I work contracts for the Bureau."

At that, the sourness in Kialla's face melted away and she actually sighed in relief. "A contractor! I see! Well, thank the stars for *that*."

"I...take it you're not a fan of Torril's bastions of order?"

"Hah!" Kialla barked. "Not a *fan*? That hypocritical bunch of—"

"Aaalright. Let's not get started on the many disagreements we have with the Seat, just now," Piria interrupted, drawing both pairs of eyes to her.

"Still an optimist," the older woman muttered with a wistful grin. "Just like your mother. She always thought the best of them. Even when I assured her I'd seen it all before, back in Nen Kimiin."

"Nen Kimiin is a *very* different place," Piria said.

"Politics is the same, everywhere, Pestle," Kialla returned, making what almost seemed an unconscious step forward to scrutinise Piria's face, her ears, her hair. It was uncomfortable and Piria stiffened a little before — to her relief — the woman stepped off, again. "Amazing, how alike you look, now," she said. "Of course, her hair came down past her shoulders, later on, but when we met, it was short, like yours..."

A short silence fell as the trio stood there in the kitchen, and Piria noticed Kialla start fidgeting with her teacup before the woman cleared her throat. "You said there was a break-in at the museum?"

"Yes."

"And Kabonn...is he alright?"

Now it was Akteron's turn to cock an eyebrow.

"He's fine," Piria replied. "Other than being slightly

traumatised by the loss of his three relics. We've been checking in with him. In fact, we have another meeting this morning. In an hour or so."

"You know the curator personally, Ms. Nooma?" Akteron asked.

"Oh, goodness, yes. We were an item, cycles ago. I'd often help his team clean up newly acquired artefacts. His methods were so outdated. They were still using brushes and rubber bulbs when I stepped in. Imagine! In this span and cycle! Luckily I was able to show them what use pulvichemy could be." Kialla smiled and put her teacup down. "Anyway. Good. Good that you're helping. Oh, the poor man, I feel for him. Losing something like that...for him, it'd be like losing a hand."

"Three hands," Piria said, realising at once how stupid that smart remark sounded. "But, actually his artefacts are not why we're here. Not directly, at least."

"Oh? Go on..."

"Well," Piria began, leaning against the kitchen bench. "I know it was a while ago, now. Around three cycles, I think. But I wondered if you could tell me what happened with that last round of research I sent you for review?"

"Last round of research..." Kialla's eyes flicked to the bench-top as she tried to recall. "Last round...remind me of the title? Or the abstract?"

"'*A potential new, non-destructive softening-paste and its applications in jewel-crafting,*' or something similar," Piria said, unable to recall the exact wording. "It was the only paper I never heard back from you about. I thought it might have been lost in your pile, perhaps?"

Kialla winced. "No, no...it's not in the pile."

Piria watched the woman take a breath, as if she were preparing to lift the next sentence. "I think I should preface this by telling you that I was not entirely in my right mind, when your envelope arrived. Firstly, I had just lost Serotonin."

Akteron looked to Piria and began opening his mouth but she held up a hand to him.

"I'm sorry, I didn't know."

Kialla nodded. "Yes. Poor little thing caught a kind of bird-flu and at his age, well-...but no matter, I've got Dopamine, now." She flashed a weak smile. "Anyway, atop that, that very same span, the educaria decided to terminate my residence as a professor."

"Wait, what? They *fired* you?"

"Mmm. Oh, I fought it," Kialla replied coolly. "I kicked up so much sand I thought I'd bury the whole institution. Students protested on my behalf. Other professors stepped in to defend me. Even Kabonn tried to lend a helping voice. But it all came to nothing. In the end I had to pack up. And during that nightmare I still had to carry on with my research." She shook her head. "I simply didn't have time to review your work and by the time the silt settled, I was in no state to do so. Over time, I eventually forgot about it. I do apologise, really, I do."

"What was their reasoning, though? To let you go? If you don't mind my asking," Akteron asked.

Kialla looked to him. "Oh, there are some political issues which the Seat would rather prominent professors keep silent about. But I've always been rather politically minded and was... less than silent."

"Still," Piria said, "that isn't the end, is it?"

"No." Kialla sighed. "And now comes the worst part. You see, I know where I put your papers. They were with all the other submissions, set aside and awaiting review. And then...goodness, I should have written to you, but I was in such a state after my door was kicked down..."

Akteron straightened. "Excuse me?"

"You were *robbed*?" Piria echoed. "Here? In the centre of town?"

"Yes," Kialla confirmed, nodding towards the small study

across the living room, inside which a small lantern was flickering, perhaps from some early morning reading. "About three cycles ago, as it happens. The thief took most of my jewellery, not that I had much, and all of my cutlery. Then he turned his sights on my workroom, where, as you've no doubt gathered, he nabbed that stack, including your research."

CHAPTER SEVENTEEN
TYROLI BOMBALLION

"Right," Piria said, kneeling in Kialla's workroom and studying the dusty floorboards where a pile of research had stood, three cycles before.

A good deal larger than the sitting room, the workroom had shelves along every wall and a gigantic table filling the centre, but was easy enough for Piria to navigate, as she had copied the layout for her own lab.

"So, we're talking a formidable stack of paper," Piria said. "And the thief took the lot?"

Behind her, Kialla leaned on the doorframe and spectated.

"Mmm. Yours and others'. And a good deal of my own," she replied, nodding towards her desk. "Scoundrel even took my writ of passage for Nen Kimiin. Not that I've the mind to return there, really. All the same, it's an awful nuisance and I'm still not sure why he did it."

"It does sound strange," Akteron agreed. "If he were just looking to make an easy profit, papers and cutlery weren't exactly the best choices."

"Oh, research *can* fetch a fine price if sold to the right party," Kialla added with a skeptical head bob, "but one has to know what they've gotten their hands on, first. They figured he might also try to ransom the research back to me, but that never happened. *My* conclusion was, he noticed the different names on all the papers, realised they were all experimental and unverified formulae, and found hawking them unworthy of his time."

"And when you say 'they'..." Akteron began.

"Oh, I notified the Bureau at once, of course," Kialla replied. "Political disagreements aside, it's the only bunch one can really trust to handle matters like this."

"And they came and checked the scene right after it happened?" Piria asked.

"As soon as I came home and realised what I was seeing, I sent a runner," Kialla replied. "Bureau was here within the hour."

"So, you weren't at home, during the actual break-in?"

"No, no. It was still early evening and I'd been out suppering in Subuur Street with an old colleague. It happened around final bell, they think."

"That is very bold," Akteron noted. He had been carefully inspecting Kialla's work-desk, hands running over the edges and making efforts not to disturb anything, Piria wasn't certain why. Probably out of the reverent fear Piria herself had instilled in him for The Cave, because Kialla certainly hadn't just left things as they were after the theft, three cycles ago.

"And what was the Bureau's conclusion?" Akteron asked, straightening to note the windowless walls and rub some dust between his fingers. "Were they able to petition a vision of the theft?"

"Yes," Kialla replied, "the vision-window was still open. We saw enough, despite one hiccough. An agent with an odd name... what was it-...*Traxer?* Yes, that was it. Well, his Sharak decided to form the man in the vision out of brick dust. As you can imagine, it's difficult to see what someone's fingers are pinching when everything is just a swirling, red jumble. But they did get a rough description. Very heavy-set. And tall. About your height," she nodded to Akteron. "Still, the lead official was so unimpressed, he gave Traxer a good dressing down right there in the-...*oh,* not you, too." Akteron had cracked a small, sympathetic grin. "What is it about this fellow that makes everyone so damned happy?"

"Apologies, Ms. Nooma. It's just that you reminded me how confusing the Bureau's terminology is. '*Traxer*' isn't a name. It's a position. A traxer is an agent responsible for petitioning visions at a crime-scene. Comes from *tracking* or *tracing*. Usually, it's an agent trained in specificity and with a strong welding."

"Oh," Kialla started. "I see. I had wondered what sparked the snickering each time I offered him anything. The Bureau team sounded like a bunch of cachaks."

"And after the petition, what then?" Piria re-routed from the distraction, rising at last from her crouch. "Did the Bureau discover anything of any use?"

"Last I heard, they were '*still working on it.*'" Kialla gave an incredulous huff. "That was two cycles ago."

"They didn't find *anything?*" Akteron asked.

She shook her head. "Apart from the most obvious clues, no. They realised the door had been kicked down by virtue of its hinges being ripped from the frame and boot marks in the wood...but it was never a very solid thing, I admit. I rectified that with the replacement. Let's see...oh yes, and they also tried to identify the footprints that had been stomped through the house. With no luck." Kialla paused, a curious look crossing her face. "Oh...though, oddly enough, now that I recall it all, there was something I noticed when I returned home. It had faded by the time the Bureau arrived but I remember a distinct, lingering odour in the air. Lanoor, I believe."

"Lanoor?" Piria said, suddenly narrowing her eyes. "As in, lanoor cologne?"

"Mmm. That's what I thought, at the time. I know it sounds strange."

"Actually...no. That doesn't sound strange. It sounds probable."

"Ri?" Akteron said, turning to her. "I'm not following."

"Who's the only person you can think of with that physical description? As tall as you but thicker. Who not only has an interest in pulvichemy, but routinely *douses* himself in lanoor cologne?"

"Oh, *pfaff*," he said. "I know you can't stand the guy, but to suggest that he stole your research...that he was involved in the museum business? That just doesn't feel right."

"*Feeling* has nothing to do with it..." Piria replied, perhaps a little too forcefully, for Akteron fell silent. An awkward breath then passed before Piria turned to where those papers had sat.

"Sure. It might be a bung-lead," she said, "but it's definitely worth paying him a visit. I mean, the facts suggest my formula was used in this theft, and lo-and-behold, the person Kialla just described would have every reason to get his gritty claws on some new research."

Akteron didn't argue with that.

"Oh! You say your formula was *used?*" Kialla now asked, a twinkle blooming in her eyes.

That sudden enthusiasm wasn't entirely unexpected, for Piria had realised long ago that to liven Kialla up, all one had to do was suggest a field-test of some research. The greying academic loved nothing more than seeing formulas and ideas leap from paper to application, and it was understandable. Piria loved the problems, the numbers and the possibilities, too, but nobody could deny it was always more rewarding to watch sparks fly...

"That's my conclusion at this point. Yes," Piria replied. "That with slight modification, my formula allowed the thief to enter the museum."

Kialla nodded and all too soon, a look of worry had replaced that momentary joy.

"What's wrong?"

"I never thought I'd say this," Kialla began, "but sometimes, I feel Torril is losing that shining, gold-gilded lustre they insist it still has. Sometimes, it's like I can *feel* things changing."

"From what we've seen these last two days, I can't disagree," Akteron said, rubbing his eyes and blinking as if to dispel a headache.

"We should go," Piria said. "Ki, thank you so much for the help. And don't worry about the research. Maybe we can track it down."

"Of course, my heart," Kialla said, eyeing Piria as if those hadn't truly been the words she'd wished to summon. A few seconds later, Piria crossed the room and brought her into an embrace.

———◼———

"I'm just not sure all of this feels right," Akteron repeated as he and Piria descended the front steps of Kialla's apartment, back into the quiet, morning streets. A startled pterenar darted away as they did, claws clacking on the cobblestones until it reached the refuge of a nearby park.

Piria merely hummed in response as they turned the next corner to see the Bureau of Security's white stone bulk appear, looming over the otherwise low cityscape. But that place could wait. There was another stop to make, first.

"Alright, what's the matter?" Akteron must have sensed her frustration. "Did I say something wrong?"

Piria hesitated, kicking a small seedpod aside. "Have you ever considered, that-..." No, that wasn't the way she wanted to phrase it. "I'm all for a leap, now and then. But don't you ever worry that *relying* on intuition is a bit of a risk? Don't you worry that you might end up wasting a bunch of time or worse, that you'll make some awful mistake?"

"That could happen whether I rely on intuition or not, couldn't it? Intuition is sometimes the only thread that can pull things together."

Piria stuck both hands into her donvul pockets.

"You think that's bollocks?"

"I don't think it's *bollocks*, exactly..."

He chuckled. "Ri, this isn't Nen Kimiin. I'm not the Triarchy. You're allowed to question me and the way I work." He brushed a tangled braid of hanging vines aside. "When we agreed to be partners in this, we each agreed to bring our own strengths to the game. And while it's true that I'm actually *all* strengths... brilliant detective and all that"— he proudly adjusted his donvul —"I trust *you*, as my *possible, maybe, almost,* intellectual equal, to tell me if I've screwed up, somewhere. So, let-loose."

His grin let her know he was only half serious, but Piria didn't laugh.

"I just worry that even when sufficient evidence presents itself, even when enough data has been collected to make a solid conclusion, you sometimes pass it off in favour of a feeling, because *'intuition'* tells you otherwise."

"Evidence and data *can* be misleading," he said with a shrug, "and we have gut feelings for a reason."

"Perhaps. Maybe." She shook her head. "Still, that doesn't mean you can't step back, now and then. That you can't take a good look at correlations? Draw a couple of calculated inferences, or plot out some likely trajectories from what you *know* is true?"

"Oh, absolutely not," Akteron agreed. "It sounds like a fine way to solve cases..."

"But...?"

"...it also sounds slow," he said, the pair crossing the main avenue and evading a few clattering coaches. "If there's one thing I've learned these last few cycles, it's that on every case, the culprit isn't your only enemy. The other enemy is time. If a petition-window closes, you're going into the investigation blind. Leave too *much* time, and that culprit might vanish...the case might *never* be solved." They peeled into a side-street which Piria knew would drop them amidst wagon-stalls and vendors, hawking every kind of curiosity. "If you don't grab that lead as soon as you see its tail poking out, you won't see it again. So, that's what I do."

"I think reaching out and grabbing a tail before you've seen the head is haphazard, at best..."

"Fair. But think about Bozik's, last night. Where would we have been if we hadn't looked to instinct, there? As unappealing as it might sound, often, there just isn't time to 'logic things out'. Sometimes, you just have to move."

The shouts of vendors permeated the air as the pair entered a colonnade of wagons whose awnings shaded spices, herbs, sauces, oils, and rare, exotic ingredients from the morning sun. A fragrant wall of scent hit them as they dodged around customers bearing baskets, all here at opening time for the best pickings.

"...but we wouldn't have known to move if I hadn't made the magamium connection," Piria countered, "by thinking things out."

"We'd still have seen the sparks." Akteron shrugged. "Look, I know you're no stranger to hunting for answers. To hacking and slashing through math and formula to get to them. It's totally valid in science. But wouldn't you say that most real-life situations don't need math?" He gestured to a stall as they passed by. "If you pick up a pair of gelsi-roots at the market, you don't have to say one root plus another equals two roots. Right? You just know."

"That's a terrible example. But I think what you mean to say is that running from sparks is an instinctual answer."

"That's what I meant."

"So. Perhaps the conclusion here is that this game needs both?"

"Sounds like a good compromise." He nodded, ducking some

hanging bowls filled with dates, then added, "...but also that instinct is better than math."

She gave an amused snort. "Seriously, Ro. We need to be careful, because if we do use instinct when we *should* have used math, that might lose us the game, entirely..."

At those words, the cheeky grin on Akteron's face faltered and Piria felt her point had been received.

"I'll keep it in mind."

Piria nodded, then spotting the large, red and white striped sail mounted atop the wagon she'd been searching for.

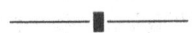

"Oh, ho! Look who we have, here," a deep, buttery voice announced, its top-heavy owner bouncing on his feet as Piria and Akteron approached through a gap in the crowd.

Tyroli Bomballion stood before his wagon, cheeks rouged, that voluminous, almost enviable goatee and curled moustache presiding over a thin-lipped smile. And...*beaks in the night,* even a good ten paces away, Piria was hit by a punch of lanoor cologne.

"Now, remember," Akteron whispered as two stall-goers passed in front of them, "don't let him get to you...stay in control."

Piria merely grunted.

It hadn't been hard to locate the oaf. Amidst the otherwise subdued-colours of Spicepot Alley's parade of stalls, Tyroli's cried out like a brigaree at dawn. Fitting, really, for it had always seemed that instead of luring buyers by virtue of the quality or rarity of his offerings, the man's strategy was to shock and stun. To deafen or dazzle or-...*scent* people into a sale.

"I did wonder when you might admit defeat and defer to my

superiority," he rumbled operatically as the two neared his awning — also red and white, to match the sail. "But tell me, why did it take so long? It was obvious, even two span ago when you set up that sorry excuse for a stall, that you could not hope to best me at this business. You had no truly interesting powders, no allure, no *flair* and thus, no customers. It is a cruel reality that, in life, a lack of talent is all it takes for dreams to turn to dust."

"Perhaps this marketplace just wasn't for me," she replied lightly eyeing the rows of common powders, some in large flasks, some in phials, all filling the backboard of the stall.

Below these, in turn, was a sign which cried, *'TYROLI'S MARVELLOUS CREATIONS!'* above a procession of jars, each filled with coloured formulae.

"It felt a little cold here, after I was accused of being a swindler," she went on, leaning to inspect one. "After word mysteriously spread through the market that I had stolen your mixtures and was passing them off as my own."

"A damning accusation, to be sure!" Tyroli said, his face falling with exaggerated sympathy. "But the truth does have a way of worming itself out of the woodwork, does it not?"

"It does." Piria turned to look the man in his glittering, green eyes. "Including the truth that bad things seem to happen to *any* competing pulchivist who sets up shop, here. Odd, that another stall owner told me you'd loosened their wagon-wheels, or that you'd had market permits issued so that stalls get placed behind trees. That others' powders mysteriously grow damp and moldy..." She gave him a look up and down. "Perhaps we can add 'sabotage' to the reasons dreams turn to dust, then."

"I am *highly* offended that you were taken by such scandalous nonsense, madame!" The man brought a hand to his heart as if injured. "But come, *come.* Let us dispense with our past grievances. You are clearly here for one of my *marvellous creations*, are you not? To see what a truly masterful pulvichist is capable of accomplishing? Perhaps a powder to cure aggression?"

"I'd happily buy one to cure dishonesty."

A passing customer cocked her head at that and Tyroli's face flashed annoyance, his jovial veneer cracking. "If you are interested in *nothing*," he said in a low growl, "then move on. I have business, here."

"Oh, I am interested in something. I'm just not sure what your price will be."

"Try me..."

Another customer wandered up to the stall and Tyroli brushed down his bright, red vest, eyeing the man and clearly preparing a greeting, though his lips remained drawn into a flat line.

"Alright," Piria said. "Does the name Kialla Nooma Kasbri ring any bells?"

"No. I've never heard that name," he replied, eyes on the newcomer.

"Oh, please." Piria leant into his gaze. "Three cycles ago, a small house on Kaluur Street? You were certainly there. The boot-marks in the door and your cologne were recorded by the Bureau of Security."

A flicker of doubt.

"How could *you* know what they're-..." he began, then changed tack. "And why would I have been at this house?"

"To steal a pile of research, is my hunch. Papers on experimental pulvichemical formulae?"

"Absurd!"

Puffing up, Tyroli pointed a thumb at his own chest. "I don't need to steal! I am a master! An *artisan*!"

Piria snorted, the gesture enough to send the man into a spluttering interjection.

"Preposterous! What insolence! To suggest that I would engage in such clandestine roguery..." He straightened and fixed her with a stare, those rouged cheeks taking on a more telling red. "*Hear this!* You are impugning my honour and I will not have it! I will not! Now, I demand you leave *this instant,* or I will be forced to-..."

"...to?"

"To-...make you!" Tyroli's eyes flicked around his stall. "I will cause your hair and nails to fall out! I will give you a permanent allergy! I will numb your feet!"

The customer was long gone by now, and Tyroli spun to his phials.

"Step away from those powders, Ty. You are not going to do any such thing," Piria told him.

"Oh, just watch me!" he replied, uncorking and tipping various powders into an empty beaker at the front of the table. "You will regret ever crossing Tyroli Bomballion!"

Piria merely crossed her arms, watching as a mixture was slapped together before them.

"I do love this market," she said, peering about as the merchant added one last green-coloured powder. "It has such strict rules though, doesn't it? Restrictions on everything. But the oddest thing about it is that much of it isn't enforced-...oh, you forgot to add a pinch of zicathium..."

"I forget nothing!" Tyroli spat, stopping that beaker at which point he began shaking it about.

Piria shrugged. "No guards walking about," she went on. "No real Bureau presence..."

"Last chance!" the man announced, turning to the pair. "This is your last chance! Back away or your sorry little lives are going to become oh so miserable. In three...two..."

Akteron did take a step backwards but Piria didn't budge.

"They also forgot to rig up petition tocsins," she said, right as Tyroli lifted the beaker and threw the mixture directly at her face.

The powder shot through the air like a dusty spear, its target unmissable. Yet just before it could connect, a glittering light flashed before Piria's nose. A large, yellow bubble formed about her head and a second later, Tyroli gave a panicked cry as that powder bounced backwards.

"*Gha!*" It struck his features and he spluttered, then let loose a mighty sneeze.

"Now, really," Piria said. "That wasn't very professional."

"What-...*blurcgh!* What did you just do-...you *attacked me!*"

Piria simply shook her head. "You attacked yourself by throwing powder into a defensive, repelling hex. But that's not important. What you should really be concerned with right now is that you didn't add zicathium to that mix, as I said."

Tyroli sneezed again as she continued.

"Which means instead of an eye-watering irritant powder, as you'd intended, you just inhaled a constriction formula. Over the course of the next few minutes, that's likely going to cause your vocal cords to tighten until they snap, and you lose that lovely voice of yours. Tragic, really."

"You have no idea what my intent was," Tyroli disagreed with a sniffle, dusting powder from his moustache. "I refrained from adding...*ACHOO!*...more zicathium in an attempt to keep the formula...less potent!"

Piria sighed. "Well, it's really very simple to prove who's right," she said. "Are your eyes watering? No. And if *I'm* right, the first symptoms will be shortness of breath. Then hoarseness. You really won't have much time after that until, you know. *TWANG!*" She spread her fingers to illustrated the point.

Tyroli snorted. "*Absolute* non−" His eyes then widened as the words came out, gravelled and husky. Worse, he realised he had started panting.

"*Oh, gods*, no! *Gods!*" he exclaimed, spinning to his display shelves and eyes darting about, presumably to determine which powders he'd need to reverse it. "I...I don't know how to cure it! *By Sevellan*, I don't *know!*"

"Relax," she told him. "I'll make the antidote if you give me answers. *Proper* answers. Tell me about Kialla, tell me what you did, that evening."

"Why-...you *rotten*–!" he began, wincing as an almost comedic rasp came out, instead of his usually smooth baritone. "*Ugh!* Alright! Alright, damn you! Maybe I broke in! Maybe I stole some papers!"

Piria stepped towards him. "Good start. Keep going. And let's drop the 'maybes'."

Behind Tyroli she could see Akteron glancing from the man's now-sweaty brow to Piria, and back again. He seemed pretty concerned — probably because he wasn't keen on witnessing someone's vocal cords snapping — and she could readily admit that things had taken a rather dramatic turn. But that wasn't her fault.

Tyroli, meanwhile, was taking a moment to recall that evening, pressing his eyes together. "There was nobody there..." he said soon enough. "The locale was supposed to be empty when I went in. And it was. And the room with the papers was unlocked! I found what I needed. I took it all. Whatever I could carry."

Akteron stepped forward. "Wait. What did you say? It was *supposed* to be empty?"

"Yes, you *villain*! I was told when to enter, just as I was told where to leave the documents, afterwards. I received my instructions on rolls of paper stuck in a tree trunk..."

"Hang on." Piria raised a hand. "You want us to believe you were *blackmailed* into stealing documents from an educaria professor? That you were *forced* to do it?"

"Yes, *damnit*! It's the truth, I swear...!" Tyroli's eyes were wild and almost tearing up. "I had no idea who she was. I still don't. I left the documents at a drop-off point. They never contacted me again! Now, *help me*!"

Akteron loosed a worried glance at her, but Piria merely paced.

"What was the leverage?" she asked. "What did they threaten you with?"

"No..." Now, the man clenched his jaw and shook his head. "I will never tell you that. It's my business, my business...you have no right!"

Piria let that sit a moment as she spun through possibilities. It was true enough, Tyroli's admission to the burglary sufficed without knowing what they'd threatened him with. And the list of possibilities there could be a stadia long.

"I think he's telling the truth, Ri," Akteron said.

"Yes, I am! Please! *Please*! My-...*ugh*, voice!" the man plead, adding a number of small coughs, perhaps for dramatic effect, though his voice *had* started to grate disconcertingly.

"Alright. Just one last thing, then," Piria said, poking Tyroli's keg-like midsection with a finger. "As of right now, you will stop selling that *ridiculous* 'speak to the dead' powder. Effective immediately. Understood? No more taking advantage of people's grief. It's evil."

"More crafty and dishonest," Akteron added.

"Yes..." Tyroli wheezed, panic overcoming him. "Yes, I'll stop! I promise!"

Slowly, and after eyeing him with some doubt, Piria gave a nod. Walking back over to the powder assortment and grabbing a couple of phials, she sprang into action, mixing their contents into an empty jar before dunking it into a nearby fountain. Then, she handed it to him.

"Drink."

Tyroli nodded and did so, gulping the mix with such relief she thought he might pass out.

Ugh. To her annoyance, she was actually feeling sympathy for the scoundrel.

"That's all, then," she told him, taking Akteron by the arm before the pair about-faced. "Thanks for the help. And think about your life choices, please."

Behind them, a whimper was the only reply as the two left the salesman at his stall, hands gingerly gripping at his throat. Piria even had the impression that he just might listen to that advice.

Moments later, winding back through the marketplace and surrounded by the usual clamour of business, Akteron turned to her.

"Sorry," he said.

"For what?"

"All that stuff about your logic not feeling right. I should trust it, by now." He shrugged. "But hey, now we know with certainty that your powder was used!"

Piria brightened. "We do. And no stress. The best way to test ideas is to have them shot at. If they're punctured, then you know there's a problem."

"I see." He considered that for a moment. "Well, speaking of questioning things, wasn't it a bit savage, interrogating him as his vocal cords were about to snap?"

She chortled. "Oh, they weren't going to *snap*...not at that dosage. At worst, he'll have a sore throat for a few days, which might actually shut him up for a while. I don't see anyone objecting to that."

The chuckle he let out held relief.

"I did tell you I'd stay in control."

"You did."

She glanced at the cobbles as they walked. "And you know, strange as it sounds, this little episode might just have re-invigorated my sense of enterprise."

"Oh?"

Piria nodded. "Sure. I mean, I have a feeling he's going to take a respite from drama for a little while. So, maybe it's time I tried selling some of my formulas again? People deserve honest products. *Real* powders, which do what they say they will. I don't want people to lose faith in pulvichemy."

Akteron smiled, and it was all Piria needed to know he agreed.

CHAPTER EIGHTEEN
THE THIEF

Kabonn's cheeks were still lucent and crimson with excitement — or perhaps from the stairwells to Riallo's office, it was hard to tell — as he bent to inspect Gildran's Collar.

As his sporadic chuckles and approving mutters filled the otherwise silent space, Piria found it odd how much this compact, energy-ball of a man reminded her of Tyroli. She'd never really considered the similarities before. But she certainly appreciated the differences. This one didn't seem to have a fraudulent bone in his body. His smiles were warm and kind, and the thought of him ever trying to threaten anyone was laughable.

Then, of course, there was the way he treated these relics.

She, Akteron and Riallo could only spectate as the curator reached out timidly towards the tarnished collar as if it were some wounded bird, poking, prodding, brushing and caressing. It went on until Akteron apparently tired of watching and turned to Riallo. "There wasn't a chance to speak to you earlier," he whispered. "But last night at the firth...my ingot belt..." Gesturing to his waist, the inconspicuous, empty space was clear.

"Not stolen, I hope?" Riallo replied.

"No, it's safely at the bottom of the ocean, now. Though I imagine some paperwork will still be required..."

"Ah. Well." Riallo gave an accepting sigh. "You know how much I love dealing with the Bureau of Charge...but don't fret, I'll have a replacement arranged the moment this meeting concludes. *If* it ever concludes." Raising his eyebrows, he then pivoted. "How is it looking, curator?"

"Yes, yes. Well, I can see it's been given a bath," Kabonn replied, "and I just hope there's no remaining salt or corrosion will ruin the wondrous detailing!"

"Yes, apologies for that," Akteron began. "As we said, circumstance didn't provide any drier options."

"And we gave instructions for the Bureau to rinse it thoroughly," Piria added. "I hope that halted further damage?"

"Oh, of course it did! You two," Kabonn said, smiling as he continued his inspections. "You marvellous two! Don't think for a moment that I hold you responsible for this! Goodness, no. I cannot express how relieved I am to have it here before my eyes, once again." He stood to rest his hands on his stomach. "And let us not forget that at the end of the day, any damage that befalls an item like this only adds to its remarkable story, does it not?"

Piria found that an interesting take.

"Yes, indeed." Kabonn continued, that grin pushing his reddened cheeks into shining balls. "What a sensational adventure this collar has seen! And I hope you don't mind me adding all that you've said to its record...?"

"AARK! Off the record!" a bird squawked from the open window.

Akteron ignored it. "Of course not."

Riallo turned to reach into that ceramic pot on his desk.

"It's just a pity we couldn't have apprehended the seller. That Bozik fellow," he murmured, spreading a handful of seeds across the sill for his feathered guests. "I'd like to have caught a glimpse of his oily mug, at least. Better still to have nabbed him. That would have provided a little more closure."

Piria watched Akteron shift a little at that, and quietly cleared her throat.

The pair had retold the story to their coordinating officer without giving away the fact that Bozik had been within a lick of the Bureau at the end, and had been allowed to walk free. They'd simply said that in the confusion before and after the explosion, they weren't sure what had happened to him. Not a *lie*, exactly. Perhaps they'd been speaking philosophically, after all? Bozik *had* seemed thoughtful on that pebbled beach. Even repentant, in a way. And surely, that whole evening would furnish ample reason for the lad to consider his choices, both past and future.

That's what Akteron seemed to have hoped, anyway.

Piria was simply glad they were all still alive.

"Alright," Kabonn then said. "Well, just for certainty's sake, let's have a closer inspection…"

Once more, as he'd done with the Bell of Tongues, the curator fished the small ring with its gemstone disc from his vest pocket and, and lowering it towards the collar, he peered through.

"…somewhere…on the side," he muttered, rotating the cloth under the collar to inspect all the angles. "Ah, there, *yes!* I can see the mark. Hmm. So, this is indeed the original."

"Curator," Piria then said, stepping forward, "would you allow me to take a look, too? I've been curious about this since that first inspection of the Bell."

"Oh, naturally! Be my guest."

Piria found the item lighter than it looked as she lowered it to peer through.

"You'll know it when you see it," Kabonn told her, just as a bright spot lit up through that disc. A small symbol, not overly intricate and drawn by hand, if Piria was not mistaken, with two lines of numbers ringing its outside.

"Ah," Piria grunted thoughtfully. "So, it's obacium…*ghost-glass*, right?" Then she straightened, handing the item back to the curator.

"Quite so." He gave her an impressed glance before winking. "Sometimes, it's the old methods which work best."

"Ghost-glass?" Akteron asked.

"Yes." The curator nodded to the implement. "It's not *really* glass, mind, but a type of gemstone with interesting refractive properties. These once enabled the sending of clandestine correspondence. Very popular indeed during the Descendency."

"In Kal Brior?"

"Which other Descendency do you know of?" Kabonn chuckled, and Akteron gave a sheepish mumble as the man went on. "Once that method became too widely known, however, the glasses lost their use, considered too insecure for any serious application. People overlook them and they're quite rare, nowadays. Thus, ironically, they have regained their utility."

"What do the numbers mean?" Piria nodded to the collar.

"Oh, various details are recorded. When the item was acquired, for example. By whom, and under which category it's stored..."

"Alright," Riallo said, clapping softly. "So, if that's confirmed, let's not forget, we still have one item loose in the wild."

"Yes, indeed!" Kabonn said, shaking himself and pocketing the glass. "And now that you two have once again shown what you're capable of, I must say, I am feeling most confident about the blade."

"I'm feeling confident, myself," Akteron began. "But please remember that while we will do our best, nothing is certain, Mr. Saal."

Kabonn chuckled. "I know it's hard to tell," he said, "but I'm an optimist, lad."

He then turned and made for the door, regarding Riallo over his shoulder as he opened it. "I await your next message, Mr. Palaman. Thank you for the update and fine work! Just marvellous, this institution!"

The door clicked shut behind him.

"Right," Riallo said, pushing off his desk and turning to the pair. For a moment, he looked to be gathering his thoughts. "I'm really hoping you two have a better lead on this guy, now. Because after your last description, my team in the Identificary helpfully narrowed a list of suspects down to...well, most of Torril. They need more."

"They're in luck, then," Piria replied, "because last night, we had a chance to quiz Bozik about just that. Turns out he got a much better look at the thief than the Doraun scout did. He even smelled the guy."

"Excellent!" Riallo gave a jubilant hop and withdrew his small notepad. "All that's got to help. So, fire at will, Ms. Kii."

"Alright. Well, Bozik's account agreed with the scout's, that the guy was average-looking. Strangely, though, his estimate of the thief's height differed. Bozik said the thief was shorter than Akteron."

"That might just be because Bozik is tall, himself, and the Doraun scout was shorter than you, Ri," Akteron said. "Perhaps their perspectives were a bit different."

"Fair point. And Bozik also added that the guy had a scar, around here, on his jaw." She gestured to the place Bozik had. "Oh, but then there's the interesting part." Standing, Piria stuck both hands in her donvul pockets. "Apparently he had a kind of stink about him, too. Bozik described it as being 'damp and sour.' Though what that could mean is in the fog, to me."

Riallo paused from scribbling to cock en eyebrow. "So, what... the guy was sweaty?"

Akteron shook his head. "That's not what Bozik said. He said it was a kind of smell he couldn't place, but not sweaty. And Bozik didn't seem one to speak loosely, I don't imagine him being careless with his words."

"I agree." Piria nodded, fingering a small phial in her pocket, the sensation of which caused her nose to scrunch up for she didn't recall putting a phial in there this morning...

"Alright, so that's it?" Riallo said, his pen hovering over that pad.

"For now," Akteron told him. "That's all we know. And I realise we're running out of time, so I hope it's helpful."

The coordinating officer made his customary, final dot, then set the pen down and rubbed his forehead. "We don't have much time, no. This morning we received another letter from our friendly ambassador and this time, he's threatening to stifle some crucial trade deals if we don't deliver. I suppose the phrase, 'not helping matters' isn't in his vernacular."

Akteron shook his head. "Pity Mikana landed such a rotten egg as her successor. There I was thinking ambassadors were supposed to be diplomatic..."

Removing the phial and holding it up, Piria suddenly remembered what it was. Those granules she'd collected from the rooftop in the Clutch. She'd completely forgotten about them after that first night, having spent all her time analysing the residue from the museum wall, and they'd sat in this garment's pocket the whole time.

"Oh, there is one last thing," Akteron mentioned. "This morning we made some progress on the break-in."

"You did?" Riallo asked, eyes widening. "Howso?"

Akteron turned to Piria. "Would you like to elaborate?"

Holding onto the phial, she proceeded to explain her discovery of the tunnelling powder and how she'd made the link to the kusamium residue. She explained the initial powder's tendency to make stone rubbery, and how one, little tweak changed its nature. That molecules shifted aside only to resettle.

All the while, she kept a wary watch over Riallo lest his expression take on that glazed-over look. It typically happened when she delved too deeply into scientific explanations. So, she kept things simple.

"The takeaway from all this is that I can conclude, with relative certainty, that my powder was used."

"It all makes for a convincing theory," Riallo said.

"*Hypothesis,*" she muttered back.

"Sure. Hypothesis. The point is, I'm convinced."

Piria nodded and, glancing down at her hand, gave a frustrated sigh.

"What's that?" Riallo asked.

"Well, with everything that's been happening, I haven't had a chance to analyse these granules, yet. And I'm sure they have something to tell us."

"What granules?"

Piria held the phial over to him. "We found them in Dagger's Clutch on that rooftop. Anomalous to the scene. Definitely introduced. We assumed the thief might have tracked them in on his shoes. They aren't gemstones as far as I can tell, but are probably organic because they're malleable."

Holding the phial into a splinter of morning sunlight, Riallo squinted at the contents as Akteron's eyes brightened. "Say," he said, "you couldn't send it over to chemistry for analysis now, could you? It'd probably save some time."

Popping the cork, Riallo gave the stuff a sniff.

"Hah," he chuckled. "No need to send it down there. Boy, does that take me back..."

Akteron stood from the sideboard. "You know what that is?"

Riallo gave a knowing smile. "I don't know if you're aware, but I started my career at the Bureau in the press. Got the job after growing up in my father's typesetting house. Useful background if you're after a job in a place that worships paper..."

"So, what is it?" Piria said, eyes flitting between the phial and Riallo's own.

"It's gum. Letter-gum. Used to make ink." He popped the cork back into the phial. "I'll never forget that smell."

"*To make ink...*" Akteron repeated quietly.

"Right," Riallo said, a realisation seeming to dawn within him.

Turning to his desk, he brandished the phial as if to illustrate his next point. "This gum. It's kind of sweet when it's raw. But when it's made into ink, that smell changes..." Taking and screwing the small cap off his small inkwell, he now held it up to take a new sniff, as if proving the point to himself. "In ink-form, it stinks, and like woodsmoke, if you're close to a lot of it for long enough, that stink seeps into everything. Your clothes. Your hair. Nowadays, ink-makers add incense and herbs to mask the stench, but before that, I'd describe it as damp. And sour."

Akteron stepped over to take a whiff, then Piria, and when the two looked up, again, they both found Riallo grinning.

"You two," he said. "You've got him. This is the piece we needed. Your thief must have been exposed to this smell for a good, long while for it to stick like that. So, my guess is he's hiding out in a warehouse. An ink manufactory, most likely. There's no other explanation for these granules, nor why he'd have that smell lingering around him."

"How many manufactories are there in Torril?" Piria asked.

Placing the phial and inkwell on his desk, Riallo now spun to a document cabinet on the back wall and rifled through a stack of folders, quickly fishing one out.

- SPAP -

It was a city map which he smoothed out on his desk and eyeing it, Piria and Akteron stepped closer.

Encircling a good portion of the city was a messy ellipse, with the museum as its apparent centre.

"The Identificary drew up this perimeter based on what we knew of the thief's movements and the timeframes we had," Riallo explained. "Now we can narrow the search right down, though, because if we're right, our target had to have made these movements from one of these factories." Taking a pencil from behind his ear, he pointed about the map with the tip, tapping on four points. "These are the four ink manufactories in Torril. But two of them are on the outskirts. Too far out..." He crossed off the two points outside the walls, then ran a finger back towards the centre of Torril. "That leaves two others, both in the inner-city. And luckily for us, I happen to know that *this* one no longer makes ink out of letter-gum. They use a synthetic compound, instead, which doesn't smell." Crossing it out, his fingertip finally fell onto the last location. "That leaves just one. Torril's main supplier. At least, it *was,* until just over a cycle ago when a fire forced the owner to close up. It's been abandoned, ever since." Riallo lifted his hands from the map and all three agents turned their eyes to each other.

"So?" Akteron said. "What are we standing around the desk for? That's the place! We need to get going–"

"Hold on. Just one-second," Riallo added, straightening again. "Listen, Akteron, I know you want this. But you can't just go barreling in there, alone. Not again. And *especially* not in that state." He met eyes with the young detective. "Let's also remember, this is now an arrest attempt. And *if* the guy is there, and *if* he does have this last relic, this is his turf. He could be armed, he might have set up wards..."

Akteron clenched his jaw, clearly desperate to move lest they miss a chance and Piria knew what he was feeling, but she also knew that now was not the time to make any rash decisions.

"I agree with Riallo," she said, turning to Akteron with a sympathetic shrug. "And who knows if the guy is alone, or not? Last night we miscalculated and almost lost more than the collar. If anything like that happens again..." She trailed off, looking him in the eyes. "We need backup on this."

The argument was logical enough. Akteron nodded.

"Let's do it," he said. "Though, I wonder if I could have a quick look at your requisitions cabinet, before we go?"

"...and I'm going to need to stop by the apartment," Piria added.

Riallo gave them both an uncertain look. "Sure, and sure... *after* I send word to get a team together. And my request would *then* be to prepare for another of Kabonn's hugs..."

CHAPTER NINETEEN
FOLLOW THE FISHERMAN

"Alright, listen up. I know we had no time to prep back at the Bureau, but that's emergency stings, for you. So, here's how this is going to work..."

Riallo's voice was low and controlled as he spoke to the semi-circle of grey-clad agents in a dead-ended street, just a brick-toss from the towering, blackened doors of what was once Torril's largest ink-manufactory.

Still, Piria honestly felt the officer needed to lay off the freshleaf for a while if the intensity in his eyes was anything to go by. Darting about like a skilithee in the sun, they betrayed an energy so potent Piria felt he might soon start emitting light and she had only seen him like this once before. Last night, at the Holes.

Clearly, then, Riallo's true passions didn't really lie with desks and paperwork...

Nearby at the end of the alley, Piria caught glimpses of the city basking in the glowing bustle of late afternoon, an almost constant stream of seller's carts clattering by in the main avenue while birds above roused themselves for the day's finale.

Closer to her, though, the blackened structures were lonely and silent as a Bureau briefing room at midnight. Only the occasional, stubborn sprig of greenery poking through various cracks, as if the jungle were testing this place for re-conquest.

"The city archives tried," Riallo was saying, "but turned up nothing on the floor-plans of the factory for us, which *is* a minor setback." He raised his hands as if to absolve himself. "Still, I know these older factories. They often follow older city regulations, which means they all have a similar layout, and *that* means if you listen closely, nobody will get lost, in there."

Brushing hair from her face, Piria surveyed Riallo's team as he explained their entry procedure and tried to recall what Akteron had told her.

They were eight, including Riallo, Akteron and herself, and all the others looked as if they'd had heard this speech every day of their lives. Perhaps they had. It didn't stop them from listening again with a quiet respect.

The two farthest from Piria, a young man and sharp-jawed woman, were hefty with scarred faces. These were the team's muscle, the *bullies*, and it didn't take more than a glance to verify that. They looked like they dusted their bowls of breakfast-rocks with iron doorknobs...

Good that they were on her side.

The next figure was the total opposite, a lithe whit of a woman whom Akteron had pointed out as the team's *nexer*, responsible for bringing things under control if they got out of hand. Ochre-coloured hair rolled into three buns, she stood tall in sleek, pliant-looking boots and fingerless gloves. And while her no-nonsense expression made Piria uncomfortable, the real source of discomfort was her attire, for ankle to neck, the woman was bound in flexible cloth, leaving her ingot-belt fully exposed.

Piria crinkled her nose at the sight. Still, Akteron had mentioned that this woman was also the operation's *springleg*, a role which would benefit from not having any jewellery or flowing garments to get in the way at a crucial moment. Springlegs *did* need to be nimble. Capable of crawling through gaps, vaulting obstacles, or scaling structures, so Piria decided practicality made the exposed belt acceptable enough.

"Also remember," Riallo's voice cut through her musings, "the structure is heavily fire-damaged. That means, don't move any rubble or lean on anything, including the walls. Stay sharp! We don't want the place coming down on us."

Piria noted that before turning her eyes to the seventh figure in their lineup — their *physician*. Piria hadn't needed Akteron's help to determine that role. Tall and rosy-cheeked, this woman carried a pair of the usual aid-bags fixed at her hips, the straps of which were slung from her shoulders to form an 'X' across her torso. Unremarkable, really.

Ah. But then there was the final member.

Piria cocked her head as she eyed him, a wrinkled antique of a human with a grey tuft of hair squashed under his flat-cap and a stubbled, off-centre jaw. It was skewed like a broken clamshell, and the way he stood — gripping a metal rod planted before him — whispered that he might *actually* have heard this speech a hundred times.

If Piria understood correctly, this feeble sod would be the first into the building. He was their *fisherman*–

"All making sense?" Akteron whispered and Piria jumped.

He chuckled and leaned closer, one hand inadvertently adjusting the ingot-belt Riallo had sourced for him as if he were bothered by the feeling of the unfamiliar metals. "Pre-sting jitters? I still get them sometimes. Don't worry, this is all just routine–"

"Hey," Riallo turned to him, keeping his voice low, "you're either part of this team, or you're not." He gestured to the semi-circle and Akteron nodded, stepping forward to join them.

Piria did the same, only to find Riallo holding up a hand to her. "Ms. Kii, you'll be hanging back with me, today."

"Oh. I was...hoping I could join the fisherman at the front, actually."

"What? No. No way I'm putting you at the head..." That official tone then gave way to a more personal one. "You have zero experience here, and he's the most vulnerable of the lot of us..."

The old man with the rod snickered.

"Put her with me," he argued, kipping his head towards the building. "She'll be fine. Look at this place. Nothin' to it. True 'nough, this is my four-hun'red and twenny-third run and I'm still here, ain't I?"

Both Riallo and Piria turned to regard him, Riallo's face showing some shock.

"What, you dun' keep count?" the fisherman asked.

"Deg, since when do you *speak*?" Riallo replied, and using the moment to her advantage, Piria cut in.

"Let me up front with Deg. I want to know how this works," she said. "I won't get in the way. I'll hang back. Really! You don't know how valuable this will be for my research."

A little voice inside Piria's head said this wasn't entirely honest, but she gently corked it. In truth, she was doubtful she'd gain anything except confirmation, because from what she'd seen and from what Akteron had told her in the half-cycle they'd been working together, it seemed most of the Bureau's methods were as musty and outdated as the wallpaper in Riallo's office. This one was probably no exception. Still, to be *sure*, she wanted to see it all. Up close and first-hand. The whole process.

The fisherman's job was simple. He was in charge of sweeping the area ahead of the team for dangerous wards, and using that metal rod of his, he'd be able to feel out anything with the potential to do damage.

It looked like slow, old technology, yet Piria suspected that a sufficiently well-timed comment to a well-chosen official could have the Bureau using a far more efficient, far more practical solution in the future. Namely, the one she'd come up with.

But she had to keep all that quiet. Any business proposal had to be well researched, after all. She had to be *sure*.

Riallo cleared his throat, apparently having decided.

"Fine. Fine," he said, turning back to his crew. "Let's do it, then. Standard formation. Deg, you and Ms. Kii will be taking the lead. Bullies next. Tis, you're after them." He nodded at the linen-wrapped springleg-slash-nexer, who also gave him a silent nod. "Akteron, at the rear, before me. Alright?"

Without another word, all then turned towards the charred warehouse doors.

———————■———————

A dampened, rhythmic dripping accompanied a low, moaning draught in the dank space, but Piria barely noticed either.

Her eyes were locked onto Deg's metal detector-rod as the man trod cautiously ahead, following a narrow corridor through rubble and under blackened support beams strewn about like a giant's matchstick set.

Clearly, this path had been cleared by someone, however, for outside it the destruction was total. Barrels and crates which had once been stacked now formed dark, organic-looking clumps of mouldering debris, while some of the huge workbenches still stood in position but looked intangible. As if their physical forms were absent and only shadow-duplicates remained.

It was cold. It was musty, and even the slivers of daylight which streamed through the sagging ceiling seemed to hold no heat. And lastly, as expected, an ever-present tang hung in the air, not unlike an old can of pickled dartfins. Piria had given a few disdainful sniffs as soon as they'd entered, sleeve held to her face for the first twenty paces before she realised it was better to breathe. Soon afterwards, she was surprised to find she'd already grown used to it. She just hoped it wouldn't seep into her clothes.

– KOOSH, KOOSH, KOOSH –

Each footstep pressed into a thick layer of ash and dirt, the occasional, rogue feather twirling in her wake, and just a few paces behind, Riallo's group were trailing in formation.

They had proved vigilant and well organised so far — even if they looked like the remnants of some failed sea-voyage — and Piria had to admit that this went against her initial impressions. The occasional glance over her shoulder had also revealed something remarkable. A kind of silent language they all spoke. Each of the team were able to coordinate and communicate with just a bent finger or brief hand gesture.

Keep low. Watch that hole in the floor. Avoid the shattered glass, there, they seemed to be saying, filling the room with silent conversation.

Ah. And then, there was Deg.

The crumpled codger plodded on without so much as blinking, it seemed. Focus sharp as glass, that rod extended before him, he didn't turn, didn't falter, didn't speak, just focused on the path through the rubble and every few paces, repeated a set of movements, the detector making a square in the air. Up, left, down, right. Then, he made a wide sweep from side to side.

Yes. Piria was alarmed at how accurate her suspicions had been.

The rod itself was nothing special. Near the handle, the shaft was dinged and rusted, and from the other end stuck two metal prongs, strung with what seemed a lattice of delicate metal strings like those of a musical instrument. These were undoubtedly sensitive, designed to send a vibration down the staff if any ward were encountered.

But...was this *really* how the Bureau handled situations like these?

Well. Piria *had* insisted she be placed up front, and now she had to try and look fascinated at what she was seeing. Especially with the whole darned team a mere four paces behind and scrutinising every movement.

Taking a quiet breath, she traced their trajectory around another mound of indiscernible, charred objects, then allowed her eyes to sweep upwards.

This place was bigger than she'd expected. Two storeys high, at least, the back wall far enough away that details faded into the blackness.

To one side, the warehouse seemed to have been partitioned by walls to create a series of open-ended areas, presumably where different processes of ink-making were carried out, but most of those dividing walls had crumbled. The entire other side of the place was one long stretch of doors. Likely storage rooms.

Before her, Deg started his cycle of movements again and Piria glanced back to see Akteron and Riallo in quiet discussion–

"Whadd'l tell ya?" Deg suddenly whispered, causing Piria to gasp.

He continued his steady plodding. "Nothing happenin' in here but dust." Then, he nodded to the floor. "*And* footsteps...look."

Following his gesture, Piria could just make them out. A faint series of depressions, spaced out regularly in the soot and leading off through the debris, ahead.

"That's what we're followin'," Deg muttered. "Someone's been here. And recently, by the looks of things. These'll lead us through any wards still in place. Though I'm pretty certain we're givin' this feller a little too much credit..."

Piria gave a thoughtful hum.

So, the thief might actually be here, then.

Taking a corner, the pair ducked a fallen piece of the ceiling lying above their path, and standing straight again, Piria whispered, "And what happens when we get to the end?"

"Ah, now," Deg whispered back, jiggling the rod as if it were giving him a problem. "When we get to the end, that's when–"

The flash was so sudden and the heat so strong that Piria was thrown backwards. Head striking something which caused a metallic taste in her mouth and a ringing to her ears, she found the world turning black for a moment, before opening her eyes to find strands of her hair on fire.

Deg didn't even have time to scream.

Not a heartbeat had passed before a pillar of flame had engulfed him and a roar flooded the silent warehouse. What followed was a deep groan of metal and the clupper of more brickwork collapsing.

Then, Piria felt hands dragging her backwards.

Muffled calls filled her ears over the sound of booms and crashes as she was slid away from the immediate danger, and all the while, the pillar of fire that was Deg raged furiously on the path, ahead.

———■———

"So, that's it," Riallo said, a hand kneading his forehead as he paced in a tight line. "Phantom wards? That's probably what burned the warehouse down in the first place..."

Piria blinked.

Since being dragged, she hadn't really been aware of her surroundings, neither awake nor asleep, as if she'd been floating somewhere else. But all at once, it was as if her mind had been switched back on and she found Akteron kneeling beside her, a hand on her shoulder.

"No wards should still be active, here..." Akteron told him. "Right? How are they still active? And *why*?"

"That's what phantom wards *are*, Mr. Uusei," Riallo answered impatiently. "Wards which linger long after they should have diffused...it's been more than a cycle since this place was destroyed, though. I didn't *really* expect any."

"Then why bring Deg along?" the muscular bully-woman piped up, her hands busy bandaging the physician's shoulder. Piria could now see that she was sitting propped up on the floor, clothing covered in blood and those previously rosy cheeks of hers, pale as moonlight.

Also...

Piria blinked again to make sure that wasn't just her blurry vision. But, no. There was a wicked shard of wood sticking clean through the physician's shoulder. Wide-eyed and panting in shallow breaths, the woman was definitely in shock.

Piria forced a deep breath of her own.

Pull yourself together.

"You know why, Mira," the male bully answered, voice steady. "Standard procedure. And if he hadn't been here, that would have been us..."

"That's not the real issue," the nexer, Tis, added through her teeth. "Who cares *why* the wards are still here? Our problem is *where* they are, and how we get Suria out, now..." She shot a pained glance at the physician.

Riallo nodded, that hand running over his head. "Yes. Right. Yes. This sting is over. Accident aside, that racket will have been heard half way to Kriolar and even if he *was* here, our target will have bolted, sure as the sky in Torril is green..."

With an exasperated breath, Akteron now looked to the smoking mass where Deg had stood, then at the ground beside Piria's legs. "*No*," he muttered, almost as if he didn't want to. "There has to be *something* here. We...I can't just leave. I'm sorry about Deg, I am...but I need some kind of proof, one way or the other. I need to know if he was here at all. We're so close!"

"Ro–" Piria began to talk him back from the delicate moment he was inadvertently stomping into, when Tis cut her off.

"You *what*?" the nexer said through her teeth. "You want to *explore*? To go wandering, totally blind, through a field of unseeable, deadly wards, all while Suria bleeds out? In the hopes that you'll find...what, *evidence*? All this guy's plans laid out on a table? A map to his next hideout? Don't be an imbecile."

"No way I'm risking it," the male bully agreed. "Without Deg we don't have a chance. All we know for certain is the way back out."

Bumping his shoulder, Mira, his partner then nodded back towards the warehouse entrance. "Actually," she said, "I wouldn't count on that."

Following that nod, Piria saw that the path back had been covered with newly fallen debris. Worse, it appeared the door they'd entered through was...*gone*. The structure around it had collapsed, erasing the portal completely. A tangled, metal roof truss stuck from the resulting brick-heap like some kind of cenotaph.

Silence lingered as each each person spun through the implications, before a waft of burning flesh made Piria dry-wretch.

Akteron rubbed her shoulder. "Still with us?" he asked, then apparently caught the same stench. "*Ugh-*...oh, *Sevellan*...that poor guy."

"I'm fine," Piria managed, trying to ignore it, and the fact that her tongue was tingling, for some reason.

"We could try to petition the entrance clear..." Tis suggested, again through her teeth. "We'd have enough charge if we teamed-up..."

Huh. It seemed she always spoke that way.

"The issue isn't the charge we'd need," Mira said back. "It's that I don't have a good enough welding for that."

"Neither do I," her partner added. "Prolly do more harm than good."

Above the team, a large support beam groaned menacingly.

"Look," Riallo said, trying to salvage focus. "That will take too much time and I don't think we can afford to linger, here.

There's nothing we can do for Deg and this whole place really might come down, now. Especially if we start shifting things about." He stepped on a little pyramid of bricks and craned his head. "I'm pretty certain there's a loading dock at the rear. If we can just get back there"— his eyes ran across the nearest wall — "perhaps through the side-rooms...that's our best bet of getting out."

"This doesn't fix the problem of the wards," Tis spoke up again.

"What would your alternative be?" Riallo replied with a hint of annoyance and just then, a brick pillar nearby toppled to the ground, throwing up a plume of dust.

Dismounting his perch, Riallo motioned towards it with one hand as if it proved his argument, and it was then that Piria remembered why she'd made that detour before they'd arrived. Why she'd insisted on stopping by her apartment, on the way to the warehouse.

In truth, she'd been intending to keep this for a quiet, isolated test if they found what they were looking for but-...well, that was looking unlikely, now.

"Riallo," she said, patting her donvul and locating the small phial.

Glancing down at her, Riallo's worried expression deepened. "Is she going to pass out?"

"No," Piria answered, withdrawing the vessel and thanking Zoilla it was still intact. "It's just that I might have a solution to the ward problem."

Piria saw her coordinating officer eyeing the phial as she gave a few more blinks to clear her vision. It didn't quite work. Any light which met her cornea still gave off a faint aura.

She patted Akteron's arm. "Help me up?"

He did so and pouring a sprinkling of powder into her palm, Piria closed it tight. With far more apprehension than she showed, she then walked back towards Deg's partially buried, smoking remains.

"Ms. Kii...?" Riallo's voice began.

She didn't answer.

Great Wastes...

The smell was almost unbearable and Piria couldn't bring herself to look down. She thus paused not far from where the fisherman had stood and, checking that Riallo was watching, held up her clenched fist.

Riallo was watching. Indeed, except for the physician, the entire group had their eyes on her.

Close to Deg as she would dare, Piria gave the best puff she could muster.

The powder dispersed on her breath and not a moment later, there was a sharp crackling sound. Lilac-coloured sparks lit up the dark air, drawing out a series of lines and casting a strange luminance about the smoking corridor before dispersing again.

Before they could fade, Piria noted which direction those lines ran...

"It's the same mix I used at official Gaussi's apartment, when we apprehended that textile thief," she explained over her shoulder. "It just showed us that there's still a very strong, very active fire protection ward, right here." She lowered her voice again. "If that wasn't already clear..."

Unable to stand near the stench of burnt flesh any longer, she retreated to the group to find Riallo's mouth open, trying to find words.

"You-...you had this the *whole time*?" Tis hissed. "You had that and you let Deg die? And Suria...you *dirty, two-faced*–"

"*Tisria!*" Riallo growled and raised a hand to her before things escalated. "Please."

When satisfied the nexer wouldn't pursue it, he lowered his finger. "We are *all* in shock, right now, but as horrible as that was, we are still a Security Bureau team. Maintain decorum. I'm sure Ms. Kii felt our fisherman had things under control." He nodded to Piria. "Right, Ms. Kii? Care to explain your thoughts? *Quickly?*"

Tis twisted her face into a new kind of snarl and clenched her fists, and those two gestures alone told Piria that her next words were very important, here. Above, the beam gave another low groan and a shower of dust cascaded to the floor, nearby.

"I didn't know...that the situation would be like this," she began, then cleared her throat to start over. "This powder wasn't meant for this purpose. It was just meant for a test and we don't have enough to dust the entire warehouse...nor even a path through it."

Tis slowly unclenched a fist, though her face remained furrowed in all the wrong places.

"So what good is it, then?" Mira, the bully woman, asked.

Reaching into the rubble, Piria pulled a blackened, wooden stick free and studied the end. Had the situation not been so grim, the irony of what she was about to do might have been amusing, but she felt only nausea as she spat on the end of that stick, then proceeded to pour a trickle of the precious, remaining powder onto it, careful to not to waste any.

Holding it out before her, she then studied the stick with an uncertain wince.

"Now, we have our own detector...like Deg's."

Nobody said a word, but their faces were more than enough to tell Piria what they were thinking.

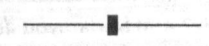

Piria paused for a moment, a tickle of sweat running down her forehead as she noticed that her shirt had become damp.

They'd taken an alternate route, following Riallo's suggestion that the back rooms might be the best way out, and left Deg's smoking remains behind.

Now, however, she was unsure.

Before them stood two, towering brick pillars, both supporting one another in a precarious, inverted *V.* Atop them, in turn, lay a trio of blackened support beams. A mere sneeze looked enough to topple the structure, yet the only way forward was to pass underneath.

But the odds of these things falling were slim, weren't they? The pillars had been here before the ward had gone off, after all, and they'd survived that blast, just fine...

Holding a breath, Piria forced her legs to move, one after the other, and kept her eyes before her, focus sharp as a shard of glass.

Treading through the murk, she made the same set of movements with that stick she held. Up, left, down, right, then a wide sweep, side to side. Then, she did it again.

Ignore the pillars. Ignore them. You have to make sure the way is clear.

A pace behind, Akteron was her shadow, the official formation broken, now. His presence was reassuring but Piria still felt an awful lump lodged in her chest.

If anything happened and Akteron was caught in that raging fire like Deg had been...

Deg. She couldn't help thinking that his death had been her fault. That if she had only stopped talking to him, he'd still be here. That if she hadn't distracted him, he'd have pulled back in time. Tis was right. She should have spoken up earlier. Told them about her powder–

Hey. She gritted her teeth. *No need for that...*

No. Through the distracting weight of her mistake, Piria reminded herself that right now, six other lives were depending on her.

So, she kept her eyes on the end of that stick, and began the cycle of movements again.

Nearby, Akteron cleared his throat softly, clearly trying not to startle her before he whispered, "Alright, Ri...which way?"

Piria paused again and raised her eyes to find they'd reached a fork. Both paths seemed to lead towards the back wall but the sun was too low to cast light into the place, now, and shadows crawled over everything. Still, at the end of one, she could just see a door.

"To the door?" Akteron asked.

"I'm not sure," Piria replied, glancing over her shoulder and trying to estimate where they had been when that ward had been triggered. Doing so, her eyes caught the two bullies carrying Suria.

"I'm not sure..."

"Why not?"

Piria turned back to him. "When the powder reacted to the ward, earlier, I checked the direction the lines ran..." She closed her eyes and tried to remember the hints of the invisible barrier she'd glimpsed. "It seemed to run perpendicular to our way, meaning it cut right across the warehouse."

If she was right, then Riallo's suggestion — that they make for the back and move through the storage rooms to reach the loading bay — would definitely prove a far safer bet than being out here in the main hall.

"No way the ward would stretch this far, though..." Akteron said, gesturing across the path. "It can't be that big..."

"That was my initial thought, too," Piria said. "But phantom wards behave oddly and it's been active a long time. It might have warped or shifted. Perhaps there are even more than one..."

Akteron frowned. "I really hope not."

A silence filled the air.

"Hey, is there a problem? We need to keep moving," Riallo's voice floated to them.

"All fine," Piria replied, staying where she was. "I just can't be sure."

Akteron lay a hand on her shoulder. "Ri," he said. "Look at me."

Slowly, she turned to meet his eyes.

"You have this. I know you do, but I can see you're looking for something to calculate and it's going to interfere with your dowsing." He nodded to the stick. "Just focus on what that's telling you. Let math and inferences take a back seat, now, and trust in feeling, because that's what's going to stop us from exploding...alright?"

Of all the things she had expected him to say, that hadn't been it. Still, perhaps he had a point.

"...alright."

Turning, she forced herself to step again. To move slowly for the door, Akteron falling in behind, and at every cautious tread, Piria watched the end of her stick for a flash or purple, wondering how quickly she'd have to drop it before she was set alight by a wall of furious flame.

Once or twice, as particles of powder fell from the tip she even swore they crackled alight as a draught took them off over the rubble.

Then, she noticed it.

A tingle. The slightest, lightest shudder of resistance and for just for a heartbeat, the stick's end lit up.

Piria held her breath.

"Ro..." she whispered, not daring to move.

"I'm here."

"In my pocket," she said, "take out the phial, and blow the last of the powder into the air before me, please."

Carefully, slowly, Akteron did as he was told.

As sweat prickled across her forehead, she heard him unstopping the vessel. Then, she saw him lifting his hand as she'd done earlier. Finally, with a forceful puff, Akteron sent her remaining powder into the warehouse's dank air.

The faintest crackling sound, and Piria gasped as a web of purple flashed before them.

The ward-lines were *right there*, a wall cutting diagonally across their path, and the stick was embedded in it, almost up to her hand.

Had she taken even one more step...

"What do I do?" she whispered, still not daring to budge.

Akteron didn't reply but, to her surprise, gave what sounded like an amused chuckle.

"What?" she whispered more urgently, eyes still locked onto the stick.

A moment later, Akteron's hands passed her head again and she realised he was reaching up towards the wards, a slender, metal object in hand.

"What are you-...."

– *KSIP! KSIP!* –

Piria watched as he snipped the air before her, lines of purple light pulsing outwards from the four blades before falling in showers of small sparks to the ground.

"The *decessors*," Riallo muttered from behind them. "So that's what you were-...I really did not give you permission to take those from my requisitions room! And the *paperwork*...!"

Akteron continued snipping away above Piria's stick. "You're really saying that *now*?"

Riallo quietened and Akteron stepped around his partner, not stopping the process. The occasional pulse of light from snipped bonds revealing that he was, in effect, slowly creating a doorway in the air before them.

"You're ok, Ri," he told her soon enough, and, laying a hand on hers, helped her lower that stick. "It's gone."

The movement caused her to exhale, but when she looked up again, only the dank warehouse confronted them, all traces of purple light gone.

Without warning, Akteron then stuck out a hand and waved it

about, drawing tense noises from the team and causing Piria's jaw to tighten. When nothing happened, he flashed her a feeble smile.

"That was stupid," was all she said.

It didn't take long for each one of the team to pass through Akteron's 'doorway,' the young detective standing in place to guide them, and when at last they were all through, Riallo called for a regroup.

"Well," he began. "We're alive. And I'm still betting on the way out being through these back chambers." He gestured to the wall beside them, where an open door stood like a slice of night, through which Akteron stepped, apparently to check for switches. Finding nothing, he turned back to the others.

"Worth a try..."

Their coordinating officer shook his head. "Even if this place was hooked up with modern lamps, they'd be useless, now. The city cut the lines a while ago." Lifting the hem of his donvul, he then exposed a few ingots. "No problem. I'll handle this one."

Taking a step backwards, the team allowed Riallo some space and the officer closed his eyes.

"Evenin', Helbaara..."

Piria raised her eyebrows. She'd never seen Riallo commune with his Sharak before and his informality was unexpected. Still, not a moment after the words left his lips, a cool draught seemed to descend around everyone and the soft, ambient sounds in the hall became slightly muffled.

Helbaara was listening.

"I need a good source of illumination. Something I can carry," Riallo said, looking around on the floor before Tisria stepped over, holding a bunch of cloth she'd apparently unravelled from one arm. Taking it, Riallo nodded thanks and then yanked a small metal chair leg from the rubble. He then wound the cloth around one end.

"How about making a torch out of this?" he said to the air.

"And I can offer...let's say one ingot?"

There was a pause, before the air shifted again, and suddenly, the chair-leg in Riallo's hand started to glow. Hissing a little, the officer flipped the object to hold it by the linen cloth as the metal apparently heated up.

He then gave an awkward huff.

"*Erm.* Excellent...thank you, Helbaara."

Despite the awful predicament they were still in, Piria surpressed a smile. That was just the way with Sharak, wasn't it? You never knew how they might choose to manifest a petition. It was the very reason specificity was so important.

Riallo then turned to the team. "Alright. Well, as we don't know how long my *chair-leg* will glow...let's move it."

"But what if we hit that ward, again?" one of the team asked. "Or there's another one?"

Riallo shrugged. "Nothing for it," he said. "We have no detector, and I believe we're out of powder, now."

Piria nodded, her expression grim. "We are. But it's highly unlikely that we'll hit that barrier again...I mean, what's the first thing you learn about wards in the Idmaion?"

When nobody answered, she then glanced through the doorway ahead and said, "That they can't run through solid objects. Right?"

There was a grumble of agreement before Mira piped up. "Can we at least petition to see if there are any more?"

Piria sighed. "What's the *second* thing you learn at the Idmaion?"

She was surprised to hear the male bully clearing his throat.

"That wards are only visible to the person who lays them," he said quietly.

"Right." Piria nodded, annoyed by the lack of rudimentary knowledge around her. Because...*seriously?* These were the basics!

More importantly, though, did *nobody* realise the truly,

revolutionary potential of her powder? Even after that demonstration? Surely, they weren't thinking clearly. Surely, they were all in shock.

"So, instead of wasting charge," she went on, "let's just hope the one Akteron snipped was an isolated instance…"

At that moment and still held aloft by the two bullies, the physician gave a weak moan which seemed to press the urgency of things. Bucking his head impatiently towards the doorway, Riallo entered and Piria followed, just behind. She was surprised to find the chair-leg bright enough to illuminate the whole space. And yet, there was something about that light…

Lumstone-lanterns were also commonly blue, but this glow Helbaara had conjured was…well, eerie. As if it didn't belong, here.

Tisria and the bullies were next, treading with caution and manoeuvring their patient between rows of shelves of blackened vats, dark-glass jars, and lumps of some congealed, oily looking substance. Despite clearly having been baked by the heat from the main warehouse, everything was still ordered and tidy, and the floor was mostly clear of litter and debris. Oddly, the faint aroma of calmwood also hung in the air.

Piria didn't complain. It was a very welcome smell, indeed.

"The shelving units must have held the roof up," Akteron noted, glancing to the metal constructions.

"Still, I'm praying that these storerooms are all connected," Riallo said. "If they're intact, we'll have a clear run right to the loading bay-…*ah*, there!"

Piria rounded the next column of shelves to see him pointing out a door, heavy and metal. And wide open.

Akteron huffed. "No good having fire-proof doors if you don't close them."

"*Thank…the Blue Robes…*" the physician muttered, and even though they were probably words spoken in delirium, Piria had to agree. She entered the next room with Riallo at her heels, his blue light first revealing a large, intact wooden crate.

"Another storeroom?" he asked.

"No," Piria muttered back, squinting. It wasn't a crate. It was a desk. And old, close-ended business desk. Shaking her head, she tried to make out the rest of the room. "It looks more like an office or–...*Nine Gods!*"

Her free hand shot to her mouth as Riallo and Akteron moved to her side, and all three gazed down at the floor.

Revealed in that pale, blue light was the body of a man, splayed out in a dark pool of what seemed his own blood. His mouth was ajar and his eyes were wide open, staring lifelessly into the darkness.

And beside his limp hand, glinting in the chair-leg's glow, lay the Umbral Blade.

CHAPTER TWENTY
ILLUMINATION

Only the sight of a dead body could squeeze a religious word out of Piria.

That was Akteron's first thought.

His second thought had been to make sure that this dead man was alone, and that no hidden killer was about to leap from the shadows and assail them, too. It quickly became apparent, however, that this man's only companions were silence and darkness.

A tense moment had then hung in the air as the rest of the crew filtered into the morbid space, and Tisria and the two bullies, Mira and Toldan, had petitioned more light. Though Mira's request had gone unanswered, the others' Sharak had responded swiftly and the room was now filled with warm illumination that seemed to beat back the unsettling blue glow of Riallo's chair-leg.

Still, there had been no time for them to gawk or mourn.

With Suria's life hanging in the balance, Tisria had hustled onwards through one, final doorway where, with muttered thanks to the divine, the damaged remains of the loading bay had come into view. The door and its rusted counterweight had been wrenched, with no small effort, out of its jammed position, and half the team were now in a coach and safely on the way to an infirmary.

Riallo's orders to them were that the Bureau dispatch a larger unit to secure the warehouse, after which a proper investigation could be carried out.

In the meantime, he, Piria and Akteron were left standing in the steady light emanating from a stone bowl and a twisted old boot, the body of an unknown man at their feet.

Akteron had only seen two dead bodies in his life before now — an odd fact which had bubbled into his mind as he stood and took in the scene. And despite the grisly nature of it all, he found himself unusually calm. Somehow, it all reminded him less of a crime scene and more of the renewal ceremonies he'd witnessed back in Kriolar. Those quiet, candlelit, morning gatherings, where godmouths prepared the deceased to meet Kendara and Kusenni, the divinities of diffusion and rebirth.

Of course, at renewal ceremonies, the bodies of those being prepared weren't lying on the ground, soaked in blood–

"About your height. About your weight." Piria cut into his musings.

"Beak-like nose. Large eyebrows, one burned-off. Scar on his jaw," Akteron added, standing from a crouch. "And look, he even has a wound on his upper arm, probably from that arrow. This is our guy."

Beside him, Riallo shook his head. "*Great Wastes.* This is grim stuff. Grim…"

Akteron had to agree. "It is. Taking his own life? That's rough as rocks, on its own. But doing that by stabbing yourself in the stomach?" Glancing at Piria, he saw her giving him that look. "Just a possibility," added. "It could be murder. We'll have to petition a vision to be certain."

"Let's wait for the other team to arrive before doing that," Riallo said. "And at any rate, it seems fair to say he died from blood-loss after that wound was made."

"Actually…I don't know about that." Stepping back, Piria made a couple of careful treads around the body, eyeing the floor, then the man's clothing. "Look, no signs of movement after he hit the ground. There's no smears on the floor near his arms or legs, or his head, for that matter. Which means he wasn't writhing about," she pointed to his donvul sleeve, the blood having soaked through only the bottom half. "I think...I think it's possible he was already dead when he fell."

"How could that be?" Riallo asked.

She shrugged. "I'm not sure. I'm no physician. But my guess is it depends on what he struck with the blade. I mean, stabbing anything in there would be pretty dire, and I know there's an important nerve around the heart which connects all the main organs to the brain...if he nicked that, I think it would have been over quickly."

Riallo gave a thoughtful hum.

Akteron, however, was still studying the man's vital fluid, which had spread a good arm's length from the body. "Does it seem like the blood is still wet, to you?"

Piria and Riallo both bent down to look.

"Hard to sa–" Piria began as Akteron pressed a finger into it. "Akteron! *Great Wastes*, that's disgusting."

"It *is* still wet," Akteron confirmed, rubbing, then pressing his fingers together. "Cold, of course...but it hasn't dried up, yet. That would mean this guy must have kicked-off recently, right?"

Piria's disgust at Akteron's blatant disregard of procedure now melted into curiosity. "How recently? Are we talking minutes? Hours?"

With a groan, she then drew a small handkerchief from her pocket and handed it over.

"Well, that shouldn't be too hard to guess," Riallo muttered. "I've seen my fair share of crime scenes and-...*hmm,* it's a relatively thick layer. It's also cool and slightly humid, in here." He cocked his head. "Off the cuff, I'd put the death at say, fifteen...maybe twenty hours ago?"

"Less than a day, then," Akteron added, spitting into the

fabric and using it to clean his fingers.

"*Ugh.* That was one of my favourites..." Piria muttered. "This is *just* like that time with the cachak guano."

"I did tell you"— Akteron pocketed the soiled kerchief absently —"that it would have washed right out. It only stains if you let it sit there for a whole day."

"It stained."

"Because you let it sit there for a whole day!"

Riallo muttered something and held up his hands. "Alright," he said. "Let's not forget there's another, major piece of all this staring us in the face."

Yes, of course.

A small silence fell as all three regarded the weapon lying in the pool of blood at their feet.

"The blade," Akteron muttered.

Taking Mira's glowing stone bowl, he knelt down beside the relic.

"Don't you dare touch that," Piria warned.

Akteron snorted. Then, he shifted his head to inspect the object from various angles. "So, this is it..."

Strange, that despite the gruesome setting and despite bearing a mantle of blood, the relic was...how could he put it? *Undiminished.* As if it wasn't really part of all this, but some foreign element, dropped amidst the horror.

No, that's precisely what it is, he corrected his own thought. And 'foreign' was the operative word...

Its metal handle was fashioned into a human figure, clad in some ancient style of dress, with an unusual headpiece resting gently, regally atop its elongated face. That face's features were barely distinguishable, smoothed into mere whispers of past detail, but they still gave an impression of serenity, even so.

The blade proper began at the figure's feet, and it was not completely smooth. Age had clearly left its gifts for all to see, notches and depressions marking that gleaming, black, glassy surface. Yet even they couldn't detract from its splendid form.

And it was for that reason, that like the bell, and like the collar, this object seemed all the more terrifying to Akteron.

"This is it," he repeated quietly.

Piria gave a nod and straightened. "Also, I think it's pretty obvious our thief was living here." She peered at a musty, stained mattress and blanket against the back wall. "There's foodstuffs in this box. He had a makeshift stove. Clothing and books in this chest, over here. And-...*eeuch*. I'm not going near that pile of...whatever *that* is, in the corner."

Riallo scratched his head, following her gestures. "How *could* anyone live here?"

"Well, it's certainly off the grid and that's what he must have wanted," Akteron replied.

Standing, at last, he then set the glowing bowl down on the large, wooden desk nearby, dusted his hands off, and stifled a strong desire to pluck the blade from where it lay.

To feel it, in hand...

Inspecting the desk, instead, he found most of its panels blackened and that two drawers out of its original four were missing. The two remaining drawers were intact, however, and sliding them open, Akteron could see vague shapes, inside.

"Riallo, could you hold up that bowl?"

Riallo did so.

"Candles...some quills...ink...a few sheets of paper," Akteron said, shifting things about, "and-...*huh*. It looks like...old catalogues?" He plucked one out. "Old museum catalogues."

"No chance that's a coincidence," Piria said, peering over his shoulder. "Maybe to research the objects before the theft?"

"Well, let's see," Akteron added, plucking one of the booklets out and holding it to the chair-leg's glow. "No, it can't be research. They're way too old. Look at this one, from 4,376..."

"Twelve cycles ago," she said.

"Hmm."

Rummaging in the drawer, Riallo plucked out three more booklets for him. "Similar to the first...all from the same, three cycle period."

"So, why in Aliru would this guy have kept these?" Piria asked. "He barely has two ingots to press together, yet he keeps some decade-old museum booklets?"

"Beats me." Akteron shrugged, placing the catalogues down on the desk. "Maybe they were already here in the desk when the guy found it. What's more important right now is the petition window, though." Turning back to the body, he then fingered his ingot-belt. "I know there's a team on the way but who knows when they'll arrive? This guy's been dead for a almost a day, already, and if we wait much longer, chances that we'll see anything useful are slim to none."

"You're right," Riallo said. "And I suppose you have two witnesses, enough for official verification. So, be my guest."

One of the things children learned very early on at the Idmaion was that petitioning was a game of uncertainty. Sure, those gifted with a solid welding saw that uncertainty reduced. Further, specificity — the careful phrasing of petitions to minimise ambiguity — certainly helped. But all that was irrelevant if, to begin with, there was no charge to offer one's Sharak.

It was to Akteron's dismay, then, when his fingers brushed over the newly acquired ingots at his waist to find that the charge he'd just been granted at the Bureau was more or less gone.

He'd checked a second time just to be sure, but when still no tingling, static buzz could be sensed, he finally removed the belt to inspect it closely.

The culprit was settled innocently between the others and identifiable only when removed. A silenced ingot.

Even in the dim light of the storeroom, Akteron could see the telltale, forking tendrils which crept over its surface, the tarnishing, pervasive blight known as *alkismia,* which plagued older ingots forged before the Bureau of Charge had implemented the new standard.

Like holes in a pipe, affected ingots like these leaked charge swiftly, then drew from neighbours until all were emptied.

– KTINGGTINGG –

Hissing a profanity, Akteron cast the bung-ingot into the darkness where it could do no more damage.

"I'm sorry, Akteron," Riallo told him, again. "This is on me. I didn't check them all before we left the Bureau. But if you say three of them are still full…"

"That's not going to be enough…" Akteron muttered.

Checking her own belt, Piria then looked up hopefully. "I still have half a belt. We can transfer."

"You know I'd offer you my remaining charge too," Riallo added, "but procedure…" He trailed off, and Akteron gave an understanding nod.

The Bureau's playbook required one member to keep at least that much charge in case of emergencies, and while Akteron did have an opinion on what, *exactly,* constituted an emergency, he didn't want to get embroiled in some inquiry about it.

"We'll be fine," he said simply.

Still, his brow remained creased.

From experience, he knew that petitioning a vision so late into the window was foolish, for the cost of such petitions increased almost exponentially the longer one waited. And that was assuming, of course, that the window hadn't already closed.

As he transferred the remaining charge from Piria's belt to his own and flipped curses about inside, therefore, Akteron could only hope that Kandaar was feeling charitable. But the truth was, he had no idea how Kandaar was feeling. And that led to the next complication.

It became apparent upon opening the communion, first with an odd, prickling sensation which ran down his neck. Then a cold draught which descended upon them, so strong it had actually rippled his donvul.

Kandaar was listening, and yet...Akteron realised at once that something wasn't as it should be.

"Kandaar, I kindly ask you to show us the space we now stand in," he spoke to the air, anyway, "as the man lying before us died. We wish to see his actions just prior to death, and the moment of his passing."

Stillness.

A stillness hung in the cool, musty room, almost as if Kandaar hadn't heard. Or perhaps he was considering the request?

Akteron cocked his head.

Faintly, he could discern a friction threading the air. Almost as if the room were charging with static. Out of nowhere, he was then met with a pulse. A gentle, but obvious pulse which rocked him on his feet.

He opened his eyes.

"What is it?" Riallo asked.

"The petition..." Akteron uttered. "Kandaar denied the petition."

"He *denied* it?"

"Because the window is closed?" Piria ventured.

"No," Akteron said, still in shock. "It's something else. He's-... it's as if he's irritated. Or worried. I can feel it."

That much was true. Yet, beneath those words Akteron also found a memory rearing its head. A memory of loneliness. Of abandonment. Of fear. It sank like a stone into his stomach and he could feel its weight. This was the first time Kandaar had refused a petition since that night, after all.

Akteron's hands started to tremble.

"So, ask again," Riallo suggested.

Akteron shook his head. He pushed the memory down and shook his hands. Tonight wasn't that night, and he couldn't let himself be carried away by the past...

Stepping back from the thief, he took a breath and let it out slowly, trying to expel the unwanted distraction, trying to focus.

Then, he surveyed the body anew.

His eyes traced over the musty, dirt-flecked clothing. The man's tousled, oily hair, and finally fell onto the blade, glinting where it lay in that slick of blood.

"Ri," he started, now clasping his hands together to steady them. "What was it Ikta told us...at the place?"

She stepped over to him. "About what?"

"About the blade. She said it was important that we retrieve it but also that it was jealous of death or something?"

Piria shook her head. "No, she said the Rootmind sensed a black stone 'of which *death* was covetous.'"

"Rootmind?" Riallo piped up.

"Irrelevant, though." Akteron ignored the officer. "That's just a poetic way of saying the blade was dangerous, right?" He bent down and without touching the blade, eyed it closely. "Why would death be covetous of it? Because it's so effective?"

"Who knows?" Piria said. "I think it's also clear that Ikta and Rama like a little drama, so reading into their wording too much might be a mistake." She gave a thoughtful hum. "What about the people of the Ularar, though? Where Kabonn said the blade supposedly came from...what are their beliefs?"

"Truthfully, I don't know much more about them than what I said, back in the Bureau," Akteron admitted.

"I don't see what this has to do with what's before us," Riallo said. "I think we need to try the petition again. Maybe you just had bad timing?"

Akteron grunted doubtfully, fearful that he was about to test

Kandaar's patience. But he was also keenly aware that Kandaar was their only hope of seeing what had happened, here.

"Alright," he relented with a sigh. "Let's try it one more time, then. But if he denies it now, there's not much I can do."

As before, the others stepped back to give him space.

Akteron didn't speak straight away. The words just didn't seem to come and after a moment of reflection, he realised that he couldn't shake that coldness.

He'd always been so certain of his bond with Kandaar. So confident, and apart from that one time, he had never doubted that his companion would answer when he called.

After all, they'd welded when Akteron was barely four — early enough that he had never really known anything else.

But now that he'd *remembered* what was buried, deep within, doubt was splitting that confidence down the centre. What would it be like, to lose what he'd always carried like an extra donvul about his shoulders? Something he'd always taken for granted?

The possibility was almost unbearable.

Riallo cleared his throat and the young agent realised he'd been staring at the thief's open-mouthed face.

"Sorry," he said, redirecting his gaze to the roof. "Ath viraan, Kandaar..."

The cold breeze descended, again. This time, it wasn't as strong.

"My respects. And I apologise for whatever I did to offend you. But I really need your assistance. I need to know what happened, here. Could you please show us the space we now stand in, as the man before us received the wound in his stomach? As he fell to the ground? I offer however many ingots you need in return for the clearest vision you can give us."

Akteron heard Riallo inhale at the open-handed offer and there was another small pause. Clenching his jaw, Akteron's fingertips pressed to the metal chips at his belt while another silence filled the room.

Then, a tingle. A buzzing from every charged ingot he had and with a gasp, he opened his eyes.

Great Wastes, Kandaar was taking the lot...*but thank Sevellan.*

"He accepted it," Piria said, watching Akteron's face.

Together with Riallo, they then hoisted the objects Tisria and Toldan's Sharak had imbued with light to brighten the room.

The vision began, at once. So swiftly, in fact, that Akteron, still awash with relief, didn't realise he'd neglected to specify something important until it was too late.

Kandaar wasn't to blame, either. How could he know that his choice would cause the three humans in that room to watch on helplessly, and with muted horror? The Sharak had simply selected the most practical, non-living matter available, after all...

"No..." Riallo uttered as, beneath the thief, that pool of blood began to ripple.

A moment later, and the entire mass was peeling off the floor, beginning to swirl about and swiftly forming into a human-shaped mass. A hollow, red shell, glinting dully in the soft lights.

It was disquieting, but Akteron couldn't ignore the likeness to the body before them. It was uncanny. Suddenly, in this dank room and before the three stood a dead man, monotone but complete with clothing and scraggly hair.

Face grim, this bloody effigy stood, rippling slightly, in his outstretched hands the Umbral Blade, unassuming and benign. As if it were being offered to someone.

This, simple gesture made it clear to Akteron — as it must have to the others — that the last few moments of this man's life were more complex than previously surmised, for in no way was this an act carried out in the throes of madness. Nor did it seem to be done in the black and twisting pain of despair.

Now, Akteron could also see the man's mouth moving. He was speaking, eyes staring keenly ahead and face, calm.

"Piria..." Akteron muttered, realising immediately what they were witnessing.

"It's a ritual," Piria muttered back. "Some kind of ritual. He's trying to petition, or incant..."

"In his final words?" Riallo followed. "Or perhaps it's an atonement? Asking the divinities for aid in his transition?"

Perhaps.

And as the three watched on, time seemed to slow and painful anticipation crept over them all. Each knew where this was heading for the result lay before them, yet none could really bring themselves to accept it until their eyes witnessed the act.

Calmly, the bloody-thief closed one palm around the blade's handle. Then the other. Speaking on, eyes staring ahead, he lowered the blade and rotated that tip towards his body, making no attempt to look down, nor to emote at all. It was as if he had sunk into some kind of stupor or trance, and Akteron wondered if he were merely carrying out rehearsed movements.

A mere heartbeat later and that notion was destroyed, for a hint of fear crossed the thief's face. He swallowed. He *was* aware, and more than that, he was afraid.

The blade rammed home.

Piria took Akteron's hand and his stomach lurched as the man somehow held the weapon in place in his own chest, face twisting in a silent scream. And next came something which Akteron felt would accompany him until the day he died, for while locked in the action of his own destruction, the man's pained expression vanished and a horrid, unnatural grin bloomed.

It lingered barely a heartbeat, until life apparently left him and the blade was let go, clattering to rest on the floor.

Expecting the bloody scene to play to its end, Akteron was astonished when Kandaar suddenly relinquished control of the vision, the figure dropping to slap heavily atop the real thief.

"*Gods!*" Riallo cried, raising a hand to shield his face. Piria gave a horrified cry, too, stepping back as blood spattered against them.

Akteron could only stare, wide-eyed at the now soaked corpse at their feet.

CHAPTER TWENTY ONE
COMMUNION

"Well, you did a fabulous job of mucking up each and every useable speck of evidence," Akteron heard Nomos woof.

Glancing over, he saw the man's thick moustache wiggle as he did that pouty thing he did whenever he was annoyed. "And Tis tells me you let those *contractors* lead on this one? Bit off more than you could all chew, I'd say. Should have left this one to the pros–"

"Nomos, not now," Riallo replied in a low voice. "None of this is their fault and I'm very aware of what went wrong."

"What went *wrong?* One agent *incinerated.* One half skewered? A building in ruins and a body covered in–"

"We handled tonight the only way we could," Riallo said firmly. "Listen, my team really got dragged through the swamp on this one, and your tasker insisted this was only a level-*two* manoeuvre. If we'd known..." His voice trailed off as he drew Nomos and his twitchy moustache away from where Piria and Akteron sat, their shoulders covered with thin blankets against the night's cool.

Akteron was relieved that he couldn't hear what followed but in truth, the discussion was only vaguely apparent on his periphery.

His gaze wandered back to the warehouse.

Security Bureau agents were swarming about it like a stinger's hive, the backup team having arrived in force.

They'd wasted no time setting up huge, barrel-like lumstone-lanterns to illuminate the blackened outsides of the building, directly after which, pairs of fisherman had spread out and swept over every inch of the structure, clearing it for the small army of grunts and specialists who filtered in at their heels.

It was impressive. There was a degree of polish here which made Riallo's own efforts seem scuffed and worn. Which made Akteron's seem amateurish. And, sitting on the low wall, at once nearby and set back from the activity, his eyes tracked it all with a sort of dull detachment, as if he were on the other side of steamed glass.

Perhaps it was shock, but a weight was tugging his thoughts downwards.

He just couldn't help thinking that if he'd been quicker, he might you have saved this lonely stranger's life. That if he'd just pushed Piria to analyse those granules sooner, he could have learned why the thief had done all this, in the first place. And might Deg also have been spared?

Of course, it was cruel and unjustified to shift the responsibility of both these men's deaths onto himself. Akteron knew that. Heck, he'd moved on this case like never before and done the best he could. Yet, even then, there was a wretched truth, staring up at him. Gnawing at his confidence. For it was clear that even his best hadn't been good enough, and...well, Bozik *had* said he was a terrible detective...

But they'd found the relic. That was something.

It had been everything, at the beginning. Back before this case had become complicated. Before it had shown him a malignant side of Torril, and a force of nature terrified of the future, and a side of him which seemed desperate for answers, even at the cost of others' wellbeing...

Akteron bit his lip as he turned his thoughts elsewhere.

There *was* still a thin ribbon of hope that some kind of silver lining could be wrenched from the ruins of all this. Answers. Not from the thief himself, of course. Nor from his Sharak, unwelded at his death. But if Akteron sniffed the right trails out...gathered enough strings, there was a chance that he and Kandaar could still cord the truth together.

Which led his mind, inexorably, to the problem of his Sharak.

Those had been no small hints, before and during the petition. His Sharak was definitely upset about something—

– *TUNGG...TUNGG...TUNGG...* –

The metallic echo of final bell began sounding through Torril's endless canopy and Akteron bit his lip too hard, tasting a metallic tang. Oddly, the taste provided a welcome distraction from his thoughts and he clung to the respite for a moment, before Piria's hand came to rest on his back.

"Now's probably not the time to mention how amazing Kandaar's vision was," she said quietly. "Despite the unconventional finale, of course..."

Akteron gave a huff and looked back to the loading bay ramp, down which the body of their thief was now being carried on a stretcher. For a moment Piria's eyes tracked it as well. Then, she removed the hand, stuffing it underneath her with the other as a kind of cushion.

"You know, you can't let this-..." she muttered, then paused, and Akteron could hear her breathing strangely. Pre-chewing words, perhaps, before they were uttered aloud.

"When I was fourteen," she began, anew, "Kovan was involved in an...*incident.*"

Akteron didn't shift his gaze from the two, yellow-robed physicians and their burden, but he found those words parting that mass enough for him to concentrate. Piria rarely discussed her father and when she did, he was referred to by name. As if he were some dusty acquaintance she'd rediscovered in her contact book. Questions on the topic were usually met with dismissive gestures or comments and Akteron had never tried to press for more.

"They didn't want people finding out or talking about it," she went on. "The Seat tried to make it disappear quickly afterwards and, well, I suppose they succeeded. But I still remember. On the day it happened, a small group somehow managed to get past Seat security and stormed his Bureau. Fanatics, riding on the waves the rebellion had stirred up down there..."

Piria spared him the obvious with that careful phrasing. Akteron didn't need to ask where these 'fanatics' had come from. They were Krio. Probably a scrappy, desperate band of youths, risking everything and hoping one last, futile attempt would somehow lead to a Seat ousting in Kriolar.

"When the runner arrived at home, mum spoke to him through the door so quietly she thought I wouldn't hear. She didn't want to worry me, but I knew it was bad just because of that. Later, I learned that the intruders had gone straight to Kovan's office. All of it was planned in advance. He and four other senior officials were taken hostage. Their aides were rounded up, and two of them...right in front of him..." Piria scrunched up her brow. "I can't imagine..."

As the two physicians carried the stretcher around the side of the warehouse and off towards the main avenue, Akteron found his eyes landing on Riallo, again. Nomos and his moustache had bounded off to woof at someone else, it seemed, and the coordinating officer was now being pestered by a bony-faced official with a notepad who appeared to be jotting down his every word.

"He was so different, afterwards," Piria continued. "He never used to question himself, before. He'd always had such confidence. But something like that. Something *that* awful..." Her voice became quiet as the memory played behind her eyes. "When I visited, I'd often find him just staring at the wall. At home, too. He was colder. Maybe he was wondering if it was his fault. Maybe he was thinking that there was something he could have done. Who knows?"

Akteron started slightly as Piria then took his hand and gave it a squeeze.

"All I know is that the look you were giving the cobblestones, just now...I remember it. And if those same thoughts are going through your head, know that they're not on your side. This is *not* your fault."

A short distance away, their thief's covered form was loaded into a coach at last, and the doors were clacked shut by the two physicians.

"I'm here. I'm on your side," Piria said, turning to look at her partner. "Alright? Don't forget that. Promise me you'll talk, if those thoughts get too loud..."

Akteron didn't realise he hadn't responded until Piria leant in front of his gaze.

"Hey, I kind of need an answer on this one..."

On her face was an uncertain smirk but Akteron noticed a barely disguised fear, underneath, too. A small, uncertain piece of Piria which he'd never seen.

Trying to smile back and failing, he instead found his arms encircling her, and rested his head on her shoulder.

"I didn't mean for our first big case together to be like this."

She leant her head on his. "It has certainly been an eye-opener."

"Usually, thefts are just thefts. Usually, they don't end in bodies."

"I know."

For a moment, they allowed the sounds of the early evening to surround them again. The clatter of the paramedic's coach rattling off down the main avenue. The mutterings of agents and officials deep in private conversations.

"*Great Wastes,*" Riallo's low voice broke the momentary peace too soon. He was speaking to his agents, though his eyes were fastened onto the bony-faced man a short distance away, currently sweeping up to Nomos to ensnare him in questions. "What a mess. What a darned mess. There's going to be one heck of a paper-stack for the Bureau to–" He paused as he caught his agent's haunted expression. "Akteron? Are you hurt?"

"He's a bit delicate," Piria replied.

"I'm just wondering how I cocked everything up so badly." Akteron added, eyeing the cobbles at his feet.

"Cocked up?" Giving a thoughtful grunt, Riallo lowered himself into a crouch. When Akteron didn't meet his eyes, he glanced back towards the warehouse, perhaps realising what his agent meant. "You didn't cock anything up, guys. Truly. Come on, this is life, not one of the Paramallion's storybooks! Real endings aren't tidy. They're unsatisfying. *Ugly*, even. You know that."

Taking a breath, Akteron allowed that to settle.

Perhaps. Perhaps that was true. When had a case ever had the outcome he'd expected? Sometimes there *were* bodies. That was simply the cold reality.

"None of us knew what we'd find, here," Riallo echoed the thought. "And honestly, I won't be forgetting that vision anytime soon. But try to look at the upside, you two solved this! And in record time, might I add. You identified the culprit, Kabonn will get his relics back, and in a couple of days, the museum can re-open. What's not to like about all that?"

Akteron gave a slow nod.

It was true, he supposed. It was a closed case, now. It was done.

Still, he couldn't shake that lingering sense of unease, and closing his eyes, all he found was the Umbral Blade, drifting about in the dark. That black, glassy point. And the figure, plunging it into his own stomach.

He opened his eyes again.

"Don't you find it all...*odd*, though?" he muttered. "Doesn't it seem—"

"Listen," Riallo cut him short, peering over his own shoulder. "Stelaron's making his rounds and getting statements from everyone. You two should split before he comes this way...not much more we can do tonight anyway, and I don't see a problem with giving your reports tomorrow, when you're not...you know, covered in blood."

"Sounds like a fine idea," Piria said, glancing towards the patchy crowd of Bureau specialists in their varying colours as if any one of them might pounce to start an interview. "When will you expect us?"

"Let's say first bell," Riallo told them as they both stood, then whispered. "I'll tell Stelaron you had to go get that bandage replaced at the infirmary. Now, scoot. Get out of here and get some sleep."

"Riallo," Akteron then managed, "could I ask you another favour?"

"What's that?"

Akteron gave Piria's hand one last squeeze and let it go. "Can you accompany Piria home? There's something I need to do."

Piria shot him an uncertain glance and Riallo seemed to mull that over, before giving a slow nod. "Sure. If that's alright with you, Ms. Kii?"

"Fine with me." She nodded, though the expression she levelled at Akteron said otherwise. "Are you sure you're—"

"I won't be long," he reassured them, already marching away from the warehouse, away from the main avenue, away from the glow of the gigantic gem-lamps and the Bureau agents drifting about.

He made instead towards the lanes that would lead him into a part of Torril which should be quiet at this time of night.

No point in letting things simmer.

It was time to talk.

———■———

Torril's Idma Temple and gardens lay inside a colossal, greenery-swathed ring-wall of ancient design, whose body of Torrilian white-stone had slowly blackened over the centuries. The patina gave the impression that the whole structure was made of shadow and oddly, it seemed the resident Sharavor were content to leave it so, for they tended to other parts of the temple with exhausting diligence.

Their efforts were clear in the manicured, garden paths which carved through the mossy ground, and the raised, cylindrical stone plinths atop which stones rested on groomed sand to mirror key celestial bodies and constellations.

Entering the ring via one of its three portals, Akteron glanced upwards to see a cloudless evening. The swathe of sky above the inner-gardens was one of the only places in Torril where the canopy didn't grow and through that aperture, the gems of the cosmos glittered brightly, suspended in a wash of dark violet. Another, white light on the surrounding treetops betrayed the coming of the moons.

Akteron had always found this place pleasant. Unlike the *Illudumes* — the Paramallion's gaudy and pompous places of worship — Idma Temples were restrained and sober. Nothing tried to convince visitors of their importance, and there was no need for the Sharavor to yammer from ornamented architecture or blare a series of chromatic horns.

Here, tropical plants with enormous, patterned leaves bobbed silently, and brilliant flowers scented the faint breaths of evening. Flaming torches spilled jittering discs of light onto thin, curving pathways, and all was quiet.

Akteron brushed a pair of fronds aside to cross one such path as a lithe young woman in light, gossamer garments came from the other direction.

"Ath laniin," she greeted with a bow.

Akteron nodded back, still following two fingers of light which led towards the tall, open doors of the ring's central structure, the Idma Temple itself, inside which the echo of tumbling water could already be heard.

He encountered no one else as he crossed the atrium and entered one of its numerous passages, branching out like petals from a flower's core. There was no token at the passage's entrance to tell him the Fell was occupied and no lantern to signal that one of the Sharavor was in there, either.

Soon, Akteron was standing quite alone in a small, rock-hewn chamber, gazing into a smooth, manmade waterfall. About an arm-span wide, the cascade's surface shimmered with the cool hues of lumstone-lanterns perched on the surrounding crags.

Akteron stretched his neck, then took a deep breath, preparing.

He couldn't recall the last time he'd visited this place but pushing all extraneous thoughts aside, he lowered himself to kneel on the small, padded floor-mat, then peered into the shimmering screen.

"Ath viraan, Kandaar."

Over the rumble, the words were barely audible.

Even so, the air swiftly cooled around him, and through the waterfall, *beyond* the waterfall, a form began to shimmer into view. It began only as a dark, nebulous blur but presently, four insect-like wings took shape, undulating slowly in the darkness. With the syrupy speed at which they moved, these could never hope to lift the creature aloft but then again, this creature did not seem to exist in the same space in which Akteron now knelt, and who knew which laws held sway, there?

The creature had no discernible head, but Akteron still felt the eyes upon him as the creature clarified further. The six, dark globes, each as large as one of Akteron's hands. They didn't seem cold nor malignant. Rather, their black, glittering depths betrayed a quiet, ponderous intelligence, each observing him from a ring-like arrangement around a fuzzy torso, from which slender limbs also extended. These fanned out on both sides to end in appendages, apparently designed more to grip, than to perform delicate tasks.

In no particular order, each of the six eyes blinked, and Kandaar was before him.

Akteron gave him a reverent nod. "I suppose we have something to sort out, don't we?"

The creatures eyes each seemed to fix on a different part of him.

"The last time I insulted you wasn't so long ago, really. At least it doesn't feel long ago. Though, I suppose four cycles have passed..." Sitting back on his haunches, he folded his hands together. "And now I've done it again, haven't I? You've never otherwise refused a petition."

The figure before Akteron simply loomed in the darkness. Akteron took a breath.

"So, tell me, Kandaar. How can I make it right? I assure you, even though these last few days may have been trying, I am not in the same place I was, then. Moreover..." he trailed off as wave passed over him. A static charge like a net being cast on his mind and body, before a scene from his childhood was pulled before his eyes.

An old instructor and one of Akteron's favourite tutors at the Idmaion now stood before him. With a single, raised finger, she issued a simple command which he'd never forgotten, and Akteron found the words coming to his lips almost on their own.

"Have faith, Akteron."

He gave a light sigh, eyeing his Sharak curiously.

"A bit ambiguous. In what?"

Another image, this time not so old, of Riallo setting a performance report on his desk. *"Don't think me cruel..."* the officer said, the words coming out of Akteron's mouth before, finally, an image of Piria floated to the surface. *"I am on your side...don't forget that,"* he muttered.

Kandaar allowed a moment to pass in silence and a prickle ran up Akteron's neck. A second later, his face flushed with heat and his hands jittered as a surge of anxiety overtook him.

Akteron knew it wasn't his own anxiety. Not really. The emotional reaction was Kandaar's doing and just one of the ways Sharak communicated, for while these beings didn't seem to have a problem understanding human speech, they had no spoken language of their own.

Unsurprising, really, since they also had no mouth, but it meant another method was needed.

The most common approach was to draw emotions, sensations and memories, cobbling together intended meaning in the mind of their human counterpart. To most people with a decent welding, this was familiar for it happened sometimes when making petitions. Still, in this Fell, the connection between human and Sharak was...*different.* Idma Temples, and these Fells, specifically, seemed to amplify communions. To intensify the interaction.

Right now, the message was clear.

"You're upset," Akteron said.

The air pulsed, slightly and he took a breath.

"I know, and again, I apologise–"

The air pulsed, again, and balancing on his haunches, that anxiety grew and Akteron had to press his hands into the ground to stop himself from shaking.

"I don't understand. What did I do? Or is it that we missed something? Something important, perhaps, back at the warehouse–...*ugh!*"

A powerful wall of static hit him, this one almost knocking him from his haunches.

"Nine Gods! Cut it *out*, would you?"

Silence.

Akteron furrowed his brow and gazed at that un-telling form, hovering before him. Serene. Unexpressive.

What in Sevellan's name...?

Kandaar had never reacted like this during past communions and with a frustrated huff, Akteron chewed his lip, again.

The rumble of the Fell continued, his Sharak's form floating placidly before him until Akteron recalled the memory-phrases he'd muttered.

"Oh. You're...looking for confirmation," he uttered. "Assurance, before you show me something. Is that it?"

A soft pulse met him, and Akteron looked into Kandaar's many eyes.

"Kandaar, of course I have faith," he replied, at last. "In you. In *us*. I've never doubted that. And I would never think you cruel–"

Before the last word had even left his lips, Akteron found himself in darkness, silent, and complete. The rumbling of the Fell was gone. It was just him and the endless black.

"Kandaar...?" he tried to say. Yet, no sound came. His voice was gone.

A few, tense heartbeats followed as the young man peered this way and that, finding nothing but cords of panic which started mixing with the unease Kandaar was still imparting.

Then, mercifully, the dark began to give way. Details began to appear in the blackness. Walls, mouldy with age, their wallpaper peeling, the wooden crossbeams between and above them sagging and brittle. A room in some tired building.

As if being viewed through water, its timbers and fixtures wavered and slowly took shape, and Akteron realised immediately what he was experiencing. Something profound. This was no mere flicker of imagery. Kandaar wasn't just prodding him to interpret things nor drawing on memories, emotions, or sensations. He had pulled Akteron *into* a scene.

Into a *memory*. And the strangest thing was, this memory wasn't Akteron's.

Quietly, swiftly, the last details emerged and unable to do more than turn his gaze about, the young man simply spectated.

Lining the back wall of the space were a series of tall, rectangular cavities. *Bookshelves*, he realised. And a window lay to one side of them, through which Akteron could discern a sign. Little blurs of light were streaming past it and could only have been raindrops, and as the wind rocked the sign back and forth, the mid-swing revealed its face, upon which was a carved image. A breaking wave.

Movement pulled Akteron's focus back into the room, where a misty, nebulous form was bobbing through the space. Halting in the centre, it slowly took shape as the rest of the scene had done and Akteron couldn't help feeling that his gaze, itself, was imparting clarity.

To prove it, he focused on the glimmer and was satisfied — then concerned — to find it sharpening into a slender but recognisable shape.

The Umbral Blade.

And bearing it was that faint, human-like mass of cloud. Seconds later, another mass materialised beside it. Then a third, lying on the ground.

The scene lurched with a sickening blur, Akteron's perception tumbling about as if inside a rolling barrel and when things settled again, the two standing forms had shifted position.

Clearly, Kandaar had moved events forward and now, Akteron found a disquieting familiarity greeting him.

There was that first figure, again. But now it bore the blade in its outstretched arms, the tip pointed towards its torso. And once again, that horrible moment of anticipation fell over Akteron, stretching out as it had done in that warehouse.

The wielder rammed that glimmering blade home.

This time, however, Akteron witnessed something new.

Something which that vision in the warehouse had not imparted. A flash of light as the blade met flesh, which rippled over the misty form of the wielder and then began to collapse to a point as the weapon fell to the floor.

Before the blade had even hit ground, however, Akteron was overcome by a sudden fatigue. Once again, it was not his own. But it was thick and heavy like an ocean wave and he knew somehow that when that wave hit, he would be pulled from this scene. That this vision would come to an end.

Before it could, he wrenched his eyes from the dissolving form and tried to regard the figure who had stepped backwards. The scene began to darken but, gaze locked upon the billowing mass, it slowly, slowly, seemed to refine itself.

Who are you? Akteron thought. *Hurry...*

Clothing appeared first. A long, straight garment crowned with a distinct, raised collar of large feathers. From this alone, Akteron could tell that a woman stood before him. Arms folded behind her back, short hair swept to one side, her head was tilted down, regarding the figure lying there. And though her face was unclear, if he had just a second or two more–

Blackness again.

Akteron felt a lurch as if he were being drawn backwards and that fatigue grew overwhelming, causing him to pant. He wasn't breathing enough air. He was suffocating!

"*Kandaar...!*" he tried to speak but still, no sound came.

Suddenly, he was looking at a street. At cobblestones, upon which a wet garment lay, water trickling from the sleeves, the fabric limp. Then the Doraun enclave, its trees on fire, the air a thick pall of smoke choking its caves. Now, a ship, foundering on a calm sea, slowly succumbing to water which crept over its deck. And before him was his own hand. His hand...within which lay the Umbral Blade! His fingers tightened around its handle. Then, Piria and Riallo stood before him, though Riallo was stumbling, falling, clutching at his throat and-...

And Piria was watching. She was holding a phial and *smiling—*

– FSHHHHHHHHH –

Akteron rocked backwards where he knelt on the floor of the Fell, the noise of the tumbling water hitting him like a sack of grain.

Sucking in a deep, blessed breath of damp air, he used one arm to steady himself, stars crawling before the gaze he turned on that sheet of water.

His Sharak was retreating into the smoothly tumbling cascade. Fading into the darkness whence he'd emerged.

"Wait..." Akteron groaned, lungs still straining. "Kandaar... wait–"

A slight shift in the air and the foreign form vanished.

No...

Akteron fell to all fours.

Just a few more seconds. A few more seconds and he'd have seen-...what, exactly? *Nine Gods*, what had he just witnessed? What had Kandaar just shown him? A nauseating heaviness hit his stomach as Piria's smile lingered. As that image of Riallo, clutching at his throat burned into his memory...

But he didn't have to accept that. It couldn't have meant anything. Just a blurred jumble of thought Kandaar must have shared accidentally as the vision ended.

And that figure. The figure who had used the blade, just as the thief had...

Akteron cursed, smacking the ground as a worried voice cut through the rumble of the Fell.

"Visitor, are you alright?" it said, and hands shook Akteron gently by the shoulders. "Visitor? Can you speak?"

Through deep breaths, Akteron nodded. "Fine. I'm fine. It's just...been...a big night."

Rocking back to his haunches again as the fatigue evaporated, he found a young man, fair-haired and clad in the light robes of a Sharavor, kneeling at his side.

"Undoubtedly. Undoubtedly," the young man said, voice awed. "It was-...you had an *insight*. Didn't you? You saw your Sharak's mind. It showed you a memory of its own?"

"Is that what happened?" Akteron managed.

"Oh, I don't doubt it! No, not at all. Though-...well, I have only read about them, and I've never *seen* anyone granted such a honour, before."

"*Honour*?" Akteron swallowed more slowly than he'd have liked. "It felt more like punishment."

"Oh, indeed not!" The young man laid a hand on his shoulder to steady him. "You misunderstand! The energy required for a Sharak to do what yours just did and the level of trust you have with him...both must be formidable. It is a he, isn't it? I couldn't help overhearing."

"You *listened*?" Akteron said.

"I didn't mean to..."

"Oh, tosh..." Akteron put a hand to his temple, for it had started aching under his bandage. "You saw my token, outside. Is that why you volunteered with the Sharavor? To spy on people's communions?"

"I regret to admit, that was one reason, yes." The young man's tone was not exactly regretful.

Akteron cocked an eyebrow. "Well, at least you're honest. Now get out."

"Yes, visitor."

The young man stood, bowed, and turned.

"Wait. Wait," Akteron then sighed. "I suppose I owe you *some* thanks for coming to assist. If I'd passed out, or if something worse had happened...what's your name, initiate?"

"Endil, visitor. Born under Kasbri."

Akteron nodded. "And you know about what I just saw? What my Sharak just did?"

The initiate glanced at the Fell. "There are books...in the Mysterion. They're forbidden to lower Sharavor but I've seen a few…"

Somehow, that didn't surprise Akteron.

"We don't understand how it works properly," he went on, "but it's surmised that Sharak have a relationship with time different to ours. That's why visions and time are interwoven. You probably know that petitioning them…the visions projected into *our* space…that they grow more expensive as the window closes?"

"As time between the event and the viewing of the event increases? Sure."

The Sharavor nodded. "Well, pulling your consciousness into *their* space? That's a whole other story. We don't know where Sharak get that charge"— he shrugged —"but they certainly don't do it on a whim."

Akteron made a swift pass over his ingots with one hand. "He didn't take any charge."

"Like I said. They don't get it from their human."

Akteron turned that over. "So, Kandaar pulled my consciousness…into his space?"

Endil nodded. "Kifvarna, one of the fontvow elders, was the first to document it. It was he who named them *insights,* and from what I saw, your experience matched his writings. You were communing normally, then you got all blurry-eyed and started babbling, and then you kind of collapsed, and the air between you and the Fell kind of…rippled."

Akteron turned his eyes to the Fell and its indifferent cascade.

"Just so you know, though," Endil added, "you probably won't hear from him for a time, now. It's possible that it injures them. Kifvarna didn't know, either. All he knows is, they go away for a while after they do this."

"What? *Injured*?" Akteron almost coughed. "They *go away*? Is he-…when will he be back?"

A shrug.

"Well…" Akteron muttered, standing, again. "That's just

great. First my ingot belt, now this..."

"But didn't he show you anything? Surely, you gained something from the vision!"

"Sure," Akteron grunted. "I got my headache back."

He didn't deem it wise to divulge details of his personal communion with this nosy kid. And that comment rang true, Akteron's head felt like he'd shaken a block of metal about in there.

"Odd," Endil then said thoughtfully. "When Kifvarna's Sharak, Goneel, did the same thing, it was because the elder had forgotten to take his daily dose of greyroot. He died later that-..." He started as Akteron entered the light for the first time. "*Nine Gods!* You're covered in blood!"

"Huh?"

Akteron raised a hand as if to check the spot the young man was staring before lowering it, again. He'd forgotten about the spattering of blood on his face and clothes, and supposed the reddened bandage over his nose didn't help matters, either. "Oh. No, it was a-...thing. Never mind. I have to go." He pointed towards the door and Endil stepped aside.

"Should I fetch the Stonewarden...?" the youth muttered, eyes lingering upon on the bloodstained garments.

"No. Actually, it would be best if you didn't tell anyone about this. I need you to keep it to yourself, alright?" Akteron fixed the young man with a stare of his own. "And know that if you don't, my Sharak has a habit of cursing others with bad luck..."

The threat was about as hollow as Akteron's boot, but who knew what Sharak were really capable of? That vision had raised a new series of unsettling possibilities.

"What kind of bad luck?" Endil almost whispered, his eyes glittering.

Oh, for the love of Sevellan...

Why did he have to cross paths with the most irreverent Sharavor in the whole stinking temple, tonight?

"Just…*ugh*," Akteron put a hand to his head, again. "Keep quiet and I won't tell the elders you were spying. Maybe I'll even tell you all about the vision, next time I'm here."

That perked Endil up. "Truly said? Then it's a deal!" He placed a palm on his forehead to seal the promise, and Akteron reluctantly did the same.

"Good," he grunted. "Now, tell me, are there any shipping equipment vendors around here…on a second storey? Or perhaps a bookseller?"

Endil's confusion was justified.

"Thought that unlikely," Akteron grumbled, and left the Fell.

CHAPTER TWENTY TWO
THE LIE

Akteron was walking.

He'd been walking since the Idma Temple and while his mind had refused to stop spinning off down dark avenues, he himself stuck to Torril's main thoroughfares.

Soft, lumstone street lanterns lit the way like wardens in the dark, seeming to guide him onwards, though they failed to illuminate all that he wished to see most.

The flashes Kandaar had shared shouldn't have been his priority. They were too nebulous and the possibilities they represented, too exhausting to tackle right now.

Still, he couldn't help fixating on that woman with the feathered collar. The woman who'd stepped backwards and allowed someone to stab themselves, a mere arm's length away...

Why hadn't she stopped him, or her? Why hadn't she intervened?

The guesses were plentiful. Perhaps she'd been instructed not to intervene? Or perhaps she'd known it would be useless to try? Or...perhaps *she'd told* the figure to make that thrust?

And what about the third form, lying still on the floor, which hadn't moved through the whole vision...

Akteron shivered despite the evening's mild stillness.

The only real way to break through all this was to find that shadowy stranger, a task which felt almost as likely as Torril's

THE TORRIL CITY MYSTERION

birdlife tweeting their evening din in Kal Brioran stage-harmonies. That woman could be anywhere by now and there was no shortage of feathered collars in this city.

It was about as cold as a lead could get.

...or was it?

Turning a corner and ducking a low-hanging branch, he recalled the room from the vision — the walls stuffed with shelves and the wave-emblazoned sign out the window — and by the time he looked up again, a familiar setting was greeting him. The lower end of the Molten Quarter, its foundries and workshops dark in the evening's silence.

He made another lap of the neighbourhood.

The intent was to calm the furore in his mind but it had little effect apart from diverting his attention, and as blocks came and went a second time, he found himself thinking of Piria.

It was no secret that Akteron was coming to rely on her presence. That voice of reason she possessed was exactly what he needed to counterbalance his own, often unfettered musings, and he could always count on a refreshing viewpoint when she was around.

He just wished she'd been there at the Idma Temple. That somehow, she'd been able to dive into Kandaar's vision alongside him. What would *she* have made of it all, through that cool, analytical lens of hers?

Submerged in thought, he entered Copperbelly Snicket and lay two fingers upon the lockstone. The front door clicked open. He trod the stairs automatically, not fully aware of where he was until seeing the single, lumstone lantern glowing innocently on the living room table and beside it, a letter.

Akteron plucked it up to find Piria's handwriting neatly running edge to edge.

Ro, didn't know when you'd be home and didn't want to be alone, tonight. Have gone to Kialla's if you need me. See you at Riallo's office tomorrow morning. Sleep well.

- Ri

Akteron set it down and ignored the call from the sofa, not daring to sit on it in his grimy, bloody state. He fetched and downed a glass of water, switched off the lantern, and went to wash off the day. To do *that* required the removal of his bandage, at last, and peeling it back he hissed as fire-like pain bloomed over his face.

Still, once the pressure was removed, there was relief.

Scrubbing the dressing to a pale brown — about as clean as it would get — he wrung it out, flicked it over his shoulder, and splashed his face. Swabbing the remaining, dried blood from his skin with a damp towel, he then finally leant towards his purple-cheeked reflection.

No. It wasn't some trick of the light...his nose was definitely off-kilter.

Well, nothing to be done about that, now. The pain was sharp as a scorolid sting at the smallest touch. The only option was to wait for a physician to deal with it, tomorrow.

Akteron wandered to the kitchen.

Sleep was looking increasingly unlikely but breakfast...well, he could prepare breakfast and knead away some of his cares. Cooking always did that.

Setting out a cutting board, some bowls, a wooden spoon and roller, he therefore set to task mixing his famed muffin-dough, the recipe for which was a closely guarded family secret. While they baked and filled the house with a sweet, bready aroma, he washed and puréed the berries, setting aside the finished coulis, then absent-mindedly took a knife and began cutting fruit. It was a careless move. The slices would brown before morning and would lose their crispness, but he was so distracted once he'd begun that he just kept going.

That is until mid-way through slicing a juicy pollom-fruit and watching liquid collect on the cutting board, when he froze.

"You shellbitten *idiot*," he muttered, "you blasted genius…"

———■———

Kabonn was bouncing on his feet, those little hands clasped before him as Riallo appeared from his small safe-room bearing a flat fabric bundle.

Setting it on the desk, the coordinating officer carefully unwrapped it to reveal the last of the museum's stolen artefacts.

"Oh, splendid! Magnificent!" Kabonn exclaimed with a clap, and Riallo stepped away, perhaps before he dizzied under the weight of adoration. "I see it's received new scratches…a couple of small nicks, but…oh, it remains sublime!"

"Yes, it's really something," Riallo added and to Akteron's surprise, there was no scepticism. Perhaps the harrowing spectacle he'd seen yesterday had manifested a genuine, newfound respect for this piece. "I had a specialist from the Bureau of Antiquities here before hours making sure it was properly cleaned before your inspection. I trust she's done an acceptable job?"

"Oh, exceptional," Kabonn replied, craning his head around the blade at every conceivable angle. "And I assume she used a pulvichemical mixture, seeing as…blood, and all that."

Riallo nodded.

The officer had already explained the story of the blade's recovery, how Akteron and Piria had tracked it down, the manner in which it had been found, and its last, awful act.

Rather than shocking or horrifying the curator, however, Akteron had found that familiar fascination crackling behind the man's eyes, just as it had done when they'd presented the collar and bell.

"With artefacts," Kabonn had remarked, *"it's all about story, without which no artefact can truly be appreciated."*

Akteron supposed that was true. Still, a story like this wasn't really what Kabonn wanted, was it? Surely, the horror of self-murder eclipsed the intrigue of antiquity or the whimsy of the blade's supposed mystical properties?

Turning the piece over, the curator removed the small circle of ghost-glass from his pocket and began his appraisal, passing it over the blade and handle. Akteron could hear Kabonn's mumbles from where he stood, leaning against the freshleaf-service.

"Indeed...this is the final, missing artefact!" the curator confirmed, straightening to address the trio. "But do tell me one thing, for I noticed you neglected to explain the most crucial component of your thrilling tale. Yes, indeed. Namely, who the culprit behind this dastardly caper *was*?"

"Ah." Clearly having expected this, Riallo walked behind his desk and retrieved a folder. "For this, it might be better if you take a seat, curator. I imagine it might come as a shock."

"Oh, my," That puckish flicker in Kabonn's eyes dimmed, and he refrained from sitting as Riallo unwound a small, string clasp and withdrew a flutter of papers from the folder.

"After our discovery at the warehouse last night, I spent some time in the Identificary," the officer explained. "I was there all night with two of my aides, but just before dawn, we finally found a match." He slapped the documents onto his desk so the three could see, and Akteron wandered over to take a look. "The man we found in the warehouse was a thirty-three cycle-old former academic. Sharak's name was Tarogaar."

Even at this scrap of information, Kabonn's expression sank.

"*Oh*," he muttered. "You don't mean-..."

Piria stepped over to guide the curator to that chair, after all.

"Tolann Vereii Nisbri," Riallo confirmed. "Previously an employee at the Torril City Museum."

Akteron and Piria exchanged a confused glance.

"...he wasn't just an employee," Kabonn elaborated, shaking his head. "He was assistant curator and had a bright future."

"...before the Whiteglove Scandal," Riallo prompted. "Before he was expelled from the museum community in disgrace."

"The Whiteglove what, now?" Akteron asked. "Slow down. I'm not following. Who is this guy?"

The curator simply nodded and in his eyes, Akteron could see an old pain resurfacing. "First of all," he said, "be a good fellow and pour me the strongest drink on that side-table."

Glancing to Riallo, who nodded, Akteron turned to fix a glass of a deep purple, finely aged Thundertip Kassoon he'd always been rather curious to try, himself.

"Anyone else?" he asked.

The other two declined and Akteron reminded himself that it wasn't even midday-bell...

Handing it over, the curator took a sip but refrained from settling into his chair, instead perching stiffly on the edge.

"So?" Akteron prompted again.

"I want it known, right from the start," Kabonn began anew, "that had I known in what manner this affair would end for Mr. Vereii, there is much I would have done differently. Yes, I knew that my being awarded the position had hurt him...but I never imagined it would end like this."

"And by 'the position' you mean the curatorship, correct?" Riallo asked.

Kabonn nodded. "Yes. Mr. Vereii had already been eying it for some cycles before I arrived and became the second assistant curator. Unusual, to have two, I agree, yet with the digs in Satholar and Ularar turning up relics left and right as they were back then, we had too much to do."

"So," Akteron said, "Tolann was your competitor?"

"Oh, goodness, no! We were the most civil of compatriots and had a great deal in common. Honestly, it was *before* I took the position that the worst problems began," Kabonn said. "Coming from the humble background he did, and with such a dismal welding, Mr. Vereii was-...how shall I put this...*desperate*. Desperate to fit in with a circle that was not his own, you see, thinking that would improve his professional and social standing. And he did succeed in infiltrating the glittering, upper echelons for a while. At a cost."

"So, you also knew about his addiction?" Riallo asked.

"Of course," Kabonn replied. "I had my suspicions right from the off, but I respected him and his achievements enough to keep that secret."

"What addiction?" Piria asked, as a realisation dawned in her eyes. "Oh. He was *lifting?*"

Riallo scanned his papers. "The physicians noted all the most severe symptoms. Blackened inner-ears, roots of his hair burned, optical nerves damaged almost to failure. Acute charge-poisoning. They estimated he had less than a tack left."

Kabonn nodded and Akteron clicked his tongue in sympathy.

Lifting was not uncommon for those with the weakest weldings. In ancient times, many had believed that weldings were a sign of intelligence and even now, though scientifically disproved, some stigmas seemed to cling too tough to dislodge.

Unfair as it was and though unlawful to do so, those cursed with flimsy links to their Sharak were often barred from certain positions and labelled 'flawed' or 'unfit' for many tasks. Many thus turned to an illegal, chemical solution, designed to wrench the aperture between human and Sharak a little wider, to improve the flow of communication. Yet, while one might see their welding strengthened for a time, the inevitable outcomes were addiction and degeneration.

Nature, it seemed, remained the sole decider of ability, and had no qualms punishing those who tried to sidestep its boundaries.

Akteron shifted uncomfortably.

"He was a remarkable young man, despite all that," Kabonn went on. "Honestly, the things he knew...the facts, the dates, the subtleties and the most obscure, foreign anecdotes. Mr. Vereii was certainly more suitable for the curatorship than I. It is true. I can admit that now, as then."

"Then, why didn't he receive it?"

"Therein lies the tragedy. You see, though I kept his secret in the strictest confidence, and I assure you, I did, others were not so gracious. Surely, you are aware that the *Bureau of Culture Toast* is the do of the cycle? Well, it was a somewhat outspoken professor who took it upon himself to reveal the details of Mr. Vereii's compulsion to all in attendance. A manoeuvre which, if you'll excuse my saying so, was one of exceptional bastardliness."

Taking another, somewhat larger sip, Kabonn shook his head. "It was this revelation which sparked the scandal to which you earlier referred, for an addiction such as Mr. Vereii's is not cheap, and regrettably, it was soon discovered that museum artefacts were being sold out of the storeroom to cover the expenses."

Peering across the room, Akteron saw that both Piria and Riallo were listening, grim faced.

"I had previously told Mr. Vereii that I would support him through his affliction, that I understood and would defend him, if need be. But then I was offered the position. In my excitement, and being too young, proud, and stupid to consider anything else, I took it. I didn't hesitate. I even held a party." He gave a light huff. "Well, I suppose you can see where this is heading. Once the scandal had come to light, it then fell to me to dismiss him publicly." His eyes were apparently seeing this moment as they stared into his almost empty glass. "The way he looked at me, that day. It was as if he'd lost his last friend. Many times over the ensuing cycles, I considered seeking him out. Expressing my profound regret. But no affliction is devoid of hazard to others, it seems, and cowardice is no exception..."

He let that sit, and for a moment only the muffled footsteps of staff in the halls outside filled the air.

"He was arrested after the scandal, right?" Piria asked.

"Right," Riallo replied, "but never punished for the thefts. In fact, he escaped before his trial."

"With help?"

Riallo shook his head. "Dumb luck. The escort forgot to lock the doors of his transport. It seems he's been living underground since then."

"Planning this theft? Does this make sense?"

"Well," Kabonn tilted his head. "Of anyone I know, Mr. Vereii did absolutely possess the skills and knowledge to carry out such a stunt. I don't doubt it for a moment. And I must say, there is some justice in it all."

"Justice? What do you mean?" Riallo asked.

"Clearly, he wished to disgrace me, at the end. And to that I say, fair play, lad. I do deserve it." A resolute look crossed Kabonn's face, and he set his glass down. "I took the curatorship at his expense, I betrayed him. And the weight has sat on my shoulders long enough." He then slapped one knee. "So, it's settled. After this exhibition, I shall make a statement. I will step down as curator and pass the mantle on to someone more deserving."

"Mr. Saal," Akteron said. "Let's not jump to such...decisive conclusions. Not just yet. We still can't be certain if this was revenge or if it was all done for another reason and I don't think punishing yourself is fair until we are."

Piria looked set to agree before Kabonn raised a hand.

"That's kind of you, both," he said, standing and brushing

down his vest. "But a story *will* break and the media will come to their own conclusions. To be honest, I've had a good run, and I couldn't bear being cast as a villain. I don't think I could stand it as long as he did." As he took a shaky breath, a familiar smile crossed his face. "I thank you. All of you, for your incredible efforts. You are a credit to your Bureau Ms. Kii, Mr. Uusei, Mr. Palaman...so, if I am no longer required?"

Glancing at Riallo, the officer gave a slow nod.

At that, the curator of the Torril City Museum made for the door. "I will be in touch about the relics' return to the museum. And I do hope you can all come to the exhibition. I'm sure it will be spectacular!"

– CATACK –

The door closed, and Akteron, Piria, and Riallo were left standing around the office in silence.

In turn, each one of them glanced at the empty glass, sitting on Riallo's low table.

"Well," Akteron said, "before we all get too close to that bottle of Thundertip Kassoon, ourselves, Piria, I assume you'd like to try out your powder?"

------■------

Riallo's safe-room was a small space tacked onto his office and accessible through a metal door. Inside, three huge cabinets filled the walls, one of which, Akteron knew, contained seized items related to ongoing investigations or which hadn't yet been claimed by the Bureau's processes and impounded.

He had only really received mumbled, evasive answers about the exact contents of the other two. But at his request and as per their agreement, Riallo had touched the lockstone and opened the first cabinet, allowing Piria to view the three treasures up close, one last time.

Outside their ceremonial, glass confines, Akteron had to admit that each relic looked pretty innocuous sitting on the officer's desk. Neither could he help feeling an attachment to them, even if it wasn't pleasant.

Riallo, on the other hand, still seemed to carry that new note of wary respect he'd found. And Piria regarded the pieces with a cool, calm intensity. A kind of patient determination which, to Akteron, always signalled that she was close to breaking one of her bigger questions open.

"There they are, Ms. Ki," Riallo said, stepping back and motioning with one hand, "be my guest."

Piria nodded.

The agreement she'd set upon starting her work for the Bureau was simple. It stated that at the end of applicable cases, she be allowed to test her powders, on the proviso they leave no physical or magickal trace, of course.

Riallo would never usually have granted such a request, but when Akteron had stepped in and been adamant that he would refrain from cooking Riallo that occasional and much vaunted mushroom casserole otherwise, the threat had been taken very seriously.

Now, well-prepared and with a twinkle in eye, Piria whipped a notepad and pencil from one donvul pocket, followed by a glass phial, a ruler, and a pair of standard, experimental gloves.

Topping off the kit, she retrieved a small stand, and as Akteron watched her affix the ruler on its side to point vertically, he suspected that under the cool patience, Piria had been itching to test whatever powder this was. Probably since they'd first set eyes on those smashed cases. Her hands *were* jittering slightly, after all.

Still, Piria didn't allow herself to rush.

Studying each of the objects carefully, perhaps in order to estimate their size or weight, she uncorked the phial, and deliberating on a good spot to sprinkle its contents, measured out some powder in to one, gloved hand.

"What are we watching, here?" asked Riallo.

"The reaction will be simple enough," Piria told him. "Upon contact, the mixture should create a spark-plume."

"...and this tells us, what?"

Reaching over, Piria dropped the powder onto the Bell of Tongues and pulled her hand clear as a small spiral of orange sparks crackled into the air, rising up alongside the ruler.

"*Around...1,900?*" she muttered, scrawling the results on that notepad as the plume faded. "Exactly what Kabonn said. A good sign."

Akteron now realised which powder this was, and also knew how many hours, days, span, cycles must have been behind it. Once again, Piria had put a little piece of her soul into its creation, as she always did, and the results were accordingly spectacular.

"You repurposed the rotten-food powder into a dating-powder..." he said.

Piria grinned but didn't answer until she'd finished jotting. "For now, it only reacts to metal. I have no idea what would be required for a reaction with stone." She then looked to Riallo. "The idea is that it picks up and reacts to a unique, residual signature left when the metal was smelted. Took me forever to locate."

Even Riallo raised his eyebrows. "Ms. Kii, this is really impressive."

"It's also very confidential, Mr. Palaman."

"Of course. My lips are sealed."

Next was Gildran's Collar, and Piria measured out her guesstimate more quickly.

"Each of these markings"— she nodded to the ruler — "represents a hundred cycles. Roughly. There's a growing margin of error the further back one goes, but it's negligible.

Plus or minus twenty, maybe thirty cycles." She dropped the powder and the crackling line extended into the air. "So... although the museum placard put this relic at around 2,300"— she squinted while tallying the number —"Kabonn might be interested to know that the collar is quite a lot older than that."

Akteron's eyes had been on the ruler too, before the plume faded. "Can that really be true? Cycle 1,400?"

Piria shrugged. "I need more samples to be sure *exactly* how accurate all this is. Plus, a list of all the elements that might interfere with the reaction. But I haven't had any results that have been wildly off, yet. I'd say it's a pretty good indicator."

"Amazing," Riallo's eyes were glinting with curiosity. "So, now, the blade."

"And lucky for us, the handle is metal," Piria added, measuring out a final dose of powder and releasing it onto the carefully worked design.

All three pairs of eyes watched as the plume of sparks zipped upwards, spiralling to the very top of the ruler, where it faded.

"Yikes," Piria said, eyes wide. "Well, Kabonn was certainly right about it being old. Cycle eight hundred, thereabouts. This thing has seen a lot."

"It sure has," Riallo agreed.

Beside them, however, Akteron had furrowed his brow.

"But like I said," Piria said, removing her gloves and stopping that phial, then putting it back in her pocket, "it might be off by forty cycles or so."

Riallo reached to take the cloth and bundle it back up, Akteron reached out to stop him.

"Wait a second. Before you take it away. Could I...test something, too?"

The man half sighed. "*You two* are bending the rules enough as it is. I can't have every agent-...*hey*! What are you doing?"

As he'd spoken, Akteron had reached into his fruit bowl and taken a particularly crisp looking eklon, setting it on the leather square Riallo habitually opened letters upon.

"Oh, no. *No, no*. I can't let you use the relic to make lunch! I'll get you a shiny new kitchen knife to celebrate closing the case, instead, how about that?"

Akteron made a calming gesture. "I just need a few seconds."

Giving a concerned groan, Riallo took a breath, held it, then exhaled, motioning to the relic. "Well, I can't deny I have been itching to try the blade out, myself. Just keep it quick."

Plucking the weapon from where it lay, Akteron found the handle cold, solid, and heavy in his grip. Despite the two bowed arms sticking out on each side, it also moulded nicely to his palm. Strange, to think that this item had passed through so many other hands, before his...

"What can you tell me..." he then muttered, lining the blade's edge up and setting it carefully upon the eklon.

And without so much as a suggestion of weight, it began to slice through. The fruit fell aside in two clean pieces and Akteron let out a small gasp.

"Great. Wonderful," Riallo commented, reaching his desk drawer and withdrawing a handkerchief. "So, that was fun. And nobody ever has to know we just did it. Now, if you please...?"

"I wasn't wrong," Akteron muttered, eyes lost in thought. "I understand."

"Huh?" Piria asked. "What do you understand?"

"All the pieces that didn't fit," Akteron said, setting the blade down. "All the things I couldn't make sense of..."

Stepping towards him and perhaps sensing his concern, Piria met his eyes. "What are you talking about?"

"It's been so easy, hasn't it?" he asked. "Retrieving all the relics? They were stolen, only to be jettisoned or sold off at obvious places. The bell was dropped and then *left* at Dagger's Clutch. Bozik was almost *given* the collar...the only one of the three that seems to have been stolen for a *reason* was the blade. And that's odd, isn't it? I mean, someone could knock themselves off with a frypan if they really wanted to. Using the Umbral Blade to do it is so complicated and unnecessary it raises a serious question."

Riallo bobbed his head. "I thought that part was simple enough," he countered. "Tolann was an artefact enthusiast, he knew about the blade and the museum's layout, he wanted to shame Kabonn, he was sick and wasn't going to last much longer. It all fits…"

"That's *precisely* the problem," Akteron replied. "Set the guy's motives aside for a moment. Step back. It's clear that even if this guy had the knowledge, the skills, the desire to pull this off, the theft took *resources* he definitely didn't have. You said it yourself, that tunnelling powder is ridiculously expensive to make, right?"

Piria nodded.

"Well, how did he do it, then? Because this guy was the very image of down-and-out," Akteron continued. "That means we have a hole. And no matter how I tried to spin things, I couldn't fill it with any good explanation until just now. Well, until last night, really."

"When you discovered…what?" Riallo prompted.

"That the whole caper. All of it was a distraction."

A small silence filled the room.

"We were so busy running about, so focused on retrieving the relics that we didn't give proper time to address the bigger question. The obvious question which the *how* and *why* inevitably led to…"

"You think Tolann had help?" Piria asked.

"That's part of it. Maybe. Or maybe he was used. I'm not sure. I'm only certain this wasn't done by him, alone."

"Gods," Riallo uttered. "Are you sure? How did we miss this?"

"It doesn't matter," Akteron continued. "Because we didn't miss the most important thing. I mean, I don't care what it's made of, no knife ever could remain this sharp after three thousand cycles…"

Both Piria and Riallo realised then what he meant, and all three of them turned to regard the Umbral Blade.

"It's a fake," Akteron said.

CHAPTER TWENTY THREE
CRACK! POW! KERSPLASH!

The implication of Akteron's words had barely landed as the tense silence was broken by one of the birds on Riallo's windowsill.

"AARK! It's a fake!" it mimicked, waggling its wings.

Riallo ignored it, and the three regarded that most ancient blade on the desk before them which, now, might not actually be so ancient, after all.

"Alright," he said, "but if that's true, then why didn't the dating powder give an anomalous date?"

"It did," Akteron replied, "the date was off."

"How can you be sure?"

"Because we know when the blade was supposed to have been made, 'under the converging moons in cycle five forty-two'. That's what Kabonn told us in the briefing, remember? So, even if your powder had an error margin of a hundred cycles, Ri, cycle eight-hundred it still a fair way from that date."

"Alright. But that means..." Riallo began, "you're saying someone replaced the real blade with another, identical looking blade, made around the same time?"

"Not necessarily." Piria picked up the thread for Akteron. "Consider that when painting forgers create fakes, they go to great lengths to use contemporaneous materials...materials sourced from as close to the original as possible." She glanced at the blade. "The same goes for making petition-moulded fakes. You need to begin with an object similar in form to the one you're looking to replicate, otherwise the results are too unpredictable." Hey eyebrows narrowed as she kept thinking aloud. "Then, yes, there's the problem of dating. Under a scope you can spot a recently made forgery easily enough because the patina, the corrosion patterns...they'd be absent. But using an object from a similar *date*? That's clever...it would baffle any conventional technique." She turned back to Akteron. "There's no reason to suppose that couldn't have been done, here."

"And if that's the case, then let's agree that whoever did this made a really, really good forgery," Akteron added, "I mean, this thing fooled Kabonn. Even the museum mark is there. It's not the *visual* result, therefore, but the *materials* that are the problem. The blade isn't *quite* old enough, as your powder demonstrated." He gave an almost amused huff. "Oh, and of course, then there's the most glaring mistake, because even after all this work, whoever did it forgot to dull the thing. It's as if the petition only specified that it had to *look* exactly alike..."

Riallo gave an appreciative nod and strode over to the sideboard to pour himself a glass of Kassoon.

"So," he said after a generous sip, "we have to tell Kabonn about all this."

"No. That's exactly what we don't do."

"I'm sorry-...*what*? Why?" Riallo lowered his glass.

"We don't tell him. We don't tell anyone," Akteron started to pace. "We let Kabonn put the blade on display. He couldn't tell it was a fake, so we don't reveal otherwise. That allows the museum to re-open and it sends a message, that we have no idea we've been duped. We carry on as usual...as if the case were closed. And whoever did this will think they got away with it all."

"...which will make it easier for us to track them down," Piria finished. "They'll drop their guard if they think they were successful."

"That's it. Nobody needs to know it's a fake."

"AARK! A fake!" The bird on the sill had been standing there and waiting for seeds throughout the discussion, but suddenly, it flapped its wings and launched off, that long, silken tail trailing behind it. Cocking a brow, Piria wandered over to the window and stuck her head out.

"What's wrong?" Akteron asked.

"That tektek," she said. "I know this sounds ridiculous...but I think it was *listening*. It's landing on a sill of the office a few doors down, now."

"Huh? How many doors down?" Riallo asked.

"Mmm, two? No...three."

"None of those offices are in use."

At that, all three of them shared a glance.

"Looks like you might have a new lead already," Riallo said quietly. "Quickly, now."

Akteron was already grabbing his donvul from the back of a chair as the officer clicked and threw him a stunshot.

"You coming?" Akteron asked, holstering it, but Riallo shook his head, gesturing to the relics on his desk and the open, unsecured requisitions room.

The young detective joined Piria as she opened the door and entered the hallway of the Bureau, and they were just in time to hear another door clicking shut, ahead, and to see a man, dressed in a smart looking ensemble and making towards the stairs.

"We can't lose him..." Piria said, breaking into a run.

"We won't," Akteron replied, keeping pace even though every step caused his nose and head to throb. Now though, pain was the last thing on his mind.

"We can't draw attention to ourselves or let him know we're tailing," he whispered. "Keep some distance."

Down into the Bureau's atrium, out the front door and

through the U-shaped drive they tailed their only suspect, narrowly missing being caught out by the occasional, odd glance he cast over his shoulder. But they remained unseen.

Led down the bustling, morning streets, around corners and through shops and stalls opening for the day, they made sure to keep him in sight, not to fall too far behind, and eventually the man slowed his pace, probably feeling he was in the clear.

He veered from the sidewalk into a small alley and only now did the pair pause to peek around the corner behind him.

He hadn't gone far and had halted by a drainpipe, his back to them while in his fingers he held what appeared to be...a chewing-coal tin.

"It's a drop point," Akteron whispered, watching their target withdraw a slip of paper from one pocket. Sliding the tin open, the stranger then swapped out this slip for one inside, and snapped it shut, again.

Before he could reach up to deposit the small package into the drainpipe, however, Piria uttered, *"Not a chance,"* and darted into the alley, fingers on her ingot belt. "Bureau of Security!" she yelled.

"Piri–"

Ugh. Why did she *always* do that? Withdrawing his stunshot, Akteron entered the alley in pursuit.

The element of surprise was theirs, it seemed, for spinning with a snarl, the man reached to his own belt.

"Don't!" Piria warned. "Hands off the ingots, and drop that tin."

He didn't do either, deciding instead to turn and bolt–

At once, though, he lost his balance. The man collapsed to the cobbles with a heavy – *KTUNK!* – feet still planted where they were, and it took a moment for Akteron to realise that Piria had petitioned to fix them in position.

"I said drop the tin," she repeated, mere paces away but not approaching lest he pulled a weapon. Akteron was then by her side, stunshot fixed at the man's chest.

"I think you'd better do what she asked," he pressed.

The man merely mumbled through his teeth.

And *vanished.*

"What-?" Piria cocked her head. "Did he just-..."

Akteron didn't have time to answer before the stunshot in his fingers became hot. Really hot. As a sizzling heat burned his fingers he was forced to drop it.

"*Blasted...*" he uttered, shaking off his hand. But marching across the alley and not deceived, he then reached down and grabbed something invisible on the cobbles. With a grunt, the stranger was yanked from beneath the cloaking hex he'd petitioned.

"He's using prepped petitions, like nexers do," Akteron warned, as Piria tried unsuccessfully to grab that stunshot and found her skin sizzling at the touch.

"*Poisonberry–*" Their suspect attempted to make another petition but Akteron reached down and tore the man's ingot belt from his waist. Small, metal chips scattered about the alley with a cold tinkling–

– *KNACK!* –

Akteron found a fist connecting with his jaw. He loosed a pained groan and released his assailant as another met his nose and sent more pain surging across his face. But Piria was there, stepping in to grab the man's jacket where Akteron had let go.

Her captive didn't hold back. With a growl, he swung. She ducked and swung back, landed a hit on his ear, but his next blow connected and sent Piria reeling. She fell to the cobbles, blinking, blood dribbling from her mouth as the man struggled to his feet, again.

"*No...*" Akteron uttered, shaking his head to clear his vision. Their guy was going to get away, Akteron just knew it...and in his state, blinded by pain and concussed, there was little he could do to prevent it. Still, he had to do *something...*

Stepping forward, he groggily readied another punch–

A foot met his stomach. Wind blown from both lungs, Akteron lurched back and hit the alley wall but even before he could sink down, a storm of punches was loosed upon him. His cheek, his jaw, his chest...there didn't seem to be an inch of him left untouched and Akteron was breathless and on ground before he knew what had happened.

No chance...

There was no chance. Whoever this guy was, he knew how to fight and he had won. And just to make *sure* he'd won, he now pulled a knife.

Leaning to grab Akteron by the scruff of his donvul, the man levelled the weapon at his neck and growled through bloody teeth, "Akteron Uusei Nisbri...*unworthy* of Doksunn's–"

– PECK! –

A sound rang out and the man's eyes blinked in shock before he dropped his weapon. Slowly, those eyes lost focus and the stranger collapsed to the ground.

Turning to the source of the sound, Akteron found Riallo holstering a stunshot.

"Sheesh. You certainly don't waste time when you want to get beaten up," the coordinating officer said, offering a hand. "Oh, *Gods*...your *face*...and I didn't think it could get any worse."

Akteron coughed and was lifted to his feet.

"Not now," he managed. "Piria..."

"I'm fine," Piria's voice replied unsteadily. She was standing nearby, gently feeling along her jaw with one hand and was injured, but at the realisation they were both still in one piece, Akteron let out a nervous sigh.

It took a good moment for the three to collect themselves, then. For Akteron to catch his breath. But at last, spitting blood, he turned with the other two to observe the unconscious man at their feet.

"Who on Aliru is *this*, then?" Riallo said.

Their suspect was young. Perhaps a little younger than Piria, hair shaved clean on the sides to create an isolated tuft atop his head.

"No idea," Akteron replied, crouching with a wince to reach into the man's jacket and remove that tin. "He was about to... make a message drop, though. So, let's see what was so important." Sliding the container open, he retrieved the small scrap of paper. Only two words were scrawled across it.

"They know."

Riallo grunted. "Well. That helps your hypothesis, I'd say."

"Did you...just use the word *hypothesis* correctly?" Piria asked, wide-eyed.

Akteron was still busy digging about. "I don't suppose it'll be...any surprise what the second note says," he panted, "but I'd still like to know."

He pulled the second note from the same pocket.

"They took the bait..."

For a moment, none of them spoke and Akteron got to his feet again, brushing his bloody face with one sleeve and blinking as his eyes blurred. "Right, so, what do...we think? I feel it'll look suspicious if no message is dropped. I say we replace the original note and send it."

"I agree." Piria nodded, and glanced to Riallo.

"It makes sense," he said, "if we want to keep up the 'duped' act."

"Unless they're expecting this guy to check-in..."

Riallo scoffed. "No chance. This guy is coming with me to the Bureau and he's going to enjoy a few span in a holding cell while he answers some very specific questions. We'll just have to hope they don't miss him."

Akteron turned to inspect the drainpipe and as he did, his vision blurred again. "I'm going...to need a break," he said, steadying himself against the alley wall. "But...not yet. I need to see this...through. I need to know what's going on."

"You need to see a physician," Riallo gave him a worried look. "But I agree. This whole thing stinks like one heck of a rotten caper. Just have patience, Akteron. We'll get there. And it will only take one name."

"Speaking of which," Piria then said. "Ro, did this guy say your name, back there?"

Mouth opening, Akteron realised that he had. "Yes," he said, turning back to the unconscious man. "And not just mine..."

It was at this moment that he noticed that something was happening. The stranger before him had begun to jitter and by the time Akteron had opened his mouth to voice his concern, it was too late.

As they watched, their suspect's body convulsed and a horrid gurgling sound issued from his throat. Piria and Riallo stepped back as the man then seemed to *liquify*. Skin becoming transparent, his body melted like a block of butter in the sun, then burst.

Riallo barked in shock as water flooded the cobbles, running down a nearby drain. And while the other two stood staring, Akteron felt a distinct pang of dread. For there, before him now lay a wet garment, water trickling from the sleeves, the fabric limp...

How had he not recognised it, earlier?

"No," he uttered. He couldn't-...*wouldn't* accept it, for that meant accepting the other flashes he'd seen, too–

"Great Wastes..." Nearby, Riallo's eyebrows were half way up his forehead as Piria stepped over to her partner.

"Ro, are you alright?" she asked, and Akteron started at the sight of her face, mind suddenly alight with that *other* flash...

"Ro...?"

"Yes," he replied slowly, pushing the image away. "I'm fine... fine. Just a bit shocked."

"A *bit*?" Riallo's dismay was almost palpable. "Our suspect just *melted*! And now we have nothing! That was our only lead!"

Glancing back down to the soggy suit on the alley's floor, Akteron shook his head. "No-...no, we're not...in the dark just yet."

"Unless this guy had a greeting card in his pocket. I disagree."

"Well-..." Spitting blood to the cobbles, Akteron knelt to flip one side of the wet jacket open. "Not a greeting card...but there is something."

Running his hand along the inner seam, his fingers found a small, coloured tag. "This jacket," he said, glancing back up at his officer. "Would..."— he paused to swallow painfully —"you believe that I know who the tailor is?"

Riallo grunted in amusement. "I wouldn't believe anyone else."

"If I take it in..." Akteron then said, "to the tailor...there's a good chance I can get that name." A weak and bloody smile crossed his face. "Oh, and then there are...the other two leads I've scrounged together in between...episodes of almost dying."

Justifiably, Piria seemed confused by that.

"I'll fill you in once my jaw is re-hinged," he assured her.

Riallo, however, gave a loud clap. "Why, you-...that's my detective!" he crowed, grabbing Akteron by the shoulder. "I told Kabonn you were the one for this case. I *told* him!"

Ignoring the burst of pain, Akteron looked his superior in the eyes. "Wait," he said, "didn't you just pick me because...I was Krio?"

"Akteron, you don't seriously-..." Riallo looked a little hurt at the question. "That was the whole play! *Yes,* Kabonn was *adamant* that a Krio agent take the case, but you realise *I* put that idea in his head, right?"

Akteron hadn't realised.

"I couldn't admit it in front of him, of course," Riallo went on, "but when this case came up, I convinced him there was nobody else for it."

Akteron suddenly felt a slight warmth, inside. And though it might have been a burst blood vessel, he felt it as the warmth of vindication, instead.

So...Riallo did believe in him, after all.

"Still," the officer went on, clearing his throat in a businesslike way as he peered at the soaked cobbles. "I hope you both realise that the Bureau can't knowingly lie to the curator of the city museum. Nor the public. And you can't be seen working this on official time. If any of the book-keepers get wind of you using Bureau resources on a closed case, there'll be a scandal..." He took a breath, turning something over inside. "There's also the issue of this whole plot clearly being dangerous, and us having no idea who might be involved." At last, he turned back to face them. "Long story short, if we want the Bureau and whoever else to ignore further investigation, this has to be done quietly. That means you two are on your own..."

A small silence fell, and a cool breeze passed through the alley.

"Except," he then added, "I'll be helping, too. So, we *three* are on our own."

Akteron grinned, bringing a burst of pain so hot he thought his cheeks would catch fire. Still, he couldn't banish it as he reached out to give Riallo a hug.

Clasping at her donvul, he then dragged Piria in, as well.

"Hey, don't thank me just yet," Riallo told him. "I mean, you could still die."

"Yeah, you can leave me out of future hugs, too," Piria added, enduring the embrace. "But thanks..."

When Akteron eventually released them and stepped back, he was surprised to find that new warmth inside had swept his panic away. It was flooding him with hope and dulling even his pain. And in the clarity it offered, he could see into the distance. There, he caught sight of a meteor, rocketing through space and set on some unknown path, and the next step was finding out by whose hand it had been launched, and with what it was set to collide.

Turning to Piria, he nodded.

"So...are we taking the case?"

In her eyes, he could already see that cool determination blooming again.

"What are we waiting for?" she said. "Let's go find ourselves a blade."

EPILOGUE

Dianon Scaa Tesbri's hands were blistered and he stank like an old sponge.

– *SKRRRUSH* –

As he plunged his shovel into a chalky pile of dried guano again, the grating impact echoed around the cave and bats stirred in the darkness, above.

Lifting his laden shovel, Dianon took a few, shaky steps through a grove of white stalagmites and dumped the haul into a pull-wagon.

Good. It was almost full. *Almost full.* Then, *Great Wastes*, the day would be over, at last!

Thankfully, it wasn't dark, yet, but the light outside was fading and he didn't want to be down in these caves when night fell. He still had to make the long walk back to Torril along the coastal track, after all, and that track was renowned for its thieves and brigands, who–

Dianon almost laughed.

*Thieves and brigands...*had that thought really just entered his head?

Damnation, up until a few span ago, he'd been one of them! Thieving from those wealthy Seat idiots up in their fancy lodgings. Taking what they didn't deserve and...*redistributing* it among Torril's more shadowy residents. The Seat had enough. They spoke of things being fair and equal, but who else had golden fixtures in their home, like Official Gaussi? A tower, like Official Si'verak? Or an enormous, sweeping garden, like Official Helar?

Dianon grunted.

Now, thanks to the two Bureau stooges who'd nabbed him, here he was, shovelling fertiliser for that lot. Probably for that same, stupid garden.

Was that irony? Dianon didn't have the smarts to know.

Brushing his forehead with one arm, the old thief wondered how much longer he could have kept it all up for, anyway. His face was already wrinkled and his nails, yellowed. He'd kept himself young with the thrill of the game all these cycles — or at least he thought he had. But that same game had aged him, too... so, really, what had he gained? A little extra charge in the Dispensary?

Pfuh...

Driving the shovel into the ground, the older man closed his eyes, allowing himself a moment to catch his breath.

Boy, it stank in here...

Spending each day in these guano-filled caves wasn't easy on the nose. And good thing he didn't have anyone waiting for him at home. Just a cold bed which also stank of bat poop, no matter how many times he washed.

He supposed there *was* that small clutch of tikkils who often showed up in the evenings. The little scoundrels who gathered about the alley window and chirped for him when he fed them. Closest things to friends he had...

Ignoring the pain in his lower back, his upper back, his shoulders, legs, neck, and body in general, Dianon bent to retrieve his pickaxe.

"*Only three more cycles of this,*" he muttered, turning back to the white pillar. "*Goodie, goodie...*"

– TINK! –

"*I can hardly feel the time passin' at all.*"

– TINK! TINK! –

With each strike, small chunks of guano fractured off the stalagmite, only to tumble and settle around his feet in a slowly growing mound. It was hard, this stuff. Not like rock, but close. And now and then, he had to hold his breath as dust-clouds rose slowly around him, waiting for a breeze to disperse it into the cave before he continued.

"'Least they coulda done was given me a mask...bunch o' law-lovin' pricks..."

– TINK! –

Five strikes. Ten. It was around the thirtieth when he finally dropped the pickaxe again and turned to fetch his shovel.

"Evening, Dianon."

"Great, blazin'-!" The words almost caused Dianon to join the bats, above. "What in Aliru you think you're *doin'*? Comin' in here an' sneakin' up on me like that?"

Finding his breath, the sweat-soaked thief now found himself regarding two silhouettes, still as statues against the pale skies outside the cave. Their faces were indistinct, but it was clear they were finely dressed. And it certainly wasn't his overseer, that much was certain.

"Apologies for the surprise," the first figure said.

"No matter 'bout that," Dianon said, shifting his head to try and make out details. No good. The light wasn't in his favour. "Howdya know my name?"

One of the figures looked to the ground for a moment, as if considering that.

"We're here on behalf of a friend. A mutual friend, I think you'll agree..."

Dianon shook his head.

"Nahhhh," he then growled, waving them away, "I know your type. You'll come here wantin' me to do somit that sounds big 'n exciting. Then I say, *I'm in.* Then I get caught again, and end up in some other place worse'n this..." He gestured to the dripping,

dank space around them, before reaching down for the shovel again. "I'm done with it all...I just wanna do my bit here and die with my lizards, back home."

"We're aware of your predicament..." the second voice said, a woman who didn't sound very old, at all. How did they rope such a young one into all this nonsense?

She stepped forward. "We know your pain..."

Dianon grunted. "Sure you do. Bugger off. My overseer'll be back any moment..."

"Your overseer. Large fellow? Bushy moustache and a hot temper?"

"That's him. Not one to mess with, if ye get my meanin'..."

– KATINK! –

A metal object hit the ground at Dianon's feet and it took a moment for him to realise it was a bracelet, inscribed with a series of numbers.

Ooh, no. Well, that was just great...

"*You killed him...*" he muttered. "*Great Wastes.* Why? Now they'll really be after me..." He'd held it off until now. Somehow. But at the sight of that collar, a familiar pain bloomed in Dianon's chest and he raised a hand to clutch at the skin. "*Ugh.* I told you to leave me alone, *damnit!*"

"We aren't interested in thievery. We're not asking you to do a job..." the woman continued.

"Then what? What do you want?"

"We are here to offer you an *opportunity*. One which few alive will ever have..."

Dianon blinked as he tried to process that, pain searing through his ribcage. Why had they needed to get him all riled up? That just triggered it, again. His body couldn't seem to handle this type of stress, anymore, *damnit!*

Still, the figures weren't moving.

"N...not my thing."

"Just take a moment. Let's think this out, together."

Blasted-...these two weren't going to take no for an answer, were they? Well, seeing as Vinaal *was* dead — the ruthless bastard...

Dianon sighed.

"*Right...alright,*" Trying to restrain his breathing, he felt the stabbing sensation easing off. "*Ergh*...whatever it is you want, seems you want it pretty bad...an' I guess you heard I'm the quickest fingers in Torril...so, what's the job — an' how quickly can you get me new metals?" He gestured to the spot at his waist where an ingot-belt should have rested.

"We told you, there is no job. We're not interested in theft."

"Then...what in...what in *Teloran's name do* you want?"

The man stepped forward and, reaching out, carefully took Dianon's arm. "Aren't you tired of this life?" he asked, rolling back the sleeve to expose Dianon's shock-bracelet, and glancing at it for a moment. "The bondage you were born into? Your duty and toil for powers you never meet? Who never acknowledge you? Who seem to care so little for your suffering?"

Dianon gave a frustrated huff, pulling his arm free as the pain receded, at last. There was a wave of relief as his heart settled, and he took a few deep breaths just to make sure it was really over before looking back to the strangers.

Hmm. These two hated the Seat almost as much as he did, it seemed. But, well, what was new about that? So did half the continent...

"Do you not feel the crushing presence, lingering in every stone of this city?" the man continued. "Do you not wish to break free of it and create a place where *everyone* is powerful, in their own right?"

"A delusion," the old thief answered quietly. "Heard such things before. Nobody challenges the Seat...it ain't possible. Look at Kriolar."

The man gave a slightly amused chuckle.

"Don't worry about them. Worry about yourself. How about

it? A new beginning. And freedom, *true* freedom, from those who control our lives..."

Dianon eyed the woman, but she didn't move.

"And in return?"

"In return, all we want is loyalty to a friend," the man said. "Help her achieve this vision, and her success will be yours."

Dianon then glanced to the shovel, standing in the guano where he'd stuck it. At his blistered, bloody hands and yellowed nails. Then, at the dead overseer's bracelet at his feet.

What had this life brought him, really, but dead-ends? What had it ever done, except grind him down, little by little? And what if what this man said was true? If he could break free from the rule of the Seat...be powerful in his own right. That did sound good, didn't it? Delusion or not...

Worst-case scenario, he'd get arrested, again, but there was no such thing as a death-penalty in Torril — this wasn't Nen Kimiin. They'd just throw him somewhere else, have him digging or pulling or stacking, and he'd get another new boss, and on it would go. Always different. Always the same.

He shot the man a suspicious glance, fingering that shock bracelet on his own wrist. "Go on, then...who is this 'friend'?"

Even in the darkness, he could see the smile as the man answered. "She is more than I ever imagined one could be."

Dianon gave a final, light huff and shook his head. As usual with these types, *talk, talk, talk.* But he'd made his decision.

"Sounds impressive enough," he said. "Well, 'spose I'd better meet her, then, shouldn'I?"

"Is that a yes?"

Dianon grunted. "*Yes, damnit!*"

– *KTINK!* –

Dianon gasped as his bracelet suddenly popped open of its own accord, and fell to the ground.

"Wha-...that's impossible..." he muttered, rubbing his wrist. He hadn't even noticed the woman making that petition. *Great*

Wastes, though, that felt good...

Stepping over the pickaxe, the former thief dusted himself off and the woman rested a comforting hand on his shoulder. "We didn't regret our choice, Mr. Scaa. And neither will you."

And with that, Dianon Scaa Tesbri was led out of the seaside caves. He left his toil and memories of his former life behind, and as the sunlight finally faded, two strangers escorted him into the coming night.

END OF BOOK ONE

ACKNOWLEDGEMENTS

Like a lighthouse keeper, writers are often tucked out of sight for months at a time and can only hope that their work glints brightly enough to catch a passing stranger's eye. It's a pretty lonely gig, but while most writing is tackled alone, it needs collaboration to really shine. This book is the result of almost five years' work, and it wouldn't have happened without the amazing people I was so lucky to have around me, throughout.

So, to Luke, and Dale, and Matt, who showed me this was possible, whose enthusiasm kept me going, and who guided me away from bad ideas.

To Paul, Dave, and Luca, without whom I would probably never finish any project! Your interest, support, (and pressure!) were invaluable.

To Caron and Martin, who were there, cheering me on from day one.

To Stacey, whose love of fantasy and prose shows through in every line she edits, and whose questions, criticism, and feedback have made me far a better writer.

To Damien, whose knowledgable, guiding hand helped me navigate the seas of publishing.

To Mr. Grace, whose encouraging words have stuck with me since grade eight and without whom I might never have tried.

To Mo, who is really all the best things rolled into one person. The one I turn to when things go wrong, who assures me that things will all work out, and who read almost as many revisions as I did.

And finally, to you, the reader. Your support is everything and I hope this is the start of a wonderful adventure together. There are so many more to come.

Thank you.